SPARROW

MIGRATIONS

ALSO BY CARI NOGA

Plover Pilgrimage
Road Biking Michigan

SPARROW

MIGRATIONS

A Novel

CARI NOGA

LAKE UNION
PUBLISHING

Text copyright © 2013 Cari Noga
All rights reserved.

Published by Lake Union Publishing, Seattle

www.apub.com

Amazon, the Amazon logo, and Lake Union Publishing are trademarks of Amazon.com, Inc., or its affiliates.

ISBN-13: 9781477830888
ISBN-10: 147783088X

Cover design by David Drummond

Library of Congress Control Number: 2015900294

Printed in the United States of America

For me and you and a boy named Boo.

ONE

R obby Palmer was so tired of the talking.
He wedged himself farther into the point of the ferry's bow, resting his chin on the rail, absorbing the steady vibration of the engine and the soothing silence. The deck on the sightseeing cruise was almost empty, the first quiet place since he and his parents arrived in New York City two days ago.

The wind off the Hudson River gusted up, threatening to push the hood of his favorite Detroit Lions sweatshirt off his head. Robby yanked on the strings, pulling the gray fabric taut over the giant, noise-muffling headphones he wore underneath, all the while keeping his eyes on a V formation of geese he'd spotted. Their staggered black lines swooped against the blue sky like an untethered kite tail. Once, he got a kite stuck in a tree. His dad pulled it out of the branches, but the tail stayed stuck for months, flapping just like these geese. Robby turned his head to follow as they plunged lower along the river. They were fast. He wished he could be that fast. On their trip here from Detroit, the pilot had said the plane traveled more than five hundred miles per hour. How fast could geese fly?

His mom might know, but she and his dad were in the cabin. The twenty-degree weather was too cold, his dad said. They'd watch the city's sights through the cabin windows. His mom said they'd come back out for the Statue of Liberty. She was the one who had wanted to go on the boat ride in the first place. "We're on vacation. Let's try to do something fun together," he had heard her tell his dad back at the hotel.

Cold didn't bother Robby. He'd rather freeze than go back in that overheated cabin filled with jostling, oblivious people, talking loudly on their phones, talking to each other, talking, talking, always talking. Like on the subway, like the cab drivers in their different languages, like his dad's family that they came to New York to visit.

The geese swooped lower, lower, and lower, until they splashed into the Hudson, their black bodies now blending into the river's gray waves. Robby lifted his binoculars and leaned farther out over the bow's guardrail, seeking their bobbing bodies. Ahh. There they were. How many? One, two, three, four, five. He counted twelve. The same as his age. He felt pleased at the coincidence and counted again, just to be sure. Yes, twelve. It was easy to count them. They swam a lot more slowly than they flew. So why did they stop flying? He liked to swim, but if he had a choice, he would always pick flying, as high as he could, as fast as he could, the silent sky all to himself.

Hanging over the steel guardrail, Robby felt the engine's vibrations change. They were going faster. Not gradually faster. Suddenly, urgently faster. Like a chase. Were they chasing the geese? But the wind changed, too. Instead of pushing back his hood, it was now blowing against his cheek, blowing his dark bangs sideways, out of his eyes for once. The ferry was turning, turning away from the geese, the view changing from the soothing sameness of the waves to the jagged profile of the shoreline, hemmed with buildings.

Trying to keep the geese in sight, Robby turned back into the wind, pivoting toward the cabin. But instead of the geese, he saw the crowd. The jostling, oblivious passengers from the cabin. Now they held their cell phones outstretched as they erupted onto the deck. They advanced on him, a mob of adults in down coats and fleece vests cornering him in the bow, their breath puffs of white, their faces a blur of expressions. Excitement, surprise, fear, one after the other, like those face flash cards they used to make him do in school.

A woman clipped his arm, and the binoculars slipped out of his hands, flopping hard against his chest. On the other side a man jostled against him. They just kept coming. He'd read about stampedes at soccer games and day-after-Thanksgiving sales. This must be what it felt like. In the back of the throng he saw his mother, her wide eyes pinned on him, her mouth open, gesturing at her own head, pulling at her ears.

Robby couldn't hear her. The noise of the crowd seeped into his hood, under his headphones, invading his quiet. He tried to go toward her, tugging at his hood, but the surging crowd pushed him back. Another passenger, a big man, jounced against him, knocking his headphones askew, spinning him around to face back out, over the rail.

And then he saw it.

The airplane's white nose poked out of the water. Poked right at the ferry, which was churning straight toward it. With its band of black cockpit windows, the plane looked back at him like a *Star Wars* Storm Trooper mask. A submerged Storm Trooper, rising out of the river. But planes didn't belong in a real river. In a video game or a movie it could happen, probably because an enemy shot it down. He looked up, scanning the sky warily. Nothing. Robby felt a tug of anxiety over the unanswered question: How did the plane get in the river? He remembered his binoculars and lifted them to his eyes. People were lined up on the wings! The passengers! How did they get out there on the wings? He remembered the flight attendant's safety demonstration in the aisle when they left from Detroit two days ago, how she pointed out the doors to be used in the event of

3

an emergency. He couldn't see any doors in the Storm Trooper. The passengers stood in uneven rows, only some wearing life jackets. Their life jackets were under the seat cushions. They hadn't listened and forgot them. Now, backlit by the late afternoon sun, their line of silhouettes staggered by height, they looked helpless. Helpless and doomed, held captive by the Storm Trooper airplane.

Robby leaned over the railing, willing the ferry forward faster, and shrieked his first word since lunchtime. "Go!"

~

Petrified, Deborah DeWitt-Goldman stared at her stylish black pumps submerged beneath four inches of icy water. The pumps were her favorite pair, her lucky pair. She had been wearing them last year when she landed the biggest gift by a living donor couple in the history of Cornell University—any school, even medicine—a ten-million-dollar challenge gift to build a new law school. Only sixty-five million to go.

But they weren't so lucky today. Neither she nor her husband Christopher could swim—a suddenly glaring imperfection in their otherwise flawlessly planned and executed lives—and the wing felt like an ice rink. An older woman had already slipped but was hauled back up by other passengers. She was shaking now, and crying, saying she had to call her son. *Her son.* The possessive words gave Deborah a pang, as always.

It was unreal. A bad dream. It must be. How could a routine takeoff go so wrong in less than five minutes? She had had the window seat. Christopher sat beside her on the aisle, engrossed in an ornithology journal even before they were taxied to the runway. The "Fasten Seat Belts" sign glowed red. Several rows ahead, a baby cried, innocently flipping on Deborah's internal longing.

Then a muffled thud. Then another, then a third, then another and she lost count. *"Did you hear that?" "What was that?" "What's*

4

happening out there?" Questions, laced more with wonder than fear, floated around her.

Christopher lifted his head attentively. "Uh-oh," he said, leaning across her to look out the window at the ribbon of river below them.

"What is it?" she asked, the first finger of fright squeezing her stomach as she leaned beside him, her hair swinging forward to brush his cheek. "What do you see?"

"Is that smoke?" Behind them, a woman's louder, more alarmed voice rose above the murmurs.

Smoke? The fright tightened its grip. Christopher's gaze swiveled from the window back into the plane. Deborah followed his eyes. Thin smoke wafted over the seats next to the wing. Simultaneously, she realized the normal takeoff force that pressed her back into the seat was gone. They weren't climbing anymore.

They weren't climbing anymore. For a paralyzed moment her eyes held Christopher's before he turned to rummage in the seat pocket.

"We're in trouble."

"What do you mean? What happened? What's going on?" Her voice rose as the plane fell, the fear now a full fist clenching her stomach.

"They lost the engines. Read this." He shoved the plastic emergency procedures card at her. "We're going to need it."

"We're crashing? Are we going to die?" Deborah's voice caught as her hand searched for his. The specialist had said one more try was reasonable. They had to make it home!

Christopher shook his head. "All I know is it's going to be a rough, wet landing."

As he concentrated on the card, she clutched his hand. Dimly she heard the baby cry and a hushed "I love you" behind her. But their fellow passengers were mostly shocked into near-silence, watching the glittering water rising up to meet them so terrifyingly fast, until they heard the captain's incongruously monotone voice: "Brace for impact."

Now, menacing waves lapped at her ankles. Overhead, she heard the approaching chop-chop-chop of helicopters. Passengers pushed cell phone buttons, trying to reach loved ones for reassurance or good-byes, she still wasn't sure. Half of them didn't have life jackets on. Could they have survived the crash, only to drown awaiting rescue? A flight attendant hollered directions. *Remain calm. Huddle close together for warmth. Help is coming.* Deborah could still hear the baby crying. She couldn't stop thinking about their three remaining embryos, back at the clinic in Ithaca.

She tried to concentrate on the flight attendant's instructions. This was what she did, after all. She executed. The ten-million-dollar gift. The perfect marriage. *Remain calm. Help is coming.* A phalanx of vessels motored toward them. Circle Line Ferries. US Coast Guard. FDNY. Her own life jacket was securely fastened. She hadn't been able to read a word on the emergency card, so Christopher had lifted the seat cushion and found the vest, buckling it tightly about her before putting on his own. She had not brought any of her carry-on baggage with her. Others had, and already one suitcase had splashed into the river.

Her feet were freezing. She hopped from one to the other, allowing each a momentary respite from the icy river, grabbing Christopher's tweed-covered shoulder for balance, burying the other hand in her pocket. What did the flight attendant say first? *Remain calm.* The helicopters whirred louder, coming into view. Her heart sank as she saw the logos. They were news media! Where were the rescue choppers? The ferries had moved closer but were now idling.

"They're throwing up too much wake. They've got to take it slow or we'll go down after all," Christopher said, adjusting his glasses to peer more intently.

"Where are the rescue helicopters? Does the media own every chopper in New York City?" Deborah wailed, as her phone rang beneath her hand in her coat pocket.

Her sister's Seattle number was illuminated on the screen. "Helen! Oh, my God."

"Call her later." Christopher's voice was sharp. "We have to pay attention. The ferries will be moving in again."

She ignored Christopher, putting the phone to her ear. "Helen? Helen, is that you?"

"Deborah, thank God. That wasn't your plane that went down, then?" Her sister's voice was faint and broken.

"It was. It is. It is our plane, but we're OK, Helen." Tears rose in her eyes, and static buzzed in her ear. She steadied her voice so Helen would believe her. "Can you hear me? We're OK. We're waiting for help now."

"I heard you." Helen was crying. "Are you still going to come out? I need to talk to you. Here, in person."

"I don't know, Helen. What's the matter?" Tears rose up again.

"Folks, we need your attention. Phones down. Listen up." The flight attendant was hollering again.

Christopher put his hand over hers, pulling the phone from her ear. "Deborah! Pay attention! The ferries are almost here. They're going to move us any minute."

"Helen's crying. My sister's crying." So was she. As they both grappled for the phone, it tumbled from her stiff fingers, vanishing into the gray waves.

"Helen!" Deborah stooped, flailing into the water for it. A wave licked icy tentacles past her elbow.

"Deborah, never mind the phone! Look, people on the other wing are getting on the ferry."

Deborah looked across the white metal shell, glinting in the sun. Indeed, passengers were climbing up the ladder.

"Keep it together, sweetheart. Just a few more minutes to hang on!" Christopher pulled her tightly against him. She tried to return the embrace, but her stiff arms wouldn't move.

~

"Oh, my God."

Aboard the ferry, Brett Stevens's eyes opened. From the moment the captain turned the ferry, revealing the astonishing scene, silent prayers had begun automatically. *Our Father, who art in heaven. Please let everyone be unharmed. Hallowed be thy name. Please save their souls.*

Reverie and recitation now both broken by Jackie's voice, Brett stared in disbelief at the plane's white nose, starting to list sideways now.

"Oh, my God," Jackie repeated. "Can you read the name?"

"What name?" Brett looked out at the waves.

"Of the airline. On the plane!" Jackie was clutching at her fur coat.

Brett squinted. US something. US Airways.

"US Airways, I think."

"Oh, dear Lord. Dear Lord." Jackie began rifling through her purse.

"What? What is it?"

"I've got to find my plane ticket!"

"The old one? Why? What for?"

Jackie didn't answer, still pawing through her purse, searching for the ticket they had changed that morning when the thought of returning to their humdrum lives in Charlotte and Pennsylvania was too awful.

Finally she located the envelope and read aloud the printed e-ticket. "US Airways, Flight 1549. Departing LaGuardia, 3:24 p.m."

Brett's watch read 3:33 p.m. The realization sank in for both of them as their eyes met.

"That might be my plane," Jackie said, her bejeweled left hand plucking nervously at her fur collar. Brett swallowed hard and closed her eyes again, twisting her own plain wedding band hidden inside her glove. Inside, she felt her heart lightening, her soul rising. Was there ever a clearer sign? Jackie was safely there beside her instead of on that plane. They were meant to be together.

Another prayer, one of gratitude, rose to her lips as Brett laid her blond head on her lover's soft shoulder and again closed her eyes.

~

Propped up by Christopher, her feet numb in the black pumps, Deborah stared at the waves where the phone had disappeared. *I need to talk to you. In person.* She felt an intense longing to see her only, older sister, and her two nieces. Regret that she'd put off this visit to Seattle for so long rose up along with the river, nearing her knees now. All her reasons were so foolish. Superstition about flying during an in vitro fertilization cycle. Her projects at work. Christopher's projects at work. What good was all that now? She still wasn't pregnant. A new law school, a paper published in the *Journal of Field Ornithology.* Trivial. People were what was important. Relationships. Family.

The realization swept over her as coldly as the river. Would she get another chance now? She thought of the embryos, E, F, and G, the clinic had labeled them, siblings to the unsuccessfully implanted A, B, C, and D. They were so far away. What was she doing here, with these strangers? Most looked like business travelers, but there was one woman cradling an infant. The one she heard crying before, now quiet. She had apparently wrapped the baby in her own coat. As Deborah stared past the passengers in between them, the coatless mother clutched the baby close, kissing its forehead, tucking in a stray sleeve tighter, her gaze never swerving from her child.

Watching the mother, Deborah felt the internal longing yield to yearning. Yearning that had survived two years of shots and struggle and, more recently, the sense that she and Christopher no longer shared a solidarity about parenthood. This yearning was in prime form, puffing out its chest, filling every cell with certainty. Deborah still wanted to have a baby. She was tired of executing their predictable, perfect lives in Ithaca. She wanted to live them. Seize the day.

The thought seemed to thaw her frozen fingers, and she gripped the nubby tweed of Christopher's jacket. If this crash proved anything, it was that the future was promised to no one. This day, this moment, right now, was all that mattered. She tilted her head back, to look him square in the eye.

"Christopher, promise me something. Promise me that whatever it takes, we'll still have a baby."

Christopher blinked behind his glasses. "Deborah, you're upset. This isn't the time to make a decision like that."

"It's exactly the time. If we don't decide what we want at a time like this, when will we know what's really important? I want this more than anything. You know that. Promise me we'll have a baby." She wasn't begging or pleading. She was simply adamant.

"Deborah, look. It's almost our turn. The ferries are right here. When we're safe and dry and back on land, we can discuss this." Christopher's voice took on his overly reasonable tone.

She fired back. "I don't need to discuss anything! This is what I want. This could be a sign. Life is short."

"A sign? Deborah, you're sounding crazy. We've talked about all this before. We've had two strikes already. And we're not getting any younger."

"We weren't in a plane crash before! Promise me, Christopher. Promise me."

And as the icy river rose over their knees, Christopher promised.

TWO

Their ferry floated barely fifty yards from the plane. Robby watched another, already loaded with passengers, motor off. Theirs would be the next to assist. He didn't even need the binoculars anymore, they were so close. The Storm Trooper now looked more like he was sinking, instead of rising. Robby bounced up and down on his toes, impatient for something else to happen.

The ferry captain sounded impatient, too. No one had budged from the deck rails. "Ladies and gentlemen. For your own safety, clear the decks and return to your seats in the cabin. I repeat, clear the decks immediately." It was at least the tenth time he had repeated himself.

"Robby!" his mother was working her way through the crowd toward him. "Robby! Did you hear the captain? Come back inside with your father and me right away. Robby!"

But even with his headphones off now, captivated by the plane, Robby paid no attention to her or the captain. He remembered what the flight attendant said two days ago, on their flight from Detroit to New York. "In the event of a water landing, your seat cushion can be used as a flotation device." It was his first time on a plane, and he imagined landing on water. Would they have landed on Lake St. Clair? Or made it farther east, to Lake Erie? Would the water seep in the windows, or would the plane stay dry? What would happen when the door was finally opened and the water rushed in? Were there any people still left on this plane?

He tilted his head back and forth as he analyzed his own questions. Nearby, a cell phone rang just as his mother elbowed herself next to him.

"Jan here." The man on his left answered. "Yes, I'm on a ferry in the Hudson."

"Robby. We have to go back inside the cabin. Right now," his mother said from his right side.

"By the plane crash, uh-huh. Yes, I have a Twitter account," said the man on the left.

Robby pressed the binoculars harder against his eyes, trying to block the dueling conversations.

"Right *now*, Robby. The captain said so. And we need to find your dad." His mom again, now putting her hand on his arm.

"Who is this? How did you find me?" On his left the man paused. "CNN?"

This is CNN. In his head, Robby heard the Darth Vader intonations. The man's conversation was getting interesting, after all. He let the binoculars hang and turned to listen.

"How the hell did you . . ." the man broke off again.

"Really, Robby, we can't stay here. We—" Her voice climbed, sounding like it did when she wanted him to stop playing video games or turn off the TV.

Irritated, Robby shook off her hand on his arm.

"Can you use it? The picture, you mean? On TV? Well, hell, sure." The man paused again. "Go on air? Live? In five minutes? You're kidding . . . yeah, I see your helicopter. Uh-huh. Yeah. Just describe what I saw. OK, I can do that. Yeah. Yeah. All right. I'll be ready."

He hung up and looked at Robby. "They're gonna have the anchor call me back in five minutes. They say I've got the first picture of the crash."

~

Amanda Stevens unlocked her back door. "Mom? You home?" Her mother wasn't expected back until evening, but Amanda automatically did the shout-out check-in.

No one responded. Amanda slung her backpack into the closet and headed for the kitchen. She grabbed a bottle of water and a bag of pretzels. Tipping a handful into her mouth, she slid onto the stool at the kitchen counter and fired up the laptop. It was officially her mom's, there for paying bills and looking up recipes and whatever else she did online, but sixteen-year-old Amanda used it most.

She turned on her IM. No one was online yet. She checked her iGoogle page before noticing the voice mail light blinking on the landline. Her mother's voice sounded strange, disembodied from the kitchen where she spent so much time. *I'm staying another night in New York, she said. Do your homework. Have Dad order out or have leftovers for dinner. Fill the bird feeder.*

Amanda's brow furrowed. Her mom never went anywhere overnight. Now she was staying another night in New York City, where she knew no one? Just as Amanda started to call her mom back, her IM pinged. Kelsey was online. Nicole followed. They dissected the events of the day at Scranton High School for fifteen minutes before Amanda's attention wandered. She clicked back over to her iGoogle. "Plane ditched in Hudson, officials deny terrorism," she read at the top of the breaking news feed, and clicked the CNN video link.

A somber anchor began. "New Yorkers like to say they've seen it all. But at about three thirty this afternoon, most of them were proven wrong when, just before afternoon rush hour, a US Airways jet was ditched in the Hudson River minutes after takeoff from LaGuardia Airport.

"Passengers have been evacuated onto the wings and are now awaiting rescue from the chilly waters near midtown Manhattan.

13

About a half hour ago, a passenger aboard a nearby sightseeing ferry enlisted in the rescue effort posted what CNN believes is the first picture of the crash on his Twitter account. We're pleased to bring you this picture now, exclusively on CNN." Amanda turned up the volume. Was the conference near Midtown? Maybe her mom was watching live. The picture flashed on the screen. "That passenger, Janis Krums, now joins us by phone from the ferry. Welcome to CNN. Thanks for your time."

"You're welcome." A man's voice, uneven with static and background noise, piped up.

"You're on the scene that we're now showing our viewers. Tell us what you know about the accident," the anchor commanded. Amanda leaned forward. It was pretty fascinating. The plane looked almost graceful, balancing itself on the waves, passengers clustered on each wing.

"Yes. Um. Well, our ferry was headed around the island when the accident happened. Southbound, toward the Statue of Liberty. And I didn't see it crash, you know. But I was standing outside when the captain told us we were diverting. And when he turned the boat, I saw the plane."

"We expect to have live video in a few more minutes, from the CNN helicopters now on the scene. We're talking live with . . ."

Her IM pinged again, and Amanda closed the video. Abby was online now. They spent half an hour sort of working on biology homework and mostly talking about tomorrow's musical auditions. This year it was a production of *Grease*. Abby hoped for one of the Pink Lady roles, maybe even Sandra Dee. Envious of her confidence, Amanda wondered if she should even bother auditioning. At church she sang in the choir, but on the few occasions she'd given in to her urge to raise her voice above the muted mediocrity, her dad had rebuked her afterward. It wouldn't do for the pastor to look like he was showing off his daughter, he'd told her. Why bring on more nagging by auditioning? But Abby just about had her convinced to audition when Kelsey pinged her.

"Turn on your TV to the plane crash news!"

"Why?"

"Your mom is on! Channel 33. OMG."

Amanda blinked. She jumped and grabbed the remote. A reporter was standing on a boat with a microphone in the face of a man holding his cell phone and gesturing. The plane was nowhere to be seen. Other passengers milled in the background, around the deck. Amanda muted the volume and studied the people behind the man, looking for her mother's blond hair and red peacoat. Mostly she saw other men, with the exception of one tall woman wearing sunglasses and a fur coat. *Who wears fur anymore?* Amanda thought. She saw a brown-haired woman with a kid who looked a couple years younger than her, wearing a pair of giant headphones around his neck. But no red peacoat. She went back to her computer.

"You're crazy, Kels."

"I saw her! I'm sure it was her. They were interviewing some guy, and I saw her behind him. On a boat. You said she was in New York."

"No way. My mom's at some church conference about food pantries. She doesn't even like boats."

"It was her," Kelsey insisted. *"Ask her when she gets home. I gotta go now. Later."*

Amanda closed the IM window and shook her head. Kelsey was wrong, of course. That was the only thing that made sense. But as she called her mom's cell phone, which rang through to voice mail, Amanda really wished her mom was right there in the kitchen, as usual.

Brett heard the voice mail notification as she sat next to Jackie in the ferry cabin, listening to her complain that she was cold. Her home number was at the top of the list of missed calls. Brett pulled her red peacoat tighter, feeling a chill from the inside. Amanda would be home from school, getting her message about now.

"My daughter. I'll call back from outside."

"All right." Jackie shrugged, burrowing herself deeper into the fur. "I'm staying right here."

Amanda picked up on the first ring as Brett resumed pacing the deck.

"Hi, sweetie, it's me. Did you just call?"

"Yeah. I got your message. Why aren't you home?"

"Oh, I met someone from another church," Brett told her daughter. *That much is true*, she thought. Her words seemed to emerge by themselves, like lip syncing ahead of the music. "They're doing some really neat things with their food pantry, and we just wanted to talk a little bit more, find out if maybe there's a way we could work together."

"Oh. OK, I guess."

"Are you OK, honey?" Brett plugged her other ear with her finger, straining to hear. At this end of the ferry the din of the rescue effort was muted, but it was still far louder than the hotel conference room where Amanda imagined she was. When would they be allowed off the ferry, for God's sake?

"Yeah, I guess. It's just been funny around here, with you gone for three days. And then Kelsey just IMed me the weirdest thing. She said she saw you on TV."

"On TV? Me?" a stab of alarm pierced Brett. She glanced at the cameras that had invaded the ferry's deck. They'd been interviewing for at least a half hour. Until Jackie announced she was freezing, Brett had paced the deck back and forth, too keyed up to sit. She could easily have been caught in the background. *Think, Brett, think.* Amanda was still talking.

"Yeah. Are you anywhere near that plane crash? In the river? It's all over the news. Kelsey said she saw you on TV. On a boat, behind somebody else being interviewed, I guess."

"A plane crash? In a river? Here in New York?" Brett repeated Amanda's words, trying to think clearly. She couldn't be caught. Not yet. She wasn't ready. She feigned surprise. "I've been stuck in a conference room, in meetings all day. Haven't heard anything about it."

"Oh." Amanda drew out the word. "I told Kelsey she was crazy. But you are coming home tomorrow, then, right?"

"Yes. I'll be home when you get back from school." Saying something truthful momentarily soothed Brett's conscience.

"OK. See you tomorrow, then."

"Right. I love you, Amanda."

"Love you, too, Mom."

Brett flipped her phone shut and tried to breathe deeply. A close call. She couldn't recall ever lying to Amanda. Through the windows she watched Jackie, now smiling and chatting with some other passenger. She remembered the night before, and that morning. Jackie looked up, caught her eye and winked. Brett smiled back, her fear of discovery almost dissolving in the warmth of the moment.

On the river side of the ferry, Robby still hung over the guardrail, glad to have it to himself again, except for his parents. On the dock side, two dozen wet passengers were disembarking into a throng of media. Everyone else seemed more interested in them than the plane. Through the binoculars, Robby scanned the hulk of white metal, wingtip to wingtip. It didn't look menacing at all anymore, the Storm Trooper mask tilted half-in, half-out of the river.

"I don't see the engines. Are they underwater?"

"Yes, probably," his mom said.

"Nothing looks broken. Not even any windows. So how did the plane crash?" He turned the binoculars toward her. Through the lenses, the intersecting lines of her plaid coat looked like little worms on a field of dirt.

"I don't know how it crashed. I'm sure it will be all over the news," she replied.

"Was there a fire?" Robby asked.

"No."

"How do you know?"

"Well, if there was a fire it would probably still be going. Or at least we'd smell smoke. Or something. Airplane fires take a long time to put out."

"Even if you crash on water? Wouldn't the water just put it out? Like a campfire?" Robby let the binoculars hang around his neck and mimed dousing a campfire with a bucket.

"Good question! But no, it wouldn't go out that fast because of all the fuel airplanes carry. It would take a long time to burn off. Even sitting in water."

Robby considered it. Then he picked the binoculars back up and returned his gaze to the plane.

"Did they get everybody out?"

"I'm sure they did."

"How do they know?"

"Well, they have lists, you know, passenger lists, that they can check the names of everyone who was rescued against."

"Lists? Were we on a list when we came here?"

His mom nodded. "There's a special word for it. What is it—oh, shoot. It's on the tip of my tongue—"

"Huh. Cool. Who's got the list?"

"Um, well, I guess the pilot has it."

"Then isn't it in the water, too?"

"Well, the airline has a copy, too. On the computer. They can get it to the police and everyone who's responding."

"Hmmmmm." Robby stared out at the river again. A circling pigeon screeched.

Linda lobbed back answers as fast as Robby pelted questions. When he finally paused she called to Sam, who was sitting on a bench up against the cabin.

"This is amazing! I've never heard him talk so much. Ask so many questions. It's been at least ten rounds! Have you?"

Sam shook his head. Linda waited for a moment, hoping he'd join them at the railing. Fun family excursion, remember? Robby was bouncing on his toes, cataloguing everything he saw in his stage whisper voice. For once the headphones were around his neck instead of clapped over his ears. The hood of his Detroit Lions sweatshirt created a pointed silhouette that made him look elfish, more juvenile, though when he was standing straight up instead of leaning over a boat rail, Linda knew that hood would be past her shoulder.

Lately she worried more and more about Robby's increased inches, which made his autistic behaviors both harder to excuse and more imminently threatening. What would happen when she wasn't—they weren't—there to buffer him from the expectations of the neurotypical world?

Sam remained on his bench. Robby swiveled his head, binoculars still pressed to his eyes, and then pointed.

"They're back!"

"What?" Linda followed his finger.

"The geese! Swimming right by the plane."

Linda squinted, trying to see what he saw.

"I saw them before. Before the crash. Now they're back. Twelve of them. Just like me." He hopped down from the deck ledge and turned to Linda, making eye contact for a rare moment. "After we get off, can we go see the plane? On another ferry?"

"I don't think so, Robby. This whole area will be secured. They're not going to let boats near," Linda said.

From the euphoria the spasm of questions had induced, her voice segued back to the placating tone she used so often, trying to head off a meltdown. She'd been on her guard all day. Since they left home, really. At least a dozen times since Christmas it had been on the tip of her tongue to tell Sam to come alone, that his nephew's senior hockey tournament would be more fun without them. Robby relied on routines to belay him through the day, so the deviations and unfamiliar place made for ripe conditions. With the cruise being her idea, guilt made her back off about marching him into the cabin, but that was a near miss. So was their check-in at the DoubleTree in New Jersey two days ago, when they'd been out of their damn chocolate chip cookies.

"Isn't that right, Sam?" she called to her husband, seeking backup. He finally stood, joining them at the railing. "Isn't what right?"

"That this area will be secured. We won't be able to get back later."

"Oh. Right." He waved at the other side of the boat. "It looks like they're letting us off. I'm going to check it out."

Robby stayed at the railing, staring into the waves. Watching her husband drift away, absorbed in her own head, Linda finally remembered the word. *Manifests. Passenger manifests.* That was what those lists were called.

~

"We're fine," Christopher argued to the EMT conducting dockside exams. "We need to get back to LaGuardia. Our car's there."

Aboard the ferry they were given thermal blankets and coffee. Someone had even produced extra uniform sets for the ferry employees, and Christopher and Deborah both now wore the ill-fitting but dry navy pants. The EMT had confirmed all their vitals were normal. Out of danger, either from drowning or freezing, Deborah just wanted to curl up and call Helen back, but her phone was at the bottom of the river.

"Sir, the airline has to do a thorough intake of all survivors." The EMT was implacable as he steered them to a taxi line. "The Park Central Hotel's been established as a command center. They'll provide more information there."

"All right." With a loud sigh, Christopher capitulated.

Deborah felt grateful for the quiet of the cab and the blast from the heater. Behind the Plexiglas divider, the backseat felt like a cocoon amid the Midtown rush hour traffic. She closed her eyes. Christopher reached for her hand.

"You OK?"

"I think so." Her mind felt numb now. As her body thawed, she became aware of the soreness in her rib cage, where the seatbelt had restrained her as they'd smacked onto the river.

"That was pretty intense."

She nodded.

"I mean, you were pretty intense. Right at the end, just before we got on the ferry."

"I guess it's true what they say about near-death experiences. It really puts life in perspective."

"Yeah. For me, too."

"You mean about having a baby?" She opened her eyes eagerly, searching his face.

"Not exactly." He shook his head.

"Then what? What were you thinking?"

"I was thinking about how grateful I was for our lives. Together, as a couple."

She squeezed his hand. "That's sweet." What was he getting at?

"But I feel like . . . like we haven't been living them these last two years."

Her heart skipped a beat. "What do you mean?"

"Ever since we started trying to get pregnant, we've been stuck in this limbo loop. We haven't made love spontaneously since 2007. Waiting for the right time to try. Waiting to find out. Waiting to try again. The IVFs made it worse."

"Worse how?" She slid her hand out of his.

"You get so obsessed, so fixated on the results. It's total tunnel vision. And then you're so depressed."

"Well, it is depressing. Not being able to do what normal women can. Normal *couples*," Deborah amended, stressing the last word.

"I wanted children, too, but I don't think it's abnormal if we don't. Especially in our circles. We're both professionals. We do work that matters. We—"

"'Work that matters?' Christopher, are you honestly telling me that after what we just went through, work is more important than having a family?"

"I have a family already. We're a family, Deborah, you and I. I want to protect that family first."

A protest rose to Deborah's lips, but they were arriving at the hotel. Another horde of media swarmed the sidewalk. Stepping out of the cab, Deborah saw the woman she'd noticed on the wing, the mother and her baby, at the center of the cluster of microphones and cameras.

"Where are you from?" someone shouted. "How old is the baby?" another asked. "What was it like out there in the river? Isn't New York the greatest city in the world, to have handled the rescue so quickly? Do you have anything to say to family at home?"

The woman opened her mouth. The media stopped shouting, waiting breathlessly.

"Well, of course it was terrifying when the pilot told us to brace for impact," the woman said. "I just prayed my baby would be OK." She patted him—Deborah was pretty sure it was a boy—on the back and smiled at him. At his round, drooling face, not at the cameras, Deborah noted.

"Come on, Deborah. Let's go." She felt Christopher tugging her hand. She pulled it back, as mesmerized by the woman as the media.

"And now I'm just so grateful. To God, to the pilot, to the other passengers who helped me. It was a miracle. A true miracle," the woman said, shifting the baby to her other hip.

"A miracle on the Hudson," offered one of the reporters.

"That's right." The woman nodded.

Security burst from the hotel. "All right, press conference is over. We've got to get these folks inside ASAP." Shouting questions again, the media turned their cameras as the lead guard placed a protective hand on the shoulder of the woman, below the baby's head. They looked like a family, Deborah reflected with a pang, watching him shepherd them into the hotel.

Where was Christopher? There he was, already through the revolving door, inside the lobby, talking on his phone. Checking in at the university, no doubt. She knew he was waiting to hear whether his department had won a big grant application, five million dollars from the US Fish and Wildlife Service for a study on the nesting habits of migratory birds. Tunnel vision, my foot. She also noticed he had used the past tense in the cab. He'd "wanted" to have children.

Silently she walked right by him, to the registration desk. "Two beds, please."

THREE

Amanda flew around the kitchen, pouring juice, popping a bagel in the toaster, turning on the TV. She glanced out the window at their backyard bird feeder. Her mom was right, it needed refilling. She'd do it on her way out. She really wasn't late, but when she created a commotion she didn't feel so lonely. Her dad was already gone, leading a "prayer breakfast" that he'd told her about the night before over the Chinese takeout he brought home, apologizing because some counseling session had run late. He hadn't blinked when she told him her mom was staying away another night.

"Well, I guess it's father-daughter night, then. We don't do this very often, do we?" said the Reverend Richard Stevens, segueing automatically into grace over the kung pao chicken and egg rolls. "Come, Lord Jesus, be our guest. Let these gifts to us be blessed . . ."

After his "amen," silence prevailed. Amanda wouldn't have known what to talk about even if she hadn't been preoccupied with both her missing mom and the auditions.

She knew what *not* to say, though: anything about the musical. Not after that one time in the choir. At least not until she'd gotten a part. Then it could be about keeping her word to the cast and director. Fulfilling a commitment she'd made would trump the risk of appearing proud and vain.

The bagel popped up. Amanda spread cream cheese thickly, thinking. Before yesterday, when was the last time she had eaten breakfast by herself? Her mom was always there in the mornings, even as the church's food pantry consumed more of her evenings—evenings when they used to make experimental omelettes with whatever happened to be in the fridge and play Scrabble or cards or watch movies while her dad offered counseling or Bible study at the church.

So, measured by meals, it was official, Amanda thought, chewing another bite. Everyone and everything at Fellowship of Hope got a piece of her parents before she did.

The TV anchor intruded on her thoughts. "Investigators will begin to work in earnest today to learn the cause of yesterday's emergency landing in the Hudson River, which riveted New York and much of the nation for hours." The plane appeared, balancing gracefully on the waves again, the passengers backlit.

"CNN has learned that the probable cause of the crash is assumed to be a bird strike," the anchor continued.

Bird strike. The words reminded Amanda she was supposed to fill the bird feeder. Swallowing the last of the bagel, she found the bird feed sack in the pantry and lugged it outside.

Sharp cold greeted her. Filling the feeder took half the burlap bag. Back in the kitchen, the clock read 7:39 a.m. She had to get going. Dropping the sack on the floor, she searched for the TV remote. The crash story was still on.

". . . Ted Ramsey, thanks for your time this morning. Coming up next we'll have a preview of the upcoming presidential inauguration. By the way, we understand that Captain Sullenberger and his family may be on their way to that event next week, at the invitation of President-elect Obama. But let's take one more look at some of yesterday's stunning scenes."

There it was, next to the toaster. Amanda aimed the remote over the kitchen counter carefully. It was an old set. You had to press the

"Power" button just right for it to work. The shot of the plane balancing on the waves, passengers strung out along the wings, had been stylized into a logo. "Miracle on the Hudson," she read as a video montage started. She waved the remote. Come on, already. A close-up of a mother holding a baby aboard the ferry deck. The camera backed up, widening the view. A man was talking and gesturing with his phone. Behind him, a woman leaned against the deck rail, her red coat bright against the gray waves.

A red coat. *Your mom is on. OMG.* OMG. Oh, my God. But yes, it was her mom, now turning toward the camera, walking toward it, her blond hair blowing across her collar, walking behind the man on the phone. Just like Kelsey said. No way. No *way*, Amanda had said, but it was her mom in her red peacoat, right there on the deck of a ferry. Nowhere near a conference room. What was she doing there? And why didn't she say she was, after Amanda asked her straight-out?

The montage changed again, to an aerial of the emergency vessels surrounding the plane and then cut to a commercial for blood pressure medication. Finally, the remote worked, vanquishing the image from the screen. But Amanda still saw the stark fact.

Her mother had lied.

Brett stood in the lobby of the Times Square hotel, wanting to meld her body to Jackie's as they said their good-byes. Neither her hands, nor lips, nor mind were behaving like a proper pastor's wife's would. *How ironic*, Brett thought. It was Richard who had set her on course to this moment, when he said the congregation expected her to be more visible. It was important to him, to his career, he said. To their stability there in Scranton, where Amanda was doing so well in school, he said, expertly manipulating the mantra that guided her life: do what's best for Amanda.

Brett hadn't balked then, two years ago, nor did she now. She yielded to expectations, waving to Jackie's departing taxi and turning to the parking garage. *Expectations, damn expectations.* Like the church's, expecting two-for-one when they hired a pastor. Amanda was an excuse at first, but she was getting older and had some good friends. She probably needed more breathing room, anyway.

Instead of co-leading the Bible study or fund-raising for a new church carpet, she decided to expand the existing food pantry into a community meal program. Once, she and Richard had both believed social justice was a major mission of ministry. Ever since he'd accepted the pastor position at Fellowship of Hope, though, Richard had seemed to grow more judgmental and closed-minded, like the congregation. The meal program not only allowed her to re-embrace her old ideals, but it meant spending time with non-members.

She'd considered carefully how to broach this to Richard.

"The Lord has told me we're meant to serve the entire community, not just those who are already in our flock," she had told Richard.

Richard nodded solemnly. "Matthew, chapter six: 'Behold the birds of the air: for they sow not, neither do they reap, nor gather into barns; yet your heavenly Father feeds them.'" He nodded again. "God will bless your efforts, Brett."

Brett steered their eight-year-old blue Honda Accord out of the parking garage, looking for a sign to the Lincoln Tunnel. Duly blessed, she had begun to use the rudimentary kitchen facilities in the church basement to cook a weekly community dinner.

The first week, a dozen people showed up. The second week, it doubled. She created flyers and posted them at the library, at grocery stores, at the bus station. After two months, fifty people were gathering regularly. It was fulfilling. What better manifestation of church fellowship was there, after all, than sharing a meal?

Eventually, though people appreciated the meals, she learned that what was really needed was meal delivery. People whose kitchen cabinets were bare often didn't have transportation, but did still have pride. Bringing the food to them—in their homes, apartments, cars—would truly help people in Scranton who were down on their luck.

That was what had prompted Brett, again with Richard's blessing, to attend the annual Meals on Wheels Best Practice Symposium, sponsored by the East Coast Conference of Christian Sisterhood and held at the Charlotte Expo Center in downtown Charlotte, North Carolina, last September.

Ahead, she could see the tunnel brightening as she approached the New Jersey end. It reminded her of seeing Jackie that first night, at the welcome reception. She was a regular at the conference, the wife of a pastor whose star was rising on the southeast megachurch circuit, according to the conversation Brett overheard.

Her eyes had noticed other details. Jackie's lean, tan figure. Her honey-colored hair curling around her shoulders. Her perfume, when they wound up sitting next to each other at the second plenary session the next morning.

"Wasn't that so inspiring?" she remembered saying to Jackie after the presentation ended.

Jackie had turned, her eyes taking Brett in from head to toe.

"Absolutely it was," Jackie said, her southern drawl thicker and sweeter than a milkshake. "Have we met?"

"I don't think so. Brett. Brett Stevens. From Pennsylvania."

"Hell-low, Brett Stevens from Pennsylvania." Jackie had smiled, clasping Brett's pale, plain hand in between her tan ones with their coral-painted fingernails.

A pulsing sensation rippled from the handclasp up Brett's arm and down to her core. *She's a pastor's wife. Like you.* The ripple receded.

"First time?"

First time for the sensations? Brett thought back to freshman year at Penn State, in the dorms. Her roommate Donna's habit of sleeping in her panties and a T-shirt. Brett had requested a single the next semester, the semester she also met Richard.

Jackie was still looking at her.

"Pardon me?"

"First time here at the conference?"

"Oh. Uh, yes."

"Well, I'm on the welcome committee. So let me be the first to welcome you to Charlotte, Brett Stevens. I think you'll like it here."

Absorbed in her memory, Brett let the Accord drift into the left lane. A truck's horn blast brought her back to the highway, to the present cold, stark January day. So different from the humid, heavy Charlotte air. The air had had something to do with it, she was sure, heating her imagination during their first cup of coffee together that afternoon, as she watched Jackie's coral fingertips curl around the cup.

She's a pastor's wife. Like you. Someone safe, she told herself again in her room that night, after hanging up from the call she was expected to make home. *Someone harmless.*

But she was wrong, gloriously wrong. Calls, e-mails, and one other stolen day in New York last December, on the premise of Christmas shopping, followed. Then, finally, this rendezvous, under the cover of another fictitious conference. Brett had dared to suggest it after Amanda came home from school talking about registering for her SAT college exams. The offhand remark sent Brett reeling back two decades, to the Penn State dorm room. She'd denied herself all this time, on the grounds of what was right, on the grounds of being a dutiful wife, on the grounds of what was best for Amanda. Now Amanda was a year and a half away from her own life. Brett's marriage was hollow. And she didn't know what was right anymore.

Still, she had half hoped that Jackie would cancel. When they finally found themselves together, twenty floors above Manhattan, releasing those so-long-suppressed instincts, yielding to play and passion and pushing away what was best for Amanda, Brett spent three days veering from exhilaration to terror.

Three days they decided to stretch into four, pushing Jackie's return flight to Charlotte to the next day. Exhilaration. Then, the fateful decision to take the sightseeing cruise. The crash. And getting caught by the camera—according to Amanda's friend Kelsey, anyway. Terror.

Another horn blast jarred her out of her thoughts. Brett overcorrected, sending the Accord all the way into the right lane just as she crossed the state line.

"Pennsylvania Welcomes You," declared the broad blue sign. "State of Independence."

Brett registered another flash of irony, this one cruel, in the instant before the sign disappeared in her exhaust and tears.

FOUR

Sitting cross-legged on the scratchy hotel bedspread, Robby Palmer watched CNN intently. His parents wanted to go get breakfast, but he wasn't budging.

"Investigators will begin to work in earnest today to unravel the chain of events behind yesterday's emergency landing in the Hudson River, which riveted New York and much of the nation for hours," the anchor said as rescue footage unfolded on the screen.

"New York Mayor Michael Bloomberg is praising the efforts of US Airways pilot Sully Sullenberger and his crew for the textbook execution of an aviation maneuver known as 'ditching,'" the anchor went on.

"Ditching," Robby wrote in the brown notebook on his lap, underlining it. He could hear the traffic down in the street.

"All one hundred fifty passengers and five crew aboard, including one infant, were rescued unharmed from the frigid waters, estimated at only thirty-six degrees," she continued. An interview with the mother played.

Robby shifted restlessly. This was all rehash they'd been replaying since six a.m. Where was the news? From the bathroom, the rush of water stopped.

"CNN has learned that the probable cause of the crash is assumed to be a bird strike," the anchor continued. "The leading cause of crashes occurring within five minutes of takeoff or landing, these strikes are unpredictable, but rarely cause as much drama as Thursday's incident. We'll speak with an expert on bird strikes at the FAA after this short break, but first this look at some of yesterday's riveting scenes."

Robby's attention refocused. This was new. "Bird strike," he wrote in his notebook. The bathroom door opened, and his mom stepped out in a hotel robe. The fan roared behind her. He turned up the TV volume.

His dad walked over to refill his coffee, clinking the pot against the cup. "Pretty interested in this stuff, huh, Rob?" he asked. "Can I see your notebook?"

Robby drew it to his chest, leaning over protectively.

"Please?"

Robby shook his head and turned away for good measure.

"OK." Sam shrugged. "Maybe later."

As she combed her sandy hair, Linda watched her husband and son in the mirror. She felt so bad for Sam when Robby shut himself off. They ought to be used to it now. At least enough not to take it personally, seven years after he'd been slapped with that 21st century scarlet letter: "A" for autism. But Sam took it harder, maybe because he had fewer opportunities to try to connect. On events like this trip, times that were supposed to be special, it was even worse.

Linda sighed. Sam came over.

"Feeling down?" He slouched against the wall.

"Hmmm? I guess not. Nothing out of the ordinary, anyway. You?"

"Nothing out of the ordinary." He raked his fingers through his hair, then jerked a thumb at their son, lowering his voice though

Robby appeared engrossed in the news. "Think we'll get him out of here today?"

"We're not making it an option to stay. We'll do the countdown, give him the warnings as it gets time to leave. But we're not going to let a twelve-year-old control both of us."

Sam snorted in a half-disgusted, half-mocking way. "Why should today be any different?"

Linda raised her eyebrows. Sam wasn't usually sarcastic when it came to Robby. "What's going on?"

Sam sighed. His back still against the wall, he slid down to the floor. Looking down at her husband, Linda was startled to see how much gray flecked his brown hair. *Does it show up in mine, too?*

Elbows balanced on his knees, Sam held his graying head for a long minute before he spoke. "I was just thinking about dinner the other night, at Tom and Robin's. How nice it was. How normal. We played basketball before dinner, and it was Tyler's idea. At dinner I could ask him questions—and get answers. And I could just talk. I didn't have to think about how to phrase a question, or be sure I'd made eye contact first. I didn't have to pretend it doesn't matter to me when I'm ignored."

Linda stole a glance at Robby, isolated in the glow of the TV, and swallowed.

"There were no battles all evening, no hassles. It was just so, so . . . easy." Sam sighed again, wistfully. "And then watching Tyler on the ice, seeing him lead his team . . . it just crystallized everything that Robby won't do." He paused. "Can't do. Doesn't do."

He glanced at Linda.

"I'm sorry. I know I'm not helping. It's just all so different from what I was expecting. That interview they had on a minute ago, that woman who was on the plane with her baby? I felt so jealous of her. She's still got all her illusions about parenthood. And mine—ours—are just . . ." he gestured in Robby's direction, shook his head and laid it back against the wall.

Linda couldn't speak around the lump in her own throat. Instead, she sat down next to Sam, squeezing his hand. Feeling equal parts guilty, desperate, and stuck, she nodded fiercely, hoping the rhythm would force the tears back.

Robby came over. "Museum of Natural History. B or C subway line. Eighty-first Street station," he said, abruptly.

Sam looked at Linda.

"Robby, do you want to go to the museum?" she asked, rising from the floor.

Robby was already putting on his Detroit Lions sweatshirt, pulling the hood up over his head. He bobbed it once. Yes.

Uncertain, Linda looked at Sam, who shrugged and nodded.

"I'm starving, though." Sam glanced at his watch as he stood, too.

Linda walked to her suitcase. "What's at the museum, Robby?"

"Birds."

"Birds? What kind of birds?"

Shrug.

"You don't know? Why do you want to go, then?"

"Gotta find out."

"Find out what?"

"About birds. Come on, Mom!"

Linda looked at Sam. "We could go in circles all morning. You try while I get dressed."

Sam waited until the bathroom door shut behind her. "How do you know there are birds there, Robby?"

"Internet."

Robby's laptop was propped open on his bed. Sam looked at the screen, open to the "Maps and Directions" page of the American Museum of Natural History. Take the B or C subway line and get off at the 81st Street station. Robby never forgot the details, that was for sure. Sam clicked over to the home page. Nothing about birds. He tried the "Exhibitions" tab. Nothing. He clicked around another moment. Nada. He looked at his son, standing impatiently by the door.

"Robby, I can't find anything about birds at this museum."

Robby rolled his eyes and stomped over. None too gently, he sidled in between Sam and the computer and typed "Birds" into the site search bar. A list of nearly one hundred hits returned. He looked at his father, eyebrows lifted in *I-told-you-so* fashion.

Sam clicked on the first link, then the second, then the third. They all were about rare birds the museum had in its collection, but not ones that were necessarily on exhibition.

"Rob, c'mere. I don't know if this is exactly what you think it is."

"Want to go. B or C subway line. Eighty-first Street station," Robby repeated, hanging his headphones around his neck.

Linda emerged, dressed. "Lin, if we get there and they don't have what he wants, it's going to be out of control," Sam told her. "And we still haven't eaten breakfast."

Linda looked at Robby. He was jiggling the doorknob with one hand, clutching the notebook in the other, humming softly but audibly, signaling rising anxiety. "We can stop at a coffee shop. I think we've got to go with him and find out."

Deborah sat up in the hotel bed, the remnant of the nightmare that woke her washing away in the undertow of her astonishment at the time on the bedside clock: 9:04 a.m. When had she last slept past six on a weekday?

She was alone, too, the other mussed bed the only sign of Christopher and their second argument of the night before. Her gaze fell on the room service menu lying next to the clock. A yellow sun and the words "Good Morning!" marched across the top in all capital letters.

Deborah closed her eyes and flopped back on the bed. On the heels of a bad afternoon and a worse evening, a good morning seemed unlikely. After they checked in, she'd called Helen from Christopher's phone, let her know they were safe, and said she would see about rescheduling the trip to Seattle right away. As soon as she hung up, Christopher had started to argue against it.

"Your purse was on the plane. You haven't got so much as a driver's license at the moment. I don't know how you could even board a plane without ID. Plus you don't have any clothes, or credit cards to buy more."

"You've got your wallet. We could buy a few things here at the hotel. And the airline's got to make some exceptions for all the passengers like us who lost ID and luggage. We could still go," she countered.

He shook his head. "This never was a very good time for me, Deborah, so close to the start of the new semester."

"Then why did you agree in the first place?"

He sighed. "I knew it was important to you. And I thought if it was the two of us getting away like we used to, even if we did visit your sister, maybe you could see how good we are, just as us."

"Just as us?" Her throat closed. She forced herself to swallow, to say the next words. "I thought you wanted children, too."

"I'm open to children, but not at any price. And we've paid a lot these last two years, Deborah. You passed up Martha's job—"

"Not that again, Christopher." She closed her eyes.

"It's more than just financial."

"Of course it is! It's emotional, it's instinctive—"

But Christopher kept talking. "A pregnancy was already risky when we started. Now you're forty-two. If you got pregnant today, you'd be forty-three when you delivered."

"And so?" Deborah couldn't hide the tremor in her voice.

"You know as well as I do how the risks increase at this age. Pregnancy complications. A C-section birth. Down syndrome."

"I passed all the screenings just fine," Deborah said defensively.

"Two years ago you passed them. And it's been two stressful years, with these cycles that become so all-consuming. Last summer, after the second time, I don't think you left the house for the whole month of July. We go to the doctor more than we go out to dinner."

The room fell silent as they faced each other. Deborah folded her arms.

"So what are we talking about, really?"

He paused, turning to gaze out at the city lights that winked between the drapes for a long moment. "I guess—I guess I'd like to move on," he said, turning back to look at her. "Move forward with our lives. We tried. I wish it had worked out differently, too. I had some dreams about being a father. The kind of father I never had. But it's overshadowed everything long enough." He sat down beside her, covering her knee with his hand. "I'm sorry."

The impact of his words crashed inside Deborah's head. She didn't know what to say. She, who always knew what to say. When the donors shook their heads and said, "Sorry, not this year," she was always the one who still managed to walk away with a check. She clung to one word—*wish*.

She stood up, moving away from his touch. "What about the embryos we have left?" She couldn't believe she was asking, that it was possible to leave three orphans without ever experiencing parenthood.

He lifted his shoulders. "I don't know. I'm sure the clinic has some kind of policy about that."

"What kind of policy?"

"They're probably donated for research."

Deborah's stomach heaved as she imagined E, F, and G on microscope slides. "Research? Christopher, how cold can you be? We're not talking about a study at the Lab."

"Maybe they're offered to other couples. For adoption."

"Adoption? This is our potential child. Children. Ours!"

Her voice broke on the last word, and so did her body, crumpling at last under the stress of the entire day. She collapsed on one of the beds, her back to the other, curling her knees up to her still-aching ribs. "I can't talk about this anymore."

"Deborah, I love you. I'm sorry. I never wanted to hurt you." Christopher sat behind her, touching her shoulder.

"And I never thought you would," Deborah said woodenly, contracting more tightly into her fetal position, away from Christopher.

The click of the door opening roused her from the memory. Christopher appeared, carrying two Starbucks cups.

"Morning." He sat on the bed he'd slept in and pushed one cup across the nightstand to her.

"Dark roast, black."

"Thanks." Deborah took a sip.

"Sleep OK?"

She shrugged. "I've had better." She suddenly recalled her nightmare, of the baby she'd seen with his mother on the wing. In the dream he was in the water instead of his mother's arms. He seemed fine, smiling even, trying to swim to Deborah. She reached out, but the waves carried him away. Unable to swim, she was forced to watch the smiling baby bob up and down, just out of her reach.

"Me too." Christopher looked at his cup.

"Is the coffee a peace offering?"

He took a long sip. "I guess you could say that."

"I want to know what *you* would say."

He set his cup down and reached across the gap between the beds for her hand.

"It's a peace offering. But I don't know what to say after that. It's not like this is something we can compromise on. We're in two different places."

"Are we? You said yesterday that you wish it had worked out differently. We could be in the same place."

He sighed. "I don't know if I can go there again. If it didn't—"

"If it didn't, then we would be done. Right now, we still have the last three embryos."

He looked wary. "So what are you suggesting, exactly?"

"One more try. All three embryos. Just like the specialist said. If it doesn't work, then we'll be done. I promise." She squeezed his hand, as if she could imprint the pledge.

Christopher exhaled deeply, removing his glasses to massage his temples. Deborah held her breath, recognizing the habit from when he did his most serious thinking.

"All right," he said at last. "I'm not promising anything right now. But I'll think about it."

Deborah called Helen from Christopher's phone after they checked out, while he went to the airline's command center in the hotel ballroom to fill out paperwork. As her call traveled west, skipping across the Great Lakes, the Great Plains, and the Rockies to the Pacific coast, it comforted Deborah to picture a phone ringing crisply on Helen's nightstand or kitchen counter, somewhere in the scenery of her sister's blissfully normal, mundane life.

"Hello?" The voice was a bit breathless. At this hour on the West Coast, Helen was probably on her treadmill for her usual morning workout.

"Hi, Helen. It's me."

"Deborah! I keep seeing coverage of the crash. I still can't believe you were on that plane. Have you talked to anyone else? Are you and Christopher really OK?"

"We are. Really, we're fine." Physically, anyway. Her bruised psyche was something else again. "But, Helen, we'll have to figure out another time for a visit. We're going home to Ithaca. I don't even have my purse. No ID, no money, no clothes." She recited Christopher's arguments into her sister's ear. "I wish I could convince him to still come, but he says it's a bad time. And it's not a good time for us to be apart, either." She lowered her voice, not wanting to say it aloud herself.

"He's talking about wanting to stop the IVF." Her sister had been a confidante during the past two years, buoying her with optimism at the ebbs. "You'll be such great parents," she said during every conversation, her use of the future tense a gift.

Not today, though. "Oh, Deborah, I'm so sorry."

"Thanks." Deborah blinked against the tears.

"He was probably pretty shaken up by the crash, right?"

"I hope that's all it is." She sighed. "Now tell me what's going on with you. What did you need to talk to me about so badly yesterday?" The phone's low battery signal beeped. "Damn it. Helen, I'm about to lose you. I'll call you again from home."

"OK."

"I'm sorry. I really wanted to see you and the girls."

"Don't worry. It'll be fine. I love you."

"I love you, too," Deborah said bleakly, and the phone went dead.

FIVE

They climbed the stairs from the West 81st Street station, Robby two steps ahead. At sidewalk level he wheeled around, searching for a street sign. Spotting one, he took off at a near-sprint, scattering a flock of pigeons foraging by a wastebasket. Linda panted, trying to keep up. "Is this the right way, Sam?"

"I'm going to trust he knows what he's looking for. Take your time. I'll stay with him."

Sam trailed behind his son up the museum's stone steps. The doors were locked. "Museum hours: ten a.m. to five forty-five p.m.," Sam read. He glanced at his watch. "Rob, it'll be open in another half hour. Let's go get some breakfast first."

"Wanna wait here." Robby plunked down on the steps. Linda caught up, breathless.

"We've got a half hour before they open, and I'm pretty hungry," Sam said. Linda nodded. They scanned the block, spotting a diner on the corner. "Come on, Robby, let's go get something to eat. We'll get you a doughnut," Linda coaxed.

Robby shook his head. "Gonna wait."

"Robby, don't be difficult. It's cold here. You're not going to get in any sooner, and the birds will still be here if we go have some breakfast first." Sam bent down and put his hand under Robby's armpit, trying to lift him up. He was heavy, heavier than Sam expected.

Robby jerked back his arm, shaking off his father and dropping his notebook. Off balance, Sam staggered back, stumbling down several steps. Ignoring him, Robby scooped up the notebook and tore up the remaining steps to the vestibule doors, yelling as he ran.

"No, no, no, no! No breakfast. Staying here. Staying here!" At the locked doors he wedged himself into a corner, clamped his headphones on, jammed his hands into his pockets, and glared down at them.

A dozen steps below, Sam punched the air. He swore, then looked guiltily at Linda. She shook her head and shrugged.

"I'll stay with him," she said, resignation saddling each word. "You go eat. Bring me back a bagel or something."

Sam started to protest, then cut himself off. A half hour without Robby sounded pretty appealing right now. "OK. I'll be back at ten."

Before he crossed the street to the diner, Sam glanced back at his wife and son. Linda had walked up to the step where Robby was bunkered but kept a good five-foot perimeter. She looked like a sentinel up there, a watchdog ready to chase away whatever might dare to disturb or unsettle the mind and body shrouded beneath the hooded sweatshirt and headphones. Not unlike any other mother, really. The problem was that simple routines of daily life were a constant bombardment to Robby's hypersensitive sensory systems. His communication and social deficits further isolated him. Thus the mission never ended.

And Sam was the only one who could relieve her.

Robby watched his father's back retreat. Down the steps. Down the sidewalk, to the corner. The dark-green diamonds of his quilted coat blended into the newsstand. The light changed. He crossed three lanes of yellow taxis and disappeared into the diner. *Finally.*

Robby exhaled and wedged his body more firmly into his corner. He liked feeling the cool, solid stone wall behind him. Here, nothing could come up and surprise him. It felt safe. The safest place he'd found in New York. Better than the hotel with the stiff, scratchy sheets and bedspreads. Better than the subways, with the swooshing trains and chiming doors and chattering riders and the surprise invisible announcer voice. Way better than Uncle Tom and Aunt Robin's house, where they went for dinner last night, before his cousin Tyler's hockey game.

Dinner wasn't ready. Why were they invited at five if dinner wouldn't be ready for another hour? "How's it going, buddy?" his uncle had said.

"I'm not your buddy. We don't ever see each other."

"Robby!" His mother laughed, her gasp-laugh. Then she told him to go upstairs with Tyler. "I'm sorry, Tom. He's just so literal," he heard her say as he followed Tyler, sighing.

Upstairs in his room, Tyler kept asking him questions. What sports did he like? Had he ever been to a hockey game? Did he want to watch Tyler's hockey highlight DVD and learn everything?

Robby didn't answer. He asked if Tyler had any video games.

"Video games are a waste of time," Tyler said. "Turn you into a slug. Let's play hoops in the backyard?"

When Robby still didn't answer, Tyler waited, then shrugged. "Fine. I'll go ask Uncle Sam."

Tyler's room overlooked the driveway. Five minutes later, Robby heard the thump-thump-thump-thud of the basketball dribbled onto the concrete, then lofted at the rim. Thump-thump-thump-thud. A shout. A laugh—his dad's. Then the smack of a high five. More laughter. Robby had drawn the strings of his Detroit Lions hoodie tighter, until the taut gray fabric almost covered his eyes. His own cocoon there in northern New Jersey, miles and miles from home.

On the museum steps he drew the strings again, but not quite so tightly, peering through the fringe of his bangs. He wanted to be able to see his dad come back, because that would mean it was time for them to unlock the doors. Unlock the doors to this place. Let him in so he could learn about the geese from Canada. Find them and figure out just what had brought them to the Hudson River, these birds in the bird strike.

Robby chewed the hard end of the drawstring. Just minding their own business, those geese were. Like he did. But that wasn't enough for everyone else. They had to prod and intrude. And look what happened.

He tried to imagine how it would feel to hit the plane. Geese usually flew in Vs. He saw them in the fall at home, soaring above the gray suburban roofs, their long dotted lines somehow appearing simultaneously fluid and regimented.

They must have been flying like that yesterday. What happened to the geese farther back? he wondered. Did they see what happened to their leader? To the next two or three or four? Did they understand? From the docks he saw the geese swimming by the plane. Were they from the stricken flock, circling back upriver to look for their lost companions? Or did they just continue on their instinctive path southward? Who would know?

"Here comes Dad, Robby."

His mom's voice broke his concentration. Robby blinked. He had forgotten to keep watch. His dad was passing the green newsstand again, carrying a white bag. Robby felt his stomach tighten.

Finally.

～

"Amanda. Amanda. Amanda!"

Walking to her locker, Amanda felt someone at her elbow just before her earbud was lifted. Abby.

"Today's the day! Audition day! How do I look?" She twirled in front of Amanda, showing off her bouncing high ponytail. She did look like Sandra Dee, at least as Olivia Newton-John portrayed her. "Can't hurt to drop a little hint, right? I'm so nervous. I'm so glad you're coming with me."

"Oh, Ab, I don't think I can today, after all. I'm really sorry, but I've got some, uh, other stuff to do." She couldn't explain why, but Amanda didn't want to tell her Kelsey had been right about her mom being on the news.

"No way. You're not serious." Abby's face became bereft.

Amanda tried to placate her. "There's two days of auditions, right? I'll be there tomorrow. Promise."

"That's what you said about today. You know how, like, huge this is for me, right?" Abby's voice quavered. She looked mad and scared and hurt, all at once. "What's the matter with you?"

"Look, I can't really talk about it now. I'm sorry. Really, Ab, I am. I know you'll be great. But I can't tonight. I just can't."

Amanda was mad, too. Mad at her mom for being gone, and doing something strange like lying about a boat trip. Mad at Kelsey for happening to see her on TV and telling Amanda about it. Mad at CNN for not showing that clip just thirty seconds later, when she'd have been out of the house. Mad at herself for not keeping her promise to Abby, who was her best friend, after all. Maybe she could tell her a little bit.

"Look, there's something weird going on with my mom. She's been out of town the last few days. And I've just got to see her as soon as she gets home this afternoon. I'll call you tonight, OK?"

To Amanda's relief, some of the anger disappeared from Abby's face, though her tone was skeptical.

"Your mom? That can't wait till dinnertime?"

Amanda shook her head. "I've got to talk to her before my dad gets home."

Abby's eyebrows lifted as she contemplated Amanda's answer. "Huh. Can't you tell me more now?"

The bell rang, saving Amanda from answering. Abby sighed. "OK. Well, I guess I'll see you third hour, then?" They had biology together.

"Yeah." Amanda nodded, and with a little wave, turned toward her first-hour classroom.

Unpacking in her bedroom, Brett tried to settle her jangled nerves. She had hoped the miles would distance her from the trip, her near-delirious joy at being free with Jackie, free from the mask and script that she followed every day of her life in Scranton. Instead, her anxiety ratcheted up with each mile. They had not spoken about the future, whether there would be another visit, or even another phone call.

But sitting on the bed she had shared with Richard for eighteen years, Brett knew there would be. Thinking of sleeping with him in the meantime made her despondent. That night, tomorrow night, the rest of the week, the rest of their lives. She couldn't do it anymore.

She didn't fear making love. Their marriage had long ago lapsed into the platonic status where it had begun, at Penn State second semester. He was a sophomore on the other wing of her floor in her new dorm, and they wound up sitting together in the cafeteria. When he first kissed her—a chaste peck after a movie two months later—Brett was so relieved for a reason to bury the feelings Donna had stirred that she kissed back.

Now, with the memories of true passion so raw, it was the dishonesty of their mutual charade that made her shut her eyes against her reflection in the bathroom mirror, as she replaced her toothbrush and dental floss and makeup in their rightful places.

But *was* this the rightful place after all—this small-but-adequate master bathroom in a three-bedroom house in a middle-class family neighborhood in Scranton, Pennsylvania? It had been Richard's choosing, as had everything since her sophomore year, when she transferred with him to a small Bible college south of Pittsburgh, near the border with West Virginia. He felt called to study ministry, he said, and he was certain she would hear it, too, if she just gave it a chance.

Whether it was a calling or not, Brett was far more comfortable on the small campus, with its unwritten but proscribed rules of behavior, than she'd been in the anything-goes atmosphere at Penn State. And after a spring-break mission trip across the state line into West Virginia, where they spent a week toiling to build a community center for a rural church, she began to believe Richard was right. The accomplishment she felt looking at the simple wooden structure, on top of the naked gratitude from the community, was deeper and more satisfying than any academic achievement. She felt proud, too, to be with Richard, the group's unquestioned leader, whose marriage proposal she would accept six months later.

Brett stared out the window, through the bare tree limbs, down to the snow-dusted lawns. So when did that all change? When did Richard become more preoccupied with being pastor than being pastoral? When did evangelical issues edge out social justice as his priority? When did Donna resurface in her memory? How many other Donnas had she closed her eyes to, until Jackie? *Don't*, she counseled herself, as she reached into her pocket for her cell phone. Not yet. It hasn't been four hours since we said good-bye. *Amanda will be home any minute*, her conscience hollered in futility as her fingers dialed Jackie's number.

It rang several times. Jackie was still in the air en route back to Charlotte, Brett realized as her voice mail recording kicked on.

The sound of her voice—its warm, Southern lilt, even reciting the innocuous greeting—electrified Brett's body.

"Jack, it's Brett. I'm home. I miss you already. Call me—no, text me—when you get in. I'll try to call back when I can. I . . . I . . . I hope you had a good trip home," she said hastily, hearing the door open downstairs and Amanda's voice calling to her, dragging her back to her suffocating real life.

"You made me feel alive," she whispered with her last breath.

Amanda watched her mom smile as she came downstairs.

"Hi, sweetheart! I'm so glad to see you!" She pulled Amanda into a hug.

"Hi." Relief surged through Amanda. Her mom looked just the same, sounded just the same. Was that really her on that news clip? Amanda decided not to bring it up right away, after all.

"How was school? You look like you held up just fine without me. How about I make us some popcorn for a snack?"

As they walked together to the kitchen, Amanda spotted the sack of bird feed she'd dropped in the middle of the floor before school. So did her mom.

Curiously, she picked it up. "Why is this sitting out here?"

Amanda stared at the burlap sack, scrambling for an explanation. Her mom filled in.

"Your father probably meant to fill it up but got sidetracked." She glanced out the window at the feeder, nearly empty again, shaking her head as she hoisted the sack. "I guess someone needs me, anyway. Be right back."

SIX

The instant the security guard at the American Natural History Museum unlocked the revolving door, Robby was inside a compartment by himself, his breath fogging the glass. How typical, Linda thought, watching the back of his head, still cradled in the hood and headphones. They spent their lives going round and round with Robby. And like Sam said in the hotel room, they always followed, always a step behind, always separated from his world.

Inside, Robby didn't even glance at the dinosaur skeleton dominating the opulent lobby. He aimed straight for two redwood-sized granite pillars that framed the entrance to the interior.

"Robby, wait. We have to pay first," Linda called as he dodged past a security guard. Grim-faced, Sam increased his stride and caught his son in five paces, taking hold of him firmly, by both shoulders this time, turning him back toward the admission counter. "Third floor!" Robby protested. "Birds! Third floor!"

"Pay first. Then birds," Sam said, using abrupt sentences, the fewest words possible, as the behavioral psychologist advised.

"Birds!" Robby insisted, freezing his body.

Still holding his shoulders, Sam said evenly, "We pay first. Then see birds. Pay first. Or leave now." He released Robby's shoulders and waited.

This time, for his own random reasons, Robby chose to comply. Mutely he followed Sam through the line switchbacks to the admissions counter, where Linda exhaled and the guard watched curiously.

Two regular admission adult tickets and one child—Robby just edged in under the twelve and under limit—cost $48.50. "Good grief," Sam muttered, putting away his Visa.

"Come on," Linda said. "If it's half as good as he thinks it is, this will be the bargain of the vacation."

Sam shrugged, then turned back to Robby, clapping him on the back. "So, third floor, right, Rob?"

Instead of wincing and shrinking away, Robby merely nodded and fell in step beside them, even removing his headphones, which cheered Linda disproportionately. She hoped Sam noticed.

She needn't have bothered with the museum map. Robby navigated them expertly to the Frank M. Chapman Memorial Hall of North American Birds on the third floor, where he suddenly looked uncertain.

"This is it, right?" Sam walked in. "Come on, let's take a look around."

Robby walked in but barely glanced at the first few specimens on exhibit. He tucked his chin and shuffled his feet.

"What the hell's the matter now?" Sam whispered. "Robby, we're finally here. This is what you wanted to see. Take a look!"

Robby remained unengaged through the first two rooms. In the third room they found a display devoted to East Coast migration paths. Robby's head lifted. He read the entire label. Linda could follow along reading his lips.

Reaching the end of the text, he bounced up and down. "Geese!" he shouted, his voice echoing in the nearly empty hall. "Geese!" He started running from display to display, pausing to scan each, bouncing on his toes, grunting, and flapping his left fist. *The anxiety trifecta.*

"This is what I was afraid of," Sam said. "I didn't see any geese exhibition listed online."

"Let's ask him," Linda said, pointing to the next room, where a man typed industriously on a keyboard.

"Excuse me, could you tell us if you happen to have any exhibitions of geese?" Linda asked.

"Canada geese!" Robby was suddenly at her elbow. Linda jumped.

"Robby, you scared me. OK, Canada geese, then," she repeated.

"Let me check." The man's name tag said he was Thomas, a volunteer from the Bronx. Typing again, he paused, then responded with the head shake Linda dreaded. "Lots of hits, but no Canada geese showing up on display at the moment."

"The Museum's bird collection grew to become one of the greatest in the world and now holds ninety-nine percent of all known species," Robby said flatly.

"Excuse me?" Thomas looked at them over the top of his glasses.

"It's something he's read, probably on your website," Linda explained.

"I know. I'm looking at it right now. He said it word for word. That's amazing," Thomas said, looking Robby up and down.

"So find them," Robby said, resuming his toe bouncing.

"Find what?"

"Canada geese."

"We don't have that type of bird on exhibit now. I just told you."

"Ninety-nine percent of all known species are here, and you don't have that one?" Sam asked, catching on to Robby's unspoken argument. "That does seem kind of odd. It's not like a goose is some rare, exotic thing."

"Well, no, but that's what the computer says," Thomas said defensively, pointing at the screen.

"Canada geese!" Robby interjected again, his voice shrill as he yanked on his sweatshirt strings. His downward spiral was accelerating.

"Isn't there someone else we could ask?" Linda said.

"Well, I could call down to the ornithology offices, I guess," Thomas said, a note of doubt in his voice. He consulted a phone list and dialed. He hung up almost immediately. "Busy." He picked it up and tried again. "Still busy." Linda heard Robby's low moan of frustration. She hoped Thomas hadn't.

He was dialing a third time when a short, bearded older man walked quickly into the room. He passed their clustered quartet without a glance, intent on something across the room.

Spotting him, Thomas hung up. "Dr. Felk! I was just trying to reach you."

"Canada geese. Where?" Robby's voice was so loud.

Dr. Felk pivoted. "Reach me? Who are you? Thomas?" He lowered his gaze as he retraced his steps, squinting at Thomas's name tag through the bottom of his wire-framed bifocals. "I've met you before, right?"

"Yes, many times, Dr. Felk," the volunteer said. "These visitors here—"

"Canada geese! Canada geese!" Robby's pitch and intensity were increasing.

Dr. Felk turned away from Thomas, taking a long look at Robby. Bushy gray eyebrows rose just above his glasses, then dropped as he took in her son, whose hood was not only up but tight around his face, from tugging on the strings. Now one hand tugged while the other plucked nervously at the headphones around his neck.

"Visitors. I see. Yes. You're interested in Canada geese, young man?"

Mutely, Robby nodded. *Hang in there*, Linda thought.

"Wonderful. You've come to the right place. Follow me." The old man reached out toward Robby's shoulder, as if to pilot him, Linda thought anxiously. But no, his hand was merely extended in a beckoning gesture, summoning them to follow him out of the gallery, the way he had entered. Robby trotted along compliantly.

"Uh, sir? Sir? Excuse me," Thomas called after him nervously.

"Yes? What is it, Thomas?" Felk halted and looked over his shoulder.

"Sir, the computer says we don't have any Canada geese on exhibit. I did a search."

"You did, did you?"

Thomas nodded. Felk snorted, a sound that turned into a cough.

"Can't trust computers to know a museum, Thomas. I've been working here thirty-five years. Been through this place top to bottom. Trust me, we have Canada geese. I'll take it from here."

Shaking his head and muttering again, Felk led them to a service elevator and jabbed the down button. "Nobody's asked about a damn bird in six months. Everyone wants the dinosaurs, the IMAX, the gift shop. You want to see a Canada goose, son? All right, then. What's your name?"

"Robby," said Robby, uncharacteristically responding before either Sam or Linda spoke.

"Nice to meet you, Robby." The elevator doors opened. Again, Felk gestured, indicating they should enter first. Inside he pressed the button labeled "B." "I'm Arthur Felk, chief ornithologist here at the museum. Been in charge of the birds around here since before Thomas back there was born."

"Linda Palmer," Linda said, extending her hand as the elevator lurched downward. "My husband, Sam. We're visiting from Detroit."

Felk shook their hands, but Robby was clearly where his interest lay. "What do you want to know about Canada geese?"

"Plane crash."

Felk's brow furrowed. "Plane crash? Don't follow you, son."

"Geese make planes crash. Like yesterday's."

"Yesterday's? That one over in the river?" Another cough.

"We were on a ferry in the river when it happened. Robby's been a little, well, obsessed with it since. He has autism," Linda started to explain. "I don't know how much you know about autism, but . . ."

Felk held up his hand, cutting her off. "So they're saying it was a bird strike? I hadn't heard that yet. Well, I'll show you what we've got in our collection now. But you might want to come back another day, because it's likely those engines will be headed this way, once the FAA's done with them, anyway."

"Excuse me?" Sam spoke up. "Why would an engine be of interest to a natural history museum?"

"Wouldn't. It's what's *in* the engine they want us to look at. We'll take it apart, do scrapings for DNA. Try to confirm the species. Cross-reference with known nesting sites in the crash area." The elevator bumped to a stop.

Linda's face pulled back in disgust, but as they stepped out into the museum basement, she read fascination on Robby's. Felk saw it, too.

"Pretty neat, right? The more we know about birds, the better we get at preventing bird strikes. There are thousands per year, you know."

"Thousands?" Robby's face clouded, and he covered his ears. "That's a lot of dead birds."

"Far too many," Felk agreed. "That's why we keep trying to learn more."

Energetically, Felk led them down a long hall. Sam increased his pace to keep up.

"Look, Dr. Felk, it's very kind of you to take the time with us. But you must be busy—"

"I'm perfectly capable of managing my schedule, thank you for your concern," Felk said. "I've got plenty of time for a bright boy like your son, who shows enough sense to take an interest in birds. They're our most highly evolved species, you know."

Sam stopped short. Linda read chagrin on his face. Felk suddenly stopped, too, then pulled out a key ring, inserting one in a door with "Ornithology Archives" etched in a frosted glass pane.

"Here we are," he said, swinging it open.

~

Deborah turned on the radio as Christopher drove northward. The long-term parking lot at LaGuardia was an hour of silence behind them.

". . . the probable cause of the crash is assumed to be a bird strike. The leading cause of crashes occurring within five minutes of takeoff or landing, these strikes are unpredictable. We'll speak with an expert on bird strikes at the FAA after . . ."

Quickly, she turned it back off. The crash was now history. She wanted to think about the future.

"It'll be Ramsey," Christopher turned the radio back on.

"What?"

"Ted Ramsey. The FAA expert on bird strikes. We've had him up a few times. Peter's hoping to get some grant money out of him."

"Christopher, I really don't want to hear any more about the crash."

"Just this interview, Deborah."

The anchor returned. "We'd like to welcome Ted Ramsey of the FAA, an expert on bird strikes."

"I knew it." Christopher smiled triumphantly and turned up the volume.

Sighing, Deborah tuned it out, turning her gaze to the window. It was a brilliant winter day, the sun glinting off the snow-covered landscape. Despite the sun, the day was all hard, rigid edges—the flat plane of cold glass through which the black road sliced through stark white fields that met a cloudless, fiercely blue sky at the unyielding line of the horizon.

The view mirrored the boundaries confining her own future. Forty-two years old, going on forty-three. Two failed IVF cycles. Three embryos left. A husband drawing a line in the sand. Deborah sighed again as Christopher snapped off the radio.

"Interesting."

"What's that?" asked Deborah, glad to turn away from the window.

"Ted's theory. That as planes age, the metal fatigue of the engines makes them more vulnerable to damage in strikes."

"Metal fatigue. I always thought that was such a strange phrase," Deborah said. "Kind of scary, really."

"How so?"

"It sounds like a contradiction. Metal's solid. Hard. It's not supposed to wear out."

"Everything wears out, eventually."

"Ithaca 100 miles." The road sign flashed past the window, reminding Deborah that their regular lives lay ahead. She cleared her throat. "It feels like we're not talking about the engine anymore."

"Aren't we?"

"I mean, that's how you sounded in the hotel, talking about the IVF. Worn out. Fatigued."

"Definitely," he said without hesitating.

"So it's not that you've changed your mind about wanting kids, really. You're just worn down by the process?"

"I don't know that you can separate the two things. And the first doesn't seem worth the second."

"But you've never really told me that before."

"Not explicitly, maybe, but . . ."

"You said that it's been my fixation, my preoccupation, with getting pregnant that bothered you the most."

"Well, yeeess." Christopher stretched out his words. "That and the time passing. I'm forty-five. You're forty-two. The risks keep getting higher at our ages."

"You're projecting that. Looking at the overall statistics and data, not at us as case studies. We're both healthy. The specialist in New York said my heart rate and blood pressure and diet and exercise habits put my body at age thirty-eight."

"That's true," Christopher said, thoughtfully.

His tone was different. The note of pessimism that had been there since yesterday was gone.

"So if the real problem is the process, and how I handle it, let's try to fix that. Not throw the baby out with the bathwater."

Christopher was silent.

"That's a joke, Christopher." She elbowed him gently.

Obligingly, he turned up the corners of his mouth.

"What are you thinking? Doesn't that make sense? Especially since we have the three remaining embryos?" She waited, willing him to see it the way she did.

"It sounds good. But tell me what it means."

"I'll get rid of all the fertility books. Drop out of the Facebook groups. Take up yoga, maybe. And we'll have mandatory date nights. After every doctor's appointment," she added.

This time he smiled for real.

"And I don't think you give me quite enough credit for seeing the forest. Sure, I wanted to visit Helen and the girls on the trip. But I wanted to go wine tasting and bike riding and bird watching with you, too. I found some good places on the Seattle Audubon site."

He exhaled. "That sounds nice."

"And last summer I *did* get out of the house at least once. We went to the dean's summer picnic. That's where you and Michael hatched the plan for the big Fish and Wildlife grant. The one that's pending right now, isn't it?"

He nodded.

"Any updates?"

"I checked before we left the hotel. Not yet."

"You've been waiting for what, like, three months?"

He nodded. "And it was three months of writing before that."

"Which could also be contributing to your stress and fatigue, right?"

He nodded again.

"So. Let's finish what we started. Try one more cycle. If it doesn't work, then we'll stop. I promise."

She couldn't bear to watch him decide and turned her gaze back to the window. The landscape had softened as they approached Ithaca. She watched a flock of birds soar through a cleft between the hills.

Christopher was silent for another frozen mile, then finally spoke. "All right. Make the appointment with the clinic. We'll try again. One last time."

SEVEN

Robby stroked the black wing of the taxidermied bird. The feathers felt so sleek. And it was so big. Dr. Felk said it was a male. So that made it a gander, not a goose. Watching from a distance, he never would have thought one could be so big. Their neighbors at home, the Petersons, had a little dog, Trixie. She was one of those yappy dogs that tore all around the yard a lot. This gander was way bigger than Trixie.

"Look at the time. I told your parents a half hour, and here it's past an hour. They'll think I've apprenticed you." Dr. Felk glanced at his watch. "We'd better go."

Robby kept his hand on the gander. "Don't want to go." The archives were crowded with shelves stuffed with bird skulls and models of wings and boxes of books, papers, maps, and more that they had barely begun to explore. Old dust hung thick. Even the city's noises were muffled here below the street. He hadn't needed his headphones once.

Dr. Felk adjusted his glasses, gazing around the room.

"I know. Heaven down here, isn't it?"

Robby nodded. The gander's beady eye seemed to meet his. Wouldn't the geese have seen the plane? Couldn't they have diverted?

"Robby." Dr. Felk's hand touched his shoulder, and he flinched involuntarily. "I've enjoyed having you here. I wish we could stay longer, too. But you live in Detroit. If I'm going to help you learn more long-distance, I have to talk to your parents. Convince them. You understand—" A coughing spasm seized the rest of Dr. Felk's sentence.

His parents, Detroit, home. All far away.

"You understand, right, Robby?" Dr. Felk stifled another cough and leaned forward, not touching him this time. Robby sighed. He didn't want to leave. But he liked Dr. Felk. He bargained. "Fifteen more minutes."

Dr. Felk scratched his gray beard. "Ten. Deal?"

"Deal," Robby agreed.

Watching him with a faraway look in his eyes, Dr. Felk reached for his cell phone and dialed. "Jim? Arthur Felk. How's everything in DC?" He coughed again. "Sorry. Listen, I need a favor."

In the museum food court, Linda swallowed the last of her second cup of coffee.

"Do you think we should go look for them?" she asked Sam. "It's been an hour."

He glanced up from his *New York Times*. "Has it?" His eyes moved over her shoulder. "Here they come now."

Relieved, Linda turned. In the twenty paces to their table, she saw Robby nod, smile, and gesture. Compared to his usual blank expression, he looked animated, she thought.

"This has been the best morning I've had at work in a long time, thanks to this young man," Felk announced as they got closer. He put his hand on Robby's shoulder, drawing him alongside. Robby flinched, Linda noticed, but allowed the touch. And he positively glowed.

"Robby, why don't you get a drink or a snack. Tell them to charge it to me. I want to talk to your parents," Felk said. Sam opened his mouth, but Robby nodded and disappeared.

Felk sat down. "Mr. and Mrs. Palmer, I must tell you Robby is a prodigy. He's got a wonderful curiosity. Asks good questions. Amazing memory. Truly amazing. He's got all the makings of a scientist."

"You think so?" Linda, who clung to the hope that Robby's autism cloaked genius, wanted to believe him. Desperately, she wanted to believe him. "Biology is his favorite subject in school."

Felk nodded. "I think he just needed to find a subject that would capture his interest. Today I think he might have found it."

"You mean birds?" Sam asked, sounding skeptical. Felk nodded emphatically.

"But he sees birds every day. He never expressed any special interest before. Why all of a sudden?" Linda scanned the cafeteria line, seeking Robby's hooded head.

"The plane crash. You know, of course, living with Robby, how it is with autistics. They're in their own world. Sometimes it takes something very dramatic to penetrate that, to make an impact. I think the plane crash may have done that for Robby."

"You're familiar with autism?" Linda leaned forward. "When I mentioned it before, you said you weren't."

"I didn't say whether I was or wasn't. I just didn't want you to go ahead and tell me everything you think you know is true about Robby because somebody, somewhere, told you that."

Sam spoke up, sounding irritated. "Now wait a second. What do you know—"

Chagrined but curious, Linda placed her hand on Sam's arm, cutting him off. "Tell us more."

Felk nodded at Sam. "I don't mean to claim I know Robby, or what's best for him. But I know some of his characteristics would allow him to flourish in a scientific environment.

61

"For a scientist, the ability to recall details is critical. Robby excels at it. On the elevator ride back up I asked him to list some of the species in *Anserinae*, which are in the same family with Canada geese, as well as swans and other geese. Though we spent only a few minutes looking at those images, he answered perfectly. In that archive room we've got records dating back before the museum's founding, in 1869. I have no doubt that, if given free rein to roam in there for, say, a week, Robby would be able to transfer whatever was relevant to his interests to his own head."

"He does have a photographic memory, doesn't he, Sam?" Linda's voice swelled with hope.

"And then there's his curiosity. That's the most encouraging part. Rote memory and how the pieces work individually isn't his goal; he wants to know more and put the whole picture together.

"The plane crash is key. He wants to know more about that, about how it affected the geese, how the geese affected it. I don't know much about aviation, but I called a friend who works at the Smithsonian Air and Space Museum. He's probably not the guy, either, to be honest. But he could refer you to someone at a place with more modern aircraft. Maybe on an air base."

"An air base?" Sam echoed in disbelief. "Are you kidding?"

"You're doing all that for Robby? Why?" Linda said simultaneously, her eyes shining with fledgling hope.

Felk shifted in his seat, regarding them. He started to reply when Linda glimpsed Robby bearing a wobbly tray in her peripheral vision. She turned, holding her breath. The unfamiliar cafeteria was a sensory minefield.

Teetering with an unbalanced load of notebook, doughnut, and chocolate milk, Robby stared at the red plastic rectangle as if it were a map back to their table when the metal leg of a stray chair thwarted him. Tray, milk, doughnut, and book clattered to the tile floor, turning heads from all corners.

Sam touched his forehead to his palm, closing his eyes and shaking his head. Robby snatched the notebook away from the brown stream of the milk, then sat right down on the floor, backing away. Clucking in dismay, Linda leaped to assist. Felk followed her, but brushed past them to the cashier, who nodded and spoke into a radio.

Felk returned to the spilled milk and pointed Robby back toward the cafeteria line. He removed the wad of napkins Linda was swabbing the brown puddle with and ushered her back to their table.

"I'm so sorry. Crowded places are so challenging for him. I'm so sorry."

"Please. It was an accident. The custodians will take care of it." He dropped the napkins into a trash can. "Now where were we?" He sat back down heavily.

"The air base," Sam said skeptically. "I'm not seeing the point of that."

Felk looked surprised. "Why, it would be a place for Robby to learn about planes, of course."

"Of course." Sam repeated, heavy on the sarcasm. "Robby has significant auditory sensitivities. You must have noticed the headphones. I can't think of a worse place for him."

"Sam, let's just hear him out, for heaven's sake!" Linda said.

"Mr. Palmer, I'm not telling you what to do with your son," Felk said. "I'm just offering options. Robby's got an instinct for birds and their behavior. I should know. I've spent my professional career with some of the most illustrious ornithologists in the field. I *am* one of the most illustrious. In my opinion, it would be criminal not to indulge that interest."

"Just options, huh?" Sam whispered to Linda, as Robby returned with a second tray.

Felk stood up. "I've given Robby my card. You still have it, right, son?"

Robby nodded.

"And I've got Robby's e-mail. I'll be in touch." Felk nodded at them both, then held out his hand to Robby. "Robby, it was a privilege to meet you. I expect to be seeing you in the future. Check out those websites I gave you, and the reference books. Sibley's guides are the best. See if you can find a local Audubon club. Just keep up with the birds and it'll all work out fine."

"OK." Robby shook his hand, his brown eyes gazing straight up into Felk's blue ones.

Witnessing that eye contact, Linda vowed to do whatever it took to nurture her son's interest, and pretended she didn't hear Sam muttering they should have skipped the sightseeing cruise and gone to the Empire State Building instead.

~

Richard had meetings at church that evening, so Brett made Western omelettes for herself and Amanda. The phone rang just as they were finishing. Amanda's friend Abby was so excited Brett could hear her, too.

"It went great. Mrs. Hamilton said my voice was one of the best in the choir, and she asked me to rehearse 'You're the One that I Want' tonight and perform it when they audition the leads tomorrow! I could have died, I was so excited. Amanda, I could be Sandra! And we're only juniors."

"That's so cool, Ab. You'd be great," Amanda said, walking down the hall, toward her room.

Brett rinsed the dishes, musing. Auditions. She thought back. Amanda mentioned something about musical auditions last week. Were they today? She chastised herself for not knowing for sure.

She filled the dishwasher quickly, then walked down to Amanda's room. Hesitating, she listened. The phone conversation must be over. She knocked lightly and peeked in. "OK to come in?"

"I guess." Amanda didn't move on the bed. The phone receiver lay facedown next to her.

Brett wedged herself into the small space left between her daughter's feet and the end of the bed. "Was that Abby?"

Amanda nodded.

"What's new with her?"

"She got asked to audition for one of the leads in the musical today."

"Good for her." Brett paused. "Weren't you going to audition, too?"

"Yeah, probably. Abby said I can still do it tomorrow."

"Oh, OK." Brett reviewed her daughter's response, evaluating whether to probe further.

"I just wanted to come home and see you this afternoon, is all," Amanda suddenly added.

"Really? You wanted to come home instead of hang out with your friends?" Brett patted her leg, wondering if that really was a good thing for a sixteen-year-old girl. Amanda pulled her knees up quickly and picked up the phone.

"Mom?" She was fidgeting with it, turning it around in her hands. "Yes?"

"You know how I asked you about being on the news yesterday, being on the boat?"

"Mmm-hmmm." Brett sat up straighter, feeling suddenly wide-awake.

"You said you weren't. But this morning, on the news, they were rerunning the crash coverage and . . . and I saw you."

"Saw me?" Brett's throat closed.

"On a boat. Just like Kelsey said."

Brett's heart thumped. Here it was already, the moment of confrontation. She knew it would come eventually, but she had only scripted Richard opposite her. It was harder with Amanda, who had stopped fidgeting with the phone and pinned her with an unwavering stare. Brett sighed and nodded, almost imperceptibly.

"So I was right."

Brett nodded again, more distinctly.

"Why did you tell me you weren't? What's the big deal? So you decided to blow off the conference and do something fun." Amanda shrugged.

There it was. The life raft of the next lie laid, so innocently, by her own daughter. *Amanda thinks I was just playing hooky. She didn't notice anything between me and Jackie.* So easy to step into, to maintain the charade a little bit longer. Of course it was wrong to lie. But it was her duty to protect her daughter, too. Wasn't it? *Just for a little while longer. Until I talk to Jackie. Until we figure this out.*

She shrugged, too. "I don't know, Amanda. I was so surprised when you asked. With the plane crash, everything was so confusing. And scary."

She's not convinced. Think of something else.

"And going to the conference was expensive, so it was important that I make it worthwhile. I didn't want you to think we were wasting time, or money. I'm sorry."

"'We?'"

Brett's heart pounded again. *I. I meant I. I didn't want you to think I was wasting time or money.* This was how the devil used lies— like a web, snaring you with another and another and another, until you were hopelessly entangled. On the ferry, with Amanda far away, it was easier to lie. Face-to-face, here in her room, it was almost physically painful.

She stood up, folding her arms, cupping her elbows tightly, as her thoughts galloped, back to New York, back to Jackie. Was she lying to her family, too? What sacrifices was she making?

"Mom?" Amanda's voice brought her back to the bedroom.

Brett looked down at her daughter. So trusting. She cleared her throat, and stepped in deeper.

"Yes, we. Me and Mrs. Longwood. Jackie Longwood. We were on the ferry together. I met her at the conference. She's from a church in North Carolina. Charlotte." On the firmer ground of the truth—albeit incomplete—Brett spoke more quickly now. "They've had a meal program and a delivery service for a long time. Much longer than we have. I wanted to learn more about how they did it all."

"Oh." Amanda's brow furrowed. "But, then, why were you on the ferry? Couldn't you just talk at the hotel?"

Brett thought rapidly.

"It was Jackie's idea. It was her first trip to New York. She wanted to take the sightseeing trip. I figured we could talk on the boat just as well as inside a hotel, so why not?"

The furrow on Amanda's forehead smoothed, but didn't erase. Brett felt exposed in the gaping silence, willing her daughter to accept her explanation. The back door opened.

"Anybody home?" Richard's voice filled in the void.

Brett stiffened. She opened Amanda's door. The hallway stretched like a ship's plank. What if he had seen the news, too?

In the kitchen, Richard was loosening his tie, glancing at the paper. "Hi."

"Welcome back." His mouth smiled, but not his eyes as he leaned forward to kiss her cheek. "How was the big city?"

"Fine," Brett said, looking back at Amanda's door. She'd expected her daughter to follow, but she hadn't. Hmm.

" 'Fine?' Four days away, and that's all you have to say?" Richard poked his head into the refrigerator, emerging with leftover Chinese.

"No, of course not. I've got lots to tell you. I—"

Richard held up his hand, cutting her off. Sitting down, he closed his eyes and bowed his head. "Come, Lord Jesus . . ."

The familiar grace rumpled Brett's mood. Couldn't he skip it just once?

His eyes opened. "All right, tell me all about it. What did you learn that might help us set up a mobile meal program here? Did you make any connections?"

"I think I did make one good connection," Brett said slowly, measuring the words. She couldn't afford another "I-we" slipup. "A woman from a church down in Charlotte."

"All the way from North Carolina, huh? No kidding."

"Right. Two years ago she started a mobile program building on the community meals they served at the church. Just like we've been talking about. At first, they used a ten-year-old van with a hundred thousand miles on it and some old pizza delivery bags to keep the food hot." Brett was reciting the biography Jackie shared at the first, real conference last fall.

"Now they've got the attention of private donors. Some local car dealers just donated six brand-new delivery vans. They've got a volunteer waiting list, if you can believe that. They've even been nominated for the governor's most humanitarian nonprofit award."

"Really! I wonder if Pennsylvania has an award like that. Can't buy that kind of publicity. It would sure boost the congregation." Richard looked excited as he took another bite of cold kung pao.

Once, he would have been excited about the award for its own sake, not the publicity, Brett thought. "I don't know. I think—"

"This is a wonderful report, Brett. More than I hoped for. That hotel room might just be worth it, after all."

A vision of herself and Jackie, together in the king-size bed, emerged. Oh, that room had been so worth it. To feel so alive, so electrically alive, down to every last nerve—

"Brett?" Richard coughed. "Brett?"

The bed evaporated. "I'm sorry. What?"

"I said, what's your next step?"

"I thought I'd go down to Charlotte to see their operation myself," Brett heard herself say, without hesitating.

"A plane ticket." Richard sighed, then brightened. "Maybe we could all go. Does your friend have children? We could go over Amanda's spring break. Drive down together. Save the plane fare, get away from the cold and snow. Enjoy some family time and all help move our church forward together. Like that mission trip we took back in college, remember?"

As Richard talked himself down south, panic galloped through Brett. Was he reading her mind? Until this afternoon she hadn't thought of the mission trip in years. Even if he wasn't reading her mind, she and Jackie would be exposed. It was a crazy risk. It would be impossible.

"It would be perfect timing. Let you plan a little bit more up here, build some more success with the church meals, before making a big leap like this."

Breathe. Just breathe. And think, Brett.

"I'd have to talk to Jackie. Maybe they're busy. Or maybe spring break wouldn't be a good time for them. Maybe they'll be going on spring break themselves," Brett said. *That sounds reasonable. It'll buy me time.* Her heartbeat slowed.

"Of course, of course. It doesn't have to be spring break. That would just be convenient," Richard said. "But get in touch soon to find out what works for her, and we'll figure something out." He stood up and hugged her, the embrace feeling more like a vise to Brett. "The Lord will make this happen, Brett. I've just got a feeling about it."

He threw away the empty Chinese container and turned on the TV.

In her room, Amanda stepped back from the door, deflated. They'd never gone on a spring break vacation. So she would definitely be at auditions tomorrow. If she wasn't going anywhere for spring break, being in the musical would at least get her out of the house. Plus, it would give her something to think about besides her mom, who suddenly wanted to run all over the country instead of staying home like she'd always done.

She reached in her backpack for her copy of the lyrics. Now she just needed to make the cast.

EIGHT

Deborah and Christopher. Good afternoon." Dr. Marissa Singh strode into her office and shook their hands. "Lovely to see you again."

Deborah smiled feebly. She wondered if the fertility specialist practiced saying that with just the right tone and expression, knowing everyone who faced her in these tastefully upholstered chairs wanted to be anywhere but there.

"Tell me about your consultation in New York."

"They sent the report, right?" Puzzled, Deborah moved to the edge of her seat.

"Indeed." She lifted a medical chart. "But I'm interested in your perspective, too."

"Oh." Deborah paused, tucking her hair behind her ear. "I was encouraged. The doctor corroborated what you said about the two— the two other times. That we'd done everything right, that after transfer, it's really a matter of beating the odds. And he said with my age and health status, I'm still a good candidate." She watched the doctor, who listened impassively.

"So we'd like to discuss transferring our remaining embryos," she finished. "I asked for an evaluation when I called?"

"I have it right here," Dr. Singh said, opening another file. "Three embryos left. All rated in very good condition."

Deborah's heart leaped. The doctor seemed to read her mind.

"That could change, you know." The doctor looked up. "We'll re-evaluate when the embryos are thawed."

"We're aware of that," Christopher said, speaking for the first time.

"Good. And what do you think, Christopher? How do you feel about a third attempt?"

Deborah's heartbeat accelerated. She had kept her word. The fertility books had gone to the library. She had unliked the Facebook pages and chat groups. And except for telling him of the appointment, she had steered clear of discussing IVF, pregnancy, and babies since the drive home from New York last week.

Her husband shifted in his twin chair. He turned to her and reached out his hand. Deborah took it. He pulled their clasped hands into his lap while he held her gaze for a long minute, and then turned back to Dr. Singh.

"I'm willing to give it one more try. One last try."

Deborah exhaled audibly. The doctor regarded them both. Photographs of her family were arranged behind her on a credenza. It looked like two boys and a girl. Deborah fixed her eyes on their smiling faces, as if the doctor's own fertility could somehow permeate to her.

"All right, then." Dr. Singh flipped papers until she found a blank page. "It's just a matter of determining when the next opportunity for transfer is, then. When was your last period, Deborah?"

Half an hour later, with the transfer scheduled for February 8, they parted outside the clinic with a plan to meet for dinner at their favorite Chinese restaurant, Campus Cantonese. In between, Christopher had a late meeting on campus. Deborah decided to call Helen.

Her new phone showed one text. Julia Adams again. Christopher had introduced them at the dean's summer picnic and then gone off to hatch the grant proposal with Julia's husband, Michael, the newest member in the bio department. What a difference a decade made, Deborah had thought while half-listening to Julia's own pitch for fund-raising help for some nonprofit, remembering how she and Christopher had first paired off at the same picnic.

She deleted Julia's message. She'd figure some way out of that. As she held the phone, it rang.

"Hi, Deborah. It's Helen."

"Helen! I was just going to call you. How are you?"

"I'm—well, I'm OK. Been better, actually." She paused. "Is this an OK time for you to talk? Do you have a few minutes?"

"Sure." Deborah's brow creased. Helen sounded breathless again. But she couldn't be doing her morning workout now. "What's going on?"

She heard a long sigh. "I'm not really sure how to start."

"Just start." Deborah frowned.

Helen sighed again. "OK. Well. It started a couple months ago. I wasn't feeling so great. Tired all the time. Achy. Sore muscles." She paused again. "What felt like a sore throat. I couldn't swallow anything."

"How awful." Deborah said sympathetically. "You went to the doctor, right?"

"Right." Helen breathed deeply. "A lot of doctors, actually. My GP sent me to a specialist. That specialist sent us to another one, at the University of Washington."

She hesitated. Deborah's skin prickled. The pauses felt like a tsunami building from the West Coast, looming over flyover country, poised to crash over her on the East. *Say it. Get it out*, she silently urged her sister.

"They put me through a whole slew of tests. Genetic tests."

"OK," Deborah said, filling in the pause left for her. "And?"

"They showed I have the gene for Huntington's Disease."

Huntington's Disease. Deborah ran the name through the database of fund-raising groups she stored in her head and came up negative. That meant no awareness, no money, or both. Not good.

"I don't know—" she started.

"It's a neurological disorder. It leads to muscle degeneration, then dementia. Symptoms typically emerge between the ages of thirty-five and forty-five."

Deborah exhaled deeply. "Helen, my God, I'm so sorry. But what does it mean, exactly? Does having the gene mean you have it now? What's the treatment? What can I do?"

"I have it now. The symptoms indicate it's in the early stages." Helen paused, her voice faltering. "There's—there's no treatment. There are some things they can do to alleviate symptoms, but there's no cure."

Silence stretched over the continent again. Deborah couldn't speak.

"Deborah? Are you still there?"

"I'm here." Her voice sounded strangled, to her own ears. Helen was only forty-five. She couldn't have some fatal, untreatable disease. Not after they lost their parents so young in the car accident. It wasn't fair.

"I'm so sorry to tell you this over the phone. I wanted to tell you in person, when you came out here. That's why I was so upset after the crash. But when that didn't work out, and you started talking about another IVF cycle, I knew I had to tell you as soon as possible."

Her last sentence echoed. "Tell me because of the IVF? What does that have to do with anything?"

Helen spoke softly, sorrowfully, delivering her sentence. "Huntington's is a genetic disease, Deborah. I inherited it from Mom or Dad. And there's a fifty-fifty chance you did, too."

~

As the school bus growled away from the curb, Robby reached into his backpack for his Sibley's guide. They had bought it in New York, at a bookstore on the way back to the hotel. The bookstore was on a corner and had a revolving door just like the museum. The author was David Sibley. In the cafeteria Dr. Felk said it was the best guide there was, and so did the guide, on the cover. "More than 6,600 illustrations in all," the back cover informed him.

At least a dozen were of Canada geese. It wasn't quite as good as the stuffed gander in the basement of the museum, but it would do. He had spent the entire plane ride home reading and knew the sections about Canada geese by heart already. He flipped there again now.

"The markings of this species do not differ significantly from male to female," he read. Robby frowned as he chewed his sweatshirt string. Which were the geese in the crash? He'd already learned only females incubated eggs. What if the geese that flew into the plane were females, with eggs about to hatch? Or had babies already? Left back in a nest somewhere around the airport? What would happen to them if the mother didn't come back? Would they be safe? Would they go hungry? Would some other mother goose take care of them? Who could find out?

Dr. Felk. He'd e-mail him after school. How lucky that Dr. Felk had been at the museum that day. He had told Robby that today was his first day back after a week of being out with a bad cold.

Robby exhaled against the window, his breath fogging the cold glass, relieved by his plan.

Linda waved at Robby's hooded profile framed in the school bus window, driver's side, six rows back, as usual. She stood in the driveway, arms wrapped around herself, puffs of breath dissolving in the chilly morning air, savoring the moment alone, free of obligations, to-dos, and follow-ups.

At the end of the block, the bus turned and disappeared. Sighing, Linda turned back to the house. Twenty minutes before she was due at the sales meeting to review year-end figures. Enough time to make some calls for her unofficial job: managing Robby's autism.

On the spectrum of autism disorders, he was considered "high-functioning," somewhere between an Asperger's profile and classic autism. For the future, that meant hope that Robby would live independently. For now, it was a sentence to the no-man's-land between the neurotypical world and that of the "low-functioning"—six-year-olds who communicated in syllables, eight-year-olds still in diapers. *There but for the grace of God*, Linda thought silently at more than one heartrending parent support group meeting.

Yet there were still Robby's high-functioning meltdowns to endure, the battles for school services, the summons from school, the hours arguing with the insurance company over coverage of his therapies. And now, exposure to aviation and ornithology to arrange.

Dr. Felk's contact at the Smithsonian Air & Space Museum hadn't been able to help. But there was the Henry Ford, a museum with historical aircraft in its collection. She knew Cathy Turner at work had a nephew or niece stationed at Selfridge on the other side of town. There was bound to be an Audubon chapter around. She went to Google.

Twenty minutes later she had marked her calendar with the next meeting of the Western Wayne County Audubon Club, found out the hours and rates at the Henry Ford, and e-mailed an appeal to Blue Cross over their latest denial. She'd stop by Cathy's cube sometime that day.

Not bad progress, even though she'd pushed the clock and would be late for the sales meeting. It was worth it. She often thought of

Robby's brain as a kaleidoscope. It spun. It fractured. It was fragile. But it was also beautiful and original and bright. Dr. Felk had seen it. Maybe one of these others would, too.

Her cell phone rang as she thrust her arms into her coat.

"Mrs. Palmer? John Drake from Lindbergh School. How are you today?"

Linda's arm froze halfway through her sleeve as Robby's principal identified himself. "Fine, Mr. Drake. Is everything all right? Is Robby all right?"

"Yes, yes, everything's all right. Quite all right, in fact. Robby's teachers tell me he's been doing very well lately."

"I'm glad," Linda said cautiously.

"Yes, it's wonderful news. His behavior's improved significantly. It's been almost two months since he's been to my office. His homework is nearly always turned in complete. And of course you knew about his aptitude for math and science, but I'm hearing from his other teachers that he's keeping up this year."

"That's good to hear," Linda said, wedging the phone between her ear and shoulder as she buttoned her coat. "Mr. Drake, I'm just on my way to work. Is there something—"

"Oh, well, then, don't let me keep you. I just wanted to share the good news, and tell you that we feel the changes in Robby's—um—situation warrant revisiting his IEP."

Reaching into her purse for her keys, Linda's fingers froze again. *Revisit his IEP.* School-speak for cutting back his services. He's doing so well, might as well cut off the services that got him there.

"You want to get rid of Laura," she said abruptly. For the first time this year, they had managed to get the services of a one-on-one aide written into the Individual Education Plan. She spent one study hall period a day working with Robby.

"Now, nothing is a foregone conclusion. That's why we're convening the IEP team."

"Mr. Drake, Laura's the reason Robby's homework is complete. She's the reason he hasn't been to your office in two months. She just gets him." Linda slid into her car.

"I'm glad she's been such a positive force for Robby," the principal said smoothly. "It's my job to manage limited resources as efficiently as possible. If Robby no longer needs her—"

"He *does* still need her! He only sees her one period a day. I don't see how you can be more efficient than that," Linda protested, punching the garage door opener.

"I know this is difficult. And as I said, we're only revisiting the IEP at this point. You and your husband will have equal input on any decisions made." He paused. "How does next Wednesday work for you? One o'clock?"

The garage door creaked its way up. Her phone pulsed with a text message reminder of the meeting she would be late for. Mr. Drake waited. Silently, Linda screamed.

~

Jackie answered on the fourth ring, her throaty voice triggering a cascade of longing in Brett.

"Hell-low?"

"It's me. Brett. Can you talk?"

"Brett?" Jackie's voice hushed. "For a minute. I just got Jimmy down for a nap. Patsy's watching a *Dora* DVD."

"How was your trip home?"

"Fine. Except Jim gave me hell about that fur coat. You were right."

"Are you going to donate it?" Brett asked hopefully. The furrier in their hotel lobby had talked Jackie, who said her Southern blood was freezing in her veins, into what he swore was the deal of the century. Unlike Richard, Jackie's husband, Jim, presided over a well-to-do congregation. Still, to Brett, spending four figures on a coat felt far more sinful than what they did twenty floors above the shop.

"I guess. I don't have a place to wear it down here, anyway. But I sure did like how that fur felt." She sighed. "So, what is it? I don't have long."

"Richard wants us to come to Charlotte. Our whole family."

"What?" Jackie's voice lost its ladylike Southern-ness when she was upset. "That's impossible, Brett. Out of the question."

"I know. But he's insisting. He asked me about what I learned at the conference, what my next step was. I said I wanted to visit, come see your operation myself."

"Well, why in the world did you say that?"

"I wasn't thinking." Stung, she hesitated. "Well, maybe I was. I do want to see you again."

Jackie snorted. "On a family vacation?"

"Eventually I'll convince him that it should only be me."

"Brett, I don't know. Even just you, it's such a risk. I never imagined you comin' to Charlotte."

"I know. And I hate lying to my family about it. Especially Amanda." Brett paused, then plunged ahead. "I don't think I want to lie anymore."

"Now, what in the world are you talking about? Patsy, honey, just a minute. Hang on. I've got to get to her."

The phone clattered down. On what? A granite kitchen countertop? A desk, on top of Jackie's calendar with reminders to pick up the dry cleaning and Pasty's next checkup? An antique table in the foyer where Pastor and Mrs. Longwood met their guests? There was so much she didn't know about Jackie. Except how she felt around her. She recalled standing on the deck of the ferry together. Except for a kid absorbed with whatever was on his headphones, they were alone outside and dared to hold hands momentarily. Feeling both bold and blessed, she vowed to herself she would hide no more. Then she'd gone home and done exactly that.

"I'm back. God bless DVDs." Jackie laughed harshly. "Now tell me what you mean, you don't want to lie anymore?"

"Just that. I'm tired of pretending. Tired of the pastor's wife stuff—the sanctimony, the self-righteousness, the appearances. It's not what I signed up for."

"What do you mean?"

"When Richard and I met, back in college, we were both about social justice. About loving one another and forgiveness and telling the truth. But that's all gone now. He doesn't care about what I do with the food pantry, just that I look like I'm a supportive wife and don't go over my budget. And if anyone else in our church knew about New York, they'd freeze me out so fast—"

"Exactly! Exactly! Me too, Brett. Jim, if he found out—" Jackie's voice dropped to a whisper. "How can you even think about it?"

"I don't care about those things anymore. Keeping up appearances. I don't want my daughter to think I'm a hypocrite. I don't want her to be one, either, blindly going along with all that self-righteousness."

"Well, if that's what you want to call it. I just call it making the best of things."

"'The best of things?' Really?" Brett felt like she had in the fur shop, trying to make Jackie see what a foolish extravagance the coat was. "Jackie, look at us. You're trying to keep a secret from a four-year-old. I'm feeling guilty for talking to you in my own house. Doesn't seem like the best of things to me."

"That's big talk, Brett. Easy on the phone. Hard in the real world."

"Maybe." She sighed, remembering again lying to Amanda's face. Maybe she was more bravado than brave, and as exasperated with herself as with Jackie.

"I've been thinking a lot about the plane that crashed. Some of the people on my flight were rebooked from that one," Jackie said.

"I sat next to one man. He said the last thing he remembers was the pilot's warning, just before they hit the water. 'Brace for impact,' the pilot said. He was convinced it was a sign from God."

"The pilot giving instructions was really God?"

"I think that's what he meant."

"What was God telling him?"

"That choices matter. And life is short. When your time comes, all the choices you've made, your whole life long, will impact what happens next. So straighten out. Live a life you'll be proud of."

Divine retribution for earthly misdeeds. Christianity 101.

"So are you saying that it's over?" Brett asked incredulously. She had thought the crash was a sign, too—a sign that they were meant to be together, their stolen extra day thwarting Jackie from boarding the ill-fated flight. *Sign, sign, everywhere a sign.* The line from the old song flashed in her head. *Do this, don't do that, can't you read the sign?* Then again, everyone on the flight wound up fine. What sign could she extract from that?

Sounding exasperated, Jackie sighed. "It doesn't have to be. But we're not college kids. We live in the real world. And you know as well as I do, that world doesn't want us." Her voice wobbled. "I can give you what I did. A few days here, a few days there. Maybe even here in Charlotte. If you came when Jim's away."

"But no husband or daughter, Brett. I can't take the risk. I won't."

~

"Good morning. Today is February 8, 2009, and this is T-Day. Transfer Day. You're listening to NPR."

Deborah blinked groggily. NPR? Why was Steve Inskeep announcing her transfer? She must be dreaming. But she was awake. Wasn't she? She rolled over to look at the digital date, glowing green on the bedside clock. Indeed, it was T-day, February 8.

"Good morning."

She started. Christopher stood in their bedroom door, bearing two cups of coffee.

"That was so weird. I don't know if I was just dreaming or awake. Is that—"

"Decaf. Don't worry."

"Thanks." Forgoing caffeine and alcohol and mayonnaise and sushi, as she had since the last appointment with Dr. Singh, often felt as arbitrary as a rain dance, rituals that only deluded her into thinking she had control. Still, she followed them faithfully. What if they were right?

Christopher sat on the bed next to her, his weight solid and comforting compared to the wispy, ephemeral hope she allowed herself: that this third time would, indeed, be the charm. "Don't you have an early class?"

"I got Foster to cover it." He smiled at her, then kissed her forehead.

"What's that for?"

"Just because." He shrugged. "Because this does feel like the right thing to do. Either way, we can move forward now. And I think we're stronger for all we've gone through, too."

"Really?" She should have been ecstatic. But instead, she felt only more guilt. She hadn't told him about Helen.

It was a white lie—a lie of omission, she told herself. Since they had unwittingly accepted the risk—to both her and a baby—the first two cycles, nothing had really changed.

Deep in her soul, though, she knew she was rationalizing, knew Huntington's would be the tipping point for Christopher, pushing the risk level to unacceptable, and banishing embryos E, F, and G to the rubber gloves of the researchers in their white lab coats. And as their mother, that was the one thing she could not allow.

"Really." He stood. "Drink up and get dressed. You need a full bladder, remember?"

She gulped dutifully. It allowed for a clearer picture on the monitor. It sounded minor, but feeling like she might lose control was the worst part of the whole transfer process.

Gratitude and guilt blended and blurred the rest of the morning, as Christopher acted more devoted husband and prospective father than at either of the two previous transfers. He dropped her off at the clinic door, then went to park. As she filled out the boilerplate intake paperwork, Deborah's conscience poked her again: *Changes in health history since your last visit.* She checked none.

Dr. Singh met them with the news that E, F, and G all survived the thaw in good condition.

"You're quite sure you want to go with all three?" she asked again. Two, the standard protocol, were transferred in both previous cycles, in order to manage the risk of multiples.

Deborah nodded.

"All right. I'll see you in there."

On the ultrasound monitor, she watched as Dr. Singh moved the three tiny white blobs, one by one by one, into the bluish, warped triangular field that was her uterus. She tried to conjure up the maternal connection she felt when she had argued for this last try in the hotel room and in the car, but controlling the urge to run to the bathroom required all of her concentration.

Instead, her mind leapt randomly. Helen. Could her prognosis really be that bad? Work. Phillip was already ratcheting up the pressure, even though the law school campaign wouldn't go public for six months. The scattered red and pink hearts on the assisting nurse's scrubs. Was it special pre-Valentine's Day attire, or did she wear it regularly?

As they wheeled her out of the procedure room she felt ambivalent, frustrated, and uncomfortably full—the cocktail of gratitude and guilt churning in her gut.

NINE

Wе've got an update this Valentine's morning on the cause of the 'Miracle on the Hudson,' that plane that was ditched in the Hudson River last month, resulting in the safe evacuation of all one hundred fifty-five passengers and crew. Kimberly Jones is standing by in Washington. Kimberly?"

Brett caught the news update as she re-entered the kitchen with the sack of bird feed, now almost emptied into the feeder. She'd been so preoccupied lately she'd forgotten to fill it. They'd feast now, in her absence.

"Thanks, Bob. I'm here at an NTSB warehouse where the evidence from Flight 1549 is being collected. Investigators are telling us . . ."

She snapped off the TV. The story was more than a little foreboding two hours before the airport shuttle was due to pick her up for her trip to Charlotte, even without Jackie's preachy seatmate echoing in her head.

She was going solo on the two-night, on-site, up-close, "bugs-on-a-windshield," as Richard liked to say, tour of Jackie's food pantry and mobile meal delivery operation.

Amanda's being cast in the musical was a stroke of luck. Rehearsals meant the family trip just wouldn't work, she explained to Richard, allowing just the right amount of disappointment into her tone. But on the bright side, she said, the trip would be more productive if her attention and time weren't divided between family and food pantry.

Logical. Reasonable. Believable. But a complete lie, scheduled as the trip was to coincide with Jackie's husband being out of town. Family and food pantry operations would be secondary, as they had been for the past month. The fallout included the empty bird feeder, a wrinkled pile of Richard's Sunday shirts, and a cool distance from Amanda. Usually attuned to her daughter's moods, Brett couldn't read the reason, but it seemed to run deeper than disappointment over not going on a spring break trip.

She heard Amanda's door close down the hall. Her daughter walked into the kitchen and opened the pantry without setting down her backpack.

"Take that off and stay a while," Brett said, lamely. "I was going to make us omelettes." She waved at the counter, where diced green pepper, onions, and ham stood in neat piles on the cutting board.

Amanda finished examining the shelves and emerged with a granola bar. She wrinkled her nose. "We always have those for dinner." From the fruit bowl, she selected a banana. "Besides, Abby's picking me up. We're meeting to go over lines. I'll just take these."

"At least let me toast you a bagel. Lunch isn't for almost five hours," Brett said, glancing at the clock. "A banana won't tide you over till then."

"Mom, I'm sixteen, you know. If I wanted a bagel, I'd get it myself." She set the bulging backpack on a kitchen stool.

Brett watched her tug the zipper, trying to close the backpack around her snacks. "Here, let me help you." Abandoning the breakfast argument, she laid her hands over her daughter's. Amanda jerked hers away.

"Amanda, sweetie, what is it?"

Amanda shook her head mutely and yanked the bag, zipper still gaping, off the stool.

"Look, I know you wanted to go on this trip during spring break. But that just didn't work. With the play and all."

"I don't want you to go, either," Amanda said abruptly. "You just got back from a trip, practically."

"It's just for two nights. I'll be back Friday."

"The last trip was supposed to be just two nights. Then it was three."

"Just two this time. I promise."

"Then a plane crashed."

"Oh, Amanda. That was a flukey, crazy, thing. A one-in-a-million chance. I'll be fine."

"But I'm not!" Amanda's words burst out of her mouth, hanging in the space in between them, *like in a comic strip bubble*, Brett thought. She stared at her daughter, silenced.

Abby's horn honked. Startled, Brett started chattering, as madly as the sparrows gathering at the replenished feeder. "There's Abby. Now please don't worry. Everything's going to be fine. I'll call you tonight, and I'll see you on Friday. Love you."

Ushered out the door, Amanda tried to quell her uncertainty and fear. To shut it away in a mental vault and barricade the door. To listen to Abby, who picked up the chatter where her mom left off. To believe that everything was fine. That it was no big deal to offer an omelette for breakfast—when most people ate them, after all— when it felt like her mother was trying to make up for something.

But she couldn't quash the feeling that everything wasn't fine, that something was in fact very wrong, something she couldn't name or describe or explain except that it started the day her mom didn't come home from New York.

❦

Christopher consulted the Moosewood cookbook one more time, then closed it, satisfied. He'd followed the recipe to the letter. He'd prep the salad for his Valentine's Day dinner now. It would all be ready when Deborah got home from work.

He piled the salad ingredients on the counter and began slicing, soothed by the rhythmic motion of the knife. He was jumpier than he remembered being during either of the other two-week waits. Deborah seemed nervous, too.

It was only reasonable, he supposed. The course of their lives would alter one way or the other, in seven days. And permanently. There were no embryos H or beyond.

But having a ready explanation didn't make it any easier to weather this last limbo period. So Christopher turned to something he could control—cooking. His classes had ended early that day, and restaurants would be jammed on Valentine's Day. Plus it felt like he owed Deborah. They'd had date nights every week since New York, and actually talked about the things they used to: current events, politics, campus gossip. Over one of the dinners, Michael Adams had texted that they got the grant. They'd toasted—she with sparkling water, he with a celebratory second beer—and he felt almost like the last two years had never happened. His wife was back to her old self. His professional life was peaking. And there was the possibility of fatherhood, too. That still felt surreal. Yet in an idle moment here and there, he'd caught himself imagining hiking with a child through Sapsucker Woods, the sanctuary that surrounded the Lab, teaching him how to observe and identify the flora and fauna, how to leave no trace.

For now, though, he needed fresh Parmesan for the salad. Where was the grater? The phone rang.

"Christopher? Hi. It's Matt."

"Matt." Christopher hesitated a half second before he placed the voice as his brother-in-law's. He could count on one hand the number of times they'd talked unattended by Deborah and Helen. "Good to hear from you. How's life in Seattle?"

"We're doing all right. As good as you can expect, I guess. The girls have been really pitching in. We've got another appointment at the university next week. I just hope Helen's not too tired to keep it."

"Mmm-hhhm." Christopher mulled Matt's statement idly. *The university.* Could Deborah's nieces be old enough now to be making college visits? He hadn't thought so, but he didn't keep close track. Matt was talking again.

"So did you guys find anything out yet?"

"Not yet. We're in the middle of the two-week wait. Should know by next Friday."

There was a pause, then Matt started speaking just as he did.

"Shall I have Deborah call back when she gets home?" Christopher asked.

"Two weeks? We got our results in two days," Matt said, sounding puzzled.

Another pause. Christopher spoke first. "I didn't know you and Helen did in vitro."

"Huh?" Matt sounded impatient. "I'm talking about Helen's genetic tests."

"Helen's had genetic testing done? Why? Whatever for?" Deborah's sister was the epitome of health. The whole family was. Last year's holiday cards featured their smiling quartet bearing sequential running bibs from some local charity 10K.

Christopher heard Matt draw in a deep breath. "Because she was feeling like shit, that's why. Didn't Deborah tell you?"

Christopher frowned, feeling like his students sometimes looked: half a step behind his lecture, brows furrowed, shoulders hunched as they strained to see the projection screen, wishing they could catch up, but mostly trying not to fall further behind. "I don't know anything. Is something wrong with Helen?"

"Wow." Matt exhaled deeply. "She really didn't. I just can't—and you've gone another round with the IVF?"

"A week ago. Transferred our last three embryos." Christopher felt panicky, like the freshman who realizes she's now just one of a hundred and fifty high school valedictorians in the lecture hall. "What's going on with Helen?"

"All right." Matt's voice took on a doctor-to-patient tone. "Helen's been feeling like crap since last fall. She had a bunch of nonspecific symptoms. Fatigue was a big one. Achy muscles. She took a couple falls that banged her up. She went to her GP, who sent her to a specialist. He sent her to another, at the University of Washington. That doc recommended genetic testing."

"And?" Tension laced Christopher's voice.

"Helen tested positive for the gene that causes Huntington's disease." Matt paused. "It's an inherited neurological disease that usually doesn't show up until middle age. Muscle coordination goes first, then your mind. Most people eventually wind up needing round-the-clock care." His voice shook. "There's no cure, not even many treatment options."

"I'm so sorry, Matt." The words came automatically, but he meant them. There would be no more running bibs on the holiday cards. Life-altering news for a couple still in their forties. Like him and Deborah. His mind wound back to one word.

"You said inherited. Helen got—ahhh, acquired—this from their parents?"

"That's what they tell us. We don't know which one, though Helen thinks she remembers her dad getting a little shaky at the end, before the car accident." Matt's voice grew thoughtful. "Who knows. There never was a good explanation for that accident. Daylight, good weather. Maybe Mr. DeWitt had deteriorated more than anyone ever knew."

"Is there . . . is there a chance Deborah would have inherited it, too?" Christopher asked.

"A Huntington's-positive parent has a fifty-fifty chance of passing the gene on to a child," Matt sounded like he was reciting. "So Hannah and Mariah are both at risk now, too."

Fifty-fifty? His wife had returned to her old self just in time to be threatened with losing it again? And if she were pregnant—He stopped himself.

"I'm so sorry, Matt." Christopher repeated. "You said you have another appointment soon?"

"Yeah. Next week. I almost forgot, that's why I called. Helen told her doc about Deborah. He knew a specialist on the East Coast. At Columbia. I've got his number if you want it."

"Absolutely." Christopher hung up and grabbed his keys, leaving the vegetables still on the counter, the door banging only slightly behind him but the realization hammering in his head: Deborah had deliberately deceived him.

In the sanctuary of his office, he Googled the name. William Hirsh, MD, head of the Huntington's Disease Center of Excellence at Columbia since 1998. He oversaw five observational studies and three clinical trials. The site confirmed Matt's statistics on the chance of inheriting the disease. He read further.

"An estimated ten percent of all HD patients do not know about HD in their family."

Christopher tasted bitterness. What percentage knew and not only withheld the information from a spouse, he wondered, but went ahead with in vitro fertilization, putting another generation at risk?

His call to Hirsh's office rang through to voice mail. It was after five. Damn. He needed information, craved data.

Christopher clicked back over to the symptoms list. *Difficulties with speech, swallowing, balance, walking.* Difficulties with speech?

Deborah, who could talk a donor into doubling their intended donation? Deborah, who balanced everything on her plate and made it look easy? *Cognitive impairment. Psychiatric symptoms.* Deborah, whose sharp mind was what made her the most attractive woman he'd ever met?

A vision of Deborah in a wheelchair flashed into his mind. Her head lolled as she sipped from a straw he held to her lips. On the periphery of the vision, a faceless child screamed from a high chair for attention and food, too.

Dimly, he heard the rumble of the custodian's rolling bucket down the hall, headed his way. The vision dissolved, but Christopher felt his own lunch rise in his throat.

~

Sam pulled out of the florist's parking lot, jammed on this damp, chilly Valentine's evening. Usually he and Linda didn't do much—a card, maybe a movie if the stars aligned and they found a babysitter. But this year, ratcheting up the romance seemed in order. Ever since the New York trip, things had been tense. Like Robby, Linda regarded that ornithologist from the museum, that Dr. Felk, as some kind of infallible genie in a bottle who would magically reveal all the answers to their struggles.

Sam wasn't so sure, at least at first. So Linda had indulged Robby's every whim solo: chauffeuring him to Audubon meetings, hanging out a bird feeder, ordering field guides. Sam stood by, waiting for Robby to tire of birds. But after a month, he had to consider that Felk might have been right, pegging Robby as a budding ornithologist. *Dammit. Some dad he was.*

It had always been an effort to engage Robby, to persist when his face stayed blank, when his brown eyes looked past them, when he retreated into hood and headphones. But the belief that one day they would stumble upon the thing that would lure Robby from the bunker of his brain also bonded him and Linda. Now, apparently, it was Dr. Felk who had uncovered it. *Some dad, all right*, Sam thought again, pulling into the garage.

Like its driver the last few weeks, Linda's car was dark and quiet. Inside, Sam expected to find her in the kitchen and Robby playing video games. But the TV was off, Robby was nowhere in sight, and Linda was curled up with a book on the couch in the adjacent family room.

"Hi." Sam stepped into the kitchen, forgetting, in his surprise, to hide the flowers. "Where's Rob?" He had been dropping the "y" on Robby's name lately, his subconscious way of prodding him into growing up a bit. Robby was mostly unresponsive to it, but Sam didn't know if that was because he disliked the name or because he was usually unresponsive.

"At the Audubon club meeting," Linda looked at him over the top of her book. *The Boy Who Loved Windows*, Sam read. Under the title, the image of the back of a boy's head dominated the cover. Even from the back, he looked like Robby.

"Another one?"

"They meet every other week."

"You're not there, too?"

"Someone offered him a ride. Robby wanted to go, so I let him."

"Really?" Sam was dumbfounded. "Someone just offered? Do they know about him?"

"Sam, didn't you hear me? A friend offered a ride *and Robby wanted to go*. It's the first social engagement he's shown interest in, well, maybe ever. I coached him on greetings and thank-yous, all the usual stuff, but of course I let him go." Linda crossed her arms.

"OK, I get that, but we're still responsible. Does anyone in that club know about him?"

"About his autism?" Linda shrugged. "Everybody there has their own bird they're crazy about. Woodpeckers, ducks, hummingbirds. Or the list they're building, counting all the birds in their yard. Or the state. Whatever." She shrugged again. "With his geese thing, Robby fits right in." She stood up. "Were you bringing those for me?"

"So now we'll layer OCD on top of autism. Great." Sam spoke almost to himself, looking confused at Linda's question before he remembered the roses he was still holding. "What? Damn. Yes. I mean, happy Valentine's Day." Frustration swelled. "Shoot. I feel like we've been—off—ever since the trip to New York. I wanted to do something special this year."

Linda came into the kitchen. "And you did. They're beautiful. Thank you." She put her arms around him. Gratefully, Sam hugged her back. They embraced silently until Linda pulled away and studied Sam's face.

"You know, Sam, Robby isn't ever going to get over autism."

Sam stepped away, folding his arms. "I know that."

"I think you know it intellectually. Until New York, that's how it was for me, too. But since then, since we came home and started doing this"—Linda waved her hand—"this bird stuff, something's changed. I really accept it now."

"You think I haven't?" *A Valentine's Day attack. Nice.*

"Not completely, no. I'm not blaming you," Linda added quickly. "I think you've resigned yourself. 'My son has autism.' That's how I looked at it, anyway, until New York."

"And then we met the fantastic Dr. Felk, and suddenly it all got better, right?" Sam couldn't keep the sarcasm out of his voice.

"Yes, as a matter of fact." Linda walked around the kitchen counter, back to the family room. They faced off over the Corian.

"Look, Sam, why are you so mad? We've wished for years that Robby would find his thing, his spectrumy thing, that he would obsess about and drive us crazy talking about, but be *his*. His bridge to the rest of the world. Now he has. So it's birds. So it took someone else, a stranger, to figure it out. So what?"

"You're right. You're right. I don't know." Sam clasped his hands together on the countertop and bent forward, touching his forehead to them. Guilt nearly gagged him, but he forced out the words. "Maybe it was that dinner at my brother's. With Tyler. A hangover of wishing."

"You're still hung up on that dinner from a month ago?" Linda smacked the counter. "That's exactly what I'm trying to tell you. You've got to get past resigning yourself that our son is on the spectrum and start owning it. For yourself and for Robby."

"But—" Sam opened his mouth. Linda shook her head.

"*These* are our lives," she said, stabbing a finger on the counter. "Silences. Meltdowns. Headphones. Now birds. All of it. Things have been this way for seven years now. This is the way they're always going to be. Don't waste any more time wishing and regretting."

"Put on a happy face, and it'll all be better, huh?"

Linda exhaled harshly. "Forget it. I'm tired of arguing." She flopped onto the couch, her back to Sam, but he saw a tear glisten on her cheek.

How romantic, Sam. He followed her into the family room. "I'm sorry. I'll try harder." He scrambled for a way to get back on track. "You want to order Chinese?"

"No, thanks." She paused. "Well, I could use the fresh air. OK. I'll pick it up."

Moments after Linda left, her cell phone rang on the kitchen counter. That showed how upset she was. She never left the house without her phone. Robby's number was illuminated.

"Hello?"

"Mom?"

"No, Robby," Sam forced himself to say the whole name. "It's Dad. Your mom's out."

"Oh." Long pause. "I need a ride."

Of course. He'd probably irritated whoever he had ridden over with. "OK." He could call Linda to get him after she picked up the food. No, wait, Sam was holding her phone. He'd have to go. "I'll come get you, then. Where are you?"

Another long pause.

"Big church. Monroe Street. Paul needs a ride, too."

"Paul? Who's Paul?" But Robby had hung up.

Big church on Monroe Street. That would be the Central United Christian Church. Sam scrawled a note for Linda, leaving it next to his forgotten, forlorn flowers, and headed back to the garage.

TEN

In the Charlotte-Douglas airport, Brett followed the signs to Ground Transportation, as she and Jackie had arranged. A bucket of flowers at a snack stand sandwiched between a Starbucks and a bookstore caught her eye. Why not. It was Valentine's Day, after all. Neither she nor Richard had marked the occasion in Scranton.

Ten minutes later, exiting the airport's automatic doors into the welcome warmth of winter six hundred miles south of Scranton, she spotted Jackie through the windshield of her SUV. An even warmer feeling surged inside Brett. Clutching the cellophane-wrapped pink rose, she rapped on the window.

"Happy Valentine's Day!" The inside of the car was filled with Jackie's perfume. Reaching for her, Brett felt light-headed, intoxicated. The nagging comic strip bubble of Amanda's last words drifted away.

But Jackie shrank back, refusing to meet her eyes, pressing herself against the door. Her body language spoke volumes. Brett dropped her hands. Her smile disappeared. "What's wrong, Jackie?"

"This," Jackie said in a wobbly voice. "Us. Together. Here. Alone. I can't do it, Brett. I'm sorry." She broke down, bending her forehead to the steering wheel, her long hair curtaining her face, her tan fingers white at the knuckle as she gripped the leather-wrapped circle.

In Brett's core, the liquid warmth cooled, like an ice cube dropped in hot chocolate. Stunned, she sat momentarily mute. There could only be one explanation.

"Did Jim find out?"

"No, no, no," Jackie gasped, shaking her head vigorously. "It's me. I decided. It's too hard. I wish it could be different, Brett, I do, but I can't turn my life upside down. Jim, he, he told me the pastor of New Hope Covenant—well, that doesn't mean anything to you, but it's the biggest church in Charlotte—invited him to lunch next week. Jim thinks he's planning to retire and wants to groom Jim to take over. If there was any hint of—of—of a scandal, I'd never see Patsy and little Jimmy again. I can't do it anymore. I'm sorry, Brett, but I can't."

Jackie's words—from the mouth Brett had kissed—pummeled her. Grief and disappointment flooded forth, the ice cube's cold, sharp edges mutilating the joy and hope she had cherished for the last month.

Jackie started talking again.

"I'm sorry. I shouldn't have led you on at the conference last fall. But I was so lonely. And I thought the distance would make it safe."

"Safe," Brett repeated numbly.

"For an affair. You were up north. I could still be Mrs. Pastor here. But then you started talking about coming out, and Jim told me about New Hope Covenant. I just can't take the risk again."

"Again?" The ice cube had melted entirely, all the heat inside Brett gone.

"Five years ago was the last time. Jim was still in school then. I had lots of time to myself. She was—" Jackie interrupted herself. "Oh, what does it matter. She moved. I had two kids in four years. I was too tired to be tempted by anyone. Until you."

"Me." Her mind grappling with the confession, single words were all Brett could manage aloud. Jackie had only ever wanted an affair. Not love, not commitment. Brett was just a body.

"You were so idealistic. So sweet. *You are.* Even after I've told you all this. You're still going to come with me to the meal tonight, because we're expected. That's what I told them. Mrs. Pastor and Mrs. Stevens will be there by five o'clock. Right?" Jackie looked at Brett for the first time.

Brett stared back at the face she had caressed and kissed and fantasized about since September. Jackie looked like a mannequin now, her face frozen into her own mask. She wanted to hide Brett behind the façade of wedding rings and well-bred voices and hope no one would be the wiser. Anger kindled in the embers of her dampened desire. The comic strip bubble with Amanda's parting words drifted back. Her plea, her face, filled Brett's mind. For this she was lying to Amanda? A thorn from the rose she still clutched poked through the cellophane, pricking her palm, a physical rebuke. She turned her gaze away from Jackie, into the back seat.

She saw a pair of children's car seats. The pink fabric on the one facing forward matched the rose. The second, denim-covered for a boy, was still turned backward as very young children rode.

The sight transported Brett back in her own life, more than a decade ago, to when Richard started talking about a brother or sister for Amanda. By then there had been two more Donnas, women who even from a distance stirred her desires the way Richard no longer did, if he ever had. She hadn't been ready to face the truth then, let alone voice it, but at least she hadn't complicated life more.

"Right, Brett? Right?" Fear filled Jackie's voice.

And as quickly as it flared, Brett's fury flickered out. Jackie was Brett, ten years younger. And like Brett had then, she would only manage to fool herself and waste time. Brett even felt a faint stirring of sympathy.

"OK. It's over." As she spoke the words, Brett knew it was the right thing to say, the only thing to say.

"What?" Jackie's face was buried in a tissue. She turned to look at Brett. "Really? You're OK with this?"

Brett shifted in her seat. "I'll *be* OK. I feel kind of idiotic. What am I going to do in Charlotte for two days? But I understand. I've been in your shoes."

Jackie wiped her eyes. "When was that?"

"Oh, about ten years ago, I guess. Richard had a shot at taking over one of the biggest congregations in Pittsburgh. He was so excited, so insistent that Amanda and I look just right, play the adoring wife and daughter in the first pew."

"What happened?"

"He bombed. The Sunday he was to be the guest preacher, he just bombed. Both Amanda and I had colds, but we came. Amanda, who was about six then, coughed and sneezed through the whole sermon, and he glared at her every time. I don't know if the congregation picked up that he was furious at his own first-grader, or just thought the sermon was terrible, or both. But he got a thanks-but-no-thanks call two days later."

"Oh, no." Jackie's eyes grew large with sympathy.

Brett shrugged. "It was his dream, not mine. So we just stayed in Scranton, which was fine with me. I liked our house, and the schools are good."

"That's what I think about Charlotte, too." Jackie's voice sounded stronger now. "And we do have two kids to consider."

Brett sat back, bemused. Did Jackie think her stakes doubled because she had two children? Maybe they did. Who was she to judge, after all? But after a decade of hiding, Brett knew the life sentence of pretending was slowly snuffing her will to live. The alarm clock mocked her daily, summoning her to don her mask and hit her marks for another day.

Recalling the story of Richard's Pittsburgh audition made her realize something else. *That* was the turning point for their marriage, when being pastor became more important than pastoring his congregation, when evangelical matters started to trump social justice. Maybe his dogged pursuit of dogma would lead to another shot at a big church, but it would be without her. She couldn't live a double life anymore, not even for a beautiful daughter who depended on her, trusted her, who had organized her life around the belief that her parents were the people whose roles they played every day.

After all, wasn't a mother more than someone married to the father? Sitting in Jackie's SUV, as the jets roared overhead, Brett recalled the pilot's reported words. *Brace for impact.* She would try to do everything she could to brace Amanda. Coming out without a partner was probably easier than with, eliminating another person from the equation. When she got home, she and Amanda were overdue for a talk.

Jackie cleared her throat. "Now what?"

"Well, I came to learn about the best practices of North Carolina's award-winning food bank," Brett said to her ex-lover. "Think that part's still doable?"

"Dinner's served in two hours." Jackie said, blowing her nose and starting the engine.

Jackie's church's operation was initially underwhelming. Brett had expected a massive warehouse and a commercial kitchen, but the facilities were nothing more than she had access to back in Scranton.

"It's all organization," said Harriet, the energetic, sixty-ish volunteer showing her around. Jackie had told her Harriet "ran things" and excused herself to call her babysitter. Now, the more Harriet talked, the more Brett realized Jackie's portrayal of her own role in the food pantry was as imaginary as their future together.

"We're in a rotation to serve meals once a week. Tonight's our night. In about a half hour, this whole basement will be crawling, I'll promise you that," Harriet said.

"But the rest of it is a database and a phone tree." Harriet sat down at a new laptop that contrasted with the dated kitchen facilities. "That's how we find out what perishables the local restaurants and grocery stores need picked up. It's how we dispatch our pickup and delivery fleet. The fleet delivers to the host meal site. That church serves the show-up crowd. The church on the next night is responsible for delivering the to-go meals. That way, they can take any leftovers right to their church to serve the next night."

"How do you get all the other churches to cooperate?" Brett asked.

Harriet smiled. "I don't. Elizabeth does."

"Elizabeth? I haven't met anyone named Elizabeth yet."

"Our grant writer. From the Methodist church across town. She's the money gal, Elizabeth is. She and her husband moved to Charlotte a few years ago, when her husband got a job at UNC. She worked in fundraising for a big university up north, I forget which one. They had a couple little kids, and she stayed home for a while, but she got bored, she said. Coffee?" Harriet paused to fill a cup for herself as well.

"They went to the Methodist church, which had a little food pantry. The pastor there wanted to expand their kitchen so they could serve hot meals. Somebody found out Elizabeth knew how to write grants, and asked her to help. So she wrote something up. Cream?"

Brett shook her head. Harriet resumed.

"Six months later, the check arrives, they're installing a brand-new kitchen, commercial appliances, enough space for six cooks to work at once. Which meant they could serve three times as many as they'd thought. And the folks showed up.

"Some of the other churches started taking notice. You think Southern church women gossip?" Harriet snorted. "We're amateurs compared to the men. The other pastors around town found out what was going on over at the Methodists, and they all wanted a piece of Elizabeth."

"I can imagine," Brett said, thinking of Richard.

"But she's a smart cookie. From her job up north she had all these ideas about 'efficiency' and 'return on investment.' She wasn't going to get every pastor in town a fancy kitchen just because he flattered her. And she really cared about the results, too. She wanted that kitchen used, and she knew there were plenty of people who needed feeding around Charlotte. Not just Methodists. Not even just churchgoing folks, either."

Harriet raised her eyebrows meaningfully at Brett, then sipped her coffee.

"So she came up with this idea of rotating the meals between churches, and meal delivery. All they had then was some warming bags from a pizza delivery place and a van that must have had a hundred thousand miles on it. She got the local car dealers to donate delivery vehicles. Now all the cooking's run out of the Methodist church and delivered ready-to-eat to the other churches each night. So each pastor can crow about serving the needy, but the work's all centralized."

"She sounds amazing," Brett said, dumbfounded that Jackie had effectively plagiarized Elizabeth's identity. Theirs had to be the first food pantry seduction in history.

"Oh, she is," Harriet had more to share. "Then she got some of the restaurants and grocery stores interested in donating produce and other perishables. Of course she gave them all good PR in the congregation newsletters for doing it. She got some money somewhere else to hire a nutritionist consultant, who plans all the meals based on what's donated.

"Once the meals got a better reputation—we're talking salads, side dishes, vegetarian options, plus the main dish—she started another program, working with the hospitals. She calls it the Stork Express. All new moms who deliver at Charlotte Memorial get an offer for two weeks of meal delivery, regardless of income. While they settle in back home, you know."

"Regardless of income?" Brett frowned. "What's the point of that?"

"I asked the same thing." Harriet smiled in anticipation of the story's end. "Eighty percent of the mothers who get the delivery wind up becoming donors or volunteers within two years."

"Eighty percent." Brett breathed in the figure, recalling the many nights she spent alone in the Fellowship of Hope basement kitchen. This Elizabeth had ingeniously built a pipeline that could nearly sustain the program. "That's amazing."

"Amazing doesn't even begin to describe Elizabeth," Harriet said proudly.

"I don't suppose she's looking to relocate to Pennsylvania, by any chance?"

"Doubt it. She says she doesn't miss the weather. She was from New York, I think, upstate somewhere where it got pretty cold. Then again, nothing Elizabeth does surprises me much anymore. If you're looking to start something from scratch, you really should talk to her."

"I'll make sure I do," Brett said thoughtfully.

~

In Sam's car, the radio was tuned to the news.

"... an update on the cause of the 'Miracle on the Hudson,' that plane that was ditched in the Hudson River last month, resulting in the safe evacuation of all one hundred fifty-five passengers and crew. Kimberly Jones is standing by at the National Transportation Safety Board. Kimberly?"

"Thanks, Bob. I'm here at . . ." Sam snapped off the radio. The crash was a month ago. Wasn't it time for the media to move on?

The Central United Christian Church was fully lit, as if it were

Sunday morning instead of Wednesday night. Approaching the vestibule, Sam could see Robby with a group of adults. The self-appointed chaperones, sticking around till Dad showed up. He quickened his stride.

But no one turned as he entered. No smiles of identification and relief, no eagerness to remand custody of his son. Instead, the group continued their conversation which, Sam discovered, included Robby. Sam hung back at the door, suddenly and oddly awkward himself, hesitant to interrupt.

A tall man with glasses was holding court, talking about his trip to the Everglades. The park was a major bird migration hub, Sam learned, drawing bird lovers and photographers from around the world.

"Added the roseate spoonbill, anhinga, and purple gallinule to my list and shot 'em all with my SLR," he said. "I'm working on a presentation for the regional meeting, but you can all see the shots on my site now."

"When are regionals this year, Ed?" asked another man.

"April. Week after Easter, I think. And it's in Lansing this year, remember. I really hope we can have a good turnout."

Murmurs went around the group. "Robby, are you gonna make it to the regional Audubon meeting?" the lone woman in the cluster asked. She was much younger than the men, twenty, twenty-one, Sam judged.

"Don't know." Robby shrugged.

"Oh, you've got to come. It's the meeting for the Audubon clubs in the whole state of Michigan. Plus Indiana, Ohio, and Ontario. There's a guy from one of the Ontario clubs who's the expert on Canada geese. Ed, do you remember that guy's name? Anyway, he could tell you everything you want to know about those geese that flew into that plane in New York."

"You think?" Robby looked interested.

"Definitely."

He shrugged again. "Parents probably won't let me."

"Why not? It's educational," the woman said. "You'll learn lots more there than you would sitting in school for a couple days."

Ed nodded, turning his head to sneeze and catching sight of Sam. "Help you with something?"

All heads swiveled his way, including Robby's. To Sam's dismay, his son ducked his head and shrank into the group, as if to remain invisible to him.

"Hey, Rob," he said, using the short version deliberately. "Can you introduce me?"

Still looking at the floor, Robby jammed his hands in his pockets and shrugged yet again.

"Mr. Palmer." Ed stretched out his hand. "Pleased to meet you. Ed Anderson. Club vice president."

"Call me Sam. Likewise."

"It's nice to meet Robby's dad," Ed said, continuing to speak for the group. "We've only seen your wife so far. I've told her this before, but I'm gonna tell you now—your son is a remarkable kid."

"So we keep hearing," Sam said, watching Robby's face open and shoulders lift. It was like watching the sun dodge behind clouds— brilliant in the light of Ed's praise, then dimming when Sam spoke. Dejection swelled.

"It's true. We were just talking about the upcoming regional meeting, in Lansing. It'd be a great experience for Robby. Of course he'd need your permission to attend. I really hope you'll consider it, Sam. If it's not convenient for you to come, too, the club can take responsibility for chaperoning. We just want him to have this opportunity."

"And why's that? What's going to happen at this meeting in Lansing?"

"He'll have a chance to meet some of the most knowledgeable birders in the Midwest and Ontario," cut in the woman. "Say Robby was into some sport. Basketball. Football. Hockey. This is like the all-star game."

Hockey. An image of his nephew Tyler on skates flashed through Sam's mind. Linda would want Robby to go. So according to the roles they'd played since New York, he should at least be skeptical. Being the bad guy was getting old. Still, he didn't like feeling cornered. Robby started going to these meetings less than a month ago. Already they wanted him to go on an overnight trip a hundred miles away?

"I can see how it would be exciting," he finally said. "And I'm sure you can appreciate that my wife and I will have to talk about it first."

Linda. He remembered the Chinese food at home. Probably already cold. "Robby, we need to get going. Where's Paul?" Sam glanced at the other faces, expecting a nod.

"Not Paul," Robby said, pointing at the woman. "Paula."

Sam looked at her blankly.

"Yes, I'm the one who picked Robby up. But when we went out to my car after the meeting, I had a flat tire. Must have picked up a nail or something. I'm right on the way to your house, so if you wouldn't mind . . ."

"Of course. No trouble," Sam said automatically, trying to wrap his mind around it. Paula looked like someone they'd hire to babysit Robby, not someone who would become a friend. Did Linda know it was a young woman who had picked him up?

The two of them walked out ahead of Sam, chatting about this hotshot from Ontario.

"I heard him speak at a conference a couple years ago," Paula said. "You'll really like him, Robby. He's not just a birder, he's a conservationist. He lives on a couple hundred acres up in northern Ontario that he's worked to restore as a mating reservation. He tracks each one that's born, banding it, and logging it into his database of migration dates and mileage and all kinds of other stuff. He's been doing it for years and years."

"'Banding' them?"

Paula nodded. "Yes, he's able to band the birds' legs with an electronic chip. So he can track exactly where they are."

"What if they disappear? Like in the plane crash."

They were at the car. Paula and Robby got into the backseat. Now Sam was a chauffeur.

"Well, I guess if he loses the signal, he knows something's happened to the bird. I'm sure he can get geographic data off the chip and figure out where the bird was when the problem happened."

"So he would know if any of his geese got hit by the plane," Robby said.

Sam glanced into the backseat. "That's absurd, Robby. What are the chances—"

But Paula interrupted. "I guess he could look into his database, see if any went missing on that date, and then check the latitude and longitude coordinates on the chip."

Robby leaned forward into the front seat. "Need to go to Lansing."

Sam flicked his eyes at his son in the rearview mirror. As usual, Robby's voice was flat, devoid of inflection and urgency. But he wore his no-compromises face, his jaw set in determination.

"Your mom and I will talk about it, Robby, just like I said back at the church."

"Need to go to Lansing," Robby repeated. "Learn about the geese in the plane crash."

"We'll talk about it at home," Sam repeated. "I know you want to go. I know you want to meet this—this goose guru. But the chance that any of the geese he's tracking were involved in that plane crash are minuscule."

"I'm not so sure," Paula chimed in. "He's been banding and maintaining his database for at least twenty years. He must have thousands and thousands of birds in there now."

Sam clenched his teeth and ground out a reply. "Thank you for the information. You can see Robby's very interested in going. His mother and I will discuss it. Now where should I drop you off?"

"Turn right at the second light. Go three blocks, turn left on Springside—"

Robby interrupted, his pitch finally building. "Need to go to Lansing. Need to meet him!" His agitation was rising, too, and he bounced and twisted in his seat, straining against the seat belt.

"Middle of the block on the left. White house with a big porch, but it's hard to see. Haven't gotten around to fixing the porch light," Paula finished. As she finally registered Robby's anxiety, her voice turned soothing.

"Your dad says you'll talk about it. Don't worry. I'm sure Ed's got his e-mail, too. Even if you can't go, we'll get you in touch with him."

"Need to go!" Robby was visibly shaking in the backseat now. Sam passed the first light and glimpsed the second, still several blocks away. *Shit.*

Alarmed now, Paula squeezed herself toward the door, as far away as she could from Robby, who was now rocking back and forth, banging his head into the back of the front seat. "Need to go. Need to go," he chanted, in time to the rhythm of his rocking.

He wasn't banging that hard, Sam could tell, and the seat cushion muffled the sound to a low thump. Still, Paula's eyes were as wide as any of the gawking strangers Sam had endured over years of these meltdowns.

"Robby. Stop. Get ahold of yourself." He was watching the rearview mirror more than the road. Sam swung onto a side street and pulled over. Putting the car into park, he twisted around.

"Paula, I need to get back there with Robby."

Paula needed no urging. She darted out the back door and into the front passenger seat, burrowing into it like a frightened animal. Robby banged against the back again, jolting her forward. She stiffened, sliding herself to the edge of the seat, hunching her shoulders toward the dash. Sam felt a flash of pity. But she could take care of herself.

He slid into the backseat and pulled Robby into his arms tightly, grounding him with the pressure of the embrace, simultaneously mimicking the rocking motion that his son used to self-soothe. "You're OK. You're OK. You're OK, Robby. You're safe. You're safe. You're safe." he whispered in Robby's ear, over and over.

"Need to go to Lansing! Need to go to Lansing! Don't talk to mom. Go to Lansing!" Robby flailed against him.

"You're OK. You're safe. You're OK. You're safe." Gradually, the pressure of the hug, the rhythm of the rocking, and Sam's mantra-like words subdued Robby. Drained of resistance, his body went slack. Sam waited a full three minutes before he released his grip, allowing Robby's body to slump back on the seat. All three of them were quiet until Sam's cell phone rang. It had to be Linda.

"Hi." Sam sat up, one hand still on Robby's leg, careful to maintain a physical touchstone for him.

"Where are you? Did something happen? It's been an hour."

"Yeah, sorry. We just had to pull over. Robby—um, Robby got a little worked up about something that came up at the meeting."

Linda caught her breath. "Is he OK?"

Sam looked Robby up and down. His son stared out the black window, dazed. "Yeah, I think it's over. We're dropping off someone from the club, though, and I think she's pretty spooked." He leaned forward to look at Paula, who hunched her shoulders further. "We're not far from her house. I'll drop her off and be home in fifteen minutes."

"OK." There was a long pause. "I love you," Linda said.

"Love you, too."

Back in the driver's seat, Sam looked over at Paula, speaking quietly. "I know you and the rest of the club mean well. But Robby, he's got real issues. Real problems that whoever's responsible for him has to be able to handle."

He was silent for a few blocks, letting it sink in.

"How many of that bunch that offered to chaperone Robby would still be willing if they'd been in this car tonight?" Sam asked as he turned down Springside Street. "It's not about wanting to deny him something, especially something that's important to him. It's about fear for his safety."

Paula didn't answer. They were in front of the darkened house with a big porch. She opened the car door. A dog was barking. She paused for a moment, then seemed to change her mind. "Good night," she said, slamming the door.

In the rearview mirror, Robby sat stiffly, staring at his reflection in the black window glass, lips moving slightly, seeing something visible only to him.

The magpie ringtone Christopher had set for Deborah burst into the quiet of his office. Calling about the empty kitchen with vegetables strewn over the counter, no doubt. He let it go to voice mail, not trusting himself to talk. Two hours researching Huntington's disease online and replaying the conversation with Matt had tilted the axis of his personal world.

"Didn't Deborah tell you? Didn't Deborah tell you?" The disbelief in Matt's voice resounded in his own head. He couldn't fathom that she would deliberately withhold that kind of information from him. Not the woman he married ten years ago, when they had plotted their perfect life. Tenure. Professional respect. Financial security. And, yes, at the right time, a family. Perfect.

Had plotted. As a scientist, he was first an observer. One with a blind spot, apparently.

Parenthood was supposed to be one more plot point on their parallel life trajectories. Like everything else, they expected to achieve it with proper planning and execution. Then a year went by, punctuated every month by an increasingly despondent Deborah. Her fortieth birthday was spent researching in vitro fertilization. Renewed optimism and a mutual trust in the experts now guiding them fortified her briefly, but the two failed IVF cycles had taken her the lowest Christopher had ever seen.

He had hoped Martha's retirement, after the first, would divert her dogged determination. The top job in the law school advancement office could provide a different kind of satisfaction, he suggested.

She hadn't even asked for consideration, forcing the search committee to go outside and hire Phillip Crandall, a boss she now despised. Simultaneously, she grew more obsessed with pregnancy, scheduling the New York consultation with the most prominent reproductive endocrinologist in the state. Then came the crash and his promise and confession, and her tears and negotiating.

And in the crucible of the crash aftermath, he'd yielded. Let himself be persuaded, let himself be carried away on a wave of ancient memories, against his first instincts. And now he'd been acting like some love-blind college student the last few weeks, while she was deceiving him.

He tossed his glasses on the desk in frustration and rubbed his temples. How could she? For him, trust was the foundation of their relationship. Any relationship. Her deliberate deception, on an issue with consequences of such magnitude, repelled him.

He clung to the hope of a misunderstanding. That Helen had been misdiagnosed. Or that Matt was wrong, and Helen hadn't told Deborah, after all. If she had, that Deborah had misunderstood Helen. He wished that they had continued on to Seattle after the crash, after all. Flying cross-country with no luggage or ID now seemed minor compared to the prospect of a wife—and, potentially, a child—with an incurable genetic disease.

Sighing, he stood for the first time in two hours. His office window overlooked Sapsucker Woods. The barren trees created a maze of crisscrossed shadows as Valentine's dusk neared. A month ago it would have been dark. A month from now it would yet be light. But it was today, and the magpie was calling again.

An hour later Christopher sat in the dark garage, listening to the Volvo's engine shudder into silence. He had blasted the heater against the February chill all the way home from campus, yet he still felt numb. He forced himself to open the car door.

"There you are." Deborah put down her phone as he entered the kitchen. "I was just trying you again. Didn't you get my messages? What happened? All this salad stuff left over the counter. Were you planning to cook?"

He nodded, automatically going to close the cookbook he'd left splayed open, facedown next to the vegetables.

"Oh. Well, I was starving so I went ahead and ate some leftovers. Do you think that's a good sign? Pregnant women are supposed to be hungry all the time."

Christopher shrugged. So much for the Valentine's dinner, not that he felt remotely romantic now, anyway. "I wouldn't know."

"I guess not." She smiled. "I think it's a good sign. This time feels different, Christopher. I think it might have happened."

Fear sliced through him as he replaced the Moosewood cookbook where it belonged, in between *Molto Italiano* and Wolfgang Puck's *Live, Love, Eat*. He gazed at her still-flat abdomen underneath the gray wool of her pants, willing answers to the two unknowns. Had the embryos implanted? Did her DNA carry the Huntington's code? The odds against the former were low, the latter, even. What were the chances both could be true?

"Christopher?" She was looking at him oddly. "Are you OK?"

He raised his eyes to hers. "Matt called this afternoon. While you were still at work."

"He did?" Her voice climbed higher than the two syllables required. She cleared her throat and turned to the counter, beginning to put away the salad items. "Did he?"

"Yes."

"I'll have to call Helen back later. I wonder why he called instead. Did he leave a message?"

"He did, as a matter of fact." Christopher waited until Deborah turned back to face him. "He wanted to give us the name of a doctor. A specialist, at Columbia. Name's William Hirsh. He heads up a program they have on Huntington's disease."

Deborah's mouth formed an "O," and she dropped the salad tongs. They clattered on the porcelain tile, the tile they'd special-ordered when they'd renovated the kitchen five years ago. Quickly she ducked her head as she bent to pick them up, but not quickly enough. A flush rose on her cheeks, igniting the embers of his fury.

"I've spent the last two hours at the Lab trying to convince myself you wouldn't lie to me. Especially about something like this. Tell me I'm not wrong, Deborah. Please tell me."

Looking down at the tongs, she exhaled for a long minute before she met his eyes and shook her head. "I'm sorry, Christopher. But I couldn't."

"It's true, then." His voice sounded like a croak. "Your sister's been diagnosed with a fatal, inherited disease. One you stand a fifty-fifty chance of developing, too."

"I knew it would be a deal-breaker for you, and I couldn't abandon them." She placed her hand on her abdomen.

"And, if it turns out you're pregnant, one the child could have."

"Our child." She looked less sure of herself now. "Our child. Right?"

He opened his mouth to answer. To hurl angry, biting, savage words at her—words he'd never said to any woman before, let alone his wife. The vision from his office flashed into his head. Feeding Deborah in a wheelchair while a faceless child screamed from a high chair. He rushed to the bathroom off the kitchen, where this time he did retch.

Light-headed and weary, he rinsed his mouth and washed his face. Laying down the towel, he met Deborah's eyes in the mirror. He could read worry now, and fear.

"Christopher?" she said tentatively.

"I'm sleeping in the guest room tonight," he said.

ELEVEN

Linda set the table for their late, now-cold Valentine's dinner automatically. From the family room she could hear the TV news.

"... *we've got an update today on the cause of the 'Miracle on the Hudson,' that plane that was ditched in the Hudson River last month, resulting in the safe evacuation of all one hundred fifty-five passengers and crew. Kimberly Jones is standing by in Washington. Kimberly?"*

Intrigued, Linda walked to the living room.

"Thanks, Bob. I'm here at an NTSB warehouse where the evidence from Flight 1549 is being collected. Investigators are telling us today that inspection of the engines, fished out of the Hudson in the days after the crash and transported here on a flatbed, is now complete and the remnant of a single feather tangled in one confirms initial suspicion that the crash was indeed caused by a bird strike. I spoke with lead investigator Barbara ..."

The door opening from the garage interrupted the reporter. Hastily, Linda clicked off the TV. Best keep Robby away from anything to do with the crash and birds for the rest of the night.

"Come on in, Robby. Here we go. Mom's home, let's just go in and relax now." Sam was talking himself through the motions of the meltdown recovery as much as he was leading Robby.

"Hi, guys," Linda said cautiously, looking between them for clues. Sam looked wrung out but grimly victorious. Robby wore a defeated, hunted look. He barely looked at her, let alone greeted her, and went straight to his room. Linda's stomach sank. Why was it always them vs. him?

In the kitchen, they scooped the rice and divided egg rolls, distributing packets of soy sauce and sweet and sour silently, their memorized preferences like marital fingerprints.

"How you doing?" Linda finally asked.

He shrugged. "All right. Mostly drained. You know."

"I know." They sat down at the table. Linda hoped Sam noticed she had put his roses in a vase, an unspoken act of détente.

"So what set him off?" Linda asked.

"Some big upcoming meeting in Lansing. Do you know about this?"

Linda pondered. "I don't think so. An Audubon meeting?"

"Yeah. A regional meeting of all the clubs in the state, plus a few more. In early April. There's supposed to be some expert in Canadian geese there. They were really talking it up tonight. Robby wants to go."

Canada geese, Linda thought. *Not Canadian*. She felt like she imagined Robby must often, irritated at Sam's imprecision. But rather than correct him, she just nodded.

"Sounds OK with me."

"Really? Just like that? Our twelve-year-old autistic son wants to venture a hundred miles from home, and that's enough detail for you?"

The roses visible from the corner of her eye, Linda bit back her defense. "I take it you're not OK with it, then."

"They hit me with it as soon as I walked in the door. I felt ambushed. I tried to put them off politely, saying we'd discuss it. But that wasn't enough for them, especially this woman who gave him a ride tonight. Paula. She just wouldn't let up, going on and on about this geese guru. I kept telling Robby I wasn't saying no, but that you and I had to talk about it first. But that wasn't good enough. He just lathered himself all up, and that was it."

Linda sighed. "The old power struggle." She took a bite of her Mongolian chicken. "It's cold."

"Yeah." Sam said to both comments, stabbing a forkful of his sweet and sour.

"How did Paula react?"

"Not well." Sam took a long swallow of his water. "She was scared. It started when they were both in the backseat. I had her get in the front so I could get back there with him and calm him down. She couldn't get out of there fast enough."

Alarm bells rang in Linda's head. "Do you think she'll tell the others in the club?"

Sam cocked his head. "I *hope* she does. They need to know who they're dealing with. Especially if you want Robby to go to more meetings alone."

"If *I* want him to go alone. So we're back to that. You don't want him to choose anything you haven't preapproved."

"That's not it. I'm concerned for his safety."

"Oh, come on! He's twelve years old. Almost a teenager. He needs more than the two of us can give him, Sam. He needs his life to be about more than autism. He needs friends, peers in his life."

"Peers." Sam rolled his eyes. "I was younger than most of the crowd at that meeting."

"Stop splitting hairs. People who share his interests. You know what I mean. Why should his autism automatically limit him?"

"It shouldn't. But it should be a starting point. It's a fact of life, Linda, and taking risks doesn't change that."

"All right, then. You go to Lansing with him."

"What?"

"You heard me." Linda's voice was terse, her face tense. "Robby deserves a chance to explore this. I'm fine with him going with the club. If you think it's so risky, or they might get scared off because of what this Paula saw tonight, you have to make it happen. Talk to the president. Chaperone if you have to."

Détente disintegrated, they glared at each other. In the silence, Robby's bedroom door opened. Linda saw his computer screen illuminated on his desk. No doubt he'd read the latest news on the crash investigation, whatever that TV reporter had said. He walked up to the table and stood there, idly fingering the unopened chopsticks packets.

"What is it, Robby?" Linda asked.

He remained silent, staring at the wall behind them.

"Robby?"

He opened one of the packets, rolling a chopstick between his fingers.

"They got the engine out of the river."

"I heard that, just before you got home."

"Found a feather inside."

"Mmm-hmm."

"A goose feather. Canada goose."

Linda nodded.

"They got sucked into the engine."

"Well. Yes. That's . . . that's pretty much what happens."

"His name is Donald Baxter."

"Who's that?" Sam interjected.

"The foremost expert on Canada geese in the entire province of Ontario. Scheduled to be the speaker for the second morning session, Audubon International Midwest Regional, ten thirty a.m., April fourth, Ballroom C, Lansing Radisson."

"You Googled him," Linda said, rhetorically.

"I need to go." Robby unexpectedly pivoted from the wall, aiming this last comment at Sam.

Sam looked at his son. Robby's brown-eyed gaze had landed somewhere over his shoulder, but at least it was in his vicinity. His headphones were hanging around his neck. His hair brushed the headband, at its usual weeks-past-needing-cutting stage, because sitting still for a haircut and the touch of the barber was such an ordeal. One hand fidgeted with the chopstick. The other was buried in his sweatshirt pocket, stretching the faded blue Detroit Lions logo.

Sam remembered the game where they'd purchased it, one of those father-son outings he'd so anticipated. With his headphones on, Robby did OK through the first quarter. The Lions had even been ahead for a change. But then they started launching T-shirts into the crowd for some dumb promotion. One hit Robby on the head, and he panicked. In an attempt to soothe him and salvage the day, Sam bought the oversized, hooded sweatshirt on their way out. Maybe it had worked, since Robby wore it almost every day.

Sam felt Linda's brown eyes on him, too, telegraphing a plea. Abruptly, he decided.

"We're going, Robby. I'll take you," Sam said.

Momentarily, Robby's gaze flickered to his face. "Really?"

"Really."

Robby stared a moment longer. Captivated by the rare moment of eye contact, Sam willed it to continue.

Then came the manna from heaven. Robby smiled. "Cool. Thanks, Dad."

Back in his room, Robby closed the door feeling happy. He was going to the conference in April. He would meet Donald Baxter.

He would learn exactly what had made those geese fly into the plane engine. Then something could be done to change it. The plane engine modified. Or the airports. Or the geese. Something.

He sat down at his desk and spun his chair. Ah, that felt good. Closing his eyes, he pushed off the floor with his toe again, circling counterclockwise, allowing the rotations to reverberate up though his spine, his body swaying slightly in the seat. The chair slowed. Robby pushed himself off again, clockwise this time. Around and around, the revolutions lulling and soothing.

When the chair stopped again, he was facing the desk. He pushed aside his notebook and the thick Sibley's guide. He was learning a lot. He cringed now, recalling the email he'd sent Dr. Felk right after their trip, all worried about goslings orphaned by the crash. Duh, January wasn't breeding time. He wouldn't make a mistake like that now. Still he had a long way to go to catch up to Dr. Felk and Donald Baxter.

He scrolled through Donald Baxter's website again. Like Dr. Felk, he had gone to Cornell University, where he was something called ABD in biology. That was where his academic path ended. His dissertation was going to be on the reservation in Ontario, but running the place left him no time to write. When journals rejected his submissions on the grounds that he needed a PhD, at least as a co-author, Baxter in turn rejected the field.

All this was posted in a screed on his site that scorned peer-reviewed ornithology journals as "snobbish, unoriginal, ego-boosting echo chambers." Baxter now published all his work on his own website. As much as the scoffed-at peers would have loved to find fault with it, Baxter's work was always meticulously documented and his data replicable when the peers tried it on their own samples. That's what he said, anyway.

Robby liked that. He could relate. His favorite subject at school was biology. Technically it was supposed to be taken in eighth grade, but his mom made the school let him take it a year earlier, since the seventh grade general science class was so boring.

At first, the other, older kids were nice. That led to coaxing him to share his homework or test answers. When he refused, they made fun of him. When he didn't respond to that, they ignored him. "Ostracized. Outcast," he'd seen written on his report cards.

But like Baxter, Robby didn't care about his status with peers. He always was engaged in his head, and the questions and conversations that others, mostly his parents and teachers, used to try to draw him out were so silly and irritating that he'd never even wanted to pursue friendship with anyone.

But Paula, from the Audubon Club, was different. She was interested in birds, too. And she offered to give him rides to the meetings and stuck up for him about going to Lansing. He had her number. He would text her that he could go to Lansing, after all.

"Can come to Lansing," he typed. Waiting for her reply, he thumbed through the Sibley's, pausing to brush a finger across several of the delicate sketches and paintings that were the guide's trademark. He wished he could draw like that.

"Robby? Is that u?"

"Yeah. So I'll meet Donald Baxter."

"??" came back.

"The geese expert. i found him online."

"Oh. Cool."

"Can u ride there with us?"

"To Lansing?"

"Yeah. Me and my dad."

After a long pause the phone beeped back with Paula's reply.

"Not sure I can still go. Might have to work."

Robby frowned at his phone.

"U didn't say that before," he typed back.

"I forgot."

Robby thought for a moment before he typed back.

"Can u change it." Another long pause.

"I don't know. Gotta go. C u."

A knock startled Robby. He turned to see his mom. "Hey, Robby. Can I come in a minute?"

Robby shrugged. Instinctively, he folded his arms, hiding the phone under one elbow.

"What are you doing?" She stepped into the room and removed another pile of bird paraphernalia—more field guides, the Sears binoculars—clearing a space to sit on the bed. Reluctantly, Robby held up his phone.

"Texting?"

Robby nodded.

"With who?"

"Paula."

"The girl from the Audubon Club?" Another nod.

"Is she a friend of yours?" Robby nodded again, then shrugged.

"You don't know?"

Robby shook his head. "She said she was going to Lansing. Now she says she has to work." He could feel his worries creeping back. He spun his chair again.

"Oh. I see." His mom thought for a minute. "Well, maybe she forgot."

"That's what she said." He paused. "I don't forget things."

"You don't. But lots of people do. That doesn't make them bad. Just forgetful."

"Yeah." Robby sighed, then yawned.

"It's getting late, Robby. Time to get ready for bed."

"First I have to check the feeder."

"OK. Go ahead."

He yawned again as he pulled up the blinds. The half-empty feeder hung from the crabapple just outside his window.

"You're really getting a lot of birds," his mom said. "Didn't you fill it just this morning?"

Robby nodded, pleased with himself. "I started a yard list." He held up a notebook. Just as quickly, the smile disappeared. "No geese, though."

"No. Well, they migrate, you know."

"Sparrows, mostly." His face suddenly turned mournful. "If somebody fed them in New York, maybe the geese wouldn't have crashed into the plane."

"Oh, Robby." His mom sighed. "A bird feeder couldn't have saved them. Geese don't go to bird feeders. They were migrating, heading south. It's what they're programmed to do." She reached for one of the field guides in the pile, rifling through the pages, as if looking for words to back her up.

Robby looked out the window. "What about sparrows?"

"What about them?"

"Do they—" he paused, afraid of the answer. "Do they migrate?"

"No." His mom hesitated. "I'm pretty sure they don't, anyway. Sparrows just stay."

"They just stay." Robby nodded slowly, satisfied. He gazed out the window. "We better get more birdseed, then."

TWELVE

The wake-up call jarred Brett out of a fitful slumber at the Charlotte Airport Hampton Inn. Airport traffic and somersaulting emotions—sadness over Jackie's decision, fear about telling Amanda, uncertainty about her future—had kept her tossing and turning much of the night. She turned the water to cold before stepping into the shower. She was meeting Elizabeth the wunderkind grant writer for coffee at nine and wanted to be as alert as possible.

She was a cup ahead when Elizabeth arrived, the caffeine working as intended. "Thanks for taking the time. I understand you've got a very busy schedule."

"You're welcome." Elizabeth sat down. She wasn't at all what Brett had expected—short, more than a little overweight, with glasses and short curly hair. "What can I do for you?"

Harriet had said she would get right down to business. And Richard would expect her to report on next steps back at home. This was her chance to get answers. But beyond asking her to move to Pennsylvania, Brett couldn't think of specifics.

"I'm not sure how to answer that," she said, slowly. "I want to move my church's operation to something like what you've done here. But it seems overwhelming. We're one church in Scranton.

We don't have the network that you have to share the workload. We don't have money or anyone with skills like yours to help us get it."

"Hmm. So what do you have?" Elizabeth asked, tilting her head.

"We've got a lot of hungry people," Brett said, after a moment's thought.

"I meant the singular you. What do you, Brett, have to bring to the table? For starters, do you have the desire to build it from the ground up? From scratch, networking with the other churches, trying and failing and trying again to get money, all the while still showing up to get dinner on the table every night?"

"I think I've got to build it," Brett answered, feeling like they were talking in circles.

"But do you *want* to build it? Is that how you want to spend your time and energy? From the sound of it, all by yourself, at least for now, and possibly for the next several years? Because if you don't, then don't waste your time trying."

Elizabeth took a sip of coffee, her eyes never leaving Brett's.

"This is a lot of hard, hard work that doesn't provide much of a paycheck. So you've got to be willing to take your pay in other ways. Sure, you'll get lots of thank-yous. You'll see people feeling good, and that can make you feel good. And if you're jumping into someone else's operation, that might be enough.

"But if you're the one building it, you need more. You need drive. You need commitment. You need passion. And it has to come from within."

Brett was silent, recalling Richard's edict to get more involved at Fellowship of Hope. She picked the meal program as her project because it fulfilled some of her own ideals about charity and service. But fundamentally, she was doing it because it was expected of her as the pastor's wife. Though how much longer would that be true?

Momentarily, the rhetorical question shocked her. But yesterday she'd been planning how to come out to Amanda, hadn't she? Divorce would logically come next.

"Wheels turning, I see," Elizabeth said.

"I'm sorry. I'm probably wasting your time." Brett tried to focus. Her heart was racing, and she felt light-headed. She could do it. Break free. Live her own life.

"Not at all. I don't have another meeting until eleven, and I'd certainly rather do this up front than have you waste a whole lot of your own—and probably mine, with e-mails and phone calls—only to discover in ten, twelve, eighteen months that this really isn't your cup of tea."

She took another sip of coffee. "And don't guilt yourself into it. It's not a bad thing if this isn't what you want to do. Just be honest."

Be honest.

Brett thought back to the conversation with Jackie. She'd told her she was done pretending. She had monumental truths to tell Amanda and Richard. Might as well start with Elizabeth.

"That's a lot to think about. And not what I expected to hear," she started. "I thought you'd give me a whole list of websites on grant writing and some boilerplate advice, like 'start small.'"

Elizabeth smiled. "I surprise a lot of people. But it doesn't do anyone any good if a food pantry or a meal delivery or any other service like it starts out for the wrong reasons. People start to rely on it. Then whoever runs it burns out. People are worse off than before, because they've become dependent. 'Consider the sparrow.' My personal motto."

"Excuse me?"

"The Gospel verse. You know. The Lord watches out for the least of his creatures. Believe me, they'll flock to you, too. So you've got to be sure you're ready first."

"I see," said Brett, though she didn't really.

"You've surprised me, too. I'll tell you, from what I heard about you from Harriet, I thought you'd say you're ready to sign on to build this thing with your two bare hands."

"Really?"

"Really. She said you asked smart questions. Were good with the folks at last night's dinner. Not patronizing. Helped out with cleanup even though you didn't have to. But now it seems like you're holding back."

"That's all true." Brett pondered. "I think I am committed to the cause. Meal nights are the highlight of my week."

"Tell me about that. Tell me why."

No one had ever asked her why. For Richard, it was enough that she did it. Turning her coffee cup as she groped for words, Brett saw her face reflected in the dark-brown circle. She imagined what that fluid woman, untethered from the ties that bound her, would say.

"Part of it is that I think I'm good at it. It's not much different than what I've done at home all these years, taking care of my daughter. It's just on a bigger scale."

"And you enjoy that kind of caretaking?"

Brett frowned, thinking. "Enjoy's not quite the right word. Especially since, as a mother, I don't have any choice. But doing it for Amanda, I've learned the value in it. The importance of it. And at the food pantry, when I'm doing it voluntarily—for people who don't have anywhere else to get a nutritious meal, or a warm place to sit or a kind word—it just feels right. Like I'm doing what I'm meant to be doing."

Brett looked up from her reflection, at Elizabeth, her words gaining momentum.

"There was this mom who came in a few weeks ago. Young, probably only twenty-one, twenty-two. She had two kids, both of them coughing and sneezing. She didn't have any insurance, no doctor. I gave her directions to the local free clinic, gave her some bus passes. Last week she was back, both of the kids doing just fine."

"There." Elizabeth smiled. "Now you're not holding back."

"In college I went on a mission trip with my husband. We built a community center. Really built it. Fourteen-hour days wearing hard hats and carpenter's aprons. That was my first taste of that kind of satisfaction, of helping serve social justice, whatever you want to call it," Brett went on. "I loved it. But where I am now, this is part of the role my husband—he's the pastor—assigned. He thinks of it almost like recruitment."

"Come for the meal, stay for the sermon." Elizabeth said dryly.

"Exactly. If I could run it completely my way, yeah, I'd sign up for another hard hat."

"Hmmm." Elizabeth gave her a long look. "It's none of my business, but everything points to more to your story than you're sharing. It's fine to keep it to yourself. But if you *do* have the drive, and the ability and talent, you need to use it. There's a lot of people who can't do for themselves. Lots of sparrows."

"So you don't like being under your husband's thumb. Plenty of food pantries and meal programs, you know. Maybe it's time to see what else is out there." Elizabeth reached into her purse.

"One of my pet projects has been a little online network. Nobody's doing anything new here; we're all feeding hungry people, just finding better ways to do it. Might as well learn from each other. It's pretty rudimentary right now, but there is a jobs page."

She handed Brett a card printed with a website. Eastcoastpantries.org. "When you figure out if you're ready, check it out."

Brett accepted the card. "Thank you."

"Don't mention it." Elizabeth stood up. "I hope you'll use it."

THIRTEEN

Withdrawing the needle, Dr. Singh's nurse pressed a cotton ball on the inside of Deborah's elbow, secured it with a bandage and lifted her arm in one expert, practiced move. "Keep this elevated. I'll be right back."

Deborah watched her leave with the precious, portentous vial. The whole plodding two-week wait was down to these last glacial minutes, which she would endure alone in the exam room. With a shuddering sigh she closed her eyes, remembering being here last with Christopher, and for the first time questioning whether she'd done the right thing fourteen days ago.

At home in Cayuga Heights, Christopher remained decamped in the guest room, leaving before she awoke in the mornings, staying late at the Lab in the evenings. After she missed him two mornings, she had set her alarm an hour earlier. Padding into the kitchen, she noticed the cold coffeepot. Making coffee was one of Christopher's morning rituals.

"Are we out?" She knew they weren't. She'd bought a thirty-two-ounce can of decaf.

He glanced up from his cereal bowl and shook his head. "I was going to pick up something on campus. Early meeting."

"Oh." She crossed her arms, considering his profile. His shoulders looked tense and rigid. Sitting next to him, she laid a hand on his arm. "Christopher, we need to talk about this."

Deliberately, he moved his arm away from her touch.

"I don't know what there is to say until you get the results."

"Until *I* get the results? Christopher, if the pregnancy test is positive, we're going to have a baby. It's going to be ours."

He shook his head, pushing away the bowl. "Doesn't feel that way."

"What do you mean?"

"You say it's ours, but you're instigating all the decisions." He ticked off on his fingers. "Trying again. Three embryos. Withholding the information about Helen." He shook his head again, looking directly at her for the first time in three days. "I don't recognize you. It's like nothing I want matters anymore."

"You wanted kids, too! You told me. So you could be the father you never had."

"I did, but I'd come to terms with the fact that we probably weren't having a family. Until you maneuvered me into this last try, after the crash."

"That's not fair. I didn't know about Helen in New York."

"But you knew before the transfer. Right?"

She hesitated, then nodded.

He stared at her and threw up his hands. "How can you be so cavalier?"

"I'm not cavalier! I take my responsibility as a mother very seriously. I told you, I couldn't let anything happen to them." She'd covered her abdomen.

"Responsibility lasts a lot longer than nine months. Have you researched Huntington's? At all?"

"Helen told me about it," she said, defensively.

"She told you about the disintegration of ambulatory function? Followed by the cognitive decline? Dementia? The proportion of patients who wind up needing full-time nursing care?"

Deborah bit her lip. *Dementia? Full-time nursing care?*

"I guess not." Christopher looked grimly satisfied. "Now say we've got a baby, too. You'd both be dependent on me. Until I become a single father."

"Single father? Christopher, really, that's a bit melodramatic."

"It's a risk, Deborah. A real, bona fide risk. One that scares me. Even if you don't have the gene, the lives we've built together are gone. This kind of a breach of trust is foundational."

"We'd build a new foundation as a family. We'd have new lives. All three of us."

"All three of us," Christopher had repeated, shaking his head as he stood to leave. "I don't think I can do it, Deborah."

"Good morning, Deborah." Dr. Singh interrupted her reverie. Startled, Deborah looked up. The doctor's smile flashed brilliantly, blindingly. "I'm thrilled to tell you, the third time was the charm. You're pregnant."

Dr. Singh was reciting the lines Deborah had scripted when she first imagined this scene two years ago, and her spirit duly soared as the guard she had held over her hope vanished. But this perfunctory, three-second doctor-patient hug was not the next cue. Christopher was supposed to be here, the fact of their *fait accompli* releasing an emotional dam that would sweep him into the current of joy and anticipation where she waited, and carry them forward together.

The rest of the appointment was crowded with details—scheduling an ultrasound and choosing an OB and more. None of the teary smiles or locked gazes or fervent kisses of her imagined scene. Now she was walking to her car alone, trying to allow herself to believe it. Well, as alone as you could be when pregnant.

Pregnant. The two syllables bounced around in her head. She said it aloud. "I'm pregnant." Incredulously, Deborah touched her abdomen.

Only one embryo had successfully implanted. Dr. Singh told her that was good. The pregnancy would be less taxing, and she was more likely to carry the baby, most likely G, to term. Still, she felt a pang for the loss of E and F. She tried to push it away, to recapture that first, brief soaring sensation. She had always expected pure joy at this moment.

Now she had to tell Christopher. She glanced at her watch and turned the key in the ignition. His afternoon office hours began in twenty minutes. *Best get it over with.* The pang echoed. This wasn't how she expected to feel, either.

She drove to campus in a kind of stupor, adrift now that her script was useless. Inside Christopher's office she removed a pile of folders from the designated student chair and sat, drumming her fingers on his desk. A laptop was on sleep mode. A light on the office phone indicated there were messages waiting. His cell phone was charging on top of a pile of folders set crossways to each other, to indicate some sort of separation, she supposed. Post-it notes with reminders and to-dos were stuck on every conceivable surface. Yet across from the laptop a three-month whiteboard calendar was almost bare except for a notation April 4–5: *Midwest Regional Audubon.*

The door opened. Reading while he walked and automatically aiming for his chair, Christopher heard Deborah before he saw her.

"Pretty slow around here, huh?"

Lowering the papers, he did a double take. "Deborah. What are you doing here?"

She nodded at the whiteboard. "Doesn't look like there's much going on."

He squinted at the whiteboard and shrugged. "My calendar's loaded on my phone. I don't even know who wrote that conference up there."

"Well, I've got another date for you to save. But it's a little further out than the next quarter." Deborah scrutinized his face, hoping for something—a nod, an eyebrow lift, a cock of the head—that would show he'd been anticipating this moment.

Nothing. He was still skimming his papers.

"And that would be?" He edged around the piles to his chair, rolling to the keyboard.

"Can you guess?"

He sighed, sounding impatient. "Deborah, I'll have students here for office hours any minute. I don't have time for games."

"I'll give you a hint. Dr. Singh was the one who told me."

Christopher looked up. She felt the blood in her temples pound as he removed his glasses and massaged his own temples. She had never noticed before how his hands steepled together when he did that, as if in prayer. A minute ticked by audibly on the office wall clock.

"And?" He still wasn't looking at her, his face hidden beneath the slope of his hands.

"November ninth. Save the date for the birth of your child." Her voice turned up as she finished the sentence. Like a game show host or a telemarketer, trying to close the deal. The deal of the century. Or a lifetime, anyway. The child's lifetime. Would it be a life with two parents, or just one?

"Wow." Christopher leaned back in his chair, finally dropping his hands to his lap. Did she see the briefest smile? The sudden movement sent his chair rolling backward until it bumped into the window. Maybe not. His face was drained, as flat as the gray day behind him.

"You had a blood test. There's no doubt."

"No doubt."

"You said child. Just one?"

133

"Just one."

"Wow." He stood and turned to the window. "I never—I just never expected this to happen to us," he finished, pressing his face to the glass, steepling his hands again. To Deborah they looked like blinders, shutting her out. Her and their baby.

"What, you thought this round would fail, too?" Deborah asked.

"That's not what I meant."

"Then what? I don't understand."

"After the crash, pregnant or no, I was ready for what came next. Because we were stronger together."

Deborah looked at her lap. She could feel his impending accusations—she was wrong, she had deceived, she had betrayed—swirling like a tornado, sucking everything innocent into its path, leaving wreckage in its wake.

But she had a mighty force within her now, too. Maternal ferocity. After her own muted first reaction, she was grateful to feel some emotion, some energy about the pregnancy. At what should have been a moment of euphoria, he chose to hold a grudge against her and the baby. Based on one decision over more than a decade together, ignoring everything else that was good between them, but most important, ignoring the child.

"But I never expected you'd deceive me," Christopher said. "And that's too fundamental to move forward."

"Christopher, I don't even know what that means. I'm pregnant. We're going to be parents. This is already moving forward. Nine months and counting."

Stalemated, they stared at each other. A knock on the door broke the silence.

"That's my first appointment," Christopher said hoarsely.

"Fine. We'll talk at home, then." Deborah picked up her purse and turned toward the door.

"I won't be coming home tonight, Deborah."

His sentence was like a blade, slicing through her. She turned back. "Excuse me?"

"I need some space. Some time to think."

"Think about what?"

"Whether I can do this."

Another knock filled in for Deborah's silent shock. "Professor Goldman? You in there?"

Christopher stood up, opened the door and motioned the student in. "I'll call you in the next couple days."

FOURTEEN

Richard stood up, swallowing the last of his coffee. "I'll see you there, then, in an hour?"

"Yes." Brett sat at the kitchen table, still eating.

"Try to sit up front. You've been too far back the last couple weeks. The congregation needs to see you. Especially after those trips out of town. People don't need any excuse to gossip, you know."

Brett started, sloshing her coffee. "OK. I'll look for a better spot." She steadied her cup with both hands as she watched him pull on his jacket. *Gossip? Did someone suspect something? Did he?*

"Good. What's taking Amanda so long? Amanda!" Backing away, he called down the hall. Since she sang in the choir, Amanda left with him before Brett.

"Richard, do *you* need to see me?" Spoken aloud, her own question surprised her. After all, it didn't matter anymore, did it?

Her husband looked nonplussed. "What kind of question is that?" Jingling his keys, he looked back down the hall again.

"Amanda! Aren't you ready yet?"

Amanda appeared in her bedroom doorway.

"There you are. Come on, we're running late."

"See you later, Mom." Amanda reached for her coat as Richard stood with the door open, issuing her instructions. "Remember what I told you before about blending in with the rest of the choir."

"I know, Dad." Hearing the resignation in her voice, Brett felt angry. His manufactured family modesty was sabotaging Amanda's talent. She hadn't realized herself how good Amanda's voice was until she was cast in the play as Rizzo, the bad girl opposite Sandy, the female lead. Songs from *Grease* now echoed around the house—at least when Richard was out. He had sighed when she told him about it. Amanda should have had the chance to share that kind of news with her father. Nine out of ten would have been proud and happy. But Richard was the tenth, who would have lectured her just like he was doing now.

"It would be a poor example to the congregation to look like I'm showing off my daughter."

"I *know*, Dad. You've told me, like, a hundred times," Amanda said, as the door closed.

Carrying her dishes to the sink, Brett stared out at the bird feeder. She recalled her husband's words. *What kind of question is that?* One seeking an answer that would allow her to stay? Do the easy thing? No. She had to stop stalling. Had to tell him the truth.

But he hadn't answered her question, either. Were she and Amanda nothing more than props to him, after all? Dutiful wife in the pew, daughter in the choir? Even if their marriage had been reduced to roommate status, he was still Amanda's father. Brett wanted to know someone could matter to him.

She thought it again at church. Richard held center stage at the pulpit. In her choir robe, Amanda was upstage right. In her Sunday best, Brett sat stage left. Human bookends, propping up the head of the household. As Richard droned on, with the air of self-righteousness she had complained about to Jackie, Brett stared out the window. This mockery of a family ritual was almost painful. She tried to numb herself, her thoughts drifting.

It was her first night with Jackie. Her first time with any woman. They lay together, the incessant New York traffic muted by the twenty floors between bed and street, and by the white noise roaring in Brett's head.

". . . I'm sure I don't have to remind anyone that Valentine's Day was this week." Obligatory chuckles from the congregation barely penetrated Brett's fantasy. *The white noise was the shredding of the rigid expectations and bigoted beliefs that she had bowed to all her life: that it was wrong to be here, naked, with Jackie.*

"Now that the chocolates are gone and the roses are wilting, let us go forward thinking about God's love for us," Richard intoned. "God loves us more than we can possibly love each other—our wives, husbands, children. His love is unconditional, all-encompassing, three hundred and sixty-five days a year."

The white noise was a vacuum, sucking away past fears and future worries. Only the present time and place mattered, only Jackie smiling the smile that matched her voice—warm and lingering.

"But for us to feel that love, to experience that wonderful purity his love offers, we must be pure ourselves. We must ask for his forgiveness for the times we have failed to follow his path. We must bare our true, sinful souls to the Lord."

The white noise smoothed and buffered Brett's uncertain, clumsy response as Jackie caressed her bare skin, her soft hands tracing south from Brett's collarbone, gently, so tantalizingly gently.

"In today's bulletin you'll find a selection of Bible verses on truth and falsehood. I invite you to pray over them this week. I believe they will help you find the strength, the courage, to reveal yourself fully. I'd like to share some of my favorites.

"John, chapter four: '. . . True worshippers shall worship the Father in spirit and in truth: for the Father seeketh such to worship him.'"

On the hard pew, Brett shifted her hips, imagining Jackie's hand seeking places, hidden places, farther down her body. Her cheeks flushed. She gripped the hymnal tightly over her lap. Richard's words

ricocheted inside her head. The white noise roared louder, beginning to pulse through Brett's entire body as Jackie's phantom fingers
swept lower still.

"Proverbs, chapter eight, verse seven: 'For my mouth shall speak
truth; and wickedness is an abomination to my lips.'"

*Their mouths crushed against each other as Jackie's fingers at last
slid to where no woman's had ever been, strumming urgently, until the
white noise of pleasure and release began radiating outward, so powerful it lifted Brett up to the sky, away from her earthly yokes, toward a
joy she hadn't let herself believe existed.*

"Revelations twenty-one, eight: '. . . And all liars shall have their
part in the lake which burneth with fire and brimstone.'"

The fiery flush faded from Brett's cheeks. The white noise went
silent. In the sudden quiet of the church, she heard a cleared throat,
a restrained sneeze. She lifted her bowed head. Hotel, gone. Bed,
gone. Jackie, gone.

Looking past Richard, she found Amanda in the choir. As the
fantasy sputtered, the sermon stopped ping-ponging in her head,
settling firmly into the grooves of guilt, carved by a lifetime of pre-
tense. A lifetime that Amanda knew as truth. *Oh, God. Could she
really do it?*

"Only then, when we have honestly asked for God's forgiveness
and committed to live his way, his truth, his light, can we fully experience the grace and peace of the living God."

Richard's gaze swept across the congregation, who joined him
in fervent conclusion.

"Amen."

FIFTEEN

The bigger one was back again, this time carrying a mouthful of crumbling brown oak leaves. Staring out the window of his last-period study hall, Robby watched the male sparrow return to its nest-in-progress on the sturdy, still-bare branch of the oak outside Charles A. Lindbergh Middle School. He'd noticed the nest yesterday and was impatient all day to get to last period. It was early March, prime nesting time for sparrows in the upper Midwest, according to the Sibley's guide in the backpack at his feet.

Today the nest was much further along, a cup-shaped wad of dead grass, leaves, and scraps of paper napkin the sparrow must have foraged from the school Dumpster. Sitting in his favorite seat by the window, his notebook open on his desk, he was immediately entranced. He added a soft line with his pencil to the sketch he'd started yesterday.

"Robby. Robby. Pay attention to your work instead of the window, please. Robby. Robby. Are you listening to me?" Mr. Duvall, the study hall monitor and Robby's math teacher, was calling from his desk at the front of the room.

Irritated, Robby turned his body away from the voice, wishing for his headphones hanging in his locker. He was allowed to wear them in study hall, but he still wasn't used to having a second one.

They'd stuck him here just last week, after reassigning Laura. He could see Mr. Duvall making his way down the aisle, shaking his head. Robby pulled his notebook in close, curling his arm protectively around the top.

The teacher stopped, bodily blocking his view. "Robby, I know you've got math homework. This is the time for schoolwork, not window-watching or doodling."

"Did it." Robby leaned way to the right, so he could watch the nest-building around the teacher. The sparrow was gone again.

"You finished it? All of it? There were twenty-five problems," Mr. Duvall said skeptically.

Without taking his eyes off the window, Robby rummaged into his backpack on the floor and brought out two sheets of notebook paper. He thrust them at Mr. Duvall.

"This—this looks pretty good, Robby." Mr. Duvall said, after a moment. "All right, then."

He laid the math homework on Robby's desk, briefly covering the sketches in the notebook. Robby scooped up the problems, shoved them back in his backpack, then leaned over to shelter his notebook again.

"I didn't know you were taking any art classes. May I look?" Mr. Duvall tried to peer over Robby's elbow.

"Not art," Robby said curtly, still looking out the window.

"Not art? But they're drawings, right?"

Robby nodded.

"Drawings of what?"

"Birds."

"Would you show me? I'd like to see them."

Finally, Robby turned his head toward Mr. Duvall, meeting his eyes for a whisper of a moment before, with an exaggerated sigh, he sat back, exposing the notebook pages.

His teacher's eyes swept the pages, then glanced outside, at the nest-building scene he'd been depicting from his indoor perspective, then back to the sketchbook. His eyebrows lifted.

"Wonderful detail. Nice proportions."

He flipped a page, to a sketch of birds in flight. Robby dropped his arm over the notebook again, jabbing Mr. Duvall's hand with his elbow.

"Ow." Mr. Duvall flinched, rubbing his hand. "Sorry. I should have asked before I turned the page, right?"

Robby grunted.

"But thanks for showing me. I'm really impressed, Robby. Those drawings are really good. You should show Mr. Marshall."

Across the room there was a sudden yelp. Mr. Duvall looked up. "Hey, Trevor, Brody, Justin. Knock it off." He strode across the room.

Relieved, Robby fiddled with the pencil, finishing the window and adding a few more strokes to the nest. Why did teachers always want you to show things? He didn't need Mr. Marshall, the art teacher, or anyone else to see it. He was perfectly content to draw in his notebook and keep it to himself forever.

His parents were like that, too, especially his mom. Then after looking at it, they always wanted to talk about it. Why had he drawn that bird, that way? Was it real, or something he had seen in a book, or imagined? Why didn't he add some color? Would he like some paints or pastels so he could? Was he sure?

It was exhausting, especially since to Robby, the answers were so obvious. Everything he drew was real. Everything was drawn exactly as he saw it. He chose pencil because it worked and was readily available. Pencil was perfectly adequate for the task, so why bother with a bunch of paints and other extra stuff?

The bell rang. Robby winced. Preoccupied with his drawings, he had forgotten to keep an eye on the clock, bracing himself for the piercing peal at 3:04 p.m.

He stuffed his notebook into the backpack and waited to merge with the rest of the class before filing out past Mr. Duvall, to minimize the chance the teacher might try to resume conversation. He wasn't a bad teacher. Robby was relieved to wind up in Mr. Duvall's study hall instead of Mrs. Russell's. She taught English and was always talking about books and discovering the author's intention and stuff that didn't make any sense at all. Still, talking was talking and Robby preferred quiet.

His strategy worked, and Robby got downstairs to his locker without speaking to or looking at anyone in the teeming halls. Spinning the combination, he opened the locker and immediately clapped his headphones over his ears. The ringing echo of the bell stopped. His body relaxed. The school ordeal was over for another day.

Now he could go home, get on his computer, get back to those bird websites Dr. Felk had given him at the museum. And Donald Baxter's site. His Canada goose database, going back to 1984, was built on an open-source platform and universally downloadable. Robby spent hours sorting and sifting the columns, testing Paula's idea that the geese in the crash were from Baxter's Ontario reservation. It was looking more and more plausible, but he still hadn't been able to tell Paula about his discoveries in the data. She wasn't answering any of his texts.

The next Audubon meeting was tonight, though. Maybe she'd be there. Robby tripped down the steps of Charles A. Lindbergh Middle School, a silent island in the flow of bedlam around him, absorbed by the surprisingly pleasant thought of talking to Paula.

Outside, he walked along the west wall of his school. He wanted to look at the nest he sketched in study hall from the ground.

A bus passed him, exhaling a dingy cloud. Robby glanced at the number on the door: 657, his bus. His mom didn't know it, but he always blew off the bus ride home. He had to take it in the morning, since it arrived before she left for work. But in the afternoon, he had nearly an hour alone before she got home. One day, sometime before Christmas, he'd realized that he could simply skip the noisy, unpredictable, frightening ride with the rowdy bus crowd, walk home, and still arrive before she did.

He rounded the corner to the south side of the building. This was the teachers' parking lot and already mostly deserted. Robby stepped through the dirty lumps of melting snow. It was an unseasonably warm day, the kind of day that made you think spring might finally be here. Craning his head back, he searched the oak's branches. There it was. The sparrow was gone again.

Robby liked the new perspective. Eyeballing the distance from nest to ground gave him an appreciation for the risk the birds took, placing their eggs so high. He envied the privacy, too. One nest per tree. Plus wings to escape, to fly far, far away if it ever did get too crowded.

Setting his backpack down, Robby groped for the brown notebook and a pencil. The male sparrow came back with the female, chattering loudly. Robby pulled his headphones down to hear better. He had to beat his mother home, he remembered after they flew away again. As he tucked the notebook away, a shout startled him.

"Hey! You over there!" It was the troublemakers from study hall: Justin, Trevor, and Brody. Though he never spoke to them, Robby knew their names, like he did for all the kids in each of his six classes. He fumbled with the backpack zipper.

"You're the one Mr. Duvall was hanging all over today. He's a big fag, you know. Are you, too?" Justin, the biggest, spoke first.

The other two laughed loudly.

"Are you?"

"Yeah, are you?"

Robby tried to smile. He shook his head, trying to sidestep the three of them. Justin deftly slid with him.

"And how come you get to wear headphones, when nobody else does?" Justin was crowding closer, way too close. He grabbed the headphones from Robby's neck and stretched them wide, wider. Robby grabbed vainly as Justin slapped them around his own neck.

"You must be somebody's little boy. Somebody's doing favors for you. What are you doing for them?"

"How come you never talk?" One of the parrot sidekicks came up with an original line.

"Yeah, how come?" the other echoed.

"Maybe he writes everything down in his notebook," Justin suggested. "He's always scribbling in that. What are you writing? Maybe . . ." he grinned with inspiration, "maybe he writes little love notes to Mr. Duvall."

"Yeah!" Trevor yelled.

"Love notes to Mr. Du-vaall," Brody mimicked.

Robby couldn't comprehend the sarcasm, but he knew the situation wasn't good. Cornered, neither fight nor flight viable escapes, he wrapped his arms around his backpack, huddling behind the nylon shield.

"Let's see," said Justin, seizing the backpack from his arms.

"Mine!" Robby reached for it, but Justin easily tossed it to Trevor.

"Find that notebook."

"Sure." Yanking the zipper, Trevor dumped it upside down. Loose papers, the Sibley's guide, textbooks, and the brown notebook bounced onto the damp dirt. Robby scrambled for the notebook, but Justin snatched it away. "Gimme that, pussy."

He flipped through several pages. "You don't talk, you don't write much, either. Just draw. What is all this shit?"

"What, Justin?"

"Pictures of birds. Birds! What the hell? Page after page."

"Birds are pretty gay," ventured Brody, his first original remark, looking hopefully at Justin for approval.

"Yeah, birds are gay. Birds. Jesus H. Christ." Justin flipped through the rest of the notebook and tossed it to Trevor. "This what you and Mr. Duvall talk about?" He sneered.

"Hey, Justin, this picture's of a nest. I think it's right up in this tree," Trevor looked up. "Yeah, there it is! Right outside the study hall window."

"That's what you guys were talking about today, weren't you." Justin's voice got louder, angrier. He snatched the book from Trevor and ripped the sketches out. "Knock it down."

"No!" Robby shrieked, grabbing again for his notebook.

"Yeah!" Brody searched the ground and hurled a big stick. It fell well shy of the nest.

"Let me try." Trevor tossed it up. He got closer, but the nest remained safe.

"Pussies," Justin grabbed the stick and threw it a third time. He, too, missed the nest, instead hitting the school window. "Shit."

In a moment, Mr. Duvall's face appeared. He opened the window. "What's going on down there? Robby? Is that you? Justin, Trevor, Brody? What's the problem?"

"Bail," Justin instructed. He flung the notebook face down on a pile of snow, then crumpled the sketches and let them fall, too. "Get out of here and don't bug me no more." He pointed a finger at Robby as he backed up. He tossed the headphones next to the notebook, then turned and fled with his minions at his heels, laughing.

From above, Mr. Duvall spoke. "Robby, I'm coming down there. Don't leave." He pulled his head in and shut the window.

Quickly Robby gathered the books and papers and notebook and clamped his headphones back over his ears. He was shaking, but being seen with Mr. Duvall would clearly only make it worse.

He zipped his backpack and ran down the sidewalk. Away from Charles A. Lindbergh Middle School and the neurotypicals who ruled there—the bullies and the well-meaning. Ran and ran until he was safe, at home.

When his mother came home to drive him to the Audubon meeting, Robby said he had a stomachache and didn't want to go.

SIXTEEN

Deborah listened to her sister's phone ring. Once, twice. No voice mail clicked on; no one picked up. Three times. It was no longer a comfort to think about where her sister might be when she answered. Four. Instead, she worried Helen might not be there at all. Five. Or Matt, or Hannah and Mariah. Six. They might be at a doctor's appointment. Seven. Or, if things had worsened, at the hospital. Or—

"Hello?"

Deborah recognized her brother-in-law's voice, thick with sleep, on the eighth ring.

"Matt, it's Deborah. Did I wake you?"

"It's seven o'clock on a Saturday, Deborah. Yeah, you woke me."

"Damn. I forgot. God, why can't the whole country agree to be on the same time?" Deborah tipped her head back against the new rocking chair and closed her eyes. "Sorry."

"I'll live. This is minor. Hang on a second. What?" Deborah heard a muffled voice, then Matt's, muted. "Yes, it's Deborah. You can call her back. You should still be sleeping."

Helen. She felt guilty. She heard a sigh, then Matt's voice again in her ear. "She wants to talk to you."

"Hi." Helen sounded OK.

"Sorry I woke you guys."

"Like Matt said, no big deal."

"How are you feeling?"

"About the same. Not so bad, not so good, either."

"Oh." Helen was usually so positive. After Christopher's reaction, she wanted to talk to someone optimistic. Someone who would say congratulations. She wanted to hear that word. Needed to hear it.

"Matt said he gave Christopher the name of the specialist at Columbia. They're running some of the same trials that I'm participating in out here. Did you get an appointment?"

"Um, no. No, I didn't."

There was a pause. Deborah could feel Helen examining her answer, searching for the rational explanation.

"What, weren't they taking new patients?"

"I don't know. I didn't call."

"You didn't call?" Helen sounded dumbfounded. "You're kidding, right?"

"No," Deborah said softly.

"No? Look, Deborah, I know you're busy. You've got the big law school campaign and all that. But this isn't something to mess around with. You're two years younger. If you do have it, there's a chance to get after it so much sooner."

"You sound like Christopher."

"Well, Christopher's a smart guy."

"Smart doesn't always mean right."

Helen coughed abruptly. "What's going on, Deborah?"

Deborah took a deep breath. "I'm pregnant."

Silence stretched over the line again. Deborah waited. "Helen? Are you still there?"

"I'm here." Helen cleared her throat. "Did I hear you right? Did you just tell me—"

"I'm pregnant," Deborah repeated.

"Oh, my God." Helen exhaled heavily. "You did another round of IVF, after all."

"Yes."

"And it worked this time."

"Yes."

"You did it without getting tested first."

"Right."

"Oh, my God." Her sister's voice dropped to a moan. "Christopher was OK with this?"

Through the window, Deborah noticed the utility line that ran along the edge of their yard sagging with the weight of what appeared to be hundreds of birds. Helen's question rolled over her. "What?"

"I said, Christopher was OK with that?"

"Oh. Well, actually, it's kind of complicated."

"Try to explain." Helen sounded like she was trying to stretch her patience.

"We had seen the doctor. Before you called. That same day, actually."

"Wait. Which doctor are we talking about now?"

"Our reproductive endocrinologist. Dr. Singh. And Christopher agreed to the third try."

"OK. And then what? After you told him about me."

"I didn't tell him about you."

"You didn't tell him?" Helen voice rose, trying to stave off her dismay, Deborah knew.

"No." Deborah suddenly wanted the whole story out. "I knew that would be a deal-breaker for him. Even though the chances of Huntington's were only fifty-fifty."

"*Only* fifty-fifty?" Helen interrupted.

"And I couldn't let those embryos—our embryos—go to research, or to another couple. So I didn't tell him."

"Oh, my God."

"We had the transfer on February eighth. I felt good about it. Christopher seemed good, too. Then, when Matt called a week later, he found out about you."

"About *us*," Helen corrected.

"I suppose. So he was furious. Said I'd lied to him. Betrayed his trust."

"Didn't you?"

On her end, Deborah shrugged. Whether she did or didn't, how did that change things now? Instead, she repeated herself. "I couldn't let our embryos go." Her voice turned bitter. "But Christopher could."

"Wh-what do you mean?" Helen's voice trembled.

"He's moved out, Helen. Moved into university housing. Some apartment reserved for a visiting professorship the department decided not to fill this year. The Joseph T. Flynn Waterfowl Management Professor, as a matter of fact." She laughed in spite of herself, the sound a grotesque distortion of humor.

"Oh, my God," Helen said for the third time. "For good? Are you getting a divorce?"

"I don't know. He said he needed space. Needed time to think about it. Well, I can give him nine months." Now her laugh masked tears.

"When are you due?"

"November ninth."

"So it's early. Lots of time. Maybe it won't even—oh, never mind."

"What? Maybe it won't even what?" Deborah's ears pricked up as her eyes dried.

"Nothing. I didn't mean anything."

"Maybe I won't even carry it to term, right? After all, I've failed twice already."

"I didn't say that."

"But you were thinking it."

Helen sighed loudly. "It doesn't matter what I think. But I'm worried. This is huge, Deborah."

"I'm ready for it, Helen. Even by myself."

"Are you? Do you truly understand what a baby would do to life as you know it? Especially if it takes Christopher out of the picture?"

"It'll be hard," Deborah said, switching the phone to her other ear, rocking steadily.

"'Hard.' That's an understatement. Try to imagine what that really means, Deborah. Imagine being in a hospital, in labor, in excruciating pain—alone. Imagine living on half your income, plus the expense of day care. Imagine what four hours of sleep at a stretch—maybe for an entire night—does to your body and your brain and your relationship with the child inflicting that hell. Imagine that, night after night for months at a time."

"Wow." Deborah said in a small voice. "What happened to the sister who kept telling me I'd be a great mother?"

"I said great *parents*. There's a universe of difference. And you can't quote what I said a couple years ago when circumstances have changed completely.

"You're talking about having a baby at the age of forty-three, with an uncertain but potentially fatal disease in your future," Helen exclaimed. "Now, possibly by yourself."

In the background, Deborah heard Matt's voice, then Helen's terse reply. "I'm fine, Matt. Don't worry so much." She spoke into the phone again. "At the very least, call that Columbia doctor. Get tested. Find out where things stand. You owe it to your child now."

Deborah wanted to end the conversation. "All right. I'll call."

"OK." Suddenly, the energy seemed to drain out of her sister, and Deborah heard a stifled yawn.

"I should let you go. Go back to bed, like Matt said."

"All right." Helen hesitated a moment. "I love you."

"I love you, too."

Phone in her lap, Deborah stared out the window at the sagging utility line. *Helen hadn't said congratulations.*

She was still stewing over it the next day when she was the first to arrive for the surprise staff meeting. What could be so urgent it couldn't wait for the regularly scheduled weekly meeting? she wondered, choosing a seat by the window.

Under the blue sky, students tossed a Frisbee and walked with jackets unzipped. It was an unseasonably warm March day, the kind of day that made you believe spring might really be around the corner, even in Ithaca. Impulsively, Deborah opened the window. She felt better instantly. She could even hear birds singing.

"Really, Deborah, it's a little chilly for open windows, isn't it?" Phillip's voice instantly frosted the room. Deborah turned to her boss, rebuttal on her lips. Among other things, the cool air would stave off her afternoon drowsiness. She was startled to see Phillip accompanied by the vice president for advancement university-wide.

"Deborah." He nodded.

Something was definitely up. Reluctantly, Deborah closed the window. It wasn't worth the argument.

Angela, her assistant, and the rest of the staff filed in, exchanging puzzled glances. Phillip ended their suspense quickly.

"As you all know, we're scheduled to go public with our capital campaign in less than six months. Unfortunately, I've recently learned two of our major donors to date have reduced their support significantly." He clasped his hands before him on the table, the gesture exposing a precisely stitched monogram on the immaculate cuff beneath his usual pin-striped suit. Deborah felt acutely aware of the fact that under the table she'd kicked off her pumps, which had been pinching her feet in the afternoons.

The room absorbed the words silently for several seconds. Sonja from the annual campaign spoke first.

"How significant?"

"Five million combined."

"And how far along were we?"

"About forty million. It's more than a ten percent hit," the vice president said. "And based on what I'm seeing at other programs, you can expect more donor retrenchment. This economy is brutal."

Around the table, Deborah saw her colleagues collectively sag. Phillip, however, sat up even straighter. He considered the new law school the capstone to his career, and he would achieve it, damn the economic realities.

"So that means that our work is cut out for us," Phillip resumed. "Starting immediately. We'll be stepping up donor and alumni club visits, so most of you can plan for more travel over the next several months."

Travel. It was the thing Deborah disliked most about her job. She remembered considering it exciting, a long time ago. But even before the crash, it had become tedious. She didn't expect any renewed appeal now that she was pregnant.

Out of the corner of her eye, she saw Angela glance her way. She'd confided in her assistant after the positive pregnancy test. She needed someone she trusted to create cover for the flurry of doctor appointments she now had on her schedule, until she figured out how to break the news to Phillip. She already knew he wouldn't be happy about a maternity leave, especially since it would fall so soon after the campaign's launch.

Now she had another reason to dread going to work. Home was no sanctuary anymore, either, with Christopher's absence a constant reproach to her decision. Pregnancy was turning out to be a twilight zone. She stifled a yawn and shifted in her seat, fumbling under the table to force her feet back into the pumps.

~

"You and Dad will both be there tonight, right?" Amanda was putting on her jacket, waiting for Brett to finish ironing her costume for the final performance of *Grease*.

"Both of us. I promise. Fourth row seats, stage right," Brett assured her. She and Richard had already attended opening night together. She'd watched two more performances solo. But apparently it was also tradition for parents to attend the closing night show.

That was fine with Brett. She loved watching Amanda onstage. The role of Rizzo had uncovered a whole new dimension to her daughter, who had expected only to make the chorus. Simultaneously, Brett felt profoundly content, thrilled, and relieved as she listened to others applaud. After this experience, Amanda would not be one to hide her true self, to resign herself to meeting others' expectations.

She was already talking about studying drama in college, to the dismay of Richard, who was pushing a business degree starting at Lackawanna, Scranton's community college. So far, he was low-key about it, but Brett knew how easy it was to bend your life to the expectations of others, going along to get along. After seeing her daughter fling herself into rehearsals, however, she had new faith that Amanda's future would be of her own creation.

Chauffeuring Amanda to and from rehearsals also gave Brett plenty of time to mull her conversation with Elizabeth. It haunted her how Elizabeth peeled back her soul and gazed inside. Combined with the energy left over from her brief affair with Jackie, Brett had felt, in the days after her return from Charlotte, as if she occupied a rare window of opportunity to act.

She almost did after that one Sunday in church. *Stop stalling*, she'd told herself that morning, standing in this very same kitchen. But someone had kept Richard after the service. And the next day it was something else. Day by day, the power of her familiar, comfortable routines sedated her, closing the window. Like ironing Amanda's costume. Richard's shirts, too, were again crisp and ready for his Sunday sermons. At the backyard feeder, the sparrows were fed and happy.

And six weeks had passed with the web of lies still intact. She still slept in the bedroom with Richard, eight inches of mattress between their backs. *Still, still, still.* She had visited the job site on the business card Elizabeth had given her, but nothing seemed right.

"Almost done? I see Abby's car." Amanda was looking out the kitchen window.

"Done. Here you go."

"Thanks." Amanda took the hanger. "Remember, there's the cast party afterward. At Mrs. Hamilton's house. You said I could stay all night, right?"

"I did. You can stay all night. I'll inform your father." Brett handed Amanda her costume hanger and kissed her cheek. "Have fun. I love you."

"Love you, too. See you later." And Amanda was gone, in a swirl of starchy ruffles, flying ponytail and spring air. It was the first warm day of the year, the kind when spring seemed to truly lurk right around the corner, even in Scranton. The kind of day to open up the windows again, Brett thought, leaning over the sink to lift the sash.

Her hands carried her through the motions of making dinner and puttering about the house. Several times she paused in front of Amanda's empty bedroom. In another year and a half, she wouldn't have to ask Brett's permission to stay out all night. Despair filled her at the idea of sharing a home only with Richard. It simply wouldn't be tolerable. The truth, on the other hand, would set her on a treacherous, unknown course. Not unlike what a pilot had faced a few months ago, his plane falling out of the sky, Brett reflected.

In the costume that night, Amanda was gorgeous as the cast took their curtain call, smiling, clutching one another's hands, and crying as they clung to the feverish high of the night. Hugging Amanda, handing her flowers backstage, watching her among her friends and Mrs. Hamilton the director—who pulled her and Richard aside, telling them that Amanda had "talent, true talent that deserves to be nurtured, please call me next week"—Brett froze the images of the evening, the last one in the life she had known for almost two decades.

She and Richard walked out into the still-warm night. She rolled down the window to keep the freshness on her face. As he started the engine, she at last told the truth.

SEVENTEEN

I don't see Paula," Robby said, pressing his face to the window as Sam pulled into the parking lot of the Central United Christian Church.

"We're here a little early. Maybe she's not here yet," Sam said. "Let's go find out what the plan is."

A half-dozen other cars were already clustered in a far corner, most with trunks open. Sam recognized Ed, the man who had introduced himself at the meeting in February, and another man looking at a map. "It's a straight shot west on I-96," Ed was saying as they approached. "We can try to caravan if you want, but there's really no need."

"Where's Paula?" Robby interrupted.

"Hi, Robby, Sam. Glad you could come." Ed greeted him. Sam analyzed his voice for any trace of false heartiness but detected none.

"Where's Paula?" Robby asked a third time.

"She'll be here. She's paid up and signed up," Ed said, looking at his list. "We're still waiting on three others, too. We've got some doughnuts here, coffee, juice." He gestured to a tailgate buffet. "Help yourself."

The three others arrived, and the doughnuts were down to crumbs when Paula finally showed up. She drove an ancient, rattle-trap Toyota. Duct tape covered the taillight and held up a side-view mirror. Exhaust billowed out the back. In the dark parking lot, Sam hadn't noticed its condition the night when he'd picked up her and Robby. He wondered if Robby had driven with her in that.

"Paula, you're not driving that thing a hundred miles," Ed said with finality. "There's lots of room in other cars. Pick a ride and let's get going."

"We have room." Robby stepped up to Paula's elbow.

She smiled nervously. "Oh, thanks, Robby. But I don't want to trouble your dad. I think I'll ride with Ed."

"No trouble at all. Plenty of room," Sam offered.

"Well, but I've missed a couple meetings, and Ed and I, we need to talk about some club stuff, don't we, Ed? It'll just be easier if I ride with him. Thanks anyway." Paula tossed her overnight bag into the trunk of Ed's car and climbed into the front seat.

"All right, then. Everybody got a ride? Anybody need a map? Let's hit the road. Next stop, Lansing Radisson." Ed slid into the driver's seat, the car shifting with his weight, and slammed the door.

Ignitions sputtered to life, but Robby remained standing, watching Ed's vanishing vehicle.

"Let's go, Robby." Sam put his hands on his son's shoulders, feeling like a cop on a TV show, physically propelling the perp into the squad car. Remembering his own junior-high crushes, though, Sam reflected that Robby was more like the victim.

In the car, Robby put on his headphones and stared out the window, not speaking for almost half an hour. Highway hypnosis was lulling Sam into his own stupor when Robby finally spoke.

"Paula doesn't like me anymore." It was a statement, not a question.

"Hmmm?" Sam stalled, glancing over. Robby had taken off his headphones.

"Paula doesn't like me. Not anymore." He turned away from the window and looked at Sam. "How come?"

Shit. Sam scrambled for a good answer. An adequate answer. *Any answer.* Autism evidently didn't affect puberty. Linda had said that

Robby needed more than the two of them could give him. Paula's age put her out of bounds as a girlfriend. But they did have birds in common. Maybe he could help Robby understand some of the rules of relationships, romantic or platonic. *Linda was right*, Sam admitted. Protection could no longer be his first priority for Robby. If autism was the elephant in their lives, he deserved to know how to handle the beast.

"Robby, I think Paula does like you, actually. But I think she's scared, too."

Robby frowned. "How come?"

"Do you remember the night we gave her a ride home after the meeting? Back in February, when they first told you about this Lansing trip?"

"Uh-huh."

"What happened that night?"

"We gave her a ride home. She lives on Springside Street. In a white house. With a big porch. The light was broken. Her dog was barking."

"Right. That's her house exactly. But what happened in the car that night, Robby? What happened when we drove Paula home?"

Robby thought silently for a moment. "She told me about Donald Baxter. That he would be at this meeting."

"Right. And what else?"

Robby lapsed into a longer silence. Finally he shrugged. "Don't know."

"You don't remember?" He could remember the details of a barely visible house he'd visited one time, but not the all-systems meltdown. Sam still found it stunning how his son could recall the minute, but not the monumental.

"Uh-uh." Robby shook his head.

"OK." Sam took a deep breath. "You got upset in the car that night. You were all excited about this trip and maybe meeting Donald

Baxter and learning more about the geese and the plane crash. And I didn't say right away that you could go."

"Why not?"

"Well, your mom and I needed to talk about it first. And I tried to explain that. But you couldn't see past wanting to go on this trip. And so you got mad. And you got like you do when you're mad. You yelled. You cried. You rocked. You banged your head on the front seat," Sam felt transported back to that night as well.

"You and Paula were both sitting in the backseat, and she didn't know what to do when you got like that. When you get fixated on something like that, Robby, no one can reach you. No one can pull you back from the edge. It happens to people with autism." Sam glanced over at Robby, who was fidgeting with the headphones in his lap.

"But she didn't understand that. That's why she got scared. In about two minutes she saw you go from a regular boy, someone she liked, to this frightening, out-of-control kid, over something simple like me telling you, 'we'll see.' That's not how a normal person—" Sam hesitated, then edited himself. "That's not a normal *reaction*. And that was scary. Paula knew something was wrong. Really wrong. But she didn't know what."

They rode in silence for several minutes. "Do you remember now?" Sam asked.

"Yeah." Robby hung his headphones around his neck. "Autism makes me get like that?"

"Yes."

"But that's not my fault."

"No. Autism is something that affects your brain. Makes it work differently. You can't change it, or fix it. You just have to deal with it."

"I don't want to scare people. I didn't mean to scare Paula."

Sam blinked. He couldn't recall Robby ever expressing a desire to positively impress someone else. "Good. That's really good to hear, Robby."

"What do I do now?"

"What do you mean?"

"How do I make her like me again?"

Shit. Back to the unanswerable. "I'm not sure, Robby. She was pretty scared."

"But you said it wasn't my fault."

"She doesn't know that, though."

"Maybe I could explain?"

"Maybe." Sam thought about Robby trying to explain his own autism to a neurotypical. "I guess you could try."

He thought of something else, though he knew Linda would disapprove. She always said the NTs needed to walk halfway, too. That it was only fair those off the autism spectrum do their part to bridge the gulf toward those on it. But fairness was an irrelevant ideal to a twelve-year-old boy navigating a first crush, or whatever this was. If Paula wasn't going to walk halfway, Robby would have to go all the way.

"It might help if you apologized, too."

"OK." Robby hooked his headphones over his head. "How long till we get there?"

~

Brett waited in the kitchen for Amanda to open the door she'd exited not twenty-four hours ago. And a lifetime ago, too, Brett thought. Because life as Amanda knew it was now over.

Brett had spent the morning modifying their guest room into her bedroom, the first step in a transition to—well, she wasn't sure yet what was next. But her part in the charade was over.

Once he found out she had no intention of trying to leave with Amanda, Richard's reaction seemed more a preacher's than a husband's, saddened that she would "choose an unnatural path." But he showed little hurt or betrayal. That was perhaps the saddest thing of all. Both of them had vowed to love and to cherish each other until death did them part. And both had failed to live up to those vows.

But the absence of an angry scene carried relief, too. Now with the truth out, maybe Richard could find someone else to fulfill the vows with. Or maybe he would dive further into being pastor. Brett was utterly ambivalent about what Richard would do next. For the moment, she wasn't even worried about what she would do next. She felt like she did on the ferry before the plane crashed, circling Manhattan with Jackie. Free. A little crazy. Alive. *Happy.*

She had emptied the birdseed sack into the feeder that morning. Springtime now. Time to fend for yourselves, she thought, shaking the last seeds out. It felt good to throw away the scratchy, heavy burlap sack.

She was puttering with the dishes when Amanda walked in, still wearing her pajamas under her jacket. She carried her costume, wrinkled and crooked on its hanger, and an armful of carnations and roses, still wrapped in the cellophane in which the enterprising lobby vendor sold them.

"Have fun at the party?" Brett recognized the pink roses she had presented backstage. Amanda dropped everything in a heap by the kitchen counter and slid onto a stool.

"Oh, I had a great time. We stayed up till, I don't know, like five in the morning. Mrs. Hamilton has this great house, with a walk-out basement, and a bunch of us took sleeping bags out to her patio and slept on the lawn chairs."

"Wasn't it a little cool? It's barely April."

"Oh, a little, but not too bad. Most everybody else fell asleep, but Neil and I stayed up talking all night long. He played one of the T-birds, do you remember him?"

"Hmm. I don't think so."

"He's tall. Dark brown hair, brown eyes."

"Are some of those flowers from him?"

Amanda blushed but nodded. "Anyway, he's a senior. He said he was really glad that I tried out, and he got a chance to meet me." She sighed happily.

"I'm glad you had a good time, sweetheart. You were absolutely fantastic. Mrs. Hamilton told both your father and me that you've got real talent. For both voice and drama. Talent you should think about cultivating in college."

Amanda looked away. "She told me that, too. But the best drama schools are all out of state. New York, mostly."

"And?"

"They'd probably be too expensive, us living here, out-of-state."

"That's your dad talking. Don't get too far ahead of things, Amanda. College is a year and a half away. Let's just see what happens between now and then."

"OK." Amanda slid off the kitchen stool. "Guess I'd better put this stuff away."

"Leave it there for a minute, would you? I want to show you something." Brett's heartbeat accelerated. So far, the conversation was almost assembly line, the same kind of small talk she and Amanda shared every day. Now came the moment to cast the monkey wrench into the machinery.

"All right." Amanda followed her down the hall to the door opposite her own, the door to the little-used guest room.

Brett watched her look around, taking it all in. The treadmill that had sat unused for years was gone. The bed was cleared of the wrapping paper and Christmas decorations that had been piled there since New Year's. The formerly bare nightstand now was outfitted with a lamp, an alarm clock, a picture of Amanda as a baby, and one of her most recent school portraits.

Amanda looked confused. "What happened in here?"

Brett's hopeful smile wobbled. This was it. *Jackie was right.* It was far easier on the phone and in her imagination. She cleared her throat. "This is going to be my bedroom now."

"Your bedroom? But what about Dad?"

"He'll stay upstairs." Brett stared at her daughter earnestly, willing her to understand.

"I don't get it," Amanda said.

The monkey wrench glanced off a gear as Brett took a deep breath.

"You remember my trip to New York in January? Seeing me on the news?"

"Yeah." Amanda crossed her arms, visibly defensive. "What's that got to do with anything now?"

"Do you remember seeing the woman on the boat with me?"

"The one from the food pantry conference? The one you visited in Charlotte?"

"Right. Her name is Jackie." Brett exhaled slowly, then breathed in again. The room felt closed in and tight. She could see Amanda's face changing, the flush of excitement from the play fading, a furrow in her brow appearing.

"I actually met her at that conference I went to last year. There wasn't any conference in January."

"There wasn't?" Amanda looked totally confused.

"Jackie and I arranged to meet in New York, just the two of us." Avoiding Amanda's eyes, she plunged ahead with her confession. *No more secrets.* She wanted everything out now.

"Jackie and I just wanted to . . . to see each other. When we met last year, there was a . . . a connection between us. It wasn't anything we planned. It just happened. It was something that I had felt before, with others—other women—but always repressed."

Stealing a peripheral glance at Amanda, Brett could see her daughter's expression changing again. Astonishment. Repulsion. And fear.

"This time, though, I couldn't. She's married, too, to a pastor. Maybe that's why it seemed safer, at first. I knew she would understand why it was so hard for me . . . I thought at first we could just be . . . friends, maybe. Someone who would understand, not judge. But once we got to New York, it was clear that wasn't going to be all it was."

"What was it?" Amanda was biting her lip.

Brett took one more deep breath. "Lovers."

With a final clank, the word wedged itself into the gears that had turned Amanda's life so smoothly for sixteen years.

"Oh, my God," Amanda sat down on the bed, elbows propped on her knees, hands over her eyes. "You're a . . . a . . .you're a . . ?" Her voice shook.

Brett nodded.

"Say it." Amanda dropped her hands from her face and looked straight at her mother. "Tell me you're—you're—that word."

Guilt, sorrow, and fear churned in Brett. But washing over it all, incredibly, was a tide of pride. The worst part of all of this had been lying to Amanda. *"I don't want my daughter to think I'm a hypocrite,"* she'd told Jackie. Well, the truth was out now. The giant, elephant-in-the-living-room truth. Freed from the anchor of her secret, Brett felt weightless, almost like she was floating.

"I am a lesbian, Amanda."

"Oh, my God." Amanda hugged her knees to her chest. "Are you leaving? Are you going away with—with her?"

"No!" Alarm spread through Brett. "That's over now. I haven't talked to Jackie since February."

"Then why are you telling me?"

"I want to be honest with you. I don't want to pretend anymore."

"You were pretending to be my mom?"

"Of course not." Again, Brett's heartbeat accelerated. "This doesn't change anything between you and me. I love you. You're the best part of my marriage to your father."

"And what about him?"

"Who?"

"Dad!"

"What do you mean?"

"Are you getting divorced?" Amanda spoke abruptly, angrily.

"I—ah, well, we haven't discussed details. But this move"—Brett gestured around the room—"is a first step."

"Are you going to tell other people? People at church?"

Brett hesitated. "Well, not right away. And I won't make a public announcement, certainly. But eventually, I suppose, people will find out. Otherwise I'd still have to pretend."

"You're breaking up our family. And you don't think you're changing anything?" Amanda exclaimed, jumping up from the bed. "You're ruining my life." She swabbed roughly at a tear leaking down her cheek and turned to the door. "I'm tired. I'm going to take a nap."

Watching helplessly as the door banged behind her daughter's shaking shoulders, the pilot's famously unemotional last instructions the day of the crash resurfaced in Brett's mind. "Brace for impact."

The passengers' fright was unimaginable. But with impact, at least there was an end. The emotional free fall Brett tumbled in now felt like eternal damnation.

EIGHTEEN

In the lobby of the Lansing Radisson, Robby claimed the end of a sofa next to a giant fish tank. His dad, Ed, and some other club members lined up to check in. Paula and the rest dispersed to vending machines and the bathrooms.

Settling himself firmly into the upholstered corner, Robby felt himself relax. The rhythm of the water pump, the random but constant motion of the fish, and the blue-green tones of the water were all soothing. He dug a deck of homemade flash cards out of his backpack. On each was a goose from Donald Baxter's database.

He wanted to figure out just which geese met their deaths in the spinning blades of the Airbus engines. Using Baxter's database, he had narrowed it to ninety-eight birds that for the last three years followed a winter migration path from the reservation in Ontario down the East Coast to Hilton Head Island.

The timing was a little off. The data put most of the geese past New York City by Christmas at the latest, and the Hudson River crash took place more than three weeks later. But Baxter could explain that, Robby was sure.

In the meantime, he studied each flash card, which bore the bird's band ID number on one side and its key data points on the reverse. Each bird had a minimum of eight dates. Robby had memorized all of them for the forty-eight birds he considered the most likely victims—none of which had been observed on the migration route after January 15. He was now working on the other fifty that he considered less likely accident contenders.

He was staring at the flashcard for goose eighty-six when Paula appeared in his field of vision with a Diet Coke and a bag of M&Ms. She had her headphones on and sat down on a chair across from him.

"Hi," Robby said.

She glanced up. "Oh. Hi, Robby."

"I'm doing research." He waved the flashcard at her.

"Oh yeah?" She crossed her arms and legs, jiggling her foot.

"On the geese. You know, like you said." It was her idea, after all, that the geese had come from Donald Baxter's reservation.

"Donald Baxter's geese?"

"Uh-huh."

"What are you learning?"

"I think I know which geese caused the plane crash."

"Really?" Paula took her headphones off. She uncrossed her legs and leaned forward. "Are you going to talk to him about it here?"

Robby hadn't thought about actually speaking to Donald Baxter. But Paula was interested now, and talking to him. Maybe he should say yes. As he considered the idea, his gaze wandered past Paula, over her shoulder, to his dad in line at the registration desk. What was it his dad said in the car? What was he supposed to say to Paula? Apologize? Yes, that was it. He adjusted his gaze in the direction of her face. "My dad said to tell you I'm sorry."

"For what?"

"For that night. In the car. When we drove you home. I didn't mean to scare you."

Paula looked away. "OK."

"It's not my fault that I do that."

Paula didn't reply. Robby tried again, reciting his dad's explanation. "My brain works different. So sometimes I act different."

"OK," Paula said again, crossing her arms. Suddenly her attention swerved. "Look! There's Donald Baxter! He's here!"

A man stood in the lobby, hands on his hips. He looked like he came from Canada, Robby thought, wearing a thick parka, a cap with earflaps, and gloves. Old, too. Older than his dad, but not as old as Dr. Felk. Surveying the lobby, he appropriated a brass luggage cart and steered it back out the doors.

"Come on!" Yanking his hand, Paula pulled Robby to his feet and into the center of the lobby. He barely had time to grab his backpack. They watched Baxter maneuver the luggage cart through the parking lot to the back of an older minivan.

"Well? What are you waiting for? Go talk to him!" Paula's face was so close Robby smelled the chocolate from the M&Ms. *What if he kissed her?* The sudden urge paralyzed him.

"Robby, it's Donald Baxter! He'll be mobbed for the rest of the conference. Now's your chance. Go!" She pushed him gently. Robby stumbled a few steps, but gained enough momentum to get out the door.

Walking up behind the minivan, Robby could see it offered room for a driver and front passenger only. All the other seats had been removed to make room for Baxter's gear, which he was now piling onto the luggage cart. Two laptop bags, a digital projector, a giant portfolio bag, and a stack of a half-dozen large, clear storage tubs, each labeled with the name of the taxidermied bird inside.

"Where is that Greylag? I know I had it on my list. Where could it have gone?"

"The Greylag goose?" Robby asked. "I thought that was only found in England."

"British Isles, actually. Usually true," Baxter replied, not turning from the interior of van. "But I spotted one on my reservation last summer. Hen and a flock of eight chicks. Found the hen again last November. Idiot hunters must have got her by mistake and were too cowardly to take her, in case they got caught. So I took her. Aha. There she is."

He leaned in and tugged another large plastic bin. It wouldn't fit on the luggage cart. "Useless thing." He began rearranging his boxes. "If I use her to educate others, at least she won't have died for nothing."

Robby smiled in excitement. Just like he felt about investigating which geese crashed into the plane. "I've been using your database, and I think—"

"Hold on." Baxter stopped shifting boxes and over the top of his glasses looked directly at Robby. "Who are you?"

"Robby Palmer."

"You're here for the conference?"

Robby nodded.

"And you've been using my geese databases?"

Robby nodded again. "Canada geese database."

"Goes back to 1984. One of my best documented. Good choice. Go on."

"I think I found out which geese caused the plane crash."

"A bird strike crash?" Baxter's brow wrinkled.

Robby nodded. "In New York. In January."

Baxter's wrinkles smoothed out. "Pilot landed the damn plane in the river, right?"

"Right." Robby was bouncing up and down on his toes now. "I was there. On a boat in the river. I saw it."

"Were you now?" Baxter mumbled, more to himself. "And so?"

"So there're ninety-eight birds who migrate through New York around that time. To Hilton Head. And no data points for half of them since the crash." Robby held up his stack of flash cards.

"Interesting," Baxter glanced at the cards, but now seemed more interested in Robby. "Your conclusion?"

"They're in the engine." Robby scrutinized Baxter's face closely. This was what the whole trip came down to. The whole last two and a half months. If Baxter said he was wrong, then—well, Robby didn't even want to think about that.

"Hmm. Plausible. Certainly plausible. I'd have to review your data. Care to accompany me to my exhibition space?" Baxter didn't wait for an answer. "Here. You can carry Greta."

"Greta?"

"The Greylag goose. Come on." He handed Robby the oversize box, slammed the van doors, and steered the cart back into the lobby.

Obediently, Robby followed Baxter back into the hotel, through the lobby, and into the exhibition hall. Conference participants were setting up at booths arranged in two concentric rectangles. He forgot about Paula. He forgot about his dad. He was going to show his research to someone who understood it and find out once and for all what had happened to those birds.

"Here we are." Baxter stopped the cart next to a white-draped table in the middle of the outer rectangle. Unzipping one of the laptop bags, he powered it up and navigated to his own site, and then the Canada goose database. "Show me."

Eagerly, Robby scrolled through the long list, highlighting his chosen forty-eight from memory. Then he started pointing out their shared data points. "All of these leave Ontario around December fifth. They usually get to New York by Christmas. They're in Hilton Head by end of January. See, the records go back to 2006.

"But none of them have been observed south of New York City since January fifteenth. The date of the crash." Robby sat back and took a breath, and waited.

"But if they're in New York by Christmas, they would have been long past the Hudson River by January fifteenth," Baxter said.

Robby winced. Baxter went right for the weak link. "I was hoping you could explain that."

"I can. Those geese aren't in that plane engine. Or in the river, or anywhere near that crash." He stood up and started unloading the luggage cart. "Your theory's wrong."

Wrong. Robby shook his head. He couldn't be.

"Then why do their dates end?

Baxter shrugged. "Could be a lot of reasons. Most likely, they're not my geese."

Just like his dad had said.

Baxter continued. "If they are, you're assuming that two months without a data point is atypical. I'll have to look at the database closer, but I'm guessing that forty-eight birds with that interval isn't an anomaly. Maybe the battery in their chip died. Maybe something did happen to them, somewhere else.

"But not in that plane crash. I can guarantee it. Data doesn't lie. If those geese have been in New York by Christmas for the last three years, they're not hanging around three weeks later."

Robby slumped before the laptop. Baxter stood up. "But it was an interesting theory. You had me going for a few minutes there. Now I've gotta get myself set up for tomorrow. Better luck next time."

Robby stood up and backed away, his head ringing with Baxter's judgment and dismissiveness.

"Hey, kid, don't forget these." Baxter tossed him the flash cards. Robby caught the stack automatically and thumbed through them slowly, watching Baxter go about his preparations, already oblivious to him.

Then, abruptly, he ripped up one. Then two. Then three. When he tried to rip up the rest, the thick sheaf of paper refused to tear. He ran out of the exhibition hall, stuffing the worthless cards in his backpack, tripping over the straps, and colliding with his dad.

~

Deborah peered through the glass door of the Ithaca Ashram. A dozen women in various stages of pregnancy sat on mats, facing an instructor. She surveyed the group. Except for one next to the wall, most of them looked a good ten years younger than she. Hand on the door, she hesitated, wondering if this prenatal yoga class was really a good idea. Looking up, the instructor beckoned her to enter, forcing Deborah's decision.

"At the first class, I always like to have everyone tell a little bit about themselves and their baby: when you're due, if you have any other children, that kind of thing," she said as Deborah apologetically picked her way through the mats. She found a space between the woman by the wall, who wore a loose Cornell sweatshirt, and another who looked almost fifteen years younger, wearing a peach tank that stretched over her bump of a belly.

"I'll go first. I'm Ming Su, and as you've all noticed, I'm not pregnant." The class giggled dutifully. "But I have two children and did prenatal with both of them. I hope you'll find this class helpful with both your pregnancy and delivery.

"Now. Let's start with you," Ming Su pointed to a more-pregnant-than-Deborah brunette on the opposite side of the room. Deborah noticed a tattoo on her shoulder blade, bisected by the strap of another stretchy tank, blue this time.

"I'm Stephanie. I'm due in June, and this is my first. It's a girl, and we're going to call her Hazel."

"That's so pretty!" came a bright voice from the peach tank woman.

"It's my husband's grandmother's name."

"Lucky you. My husband's grandmother's name is Agatha," Peach Tank said. Giggles erupted around the room.

"I'm Allison. This is my second. I have a little boy who's three, and this one is a surprise," said the woman next to Stephanie. "But my husband thinks it's a boy, too," she added.

"When are you due?" Ming Su prompted.

"Oh, yes. August. August tenth."

"I'm August eleventh!" chirped Peach Tank. Deborah wished she had chosen another spot.

The third woman introduced herself. Megan, who sported a lime-green tank and tattoos on both arms as well as her left ankle, was pregnant with her first, a boy, due May 1. Another ripple went around the room as the most-pregnant among them commanded instant respect.

"You could be celebrating Mother's Day this year!" was Peach Tank's comment this time, delivered in an excited squeal.

"I'd better send my husband out now," Megan said with an eye roll that earned chuckles of appreciation. "You think he's going to remember that with a week-old newborn in the house?"

Deborah smiled gamely with the others, unease beginning to set in. Three for three married. Though she and Christopher had done nothing to change their formal status and she still wore her wedding ring, she had already started thinking of herself as a single mother. She could see Peach Tank wore a wedding band, too, as did the silent-till-now older woman on her right.

Deborah stole another glance at her. The woman looked vaguely familiar, but Deborah couldn't place her. Maybe it was just the Cornell sweatshirt. If she had any tattoos, they weren't visible. The woman smiled as she nodded at Deborah's own Cornell shirt. Feeling better, Deborah rested her hands on her belly, right hand over left, a gesture she'd found comforting lately.

Two of the next four didn't mention husbands. One of those who didn't was expecting twins. Deborah started to feel a little better.

Peach Tank was Kate, pregnant with her first, indeed due August 11. A boy, who would be named in honor of his paternal heritage, Earl Wyatt Montgomery IV. Poor kid. It was her turn.

"I'm Deborah. I'm due in November with my first. I work at Cornell."

Where did that come from, she wondered. No one else had identified an employer, though she couldn't believe none of them worked.

"Oh yeah?" Ming Su spoke up. "You're lucky. They have a great maternity leave policy. My husband worked there in grad school. A woman in his department had a baby and got four months off, then came back to work part-time for two months until summer. She got practically a whole year off."

"Well, I'm not on the faculty, so I won't get summers off," Deborah replied.

"You might decide not to go back to work, too, you know," Kate chipped in. "I know I'm not. They're little for such a short time." She sighed. "I can't imagine missing any of it."

"Me either," Megan and Stephanie spoke up simultaneously. Kate smiled happily; two more for the stay-at-home side. Deborah felt another flicker of unease. She earned the higher salary, anyway, and now with Christopher out of the picture, she had no choice but to work. She caught the eye of the older woman next to her, who gave the slightest eye roll Deborah had ever seen. She felt a surge of gratitude.

"Let's move on," Ming Su said quickly. "We've one more to go." She nodded at the woman to Deborah's right.

"I'm Julia. This is my first. I'm due August first."

"Wonderful. Thanks, Julia. Now let's begin in mountain . . ."

Her voice faded as the pieces clicked in Deborah's mind. Julia. Julia Adams. The woman who had tried to enlist her in the nonprofit cause at the dean's picnic. The one whose husband had huddled with Christopher, discussing the grant. The one whose texts she had blown off following the crash. She cast a furtive, sidelong glance. No doubt.

"Now if you ever feel tired, or light-headed or winded, you need to go into child's pose," Ming Su's voice interrupted her nagging conscience. "That's a resting pose where you're on knees and elbows . . ."

Beside her, Julia stage whispered. "Child's pose? The rest of them must have that mastered already. What are we grown-ups supposed to do?"

Deborah's surprised laugh came out like a snort. God, did that feel good. She glanced at Julia again. Maybe the unreturned texts were no big deal. Her Cornell sweatshirt was faded, like she'd had it a while. Deborah wondered if she was an alumnae, or worked on campus, too.

"Let's quiet our minds now, please," Ming Su said sternly. Peering through the curtain of her hair, Deborah saw she was looking at them. "So much for being the grown-ups," she whispered back to Julia.

"Prepare yourselves to connect with your babies," Ming Su instructed. "Close your eyes."

Reluctantly, Deborah did. She hated feeling blind.

"Set aside the world of getting ready, to-do lists, baby registries. This time is about you and your baby. Getting ready to experience birth together."

Lulled into the idea, Deborah laid her hands against her belly again, then crossed her arms, hands cupping her hip bones, and tried to imagine labor. Tried to imagine her stomach growing as big as Angela's. Tried to imagine feeling a kick from the inside. The day her assistant began her maternity leave, the baby kicked just as Deborah hugged her good-bye. Angela laughed and apologized. Deborah laughed, too. But privately she had been in awe of the power of that baby's kick on the other side of her abdomen, now more than three years ago.

Awaiting the sensation now herself was a little scary. She tried to imagine birth, to imagine pushing. Tried to imagine a baby's head emerging between her legs. Tried to imagine cuddling and comforting it, warm and wet and crying. Bringing its soft, fuzzy head to her breast to nurse. And then Deborah herself was crying softly, tasting salt as the tears ran down her cheeks.

She was scared. She was angry at Christopher. Everything he and Helen had said was true. She had no idea how she would manage alone. The pressure at work was rising. She had two out-of-state trips this month and another in May. She hadn't yet told Phillip her maternity leave would begin almost as soon as the law school campaign went public. Something brushed her arm.

It was Julia, offering a tissue. "It'll be OK," she whispered.

Gratefully, Deborah accepted the tissue. Julia's was the first voice of empathy she'd heard since February, almost two months ago. A kindred soul offering a kernel of faith. Deborah concentrated on that kernel, seeding it firmly in her own soul.

"*Namaste*, ladies." Ming Su tipped her head toward them an hour later. "See you next week."

Side by side, Deborah and Julia rolled up their mats.

"Thanks for the tissue," Deborah started. "And I'm sorry I never got back to you about your fundraising project."

Julia dismissed it with her hand. "It's fine. And I was actually kind of relieved to see someone else get overwhelmed with all this."

"Yeah? You do, too?"

"Definitely. It's a huge change, and not very much time to adjust, if you think about it. Nine months to create a creature who's going to depend on you for almost twenty years. I mean, I knew my husband for five years before we even got engaged."

"Right." Deborah wanted to head off a husband discussion. She nodded at Julia's sweatshirt. "Alumni, too?"

"Alumni. Twice, in fact. Undergrad and master's in social work. Then I put Michael through his PhD."

Deborah nodded. Michael was Christopher's colleague, the other lead on the big grant. Were they friends, too? She decided she didn't care. Julia seemed like someone who could be a friend. She hadn't had a real female friend in Ithaca in a long time, since Elizabeth moved down south.

"Listen, I'm sure you probably have plans already, but I could sure go for a cup of coffee. How about you?" Deborah asked.

Julia looked at her watch and grimaced. "Can't today. After class next week?"

"I'll be looking forward to it," Deborah said.

NINETEEN

Christopher was barely in time for Baxter's presentation. He hadn't slept well. He'd missed his connection out of Detroit and was forced to rent a car to get to Lansing. Then he learned the agenda had changed, and he was now scheduled to present immediately after Donald Baxter, who would suck all the air out of the room. To top it off, he was booked into a room next to a bank of rattling elevators.

Still, it was better than the depressing fellow's apartment, pre-furnished with an ugly '80s seafoam couch, sagging with worn-out springs, and a coffee table with permanent coffee rings. Plus the baggage of resentment and anger that he had moved in himself.

The conference room was predictably packed. The only seat left was in the middle of the back row, next to a kid wearing a Detroit Lions hoodie. Kids weren't unheard-of at these kinds of conferences, but one that young was unusual. Hoping he wouldn't fidget, Christopher squeezed into the row as Baxter was introduced.

Polite applause followed. By consensus Baxter's reputation was that of an egomaniac at best and insufferable at worst, but most of the audience, like Christopher, couldn't afford to miss what he might say.

Today he was tipping more toward his insufferable self. Christopher tried to concentrate on the presentation. It should have riveted him.

Baxter claimed to have identified a new flyway between Ontario and South Carolina.

It was one of the shortest durations documented, departing in late December and returning in mid-March. Baxter attributed it to global warming, and it was most common among birds who lived in heat-trapping urban areas. They simply didn't have to leave as early as they once did.

All of that was well-trodden in the journals. But Baxter's latest breakthrough showed a profound physiologic impact. With less distance to cover, he had documented nearly a five percent decline in the wingspan over three generations of Canada geese. Meanwhile, the birds' evolutionary instinct to feed before the long flight south continued undisturbed. With a smaller wingspan transporting the same weight, the task of flying was more taxing.

Takeoffs in particular were harder. The geese required more distance to gain their migratory altitude than they were known to need even five years ago. Nor could they fly as far or as fast without resting. So more takeoffs were required over the course of the migration route, further draining the birds.

The room was buzzing already when Baxter delivered his cliffhanger.

"Of course, the likelihood of more low-flying flocks in the future has significant implications for humans, especially in well-populated flyways like this one, which includes Toronto, the New York-New Jersey-Philadelphia area, Washington DC, and Baltimore.

"To offer just one example of a consequence, let's consider the well-documented problem of aircraft bird strikes. Most recently we had the so-called 'Miracle on the Hudson' crash this past January."

Christopher's head jerked up. Goosebumps prickled his arms. *Brace for impact.* Icy water sloshing over his ankles. Flight attendants shouting. Deborah's plaintive pleading.

"You heard it here first: When that investigation's complete it will be Canada geese from this flyway that drove that plane into the river. And we'd better hope for more hero pilots out there, folks, because my data points to many more birds flying into engines."

The buzz crescendoed. Next to Christopher, the kid in the sweatshirt jumped up and leaned forward, stabbing his finger at Baxter. "You lied!" he cried. "I was right, and you lied."

The man on the boy's other side rose, too, pushing his arm down, trying to get him to sit back down. "Robby. Stop it. Sit down."

"It was my idea, Dad! Mine! I told him yesterday!" Robby's arm fell, though he remained standing. "He said I was wrong. I knew I wasn't."

"We're leaving. Go, Robby," his father said, towing him out of the row. "Move it. I mean it. Now."

Christopher followed them out. He had no desire to sit through the Q & A that was sure to cut into his presentation time. Better to leave and try to collect his own thoughts. The father had taken the boy down the hall, but Christopher could still hear their conversation. Irritated, he pushed the button for the elevator. Apparently he'd have to go back to his room.

Sam faced off with his son.

"Robby, what's the matter with you? Why are you calling him a liar? When did you even talk to him?"

"Yesterday! When you were looking for me."

"You were having a conversation with him? What did you have to talk about?"

"His database. I've been studying it." Robby dug into his pocket and held up a thumb drive. "He asked me to tell him more."

"The conference keynote speaker?" Sam was skeptical. "Really?"

"Ask Paula! She saw him. Told me to follow him. Talk to him. And he stole my idea!"

"Robby, I know you've been obsessed with those geese since the crash, but you just can't go around accusing people . . ."

"Robby! Mr. Palmer!" The door from the conference room burst open, and an older man wearing a short-sleeved shirt with a tie hustled down the hall. Sam crinkled his forehead. The face was familiar, but Sam couldn't place him.

Robby, though, recognized him right away.

"Dr. Felk!"

Sam blinked. Indeed it was, the bearded, bespectacled ornithologist from the American Museum of Natural History who was so awed by Robby's instincts. The man responsible for bringing them here, here himself.

"Wonderful to find you here," Felk said, shaking both their hands. He gave Sam an extra pump and a pat on the back. An attaboy for bringing Robby.

"I heard the commotion and recognized Robby when I looked over. What's going on, son?"

"He stole my theory!" Robby insisted again. "I used his databases. Yesterday I told him more about the geese in the crash." His words sputtered, the sentences clipped into fragments. "Late migration date. Fly to South Carolina. No data points since the crash. I was right, Dr. Felk!

"But he said I was wrong. 'Better luck next time,' he said.

"Then, in there, he took my idea." Robby dropped to his knees in the middle of the hall and rummaged in his backpack, pulling out a handful of disorganized, torn flash cards. "I can prove it. It's all here!"

"Robby, please. Keep your voice down," Sam pleaded. Some passersby carefully threaded past the hallway tableau, studiously avoiding even a glance. Others watched furtively. Felk was listening intently. He took a flash card, then another. "You did all this research yourself?"

Robby nodded. "It's here, too." He held up the thumb drive.

"Are you free for lunch?" Felk looked between father and son.

"Yes. Tell him yes, Dad. Tell him yes!" Robby stood up, staring at Dr. Felk as if at a redeemer.

Sam hesitated. He looked at Robby's face. "All right. I suppose."

As Robby walked ahead to the hotel restaurant, Sam spoke quietly to Felk. "He's so deep into researching this crash. It's like some complete alternate reality. I'd heard autistic people could get really involved in their arcane niches, but I never expected anything like this."

Felk nodded. "I had an instinct about Robby back in January. I just want to see where he's gone with it the last couple months."

Father, son, and ornithologist sat down in a booth. Robby dumped his backpack out on the table and began reciting again the trends he'd discovered in Baxter's database of banded Canada geese.

The South Carolina–bound flock with late arrival dates in New York. The lack of data points after January 15. His group of forty-eight most likely victims. His second-tier choices. Felk listened, waving off the waitress multiple times.

After fifteen minutes, Robby finished. He sat back, as drained as after a meltdown. But though his adrenaline was obviously revved up, he'd remained coherent and in control of his body except for the outburst in the lecture hall, Sam realized.

"You've been busy the last couple months," Felk said, pushing the backpack contents around on the table. Flotsam and jetsam, Sam thought. The giant, outdated headphones; the flash cards, dingy from constant handling even before Robby ripped some; the brown notebook; a cheap solar-powered calculator.

At the bottom on the pile, Felk's fingers brushed more ripped paper—larger than the flash cards, the sheets unlined, hastily crumpled.

Seemingly idly, Felk's fingers smoothed the wrinkles. Sam leaned over to see better.

It was a sketch. A bird perched on a branch, building a nest. Done in pencil, like the flash cards. Unlike Robby's sloppy penmanship, though, the lines of the drawing were finely done, from the precise edges of the bird's beak to the variegated shading of its feathers.

Next to him, Sam felt Felk sit up straighter. "Mmm-hmm," he said, setting aside the sketch and returning to the pile, sifting through the papers more urgently now. He found another crumpled sketch, this one a close-up of the nest. Then a third of a bird in flight. He turned them to face Robby. His son ducked his head, pushing the sketches back into the larger pile.

"Robby, did you do those?" Sam tugged them back out, amazed. Linda mentioned Robby doing some drawing, but he'd never imagined anything this good. "They're wonderful. Why are they in the bottom of your backpack, crumpled up?"

Robby looked at his lap, then at the sketches sticking out of the pile. He shrugged. He looked at Felk, who held the gaze a long moment before he spoke.

"Your dad's right, Robby. Those sketches are excellent. They show attention to detail, accuracy, and skill. And they show the most important thing. Far more important than the data on your flash cards, believe it or not, or even whether you reached the right conclusion before Baxter did. They show passion."

A strange look crossed Robby's face. Embarrassment? Confusion? Both? Sam couldn't tell.

"I see your passion for birds in these sketches, Robby," Felk continued. "And that's the piece that an ornithologist must have. It's not just about the mystery of flight, the aerodynamics, the fascinating ancestry of birds that makes people dedicate their lives to studying them. There has to be a passion. A personal one.

"For me, it's hearing the rare songbirds, like the Bicknell's thrush. For the last thirty years, every spring, I go to Vermont, hoping to hear one. For Baxter, it's establishing a sanctuary on his reserve up there in Canada, providing safe haven from all the threats we humans impose."

Robby nodded slightly, his brown eyes lifting to look at Felk.

"I don't know what it is yet for you. But looking at these sketches, I know you've got that passion. You've got the head for the data, that's for sure, not to mention the intellectual curiosity. But think about these past two months. What kept you at your computer, querying that database every which way till Sunday?"

"I could imagine how they felt." Robby seemed to be talking to himself. "I saw them from the ferry. Flying along the river. Not bothering anyone."

Felk nodded. "Go on," he said, softly.

"Just there in the sky. Their home."

Felk nodded again.

Robby cleared his throat, his voice getting a bit louder. "Then comes the plane. Invading. The birds don't have a chance."

Watching the tears form in Robby's eyes, Sam felt dampness in his own.

Robby looked at Felk. "I thought if I learned about them, maybe I could help them."

Felk smiled. "You will, Robby. I would stake my recording of the Bicknell's thrush on that. And after lunch, I'm going to introduce you to someone who can help you with the first step." He looked around the restaurant. "Do you suppose we could convince the waitress we really do want to eat?"

Flagging down a waitress, he waved for Robby to order first. Sam caught Felk's eye. "I think you mean the second step, right?"

Felk's brow furrowed. "How's that?"

"You said you'd introduce him to someone who can help him with the first step." Sam held Felk's watery blue gaze. "Robby met that man three months ago. And it's past time I thanked you."

~

"Christopher! Christopher Goldman. Is that you?"

Christopher turned and smiled, the voice lifting his low spirits. Class of '56, Arthur Felk was one of Cornell's most venerated biology alumni and an institution himself at the American Museum of Natural History. The summer internship he offered there every year was one of the most competitive at Cornell. He had mentored dozens of greenhorn students who didn't know the difference between a crest and a cap into confident, credible scientists—including Christopher.

Lately Christopher wondered whether the man's age was catching up with him. Last year, he'd caught a few methodology mistakes in research Felk asked him to review before journal submission. Still, his lifetime stature was towering.

"Dr. Felk! I didn't know you were going to be here. Why didn't you get in touch? Can we meet for dinner later? A drink?"

"Arthur, please, Christopher. You know to call me Arthur now. Sort of a last-minute decision, my boy. Later, yes, indeed, we must meet. But there's something else first. You're on your way to the Expo, yes? Staffing the camp table?"

Christopher nodded.

"Excellent. I'm going to bring by some people this afternoon. Robby and Sam, boy and his dad, from here in Michigan. Met them at the museum back in January. We spent an hour down in the archives. Christopher, this kid's brilliant. Twelve years old. I've never seen so much raw potential." Felk was visibly excited, his eyes bright, his words rapid. "But it's raw, you know? I think his parents mean well, but they really don't have any idea how to help him. So he's got his local club. And this. The camp could be what cements it for him."

"Twelve years old?" Christopher shook his head. He hated to disappoint Dr. Felk. "Thirteen's the minimum age for camp."

The older man paused, his train of thought interrupted. "Really. I didn't know that. Well, maybe he's got a birthday coming up." He resumed. "Anyway. I want you to meet him. Robby Palmer. We'll be by in about an hour."

"I'll keep an eye out." They shook hands again.

Absorbed in talking to another prospect, he didn't notice Felk approach with the Palmers an hour later. So he couldn't stifle shock when he recognized the kid seated next to him at Baxter's presentation, the one who had the screaming outburst. Clad in the same oversize gray Detroit Lions sweatshirt, hood up, accompanied by the furious father who had dragged him into the hall. *This was the prodigy?*

"Robby and Sam, this is Dr. Christopher Goldman. He's the one I told you about at lunch. He's a biologist at Cornell University, the very best in the country. They run a special summer camp for young birders."

"Hi, Robby," Christopher extended his hand. He owed it to Dr. Felk to at least give the kid a chance. Robby stared at the floor, not meeting his eyes.

"Go on, Robby." The dad nudged his son, who reluctantly withdrew a hand from his pocket and wordlessly placed it in Christopher's.

Felk crouched down to Robby's eye level. "Robby, it's OK. Dr. Goldman can help you. He's an accomplished scientist. He studied with me at the museum years ago."

Robby's head lifted to look at Felk. He glanced back at Christopher, reappraising him silently, skeptically, then nodding. Ridiculously, Christopher felt reprieved.

Felk stood up. "Christopher, you're on."

"OK. Well." Christopher handed a brochure to Sam. Robby stuck his hand out and after missing a beat, Christopher handed one to him, too, suddenly wishing he'd let someone else handle this conference. Someone with kids. He didn't know how to behave around kids.

After last summer's camp, when Peter has raised the budget alarm and presented this conference as a prime recruiting opportunity, everyone in the department was surprised when Christopher not only volunteered to go, but to help with the summer camp.

Christopher tried to act noncommittal. It had been a sentimental impulse, a way to show Deborah he was trying, too, trying to prepare for potential parenthood. Well, maybe not just to show Deborah. Deep inside he did carry that imaginary video clip, of himself and a child in Sapsucker woods, each with a pair of binoculars. In the first frame he pointed where the child should look. In the next frame he crouched down with his own set level. In the third, he put his hands over the child's, gently aiming the lenses together. He hadn't even told Deborah about the camp before everything started happening: the crash, the transfer, the news about Helen, the positive pregnancy test.

Well, he was committed now. Christopher launched into his spiel, still directing his words at Sam. "Cornell's summer birding camps are considered the premier learning experience available to future generations of ornithologists. Every summer young people ages thirteen to sixteen gather on our campus to spend two weeks—"

Sam interrupted. "Thirteen? Robby's twelve."

Christopher nodded. "Thirteen's the minimum. When's his birthday?"

"October."

"Then he could come next summer."

"Coming this summer." Robby spoke for the first time.

Christopher shook his head and directed his answer at Sam again. "It'll be better if he waits a year. Gets a little more mature."

"This summer!" Robby insisted. Sam and Christopher both glanced nervously at Felk, who seemed unperturbed.

Felk looked at Christopher. "Robby and his family were visiting New York this winter when that plane crashed in the river. The one struck by the Canada geese. They were on a ferry in the Hudson, in fact. That's when Robby got interested in geese. They came to the museum afterward. That's how we met."

"You were on a ferry in the river that day?" Stunned, Christopher looked first at father, then son.

"Yes." Sam nodded. "It was a pretty pivotal experience for Robby, seeing that. You can imagine."

"I can." Christopher nodded. "I was on that plane." His voice sounded like someone else's.

"On the plane?" Sam echoed.

Robby's head whipped up as Felk spoke. "Christopher, you were a passenger? I didn't know. My God, what a thing to go through. Was Deborah with you?"

Before Christopher could nod again, Robby cut in. "Did you see them fly into the engine?"

"See the geese?"

Robby nodded.

"No. It all happened so fast, just a couple minutes after takeoff. We were—"

"Did you hear them?" Robby plunged forward with another question. "Hear them get sucked in?"

Christopher blanched, remembering. "Kind of. There were some thuds. Then the engines stalled."

"The right side first, right?" Robby was bouncing up and down on his toes. "The news said both. But the NTSB report said the right side was hit first. About ten seconds before."

"You read the NTSB report?" Christopher's attention was now fully focused on Robby.

"How did you get your hands on that?" Sam asked incredulously.

"Internet," Robby answered. "It's unusual for both engines to be taken out. Most bird strikes are single-engine events." He continued, reciting the report apparently from memory. "Were it not for pilot Sully Sullenberg's quick thinking, the outcome could have easily been tragic."

Felk jumped in. "Christopher, I think you can see Robby's pretty interested in birds. Maybe we can work around that age limit."

"I'll check into it." Christopher felt dazed, transported back to that cold day, so pivotal in his own life.

Another parent-child pair approached the booth. Felk took the cue, shepherding Robby away. "We'll read through this material. I'm sure there's plenty online, too. Christopher, how about one of your cards, too, in case Sam or Robby have questions later?"

Christopher had extended his card. As Robby reached for it, he handed Christopher the thumb drive. "Check this out, too." As their fingers brushed, the momentary touch startled him.

From a dozen steps away, Felk had called over his shoulder. "Meet me in the bar for that drink at six."

TWENTY

In the kitchen, Brett shuttled between sink and stove. Amanda was closeted in her room, Richard in his basement home office. Her only company was a pair of persistent sparrows twittering outside the window as they scrabbled for the dregs under the empty feeder.

Brett scooped the potatoes into a serving bowl. She filled the water glasses and lined up the salad dressings. Then she took a deep breath.

"Amanda, Richard! Dinner's ready."

Gathered at the table, she imagined them as a three-part Venn diagram, each one's edges barely overlapping around the oak dining set. She and Richard had bought it when she was pregnant with Amanda, still suppressing the sensations from freshman year and deluding herself that she might bear the brood that would need a seven-piece set.

Richard started the grace, extending his hands to Brett and Amanda automatically. "Come, Lord Jesus, be our guest. Let these gifts to us be blessed . . ." As she gazed at the chipped purple polish on Amanda's nails, Brett felt grateful for the hand-holding tradition, the first touch she'd had in a week. Now that she'd thrown away her life script, she was discovering there was a fine line between freeing and floundering.

"Amen," Richard said, his eyes still closed.

"Amen," Brett repeated, releasing Amanda's hand. But on the other side, Richard held on. "Lord, we come to you tonight with heavy hearts, to ask for your forgiveness and guidance to help us find our way back to your path."

Brett's head whipped toward her husband. Richard squeezed her hand tighter.

"This path Brett is choosing, Lord, I know it's unnatural. I know it's not your way. Help me to help her realize that, Lord. Help us to again be husband and wife, as you intended. Parents to Amanda. A Christian family once again."

Opening his eyes, he released their hands and picked up his fork. "Pass the potatoes please, Amanda."

"Richard." Brett felt ill. "My God. What are you saying?"

"What I believe, Brett. I've been praying about this all week. I'm not going to allow our family to disintegrate. We've turned away from God. Me too, I'll admit it. I've been swept up with being pastor, spending so much time at church. I'm praying for the strength to change, to be more humble, more fulfilled in my role at home." He turned to Amanda. "The potatoes, Amanda?"

Amanda looked as shocked as Brett felt, her hand frozen on the serving bowl.

"Richard, your prayers aren't going to change me."

"Don't underestimate the power of prayer, Brett."

He was so calm, so damn complacent.

"I don't. I've been praying for years for the strength to tell you the truth. Both of you. And I finally did." Brett's chest heaved. "John, chapter eight: *'You will know the truth, and the truth will set you free.'"*

"Don't you twist sacred Scripture. Don't tell me God played a part in this." An edge crept into Richard's voice. "It's Satan at work. He's seized your soul, Brett. Lying for all these months. And this— this—sinful behavior."

"My behavior is not your concern anymore." Brett felt like her words might singe the air, she was so angry. She saw Amanda's head swiveling between them. She looked torn between wanting to run to her room and not daring to miss a word. Watching her, Brett didn't notice Richard's clenched fist on the table until he banged it.

"Amanda, go to your room."

"Richard, she's barely started her dinner."

"This isn't a conversation for a child to hear!"

"Then why did you start it?" Brett asked, as Amanda interrupted.

"I'm almost seventeen, Dad!"

"Start it? I haven't started anything! It's you." He stood up, a condemning finger pointed at Brett. "*You* who have placed this family on the precipice." Pushing his chair back so hard it toppled over, Richard stormed out.

Bleak silence draped the dining room. Wordlessly, Amanda stood and left, too. Brett sat alone, feeling a black hole open inside her. Even the sparrows outside had deserted her.

$\sim$

Friday afternoons the Lab was always sparsely used. On days like today, the first to flirt with seventy degrees since last September, it was deserted. So the knock interrupted Christopher's concentration. He looked up from Donald Baxter's website.

"Peter. Come in." He turned away from the computer to greet the lab director.

"Thanks." Peter Hawkins removed a pile of folders from the lone visitors' chair and settled his lanky frame. "Came by to thank you for the nice job in Lansing."

"How's that?"

"Just got a call from *Audubon* magazine. They're planning a major feature on bird camp."

"Is that right?" He remembered talking at the Expo with a woman who identified herself as the Midwest editor for the nation's most widely circulated ornithology periodical. At the most he'd expected a blurb. "A big piece, huh?"

The director nodded. "They'll be on campus this summer to shoot the art. It'll probably run in the November issue. So it won't help enrollment this cycle, but it should really goose the numbers for next year."

Christopher smiled dutifully at the feeble pun. "Great. Glad I could help." He knew this was important to Peter. He was the Lab's most budget-conscious director ever, and had vowed to turn the camp from a break-even enterprise into a revenue stream.

Enrollment was too highly concentrated in the northeast states, he said. That was why he approved the Lansing conference, though travel budgets in general were being chopped across campus. The upper Midwest states and Ontario were close enough to upstate New York that parents could drive their kids to camp, meaning they wouldn't automatically rule out the program as "too far" or "too expensive" because of an airfare tacked onto tuition.

Distance and cost were all relative, Christopher thought, his mind jumping to Deborah. He remembered attending a birding conference in New Zealand several years ago—before the travel budget cuts—his first in the southern hemisphere. A presenter referred to the "fall migration north." Though it was entirely logical, his northern hemisphere–trained brain couldn't wrap itself around the fact. Now, living less than a mile from Deborah in the vacant fellow's apartment, he felt as far away and befuddled by her as he'd been at that conference in Christchurch. Hawkins was talking again.

"What's that you've got up there? Donald Baxter's site?" Peter leaned forward, frowning, gazing at the monitor behind Christopher. "I heard he was in Lansing, too."

"Uh, yeah." Christopher felt irritated at the intrusion, and at his own instinct to justify what he was doing.

"Humph. Waste of your time, if you ask me." He stood up. "I'll keep you posted on the piece. The reporter will probably want to talk to you again."

I didn't ask you, Christopher thought. "Fine," he said aloud, only wanting Peter Hawkins out of there. "Have a good weekend."

"You, too." The director finally left, his footsteps echoing.

Christopher leaned back, removing his glasses to massage his temples. Opening a drawer, he removed the thumb drive that kid gave him in Lansing. Dr. Felk's protégé, Robby Palmer.

It was practically full and an organizational nightmare. Pdfs, Excel files, notepad files, JPEGs. Except for the file extensions, the names followed no protocols Christopher knew. He sighed, exasperated.

But though the research appeared haphazard, after what Dr. Felk told him over their drink in the hotel bar, Christopher knew the contents of the drive were organized to an almost military degree of meticulousness—just Robby's own brand.

Felk was seated before a glass filled with ice when Christopher had entered at 6:05 p.m.

"What's that?"

"Scotch on the rocks."

"Make it two," he told the bartender, settling onto the stool next to the older man. Wearily he rubbed his temples.

"Long day?"

Christopher nodded, then straightened up. He didn't want to tell Felk the whole story about himself and Deborah. *Steer the conversation away.* Reaching into the pocket of his tweed jacket, he laid the thumb drive on the bar. "I need you to take this back to the boy."

"Robby."

"Yes. Robby. It would be a conflict of interest for me to look at his research before he applies. If he applies. You must know that. It would be unfair to the other—"

"Christopher." Felk held up his hand. "Keep the drive."

"Really, it's not appropriate—" Christopher began to protest again, but Dr. Felk's face stopped him. Almost translucent it was, the wrinkles and bifocals and thin lips belying his inner radiance. Christopher had seen that face before. In the crowd after his PhD commencement, a ceremony that his own father didn't bother to attend. The card with the Phoenix postmark had arrived two weeks late, and he had let Deborah open it. He sipped the drink the bartender brought, remembering. So he'd hear him out.

"So. You're convinced he's exceptional."

Felk nodded. "That morning we spent in the archives, he was a sponge. Anything to do with geese, with *Anserinae,* he just devoured. Pictures, specimens, charts—"

"If he's spending hours on Baxter's website and reading NTSB reports, he does seem to have the curiosity," Christopher said slowly. "But there's something about his manner, the way he presents himself. It's—it's off-putting," he concluded lamely.

"That's what I want to talk to you about." Felk shifted in his seat. "Robby has autism."

Christopher frowned. "I don't know much about that. It's neurological, right?"

"Right. Inhibits communication and social abilities, typically. People on the autism spectrum—and it is a huge range—also typically exhibit preoccupations with very narrow interests. Robby's is the geese that struck the plane."

"What about the hood? The wishy-washy handshake? The outburst at Baxter's presentation?"

"Sensory issues, most likely. Kids on the spectrum have sensitive systems that get overloaded easily, and they shut down. The Baxter thing was because he felt wronged. He doesn't know an appropriate way to handle it, so it came out like it did."

Christopher rattled the ice in his glass. "You think a boy with all that going on can handle bird camp?"

"Absolutely." Felk bored his gaze into Christopher's eyes. "Cognitive deficits can accompany autism. But in high-functioning kids like Robby, more often it masks intelligence. Between you and me, I'm guessing that thumb drive will show he was a least a little justified about tearing into Baxter, too."

"Why are you so interested in him, Arthur?"

Felk sat back. A long moment passed. "I had a brother who was autistic. Retarded, most people called him. No one had ever heard of 'the spectrum' back then—in the forties. He was pretty severe. Benjamin. He was four years older than me, and I talked before he did. Doctor advised my parents to put him in an institution. They agreed. With five other kids to take care of, they were overwhelmed.

"But it killed my mother. Literally." Felk stared over Christopher's head now, looking years and miles away from the bar. "The institution was probably a hundred miles from our house. She visited every chance she got and when one visit was over, she was counting the days till the next. One December a blizzard was forecast when she was scheduled to visit. Dad tried to convince her not to go, but you'd have had to lock her up to keep her from Benjamin, especially right before Christmas.

"She made it for her visit." Felk paused for a long swallow. "But she never made it home. Police never could say for sure why. The storm was over by the time she left the next day. Day was clear. Of course, they didn't plow like they do now. Maybe she was going too fast. At any rate, her car skidded off the road, into a snow bank, which buried the car. If she wasn't dead when she hit it, she was buried alive. The officer brought us her pocketbook. That was all."

"I'm sorry," Christopher said softly.

His words pulled Felk back to the present. He sighed deeply and looked at Christopher. "It broke my dad up. He started drinking. He was dead in less than ten years, his liver destroyed. So before I was out of high school, I lost both my parents, and my only brother, to the institution. And all because people were afraid of Benjamin. Afraid because he was different."

"I'm sorry," Christopher said again. He thought about Deborah, still in the early stages of her pregnancy, and the baby's hidden, developing DNA strand. Was the Huntington's gene there already? If so, would it remain dormant and benign? Or would it bide its time until the ominous threshold of thirty-five?

What about autism? The little he knew surmised a genetic role, too. His mother's cancer, too. These were the kinds of risks having children posed. He shuddered involuntarily and drained his glass.

Felk nodded, accepting his inadequate rote sympathy. "There's a happy ending, though. When we got old enough, my sisters and I transferred Benjamin to an adult group home in New Jersey. It became home for him. He lived there for more than thirty years. He got a job stocking grocery store shelves. He learned how to take the bus.

"He was a huge baseball fan. Baseball was to him what birds are to Robby. I took him to the Yankees play-offs a few years back—I think it was the highlight of his life. He died just last year."

"That's the happy ending?" Christopher looked at Felk curiously.

"Sure. Benjamin reached his potential. He was happy. He was living in the world, not locked away from it. You asked why I was interested in Robby. Benjamin is why."

He swirled the ice in his glass. "But I'm a lot older now. Robby needs somebody younger." He paused, then nodded again at the two-inch piece of plastic on the bar. "Take his drive back home, Christopher."

Christopher had hesitated one more moment, then dropped the drive into his tweed pocket.

Now he stared at the cryptic list of files. He glanced at his watch. Three o'clock on a lovely spring Friday afternoon, but he didn't have anything better to do. Randomly he opened a spreadsheet labeled "NTSBstrikes1985to2005." It took a minute to load. The document had over one thousand lines of content. Christopher peered through his glasses, digesting. He sat up straighter and scrolled down farther.

Jesus. Dr. Felk was right about Robby.

TWENTY-ONE

Deborah stepped up to the nose-pierced cashier at Ivory Tower Coffee and Smoothies, looking longingly at the silver carafes lining the counter. Beside her, Julia poked a straw into a cup of dark-pink liquid and reproached her good-naturedly. "The Berry Blast is the best."

Deborah sighed. "Make it two."

She never thought it would be so hard to give up coffee. It was nice, though, Julia's friendly needling. How long had it been since she went out with a girlfriend? Elizabeth had moved to North Carolina four years ago. There was Helen, but they only saw each other a few times a year. She'd missed friendship without realizing it, she thought, following Julia to a table.

"So, Megan's going to celebrate Mother's Day after all," Julia said.

"Yeah. She was what, almost four weeks early?" The most pregnant at last week's class, Megan, she of the arm and ankle tattoos, had not returned that week. Kate, of course, informed them that Megan had delivered early. Baby Carson was in the NICU at Cayuga Medical Center as a "precaution," but he was expected to go home later that week. The news sobered everyone at the class.

"Mmm-hmmm. But the baby was almost six pounds. Doesn't seem like he belongs in a NICU. I guess you never really know what can happen."

"I guess not," said Deborah, feeling uncomfortable. Helen had called the other night, again urging Deborah to get tested at Columbia so that she could "manage the pregnancy better," whatever that meant. "So tell me about your nonprofit."

"Oh, never mind." Julia took a long sip. "You probably get sick of people picking your brain all the time."

"No, it's OK. I'd kind of like to talk about something I know, actually. And know I'm good at. All this baby stuff unnerves me. There's so much to learn, and no way to practice before the real thing."

Julia smiled. "Yeah, who decided that? All right. We need help with fundraising. What else is new, right?"

"What's the name of the organization again? Interfaith something?"

"The Ithaca Interfaith Alliance. We run a food pantry and a community meal program. I got involved through my church."

"A food pantry? In Ithaca?"

"That's part of our problem." Julia sighed. "Everyone thinks Ithaca's a rich college town. But that's not the whole story. There is real need here. I think we get a lot of Cornell people, in fact. The grad students and the adjuncts."

Deborah stared out the window. The grass was greening up and students flowed by on bikes. She thought of the students she saw studying in the law library, buried behind piles of five-hundred-dollar books. Probably all purchased with student loan money. She'd never thought they could have a need as basic as hunger.

Julia continued. "So the churches who are Alliance members support it, collecting food from the congregations. We use their kitchen facilities for meals. But we're starting to get more and more requests for meal delivery. Attendance really dropped this last winter. We heard it was because people couldn't get out of the house."

"Because of snow? Bad weather?"

"Maybe." Julia looked pensive. "Or maybe they didn't dare drive because they hadn't paid their car insurance. Maybe they bought medicine that week, instead of gas. Or paid the heating bill."

"Really?" Deborah thought about that. "People are that bad-off?"

"Well, think about it. You know all the stats about this economy. Record unemployment, especially long-term. How long could you last without a paycheck?"

Deborah shifted in her chair. She had been thinking about exactly that lately. She still hadn't told Phillip. Under the best circumstances, he would have groused about a maternity leave, but the retrenchment from the law school donors made the timing even worse. Legally, he couldn't deny her a leave. But he could—and would, no doubt—make her life miserable right up to and after it.

"Sorry." Julia filled in for her silence. "I didn't mean to sound so self-righteous."

"Don't apologize. You believe in your cause. That's the most important thing in fundraising." Deborah paused. "I was just thinking how I'm not sure what's going to happen with my own job after the baby. And what I'd do without my paycheck."

"Mmm." Julia nodded. "One income makes it tight, that's for sure."

Deborah hesitated again. She didn't know Julia Adams well yet. But if Deborah didn't tell her she'd find out from the campus grapevine sooner or later. If her husband hadn't told her already.

"Actually, I don't know if there's another one I can count on," she said carefully, watching Julia's reaction. "Christopher and I are separated."

Devoid of judgment, Julia's eyes relieved Deborah before her words. "I'm so sorry. Going through that while you're pregnant must be very difficult."

Deborah nodded, trying to will back her tears. The other day four large packages had arrived in Cayuga Heights. Inside was both the baggage they'd carried on and checked on Flight 1549, retrieved when the plane was salvaged from the river. Her purse, with her ID and credit cards and makeup bag and keys. Christopher's red Cornell carry-on. Their matching navy rolling suitcases, a wedding gift from Helen and Matt. Inside Christopher's, the green sweater she had given him for his last birthday. Their toothbrushes—his blue, hers red.

Sorting through the detritus of their lives lived together, Deborah felt mocked. The suitcases and purse were in bad shape, but the recovered contents, which someone had dried and folded, were in amazingly good condition, even smelling sweet from sheets of fabric softener placed in between the garments. Just the opposite of her personal aftermath. Still not visibly pregnant, she looked the same as ever outside. Professional, perfect Deborah. But her insides felt as battered as the waterlogged leather and canvas as she volleyed between resenting Christopher and missing him, blaming him, and feeling guilty, anticipating motherhood and fearing it.

But just like in the class last week, Julia was holding out a tissue. And even before she'd dried her eyes, Deborah felt the tears slow. A shared burden is half a burden. Shared joy is double joy. And she had that, too, she remembered, laying her palm on her belly. She took a long sip of the smoothie. It was pretty good, after all. She smiled as she dabbed her eyes.

"I've got an ultrasound scheduled."

"What! Already?" Julia gasped.

As the spring sun streamed in through the windows, they feathered their nests together.

Chewing the end of his hooded sweatshirt string, Robby clicked "Play." Two or three low notes followed by several higher ones. He clicked again, counting silently. Six was the most high notes in a row.

He shut his eyes to block the distractions in his bedroom, concentrating as hard as he could. The low notes sounded almost like a duck's quack, short and clipped. The high notes varied, some held twice as long as the others. He clicked "Play" again.

"Whatcha doing, Robby?"

Startled, Robby opened his eyes just long enough to locate the disruption. Without a word of response to his dad, he blinked them back shut, and once more clicked "Play." The song of the Bicknell's thrush, which the website said had one of the most restricted breeding and wintering ranges in North America, was extraordinary. Just like Dr. Felk said. Below the audio link it said it was recorded by someone named William H. Gunn.

"Listening to bird songs?" His father was behind him, looking over his shoulder.

Duh, Dad. Robby swiveled his chair side to side as he pondered. How did William Gunn get the recording? Did he take a microphone out into the woods and just wait? How did Dr. Felk get his? He said he went to Vermont every year to look for it. The website said the thrush's conservation status was vulnerable. How hard would it be to find a vulnerable bird? He started to click "Play" again when his dad covered his hand on the mouse.

"Robby. I'm asking questions so I can learn, too."

Instinctively, Robby jerked his hand and swiveled his chair away from the touch. But his dad stopped him, grasping the back of the chair and crouching down next to it, at his eye level. "I want to learn, too. Can we do it together?"

Robby spit out the sweatshirt string and exhaled deeply, blowing his long dark hair out of his eyes. His dad was different since they'd gone to the Audubon conference in Lansing. He yelled less, and sighed less. Robby couldn't say why. But it had started there.

"Bicknell's thrush," he said, nodding at the screen.

"That's the one Dr. Felk likes, right?"

Robby nodded, clicking play again. The bright, clear trill filled the room.

"Pretty," his dad said.

"I want to hear it, too."

"In real life, you mean?"

Robby nodded.

"Vermont's a long ways away."

Robby shrugged. "Still want to."

"Hmm." His dad nodded at the computer screen. "Is there more?"

"Lots." The website Dr. Felk told him about, the Cornell Lab of Ornithology, had thousands and thousands of calls in its acoustic library.

"Let's look for something we can find in Michigan."

Robby looked doubtful, glancing back at the gray Bicknell's thrush.

"Let's just see. There must be something interesting here."

Robby found a US map and clicked over Michigan. The familiar mitten waved back at them, divided into sections. There was also a list of conservation status search choices: critically endangered, endangered, vulnerable, near threatened, of least concern.

"Bicknell's thrush is vulnerable," Robby said, clicking the word.

"No results found," his dad read. "Try another one."

Robby clicked near-threatened. Two names popped up.

"Piping plover and Kirtland's warbler," his dad read. "You pick."

"Piping plover." Robby decided, clicking. A bird with a pale brown back and white belly appeared, standing on sand. He clicked the audio link, recorded by Geoffrey A. Keller. The bird's mid-range peeps filled the room. Unlike the Bicknell's thrush, the notes didn't climb up the scale but were all even. A bird that went blah, blah, blah, Robby thought. *Boring.*

"I liked the Bicknell's thrush better."

"It's a beach bird," his dad said, reading ahead. "It nests up north, along Lake Michigan, mostly in the Sleeping Bear Dunes National Lakeshore. I went there when I was a kid."

"Did you see any?"

"Not that I remember." He read aloud further. "Piping plovers return in late April or early May."

"April? This month?" Robby said, feeling more excited.

"Incubation of the nest is shared by both the male and the female. Incubation is generally twenty-seven days," his dad finished.

"That means it takes twenty-seven days for the eggs to hatch?"

"I think so."

"So we could see the baby birds if we went in a month."

"You'll still be in school then. We could go in June."

"Don't want to wait until June," Robby said. June was too long to wait if they returned by early May. Like seventh grade was so important.

"They'll still be there, Robby. It says the females don't leave until mid-July."

Robby felt the anger spreading through his body, stiffening his neck, his shoulders, his arms. His hand clenched the mouse. He shook his head hard.

"Don't want to wait," he repeated.

"I promise, we'll go after school's out." His dad spun his chair so they faced each other. "Can you hear me, Robby? I promise."

Robby stared over his dad's shoulder, out the bedroom window. He could see the bird feeder hanging in the crabapple. The first buds were starting to pop.

"It's going to be OK. They'll be there, and we'll see them in June. It's going to be OK." Sounding far away, his dad's voice was smooth and even and calm. Kind of like the piping plover's song.

Robby looked away from the window, back at the computer screen. He inhaled deeply, like his mom was always telling him to do when he got mad. "In through your nose, out through your mouth," she would say, demonstrating herself.

It helped. He could relax his fingers enough to click the audio link again.

The plover's sequence of clear peeps resounded again. The first three notes did have a slight rise and fall to them, he realized, sounding almost like a series of pairs: up down, up down, up down. Then came the long, repeated even peeps. He clicked it again, looking at the image of the little brown and white bird on the sand. He liked the beach. Liked feeling sand on his feet. Liked to swim.

A long time ago he'd overheard Megan, the therapist he saw when he was six or seven, tell his mom that swimming was good for him. "The water pressure provides sensory input," she had said. Robby remembered it because no one had ever explained that water had pressure. It had scared him a little. The next time they went to the pool, he paused on the steps cautiously, waiting to feel the water squeeze around his ankles. He hadn't felt anything.

He had stepped in deeper, to his knees. Still nothing. What did Megan know, anyway? He had plunged in then, the water comforting like so few other places, enveloping his body, muffling noise, buoying him like a pillow.

As he thought about swimming, imagining seeing the piping plovers on the beach, Robby's anger stopped throbbing. His hands and arms and legs slackened. His dad's murmur gradually became louder. "It's going to be OK. They'll be there, and we'll see them in June. It's going to be OK."

The plover's last peep faded. Robby looked at his father. Straight in the eye.

"OK, deal. In June."

~

Seeing Richard's car pull into the garage, Brett unconsciously lifted her fingers from her laptop to her lips, biting her nails. Despite his declaration at dinner, Richard had retreated even further into church business as April had become May. Amanda sequestered herself at school as much as possible. Bivouacked in the former guest room, Brett barely remembered the freedom and giddiness she'd felt moving in. Richard's grace had left her with an abiding sense of nausea. He was opening the kitchen door.

"Hi."

He nodded. *He can't even bring himself to speak to me*, Brett thought, noticing how haggard her husband looked. For the first time, sympathy flickered. All Richard wanted was to go back, back to the way their lives were. And it would never happen. Nor was there solace in memories, since he now knew their perfect Christian family had been a mirage. At least she had the hope of a happier future. She was already trying some of Elizabeth's suggestions, like fresh produce donations, and the meals were running more smoothly and attracting more guests than ever before.

Richard walked around the kitchen counter, carefully keeping a perimeter between them, into the living room and dropped into his chair.

"So, what would you do with two cases of lettuce, eight pounds of carrots, half a case of bananas, and a lot of cherry tomatoes?" Brett twisted on the counter stool, speaking to the back of his head. "Marge just called after produce pickup rounds. That's tonight's haul from the restaurants and grocery stores."

Richard didn't reply, staring into space, away from her.

"Salad, yes, that's what I was thinking, too. The bananas could be a take-along, or, if they're really brown, baked into something. I—"

Richard cleared his throat, turning to face her. "Brett, this isn't working."

"What do you mean?"

"This lifestyle."

"It's not a *lifestyle*, Richard. You make it sound like—I don't know—a decorating theme. It's my life." *That I'm actually living for the first time*, she thought silently.

"That's what it feels like. We've been married for eighteen years. Together for twenty. Now, all of a sudden, you say it's all been a fraud."

All of a sudden. Brett stood and walked into the living room, facing her husband, her fists curled on her hips. "Do you think I would throw twenty years away on a whim, Richard?"

"Not the Brett I married. But the Brett I married wouldn't have lied for years, either."

"Richard, you're making this impossible!" Brett threw up her hands. "You're angry about me lying, but you don't want to hear the truth, either. I can't win for losing."

"I guess that's how you would see it. All about you," Richard said.

Through Brett's tears, his face blurred. *He was so wrong. So unfair. For twenty years it had been about nothing but him. And Amanda.*

"You know, you're not the man I married anymore, either. The man who took me on a mission trip, taught me about servant leadership and social justice, he disappeared years ago," Brett said hotly. "All you care about is being on the marquee in front of the church. Pastor Stevens. You admitted it yourself at dinner."

Richard looked chagrined, then shrugged.

"It wouldn't matter if I was just the same, would it? You're the one who says it's nature, not nurture."

Brett was silent. Richard nodded with grim satisfaction.

"Well, fine. I'm washing my hands of it. You've made your decision. It's between you and God now. But I'm not tolerating sinfulness under my roof anymore." He shook his head, leveling her with his eyes. "You move back upstairs. Or out."

TWENTY-TWO

O K, Deborah. Hop up on the table."

It was her third appointment with the OB and the first ultrasound since her pregnancy was confirmed. She hadn't been in this room yet or had this technician, whose scrubs top was covered with scattered rainbows.

Deborah wondered if Dr. Dunn required cheerily themed attire as a subconscious positive reinforcement. At the end of this first trimester, she was almost ready to allow herself to believe she would finally become a mother. Almost ready to believe it wouldn't be taken away again. Still, fear vied with anticipation as top of mind. She wanted to see the baby. Yet indulging would destroy her last fig leaf of protection. If something went wrong from here on, after she'd seen her baby, Deborah didn't know whether she could recover.

The technician pushed the power switch on a large flat screen TV angled toward the exam table.

"I'm Kristy," she introduced herself briskly, settling herself on the wheeled stool. "Just lean back now and pull up your shirt and unbutton your pants for me, please. I'm going to tuck this paper liner in here so we don't get any of the gel on your clothes." She rolled away from Deborah on the stool to the counter and pulled on rubber gloves, then took up the tube of gel.

Deborah looked down at her belly, which had thickened but not yet swelled. "This will be a little cold," Kristy warned as she squirted, then smeared it around. "All right. Let's see what we can see."

Holding a wand that looked like a tire gauge to Deborah, she began moving it in slow circles around Deborah's belly. The wand felt warm through the thick gel. The television screen changed from black to a pulsing, grayish-blue hue. "Is that the baby?" Deborah asked, leaning forward.

"Lean back, please. I need you to remain still." Deborah leaned back, her eyes never straying from the screen. "That's your uterus. I'm trying to find the baby inside. Let's try a little lower."

Deborah felt her pants tugged down farther, the wand brushing just above her pubic bone. "Ah. There we are."

A white, comma-shaped blob floated onto the screen. Instinctively trying to see better, Deborah sat up again. The picture flickered and disappeared. She leaned back before Kristy could correct her. "I'm sorry. I'm sorry. Can you get it back again? Please try to get it back."

"Relax," Kristy resumed the wand's slow motion. The blob reappeared, larger and closer this time. Deborah could see tiny webbed fingers and toes protruding from what looked like stunted arms and legs. "Ah, she's giving us a profile. Good girl," Kristy murmured.

"You can tell it's a girl?" Deborah asked. Kristy paused and squinted.

"Well, I don't see anything that would indicate a boy. How far along are you, again?"

"About twelve weeks."

"Right. Too early to say officially, then. I guess that was just a reflex. You seem like you're going to have a girl. Working here, you get a feeling for these kinds of things."

With a red laser pointer, she indicated the baby's eye socket and ear. A throbbing white dot was the heartbeat. Deborah could see the bump of the nose, and a big belly. Then, after freezing the image on the screen, Kristy wiped the gel off.

"You're all done. How many prints would you like?"

"Excuse me?" Deborah's eyes were fixed on the screen, but her mind was thinking about Christopher. She had imagined this moment so many times, sharing their first glimpse of their child. It was never supposed to be her first glimpse of their child. But Christopher knew nothing of the appointment; she was meeting Julia at the smoothie shop afterward to debrief. He would say that was another consequence of her unilateral decision to go ahead with the transfer. But hadn't he acted just as unilaterally in moving out?

"How many prints would you like? People usually want a few, for family members."

Deborah winced. So far, she was the only family her child was assured. Christopher would point out even that wasn't guaranteed, given Helen's diagnosis. "Two will be fine," she said, still watching the screen.

"Two it is." Kristy peeled off her gloves and regarded Deborah with her hands on her hips. "OK. You need a few more minutes to look at your baby. We're not busy. You go ahead. I'll be right back."

"Thank you," Deborah whispered, dimly aware of being left alone. She slid off the table and approached the screen, thoughts of Christopher fading. Her baby was real. *Her baby.* The image was like a magnetic field, drawing her inexorably toward it. There in black and white, curled up on a forty-inch screen, was a baby she could recognize, even without Kristy's guided laser tour.

With her palm she could cover the magnified image of the head. She traced along the spine, and then rested her finger over the tiny hands. It was a crystalline moment, one that captured the essence of motherhood: to protect and nurture and love, ferociously and unconditionally. Physically, the baby looked almost alien. Yet Deborah felt instantaneous attachment. Christopher should be here, she thought. Seeing is loving, no matter what secrets were within the invisible double helix that twined inside.

"Hello, baby girl," she said softly. "I can't wait to meet you."

At the reception desk, Kristy handed her the pictures. "We'll probably see you again in another six weeks or so. Be able to tell if I was right about a daughter by then."

"I'll be here," Deborah said.

Her cell phone rang as she stepped outside with her two-dimensional treasures.

"I'm running late. Be there in fifteen minutes," Julia said.

"OK."

"How did it go?"

"Perfect." Deborah answered. She carefully stepped around a puddle, not wanting to disturb the cluster of sparrows splashing there. "Just perfect."

~

"Welcome to Ithaca, Brett. We're so glad to have you here."

"Thank you." Brett shook hands with Pastor Susan Ellis. "Call me Pastor Sue," said the chair of the Ithaca Interfaith Alliance board of trustees, who had posted the Alliance's director position on Elizabeth's website.

"This is Julia Adams, another board member and volunteer," Pastor Sue continued. "She'll be participating in the interview today, too." Brett shook hands with a very pregnant woman who looked to be in her late thirties.

"Pleased to meet you both. I'm glad to be here, too," Brett said automatically. How long had it been since she'd done a job interview? Years, no question. But she didn't feel as nervous as she'd expected around these two. They were in Pastor Sue's office, a cramped cinder block box that reminded her of Richard's.

Still, there was plenty of adrenaline pumping. This job seemed so perfect. Foreordained, even. She'd visited the website a few times without luck before this posting came up, within two weeks of Richard's ultimatum. Ithaca was barely a hundred miles from Scranton. An easy weekend drive for Amanda, who was at driver's training at that very moment. And in the state of New York, home to a host of drama schools.

"We appreciate you taking the time to come up," Pastor Sue said. "We'll talk here, then go over to Immaculate Conception—that's the Catholic church scheduled to host tonight's dinner—so you can see some of our operation. Hopefully we'll have you back on the road home by seven."

"Because I'll need to be in bed by then, too," added Julia, smiling and touching her belly in a gesture Brett remembered herself.

"When are you due?"

"August first. Less than two months."

"I've been telling her she's got to work on her timing. She'll be sweating out the dog days," Pastor Sue said.

"Congratulations." Brett leaned forward eagerly. "It's really a coincidence to be meeting with you. I've been wanting to try out an idea to expand your fundraising and volunteer base."

"The sooner we do both, the better," Pastor Sue said.

"Yes, go on, please, Brett." Julia nodded.

"You can do it by offering meal delivery to new mothers."

Julia and Pastor Sue raised four eyebrows back at her.

"It's not my own idea," Brett added quickly. "I visited another church that implemented a program like that with a lot of success."

She summarized the Stork Express program Elizabeth had started in Charlotte.

"You're already doing meal preparation and delivery here. So without requiring any new resources—beyond more food—the Stork Express program expands the Alliance's reach and reputation among an entirely new audience, one that can help sustain it." She took a breath.

"What's such a wonderful coincidence is that you're already plugged into the new mom community." Brett nodded at Julia. "That would give us a head start."

Neither she nor Pastor Sue had said a word, though both scribbled notes as Brett talked. Suddenly conscious of the silence, Brett felt her nerves return. She hadn't even let them ask the first question before she started rattling on.

"I'm sorry. I'm sure you have questions for me."

Pastor Sue and Julia exchanged a look. Brett thought she detected an almost imperceptible nod. Pastor Sue turned and focused on her.

"We do." She paused. "I've never done this with a job candidate so quickly, but you make quite a first impression. You're creative, you're eager, you're connected, you're smart. You're exactly who we need at the Alliance. When can you start?"

Brett blinked. Was she serious?

"Excuse me, I'm not sure I understand. We haven't even finished the interview. You're offering me the job?"

"I am." Pastor Sue nodded. "Our executive committee empowered me to make an immediate offer, to the right candidate, of course. But I imagine you'd probably like to see a little more of the Alliance operation first. Why don't we head over to Immaculate Conception right now? We'll take the scenic route and show you a little bit of Ithaca, too."

"All right," Brett agreed, feeling a bit dazed.

Julia drove and doubled as tour guide. "You can't come to Ithaca and not see Cornell University. Of course, I'm biased. It's my alma mater and paycheck provider now."

"Don't forget Ithaca College," Pastor Sue said from the backseat. "Remember, we're headed to George's place."

"George is our board member representing Immaculate Conception. He's a pretty popular professor at Ithaca College. English Lit," Julia said. "Education is pretty much Ithaca's biggest industry. The K-12 schools have a great reputation, too."

"Do they?" Brett said neutrally.

"Careful, Julia," Pastor Sue said from the backseat.

"I know, I know." Julia waved her hand and rested it on her belly again. "We can't ask you about children. But for me, right now, schools are so important. So I'm just saying, *in case* it would happen to be important for you, the schools here are very good. Public and private."

"Thanks. I appreciate that," Brett said. She looked out the window. Amanda would be a senior this fall. A bad time to start a new school. But could Brett really move away and leave her in Scranton? In the abstract, the idea of weekend visits seemed ideal, a year not so long. Now that the job appeared to be hers for the taking, Brett didn't feel so sure of the happily-ever-after ending. Her track record predicting outcomes where Amanda was concerned hadn't been very good lately, either.

Yet Richard's ultimatum was real. This job was an excellent match for her skills. A parent with New York residency could be a real plus for Amanda in just a year. And if she was completely honest, Brett admitted she liked the idea of a fresh start in a new place. So it all came down to timing. Would it play in her favor, or against? *Sign, sign, everywhere a sign.* Brett pressed her head to the window and scanned Ithaca's leafy streets for one.

~

Deborah wrapped her hands around the teacup at Campus Cantonese, enjoying the sensation of heat seeping through the thick china into her palms. It was barely summer, but the air-conditioning in the restaurant was giving her goose bumps.

Then again, maybe it was because Christopher would show up any minute.

Since he had moved into the vacant visiting faculty apartment, they had spoken on the phone a few times, mostly to negotiate logistics about their shared bank accounts. Otherwise, Deborah left him alone, giving him the space and time he'd said he needed. She filled her days with work, yoga, outings with Julia, and planning for the baby. Moments of anxiety and feeling overwhelmed still blindsided her. At work, Phillip was still an ass. But she had a sharp, new, black-and-white vision of her future.

She had scanned and stored the ultrasound image on her work computer and stole looks at it throughout the day, as helpless to stop as any addict. The original sat in a frame on her nightstand, the first thing she saw upon awakening and the last thing at night. Staring at it, Deborah pondered the promise and mystery and fear within the black-and-white rectangle. She had never embarked on anything as uncertain and uncontrollable as motherhood. It was almost anathema to her nature. Yet she found herself facing the future with an equanimity Ming Su would applaud.

Except for the times when her mind drifted to questions like whether the baby would have straight dark hair like hers or sandy strands like Christopher's; Christopher's aptitude for science or her own extroverted personality. The quicksand of Huntington's lay around the edges of those questions, which she skirted as fast as she could.

It was for the baby's future that she asked Christopher to meet at Campus Cantonese, one of their regular restaurants. Decisions loomed—her job, their marriage, the future. She checked her purse again, making sure the envelope was still there.

"Hello, Deborah."

His voice startled her, and tea sloshed over the edge of the cup as she set it down. First freezing, now burning.

"Hello, Christopher," she said, standing awkwardly. Should she shake hands? Hug him? Kiss him on the cheek? Ambiguously she leaned toward him, letting him take the lead. He went for the middle ground, the hug. But he clasped her around the shoulders, not her waist, keeping space between her growing belly and his trim one.

He slid into the booth opposite her, his red Cornell shirt blending against the red vinyl.

"Enjoying your summer freedom?" she asked.

"Not so free this year. I'm teaching two classes."

"Really. No research?" Odd. Christopher usually cherished summer as his time to get out in the field.

"Not much. I've got one trip planned later this summer. Vermont. Dr. Felk asked me to go with him on his annual Bicknell's thrush expedition. But otherwise I'll be sticking around here."

"How is Dr. Felk?" Deborah first met the older man at their wedding. They had had him over for dinner a handful of times when he visited campus. She liked him the way you would a grandfather. Christopher had wanted to stop by the museum on their New York trip back in January, but there hadn't been time.

"He's fine. Holding his own." The waitress arrived with the teapot and a menu for Christopher. Silently she mopped up the spilled tea and refilled Deborah's cup. Deborah warmed her hands again as Christopher looked at the menu. *The lo mein. As usual*, Deborah bet with herself, hoping she would lose.

She cleared her throat. "So what prompted you to teach this summer?"

Christopher looked up. "Earning some extra money sounded like a good idea."

"Because?"

"Because of the baby, of course, Deborah."

Her heart rose on a tide of hope. "Does that mean you're coming home?"

"I didn't say that."

The tide rushed back out, Deborah fighting the undertow.

"Then what do you mean?"

"You were right what you said at my office. This is moving forward. I'm going to be a father." He stared off into space, as if reading lines he'd rehearsed. "I'll live up to that. You can bank on it. But I'm—" he swiped a finger across his eye. Was he crying? "I'm still struggling with how it started. And whether I can stay married to you."

Deborah felt like he was spinning away from the table, refracting with the sparkly specks in the booth's red vinyl.

Behind his trifold, laminated shield, he took a deep breath. "Have you had the HD test yet?"

"Have I had—what?"

"The HD test. What Helen had. The screening for Huntington's Disease."

"No."

Christopher looked taken aback, laying down his menu shield, on the offensive now. "Deborah, your genes aren't going away. After the baby, I thought for sure you'd recognize the importance of addressing your health."

"It's not after the baby yet. It's before."

"Well, technically that's true. But—"

"It's five months before, and I'm scared. You've dropped out of our lives. At least I know now you plan to send a check every once in a while. That will be a help. I assume you'll be willing to put her on your health insurance, too?" She held her breath.

"Well, yes, I suppose. But why wouldn't you just add her to yours?"

Belatedly processing the pronoun, Christopher's eyebrows shot up. "Her? You know it's a girl?"

"Yes." She reached into her purse. Her relief at his answer muted her anger, leaving her mostly sad. "Foolish as I am, I even thought you might like to see a picture."

"A girl," Christopher repeated, quietly.

"Not just a girl, Christopher." Deborah stood to leave, dropping the envelope on the table. "Your daughter."

TWENTY-THREE

How much farther?" Robby called from the backseat.

"About an hour to Traverse City," his mom answered.

"Park first! Not the hotel!" Alarmed, Robby sat up, pulling his headphones off.

His mom sighed, turning from the front passenger seat.

"I know we said we'd go to the park first, Robby. But we got a late start and—"

It was her *be reasonable, Robby*, voice. "Park first!" Robby insisted, squeezing his iPod tightly. "See the birds!" It was finally June. He'd waited and waited for June to arrive. For school to be over, to be on the road, every minute closing the distance between him and the piping plovers.

"We can make it. The Visitors Center is open until five, right?" His dad was driving.

"Sam, if we go there first, we'll pass Traverse City. By the time we get to the hotel it'll be going on seven. He'll be starving, and we'll still have to check in and—"

"You know we've got to stick to the plan, Linda," his dad said. "We can hit a drive-through." He glanced at Robby in the rearview mirror.

"We'll go to the park first, buddy. Just like we planned."

Mollified, Robby sat back. *First less yelling and sighing. Now his dad was on his side.*

"Why are we staying out in Traverse City, anyway?" his dad asked.

"I couldn't find any hotels closer. Just B and Bs," his mom said. "If Robby had a meltdown, in front of nothing but couples—"

"Right." His dad nodded.

As they droned on, Robby settled the headphones back over his ears and clicked "Play." He was listening to his "Birds of the Great Lakes" playlist, the one he had made just for the trip. It had all the regular birds he saw in the backyard—sparrows, cardinals, blue jays, plus the piping plovers, the Kirtland's warbler, and dozens of others.

It was his second playlist. He already had "Birds of New England," which started with Dr. Felk's favorite, the Bicknell's thrush. Listening to that one was usually relaxing. But today he kept glancing at his watch and then the car clock, which was two minutes ahead. Their trip was only three days long. He didn't want to waste any time.

They arrived at the Visitors Center with fifteen minutes to spare by his watch, thirteen by the car clock. Robby was outside before his dad even turned off the engine, galloping toward the entrance of the weathered, gray-blue building.

Inside he saw a lady wearing the ranger uniform he'd seen online, a gray shirt and green pants. She was standing in a little office separated from the lobby.

"Hi there. Can I help you?"

Robby stepped up to the counter between them. She had a pencil tucked behind her ear. Her name tag said she was Ruth Heron, park ranger.

"Like the lake?"

"Excuse me?" Her dark eyebrows pulled together.

"Your name. Like the lake?"

She looked down at her nametag. "Oh. No, that's Huron. H-U-R-O-N. Mine's Heron. Like the bird."

"Oh." Robby gazed past her thinking. Herons. He hadn't downloaded them yet. Would they belong on his Great Lakes playlist? Or New England?

She rested her elbows on the counter and leaned toward him. A long braid fell over her shoulder. "What's your name?"

"Robby."

"Hi, Robby. What brings you to the Sleeping Bear Dunes?"

The Sleeping Bear Dunes. Robby's brain pivoted. "Piping plovers."

Ruth cocked her head. "Do you want to see the plovers?"

Robby nodded.

"They're out in the park. Not here." She removed the pencil from behind her ear and tapped it on the counter twice as she spoke the last words.

There was a container of pencils on his side of the counter. Green, the same color as her pants. Robby took one.

"Then where?" Tap, tap.

"Well, we have multiple nesting sites."

"I want to see them all," Robby said, as the door opened behind him.

"You're welcome to do so, as long as you observe the breeding boundaries."

"Breeding boundaries?" It was his mom's voice.

"Yes." Ruth's eyes strayed to his parents. "Plovers are endangered birds, you know."

"Threatened," Robby said. "Threatened birds."

"In other locations that's true. On the East Coast, in the Great Plains. Here, they're endangered."

"That's worse, right?" His mom again.

"Yes." Ruth nodded. "And breeding's the most critical time of year. So our plover patrols fence off their nesting areas to protect them."

"What happens to them?" his dad asked.

"Predators get them." Robby answered, as Ruth opened her mouth. "Or people scare them off the nests. Throwing footballs around, leaving garbage that draws the predators."

"That's right," Ruth said. "You sound like you've been doing some research."

"That's an understatement," his dad said. "We've come up from Detroit just to see these birds."

"Is that right? Wait, I'll come out to join you." She disappeared through a doorway.

"What kind of predators?" his mom asked.

"Crows and gulls." Robby answered, bouncing on the balls of his feet, tapping the pencil again. "And raccoons, and dogs. Right?"

Ruth emerged around a corner, joining them in the lobby. The pencil was back behind her ear.

"Right." Ruth paused a moment. "Or the nests get washed out in a storm, if they're situated too close to the water's edge."

"Last year you lost four that way," Robby said.

"Right again." The ranger nodded. "But so far this year, we've been lucky."

"The patrols can't do anything about storms, though," his mom said.

"No. But they monitor the nests, make sure people observe the fenced-off perimeter. And provide the education. Most people are very respectful, really. We just get a few bad apples."

"I want to be on a patrol," Robby said.

"Oh, that's out of the question." Ruth shook her head, her dark braid flicking each shoulder. "Our monitor volunteers have all had special training. Piping plovers are very rare, special birds. Endangered, like I said. We have fewer than two dozen pairs here."

"I can learn." Robby crossed his arms, rolling the pencil behind his elbow.

His mom put her hand on his shoulder. "Robby, we're just here for a few days, you know." It was her *be reasonable* voice again.

He shrugged off her hand and looked at Ruth. "I know what a football looks like. I can pick up garbage. I can learn the rest."

"You're persistent, aren't you?" Ruth said.

"You can't even imagine," his mom said.

"And you're really interested in plovers," Ruth said.

Silently, Robby bobbed his head.

"He's in an Audubon club at home," his dad spoke up suddenly.

Robby looked up. *Again, his dad on his side.*

"He's very good at following directions. You wouldn't have to tell him what to do twice," his dad said.

The ranger hesitated, tapping her pencil again. "Monitoring I can't offer. But the local camera club's taking a plover hike tomorrow morning. Meets here at seven, before we open. You could come along to see them, anyway."

"That sounds pretty good, Robby." His mom was talking in her *isn't-that-nice* voice.

Robby hesitated. "Will we see all of them?"

"All the eggs haven't hatched yet. But we'll visit areas with both brooding chicks and nests, yes," Ruth said.

Robby thought about it. He wanted to be on the patrol. Ruth said the plovers were endangered, and that was even worse than threatened. So someone had to keep the dog walkers and kite flyers and predators away. Why couldn't they let him? He'd be the best patroller ever. No one would dare disturb the nests. Inside he felt the anger squeeze his stomach.

But the hike sounded good, too. Chicks and nests? What he read online had said all the eggs would be hatched by now. Ruth must know more, and she was going. She was OK. He would put the heron in the Great Lakes playlist. He rolled the pencil between his fingers, back and forth, thinking.

"Deal," he said.

"Morning, folks. I'm Ruth Heron, and I'll be leading our hike today." Robby glanced at his watch, pleased she was right on time. It was 6:58 a.m. Ruth wore a wide-brimmed hat and had another, single-lens device slung around her neck in addition to binoculars. His dad had given him his old Sears binoculars to wear around his neck, too. Everyone else in the group outside the Visitors Center had binoculars as well, plus a camera or two apiece.

"As you all know, the plovers are an endangered species here in the Great Lakes," Ruth said. "Their breeding season is under way, and so far this looks like a better-than-average year for fledging."

"How many nests?" asked a man with a tripod.

"Ten. With four eggs each, we'd hope to only lose half," Ruth said. Robby heard his mother gasp. "Only half? My goodness, that seems high."

"Survival of the fittest," Ruth said, flatly. "This year, though, we've had twenty-four hatch already, with a few nests still to go."

A murmur of appreciation went around the group. Robby saw Ruth smile briefly. It vanished just as quickly.

"Migration is still well over a month away, though," she said. "We'll caravan out to the north end of the park first. Most of you know the rules. Be quiet. Don't leave any trash, and pick up any that you see. Observe the roped-off breeding areas, and don't approach any plover families if you find them beyond the fence. Any questions?"

No one spoke. "All right. Take five minutes, fill up your water bottles, put on your sunscreen. We'll be out for a couple hours this morning, and it's going to get hot."

Water bottles and sunscreen. Robby looked anxiously at his mom. "Did you bring water bottles and sunscreen?"

She frowned. "I'll check in the car. Keys, Sam?"

His dad reached into his pocket as the others drifted apart. Robby jerked the strings on his sweatshirt, tightening the hood over his head, and then jammed his hands in his pockets. Would they be allowed to go on the hike if they didn't have the right stuff?

"Relax, Robby," his dad said.

Easy for him to say. He'd been waiting weeks and weeks and now, finally, the plovers were minutes away. Robby scuffed his toe into a clump of weeds growing in the sandy dirt and stooped to pick one. He had seen water bottles and sunscreen for sale in the Visitors Center yesterday, but it wasn't open yet today. Still, Ruth would have a key if they needed to get inside. Wouldn't she? He twirled the weed between his fingers, watching his mom rummage in the car.

"Ready to see your first piping plovers?"

Robby barely heard Ruth's voice beside him, shrouded in his hood and focused on the problem of water and sunscreen. Beyond the orbit of the weed's fuzzy green head, his mother slammed the car door and turned around. A water bottle dripped from one hand. In the other, a container that looked like it could be sunscreen, suspended from two fingers.

She'd found it. Robby felt limp as his anxiety drained away. They could go!

"Robby?" Ruth's hat was tilted to the side. "Ready to see your first piping plovers?"

"Yeah!" As his relief erupted, Robby jumped in the air, dropping the weed. Ruth stepped back quickly. Robby bounced on his toes, trampling the weed. A cloud of dust swirled up past his ankles.

"Here you go, Robby." His mom was there with the sticky sunscreen bottle. Robby wrinkled his nose.

"It stinks."

"Want me to do it?"

"No." He rubbed it over his face and legs, hard and fast, and thrust the bottle back at her. *Let's go, let's go. Let's go see the birds.*

"You've got a blob on your forehead. Here, let me." His mom reached for him.

Robby ducked, swatting her hand away.

"Come on, Robby."

"Linda." His dad came at them sideways, speaking quietly. "It's not worth it. Let it go."

His mom hesitated. "Fine," she said in her *not-fine* voice, capping the bottle.

"Sure you want to wear that sweatshirt?" Ruth asked. "It'll be hot on the beach."

"He'll be fine," his mom said quickly, as Robby nodded vehemently, thrusting his hands in the pocket.

"All right." Ruth shrugged. The four of them crossed the parking lot to join the rest of the group, dust clouds obscuring their feet.

"We really need rain," Ruth said, working her toe into the dusty lot. "It's been dry all spring."

"There's supposed to be a big storm tonight," volunteered an older man who carried a single-lens scope like Ruth's and wore a photographer's vest covered in pockets.

"I heard. Maybe it'll help us catch up." Ruth glanced around the group. "Everyone ready? All right. Let's go see some plovers."

In her park service truck she led the caravan out of the parking lot and turned north. Robby exhaled deeply, blowing his bangs out of his eyes. *Finally.*

After half an hour of trudging along the beach through ankle-deep sand, Sam paused to wait for Linda. Robby's gray sweatshirt receded as he trotted ahead with Ruth, oblivious to his lagging parents.

"How you doing?"

She wiped a strand of hair from her eyes. "Hot. Tired."

"At least we're not lugging camera gear like the rest of them. If this was a trail it'd be fine, but the sand just makes it brutal," Sam said. "I sink with every step."

"Life with Robby." Linda shrugged. "Even on vacation, we can't escape it."

Sam raised his eyebrows. "Not like you to be so pessimistic."

Linda sighed. "Sorry. Early onset summer blues, maybe. You know how he gets when school's out. Without those routines, he falls apart." She took a long drink from the water bottle.

"Maybe this year will be different. He's got his playlists, and the Audubon club and all."

"Yeah. But every time I let myself go there, thinking things are getting better, hoping, it blows up in my face. Stealth autism. Like with this whole birdcall obsession."

"What do you mean?"

"Oh, it was dumb. I should have known better."

"Come on. Tell me."

Linda hesitated. "OK. So, the calls, the songs, that's how birds communicate, right?"

"Right."

"Well, when Robby got so into them, after you went to that conference, I convinced myself it might make him start communicating more." She looked down at the sand, then up at Sam. "With us."

"Oh, Linda." Sam shook his head. He felt the familiar hollow gaping inside him, the hollow where the right words should be, if there were any words that could compensate for what Linda craved. "Jeez."

"But all he does is download those calls and make his playlists. Then he disappears into his headphones again. He's as isolated as ever."

She sighed. They walked silently for a moment.

"He seemed to connect with the ranger," Sam ventured.

"True." Linda's voice brightened. "I thought we were headed for a meltdown for sure yesterday, after she told him he couldn't do that patrol thing. But he kept it together."

"He's really into these birds, and she is, too." Ahead, Robby and Ruth's figures were no longer moving. Sam and Linda were gaining on the rest of the group. "Looks like we're almost there."

Ahead, the group had stopped twenty yards shy of a roped-off section of beach. The camera club members went into action, whipping out their tripods, mounting cameras, uncapping lenses. Robby lifted his binoculars to his eyes and stared out, too. *What does he see,* Sam wondered.

"Here we are. Home sweet plover home," Ruth said, raising her scope and training it down the beach. "If you'll all look for the exclosure—it looks just like a mesh box—that's down near that little spit, back from the shoreline—oh dear. Oh, no."

"What? What?" The group aimed their binoculars and scopes where Ruth had. Sam saw Ruth lower hers as the rest swept the beach. Briefly her head bowed before she spoke again, in a steady, resigned voice.

"I'm sorry, folks. If you look under the exclosure, you'll see a smashed egg. It's more speckled than the rocks around it. And I don't see any adult plovers around. It appears that this is a deserted nest."

"What happened?" the man in the photographer's vest asked.

"I wish I could tell you. Probably a predator got it—either the eggs, the parents, or both."

"But isn't the exclosure supposed to protect them?" a woman asked.

Ruth shrugged. "It doesn't always work. The parent plovers have to go in and out to feed. If something happens to one while it's out, the other abandons the nest."

"Why?" It was Linda's voice.

"That's just the way it is. Incubation is shared. Depending on the timing, the one who survives might find another mate and start a new nest."

"Really? Right away?" Linda asked.

Ruth nodded. "Plovers aren't sentimental. They find another mate and get on with it."

"There's Mother Nature for you," commented the man with the vest.

Plovers aren't sentimental, Sam thought, the hollow inside him yawning again. Like someone else he knew, he thought, glancing over at Robby.

But Robby wasn't there.

Sam's pulse quickened. Instinctively he spun to the lake. The calm dark-blue surface rippled placidly, stretching uninterrupted to the horizon. Sam felt an instant of relief, followed by another stab of alarm. Where could—

"Hey! Ruth!" It was Robby's voice. Sam looked up. His son was twenty yards down the beach, standing right next to the rope, waving.

"Ruth! Two more eggs!"

"Robby!" Linda shook her head. "You're supposed to stay back!"

But Ruth was striding across the sand. "Show me!"

The man with the photographer vest hesitated, then pulled up his tripod and followed her. Sam looked at Linda and shrugged. They jogged to the rope, where Robby was pointing.

"There, by that fallen log, about five feet from the smashed one. The log kind of shadows them right now, but I think—"

"I see them. You're right. Two eggs. You've got sharp eyes, Robby," Ruth said. "I've got to radio this in right now."

"Who do you call?" Robby asked.

"Dispatch, to send a patrol out. We need to start monitoring immediately, to determine if the parents are still around and tending the nest. If they're not, we'll collect those eggs and try to raise them in captivity."

"Will you keep them together?" Robby asked, his eyes pinned on Ruth's face.

"Definitely," Ruth said, reaching for her radio on her hip, taking in the group that had followed. "Back down the beach, now, all of you," she commanded. "We don't want to scare the parents, if they are still around."

Robby backed away, keeping his eyes on the exclosure.

Linda herded him away from the group. "Robby, you knew the rules. What made you go so close?"

"Ruth said the parents abandoned the nest."

"Yes, but—"

"And she only saw one smashed egg. There's supposed to be four." He was still walking backward.

"OK, but Robby—"

"So I had to find out about the others. I was worried about them."

"You were *worried* about them?" Linda stared at Robby.

"Yeah." Robby nodded.

"He was worried," Linda whispered, grabbing Sam's arm. "He was *worried*!"

"I stayed behind the rope," Robby said. "That was the rule. 'Observe the roped-off breeding areas.'"

Sam smiled to himself. That was the rule. Word for word.

"I had to find out," Robby repeated, looking up at Sam.

"It's OK, Robby." Squeezing Linda's hand, Sam looked over his shoulder. Ruth was tucking away her radio now, jogging toward them, her long braids swinging off her shoulders. Seeing her, too, Robby stopped.

"Monitors are on their way," she reported. "They'll look around for the fourth egg, too, but my guess is a predator got it." She turned to Robby. "Robby, I'm so glad you were here. Spotting those eggs gives us another chance. Great work." She held her hand up for a high five.

Sam watched as Robby, without a moment's hesitation, slapped hands with Ruth. And his unsentimental son smiled.

The plover patrol summoned, they continued hiking down the beach. At the next stop they watched two parent plovers tend a full brood of four chicks running around the beach. Following the photographer's cue, Robby lay on his stomach, chin propped on the sand, to get a better view.

"These four hatched day before yesterday," Ruth said.

"Really?" Linda said, surprised. "And they're already running around?"

Ruth nodded. "Plovers only stay in the nest their first hour or so."

"You're kidding," Linda said. "They don't sound very nurturing."

"You're looking at it through human eyes. It's different in the wild," Ruth said. "Now the goal is independence. These guys have to be ready for a thousand-mile flight in six to eight weeks."

Sam felt Robby at his elbow.

"Your turn to look, Dad!"

"What?"

"The plovers. Feeding and playing together." He lifted the strap over his head. "Take a look."

"Yeah?" Sam raised the binoculars to his eyes. "Show me where."

"Middle of the beach. Beyond those stones where their nest was. See it? Do you see them?"

Sam scanned the sand slowly. "No."

"Get down like this." Robby splayed himself on the sand again. Sam hesitated, then awkwardly crouched next to Robby.

"Let's take just a few more minutes. We've got one more nest to see yet," Ruth announced.

Sam panned the beach again more quickly. Frustration swelled as he recalled another journey, undertaken another day, hundreds of miles from this beach, but destined to be just as isolating. The autism evaluation team had pushed their written assessment of Robby across the conference table at him and Linda. Bold black check marks appeared next to each of the diagnostic criteria. Sam remembered the first one best:

Qualitative impairment in social interaction . . . a lack of spontaneous seeking to share enjoyment or interests . . .

Now here was Robby, spontaneously sharing his interest in these birds. And Sam couldn't find the damn things.

"Aim one eye on the water and one on the beach." It was Ruth's voice. "They're closer to the shoreline than you'd think."

Sam adjusted his gaze. Still nothing. Then he heard it, the sequence of mid-range peeps he remembered from Robby's computer. He swung the binoculars that way.

"There, Dad, right there!" Robby knocked his elbow, tilting the binoculars. And then Sam saw them: four tiny, dirty-white birds on stick legs.

"I see them! I see them, Robby. And I can hear them, too."

"Seeing an endangered species in their native habitat is a rare privilege," Ruth told the group. "Especially with their young."

"Isn't it cool, Dad? Mom, do you want to see? Let her look."

"Sure." Linda crouched down next to him, beaming.

Sam handed the binoculars over, feeling the hollow inside fill with an unfamiliar blend of flavors. Gratification. Contentment. Wonder.

"Here, take these," offered the man with the photo vest. "I've got an extra set."

"Thanks," Sam said. Alongside their son he and Linda watched, basking in the rare privilege of the moment.

TWENTY-FOUR

"Let's just stop here for a second, Christopher."

Turning, Christopher saw Arthur Felk heading toward a bench a few steps off the trail. Though he was a good twenty paces behind, Christopher could hear him panting. He frowned. They had been out for less than half an hour on the easiest path through the Sapsucker Woods sanctuary, and Felk was already winded. How could the ornithologist have thought he could handle the rocky peaks and elevations of northern Vermont?

Dr. Felk had called a few weeks ago to change their plans for the Bicknell's thrush hunt. He planned to set up an endowment, he said, and wanted to take both Christopher and Deborah out to dinner to talk it over. He'd arrive after lunch, and in the afternoon, they could explore the sanctuary instead.

"You know Deborah's in the law school advancement office. Not the Lab's," he reminded Felk.

"I know, Christopher," Felk said. "Just invite her, OK?"

Reluctantly he left a message for Deborah, but she hadn't called back. Now he wondered if they'd make it to dinner themselves. He joined Felk on the bench and held out his water bottle.

The older man nodded gratefully, taking a long drink. Sweat beaded along his brow, Christopher noticed as he tipped his head back. Even with Felk having more than two decades on Christopher, the flat, shady trail shouldn't have caused that kind of exertion.

"Dr. Felk, are you OK?"

"Fine, fine. Just give me a minute to catch my breath."

Christopher waited a minute, then two, then three. Gradually Felk's panting slowed to normal breathing. He turned his head and met Christopher's eyes, accepting his scrutiny. He seemed about to speak when a high-pitched trill pierced the quiet.

Felk turned his face upward and cupped his ear. The trill sounded again, a repeating staccato. "Tell me."

"Swamp sparrow," replied Christopher.

"No doubt," the older man replied, smiling in satisfaction. "You always had one of my best ears."

"So don't I deserve to hear the truth?"

Felk turned to look at him again. He tried to smile, but it wobbled at the corners. "Not much to tell. What you see is what you get. I'm getting old, Christopher. And slowing down."

"You're not sick?"

"Not acutely. Oh, I've got arthritis and high blood pressure. Had a bad cough last winter that took months to kick. Nothing that taking twenty years off wouldn't cure."

"How old are you?"

"I'll be seventy-five this year."

"Is that why you're up here now to set up an endowment?" Christopher asked.

"One reason. I wanted to see you, of course."

"I would have come to New York, you know."

"I know. But I wanted to see Deborah, too. She'll meet us for dinner?"

"I hope so. I left her a message. But I haven't heard back."

"You left her a message?" Felk's face turned quizzical. "You couldn't just mention it over breakfast?"

237

"I'm afraid not. Deborah and I aren't living together now," Christopher said. With the words he felt relief wash over him. Though their separation was old grist for Cornell's gossip mill, he hadn't confided in anyone since he requested use of the vacant apartment from Peter. Four months on, keeping up his professional façade as the unruffled, collected scientist while living alone in the apartment was far more draining than he'd expected.

"Christopher. I'm so sorry. What's happened?"

Felk had never married anything but his work, yet Christopher found himself telling the older man everything, interrupted only by the swamp sparrow. Their years of infertility struggles. Deborah's plea after the crash. His agreement to try one last round. Helen's diagnosis. Deborah's deceit. His departure.

Even the ultrasound picture, which had remained in his wallet since Deborah dropped it on the restaurant table.

When he was finished, Felk drew in a deep breath. He opened his mouth, then closed it, looking off in the distance. Once more the swamp sparrow's repeating trill resounded through Sapsucker Woods. Felk's face relaxed and he smiled.

"What are you thinking?" Christopher asked.

Felk turned back. He regarded Christopher for another long moment, then spoke.

"Have you had a chance to review that thumb drive from Robby Palmer?"

Christopher's mind spun at the change of subject. "The boy from the conference in Michigan?"

Felk nodded.

Christopher hesitated. "Briefly, yes. But I couldn't make heads or tails of the files. And like I told you before, if he's going to apply to bird camp next year, it would be a conflict of interest for me to review it."

Felk nodded, looking unconcerned about ethics. "Would you like to guess what my endowment is going to fund?"

"I assume ornithology research, naturally."

Felk shook his head.

"Then I'm at a loss." Christopher felt forlorn, too. Didn't Felk have anything to say about his story?

"The Benjamin J. Felk Chair in Autism Advocacy will be jointly established and awarded between the law school and the medical school."

Christopher contemplated his words. "So that's why you wanted to talk to Deborah."

"Yes."

"You're doing this for your brother."

Felk smiled again slightly, looking up into the trees. "Most people will think that. But I'm really doing it for me. Call it atonement."

"Atonement? For what happened to your brother in the institution? You were his—his savior." The religious word felt awkward on his tongue.

"No, I was too late. Oh, his life was happier after we moved him. But it wasn't appreciably better. Intervention, therapy has to come early to be effective. But it's not too late for Robby. Or the millions of kids like him."

Felk looked straight at him. "Don't let it become too late for you and Deborah and your child, either, Christopher."

Deborah stretched and yawned. She had fought off her two o'clock drowsiness, but it was coming back more powerfully now as a three thirty coma. She could duck out early; Phillip was away at a conference. Angela buzzed her line.

"I'm just on my way out, Angela."

"Sorry. There's someone here to see you."

She groaned softly. "Who is it?"

"His name's Arthur Felk. He says he's an alumnus, and he wants to set up an endowment."

Arthur Felk? Christopher's mentor, the grandfatherly ornithologist from New York?

"He's here in person?" Deborah frowned to herself. Who drove for four hours without making an appointment first?

"Standing right in front of me." Her voice dropped to a whisper. "He doesn't look so good, Deborah."

She sighed. "All right. I'll be right out."

"OK. Sir, can I get you something? Water, or perhaps iced tea?"

"Water, please, young lady." Deborah heard Felk's voice faintly before Angela hung up.

Hastily she tidied the papers on her desk, closed her e-mail window, and removed her purse from the spare chair. Good enough.

Angela telegraphed her worry as she passed the reception desk. Deborah sat down quickly, before Dr. Felk could try to get up. His face was chalky, yet he was sweating. The water bottle Angela provided was already almost empty.

"Dr. Felk? Are you all right?"

He smiled and dodged her question. "Deborah. It's been a long time."

She nodded. "I'm delighted to see you. But I'm worried. You look exhausted."

"I could say the same thing about you." He watched her intently as he drained the last of the water.

Deborah's cheeks grew hot. She placed her palm over her swollen stomach. "That's pretty common when you're pregnant."

"As it is in your seventies. I'm fine. I may have overdone it a bit with Christopher on the trails just now, but another half hour in this air conditioning and another bottle of water and I'll be as good as, well, sixty, anyway." He smiled at his joke.

"You saw Christopher?" Deborah sat up straighter.

"Just came from a hike with him at the sanctuary. Beautiful place. And that new building. Amazing what's happened around here since my day." He swallowed the last of the water. "He told me he wasn't able to reach you about dinner, so I thought I'd just stop by here."

"I'm sorry about that," Deborah said, her cheeks flushing again. "I—"

"Perhaps we could go to your office," Felk suggested. Color was returning to his own cheeks, and he was no longer sweating. On their way down the hall she got another bottle of water.

"So Angela mentioned that you're interested in setting up an endowment," she said, closing her door. "I can get you started, but the Lab has its own development staff that will need to get involved. We're honored that you—" Deborah was warming to her boilerplate donor spiel when Felk laid his hand on hers.

The unexpected gesture froze her words midsentence. Looking into the older man's kind blue eyes, she repeated herself, trying to resume the rhythm. "We're honored that you would include Cornell in your estate plans. As you know, of course, Cornell is a world-class—"

"Deborah. May I talk, please?"

"By all means." She looked at her hand, still covered by his wrinkled one. "First rule of fundraising. The donor always gets to do the talking."

He smiled, patting her hand before lifting his. "I do want to set up an endowment. But it won't have anything to do with the Lab."

"It won't?"

"I'm interested in endowing a chair that will be jointly overseen by both law and medicine. So you and your office will indeed be involved. But that's not really why I stopped by."

"Law and medicine?" Donor whims were nothing new, but for

someone who had spent a career in such a specialized field as ornithology, a deviation was unusual. "May I ask why?"

"You may. After I tell you why I did stop by."

She flushed. "I'm sorry. It's really none of my business."

"Well, we'll be even then. Because this is really none of my business, either. But, Deborah, it upsets me to hear about your situation with Christopher."

She stiffened. "I don't have a situation with Christopher anymore. He chose to move out. Out of the house. Out of my life. Our lives," she added.

"That's unfortunate. I wish he hadn't."

"I think you're talking to the wrong person, Dr. Felk."

"Oh, I told Christopher, too. Absolutely."

"And what did he say?" Deborah laid her hands on her belly. *Relax. Breathe.*

"He's still angry. About what he considers your deceit."

"I see." Deborah swallowed hard.

"I didn't come to talk about how you got here, Deborah." Felk leaned forward and laid his hand on hers again. "You did what you did to protect someone you loved. Someone vulnerable. I understand that. It's a powerful motivator."

Gratefully, Deborah nodded.

He sat back and clasped his own hands. "But I do want to talk about where you go from here. I know what it's like to grow up without a parent, though it was my mother I lost."

"I'm sorry," Deborah said softly.

He nodded. "Decades ago now, but I still remember how I felt. How lonely. Scared. Angry. I don't want your child to feel that way."

"Again, I think you're talking to the wrong person, Dr. Felk. I can't make Christopher forgive and forget. And I apparently can't convince him that the reward of parenthood is worth the risk of the unknown."

"But now that's still abstract. The baby will be real. He showed me the picture, Deborah."

"He did?"

"Keeps it in his wallet."

Deborah leaned back, digesting that.

"Have you ever heard that you learn what you need to learn when you need to learn it?" His blue eyes were locked on hers.

Deborah shook her head.

"I forget who said it, but it's true. When the baby's born, that's when Christopher will realize he's a father. I know it." Dr. Felk's face was somehow both fierce and plaintive as he implored her. "What I'm asking you to do is just keep the door open. Don't shut him out. Please, don't shut him out."

~

Brett heard a car door slam as she carried the garbage bag to the garage. Amanda stepped out of Abby's car, her hair still wet from the pool. Probably headed to work next. She had her first part-time job this summer, working at the Dairy Queen a couple blocks away. Brett's news would yank her another step into adulthood. Guilt surged as she slung the bag into the garbage can. It was supposed to be the other way around—the baby bird leaving the nest.

"Have fun at the pool?" Brett walked back across the yard to the picnic table.

"Sure." Amanda shrugged indifferently, heading for the door.

"Come and sit with me for a minute, OK?" Brett patted the picnic bench. Her hand kept time with her thumping heart.

"I've got to get ready for work. I start at five." Amanda's hand was on the doorknob.

"This won't take long. Promise."

Amanda heaved a sigh, trudged to the picnic table, and sat, dropping her duffel bag between her feet. "Well?"

Brett swallowed. Her rehearsed words had fled. "I have some news."

"Yeah?"

She wasn't going to make it easy. Brett took a deep breath and plowed ahead. "You know things have been kind of uncomfortable around here lately."

Amanda snorted. "The understatement of the year."

Brett ignored the sarcasm. "I understand you're angry. Your father, too. And since it was me who brought all this on, we decided"—she paused, swallowing hard—"we decided it would be best if I moved out."

She peered at her daughter's face. This was the crucial part to get right. She could live with the guilt if she got it right. Amanda's well-being was best served by staying in Scranton, believing it was Brett who chose to move, rather than Richard who forced her. Angry as she was at Richard, Brett couldn't make Amanda choose sides and uproot her from friends and school. Secretly, she hoped some space would allow Amanda to accept her more quickly. But drained of her defensive sarcasm, Amanda's face made her doubtful already.

"Move out? You're moving out?"

"Yes." Brett paused. "I've got a new job. I start next month."

"Next month?" Amanda whispered.

"Yes."

Amanda looked as pale as the vanilla ice cream she'd soon be serving. And Brett hadn't yet revealed the most explosive part.

"Wha—what kind of job? Where are you going to work?"

Here goes the rest of my life.

"I've been accepted as the director of a food pantry in a city in upstate New York. Ithaca, New York."

"Oh, my God." Amanda's voice cracked the gulf of her guilt wider. "New York. You're moving out—*next month*—to take a job in New York?"

Brett nodded mutely.

"What about me?"

"You'll stay here, with Dad. We talked about it. We think that's the best thing. Not to uproot you from school, especially from the drama program. Or your friends. And now your job . . ." Brett's voice trailed off, realizing how ridiculous that part sounded.

"I'll come visit, of course. And I hope you'll come visit me. Ithaca's only about a hundred miles from Scranton. And you'll be getting your license soon."

"Come visit you," Amanda repeated.

"Yes." Brett nodded eagerly. "I thought maybe we could go apartment-hunting together next week. I won't be able to afford much, but I'm hoping for at least a two-bedroom. One for you."

"My own bedroom. Like that's going to make everything OK?" Amanda exclaimed, jumping up from the table. "You couldn't get a job here in Scranton?"

"Well, I didn't really think about that, Amanda." *Don't mention Richard's ultimatum. Don't mention it. Don't mention it. Don'tmentionit.* "This opportunity came up, and it's a great match for my skills, and—"

"Not such a great match for your family. But no big deal, Amanda will be fine. She's always fine." Amanda snatched her duffel bag. "All right. You've told me your news. Congratulations. Congratulations, Mom, on your new job. I hope you'll be very happy in Ithaca." She stalked into the house, the screen door slamming behind her.

Left alone at the picnic table, Brett barely felt the heat of the June day as a chill as raw as the January wind on the Hudson River whipped at her heart.

TWENTY-FIVE

B oom.

In his bed in the dark hotel room, Robby stirred, rubbing his eyes. In his dreams, rain cascaded from the clouds like waterfalls. Waves pounded the beach. The plovers scattered, losing each other in the dark. The babies cheeped, seeking their parents. *Cheep, cheep, cheep.*

Boom.

His eyes fluttered open. Thunder. The storm the man on the hike predicted. For real.

Pushing off the blankets, he swung his feet to the floor and stood. Thud. That was his *Sibley's Guide to Birds* that he'd taken into bed, sliding to the floor. He'd been writing a postcard to Paula on top of it, telling her about the eggs. Robby winced and glanced over at the other bed. His mom and dad were indistinct lumps, shrouded under the blankets, both turned away from his bed and the window. He waited a moment, but they didn't move. The digital clock on the nightstand between the beds read 2:18 a.m.

He parted the heavy draperies. A crack of lightning flashed a zigzag line, and the sky vibrated. One, two, three, four, five. One mile. Six, seven, eight, nine, ten. Two miles. Eleven, twelve, thirteen, fourteen—

Boom.

Less than three miles away, according to the rule he learned in Mrs. Kowalski's science class. Storms usually moved west to east. So it would have already passed the park. Robby pressed his forehead to the glass. Were they safe? On the morning hike Lake Michigan was calm, but they had pictures in the Visitors Center of waves five feet high, crashing on the beach where they nested. What about the eggs? Ruth said washouts were—

Behind him, he heard a cough. His mom rolled over. Quickly, Robby slid back into bed, his back to her. He didn't want questions.

The drapes stayed parted an inch. Through the rain-spattered window he watched the sky pulse with lightning, worrying and waiting for dawn and answers.

Outside the SUV's window, orchards and fields of corn made a blur of green along the highway between Traverse City and the Sleeping Bear Dunes. "Knee high by the Fourth of July," his mom had remarked yesterday. Robby repeated the line to himself, liking the rhyme even though it was ridiculously meaningless. Whose knee?

The monochromatic view was soothing. He was still worried about the storm last night.

"They're OK, right?" he asked. The road was still wet, even though the sun had been up for hours. The storm must have been really bad out here.

"We'll see, Robby," his mom said.

It was her maddening *nonanswer* voice. Robby sighed, yanking his sweatshirt strings to tighten his hood, and pushed his feet down on the floor, willing the car to go faster. He had to find Ruth. She would know.

At the Visitors Center he sprinted across the parking lot to the building. Ruth wasn't at the admissions desk, and she wasn't in the big room with the maps and topographic models, and she wasn't in the little auditorium where a video about the park played on a continuous loop. Robby was out the door again, almost colliding with his parents. Behind them he spotted one of the white park service trucks pulling in. Through the open window he saw Ruth at the wheel.

"Ruth!" He pounded down the parking lot, behind the building, to the area reserved for park vehicles. "The plovers are OK, right? They made it through the storm."

From behind her sunglasses, Ruth stared down at him. She opened the door, climbing down to crouch beside him, at eye level. She pushed her sunglasses on top of her head. Her eyes looked shiny.

"They're OK, right?" He jerked the sweatshirt strings, drawing his hood so tight his eyelashes brushed the cinched edge.

Slowly, Ruth shook her head. "I'm sorry. The storm washed out two nests."

Robby counted up quickly as his parents joined them. "Eight eggs?"

"Six. Two were already gone."

"Well, there're still eight nests left then, right?" his mom now spoke in her brisk, *let's move on now*, voice.

"Counting the deserted one from yesterday, only seven," corrected Ruth. "It's absolutely devastating. Plus, we've not confirmed the whereabouts of the breeding adults from those nests."

"Oh," his mother said in a small voice.

"I'm so sorry, Robby," Ruth said. Still crouched down, she put her hand on his shoulder. "I wish there was something we could've done."

He twisted away from her hand, balling his fists. The throbbing was starting, his limbs turning rigid. "Any we saw yesterday?"

Ruth nodded. "The last one."

The throbbing accelerated, moving up his body, from his churning stomach to his shoulders to his ears, where it roared and pounded, drowning out the adults' voices. The last one. The four pristine eggs he had been so relieved to see, after the disappointment of the smashed one and the fear for the orphaned pair. He recalled the wave from his dream, a cold, noisy invader, thrashing the beach, sucking the eggs and their pebble nest into its swirling turbulence. It was all a waste. The exclosures and the plover patrols and coming up here. All of it. The plovers' song was silenced. The plovers were dead.

"UnnnhhhhHHH!" The throbbing poured out his mouth in a guttural roar. His arms and legs vibrated. He pounded the truck door and kicked the tires on Ruth's truck. He felt his father grab him under his armpits, trying to pull him away. Lunging for the truck's side-view mirror he held on, still kicking at the tires.

Unprotected by his summer sandals, his toe smashed against the hard rubber. Pain ascended over the throbbing, and he became deadweight, knocking his dad over backward. They both sprawled onto the damp dirt of the parking lot, Robby's keening fading to a whimper. Then silence.

Robby stared up into the blue sky. He didn't know how much time had passed. His mother's face hovered at the edges. And another woman, sunglasses on her head. She had her hands on her hips. The ranger. Ruth. He turned his head. His dad, brushing dirt off his legs, reached down to pull him up.

"That was a meltdown," he heard his mom tell Ruth. "This happens a lot when Robby gets overwhelmed. It's part of his having autism."

Ruth just stared at him. In a fluid motion she stooped to pluck a weed from the parking lot. She twirled it between her thumb and forefinger a few times. Clockwise. Counterclockwise. Clockwise. After she was sure Robby was watching her, she extended it to him.

His fingers closed over the thin stalk. The rain had nourished it, too. The stem felt stronger and looked greener than the dry, browning one he had picked yesterday. Rolling it as Ruth had, between his thumb and forefinger, he concentrated on how the movement felt, rather than the twirling, fuzzy head. With his index finger he rolled it along the pad of his thumb, one, two, three, four, five until his finger couldn't bend anymore. Then slowly he straightened it, one, two, three, four, five until the two fingers were parallel. And back, keeping the pressure even. And forward. Ruth waited.

"I understand feeling angry and sad. I am, too. But you can't let it get the better of you. There's still so much we can do to help them. Believe me." She cleared her throat. "Remember the eggs you spotted yesterday?"

Robby nodded.

"We collected those early yesterday afternoon, after our patrol volunteers monitored for four hours with no sign of the parents or the fourth egg. They're up at our captive-rearing facility now."

"What happens there?" Robby said.

"I've got a Skype call update in ten minutes. You can come to my office and see for yourself if you'd like. As long as your foot's OK."

"Yes," Robby answered instantly. Before his parents could say anything.

"Let's go," Ruth said, leading the way.

Ruth sat down in the lone desk chair that constituted the seating in her cramped office. Robby craned his neck, trying to see her laptop screen. As soon as she logged in, a man's face filled the screen.

"Morning, Ruth." He wore a T-shirt and glasses and didn't look nearly as official as Ruth.

"Hi, Josh. I've got some folks with me today. They were on the hike when we found the eggs yesterday. Robby here actually spotted them." Ruth turned the laptop slightly.

Robby saw his own face, encircled with his hood, appear next to Ruth's in a little square in the bottom corner of the screen. Right next to hers. He looked down. He hadn't realized they were practically rubbing shoulders. He took a step away. His face moved out of the square on the screen. He hesitated, then shuffled back a half step. His face reappeared.

"Hey, Robby." Josh smiled. "Good work. You gonna be a biologist someday?"

Robby shrugged, turning to Ruth. "Where are the eggs?"

"Let's ask. Fill us in, Josh?"

"Everything's great. Starting with, there's just one egg now."

Beside him, Robby felt Ruth's body tense before he heard it in her voice. "Just one? What—"

On the screen, Josh's face receded as he backed away. Now Robby could see what looked like a big plastic box with a bright light over it. Hands grabbed the laptop and carried it closer to the box. Inside, Robby could see one egg.

And one chick.

Beside him Ruth's body relaxed. He felt her hand grip his shoulder. Her voice was relieved, light.

"It's hatched. Look, Robby, it's hatched!"

"Got here a few hours ago and found this one," Josh's disembodied voice said.

"Is it male or female?" Robby asked.

"We won't know till adulthood. Unless we do DNA testing," Josh said.

"Either way, it's fantastic." Ruth leaned back against her chair, smiling.

"Wow." His mom's voice, faintly.

"Way to go, Robby." His dad's? Or Ruth's? Robby didn't know. He was riveted to the screen. He could see now why plovers belonged on beaches, where they blended with the sand and pebbles. In the stark, sterile box, the tiny chick looked so alone. It was a female, he decided. Her parents had deserted her. One sibling was smashed on the beach. One was missing. One was still in its shell.

"Will the other one hatch soon?" he asked.

"I think so," Josh's voice answered. "Eggs in a clutch usually hatch within a day or so of each other."

"What happens now?"

"They'll stay at the biological station for about thirty days," Ruth said. "They'll be able to fly then, and we'll bring them back here and release them."

"Release them?" Robby turned from the screen to look at Ruth.

"For their winter migration. They'll need to head south. Look."

From a pile of papers she grabbed a US map. The Great Lakes were dotted with Xs. So was the Atlantic coastline from North Carolina to Florida.

"We'll band these before releasing them, so we can keep track of them. Eventually they'll show up on the map."

"Back here?"

"Probably not. Nesting where they were born would lead to inbreeding. They need to find their own territory."

"Oh." Robby looked at his feet. Ruth sounded excited, and so did the man in the computer. But the odds against the tiny bird, all alone in the world, seemed huge. And his toe hurt.

"Robby, I won't lie to you. There are no guarantees. Mortality's high on the plover's first migration. We lose more than half. But we don't have a choice about whether they go. It's biology.

"But we do have a choice about what we do here. This—" Ruth swept her arm, taking in her office and the laptop, "all this doesn't happen by accident. It happens when people do the right thing. Like setting aside this park to begin with. Like watching and observing them in their habitat—just like you did yesterday. Keeping records and providing assistance when we can, like with the exclosures and the banding and the captive rearing." She paused. "Even being sad when they're harmed. Because if you weren't sad, it would mean you didn't care."

Silence filled the room. Robby could see dust floating where the sun streamed in the window. On the computer screen the little chick seemed to be pecking the bottom of the box. Then he heard something. A faint cheep. He stepped closer to the computer.

Again. Cheep, cheep.

Robby pushed back his hood and tilted his head down to hear better, closing his eyes to block any distractions.

Cheep, cheep. Louder now. And maybe stronger?

Opening his eyes, Robby's gaze fell on the map. There were lots of Xs. Lots of places for this little one to go. Lots of places where people would be on the lookout next summer. And even though they were going home later today, now he could Skype with Ruth and Josh and check in on her. Until it was time to release her.

He touched the chick on the screen so it looked like it was pecking his finger. He exhaled deeply, blowing his bangs out of his eyes. Behind him, he heard his mom sniff. Suddenly, Ruth's radio crackled.

"Platte Point patrol one to ranger. Platte Point patrol one to ranger. Over."

Ruth lifted the radio off her hip. "Ruth here. Go ahead, Platte Point. Over."

"Reporting four new chicks at Platte Point. Nest ten. We'll need to schedule the banding crew out here. Over."

"Copy that, Platte Point." Ruth pushed back her chair and looked at Robby. She had a question on her face.

Robby looked back and nodded. "Let's go."

TWENTY-SIX

Moving day, July 3, broke hot, humid, and silent. Richard had left for church. Amanda, whose cool distance had hardened to frozen estrangement over the past weeks, was spending the night at Abby's. Her heart a crater in her chest, Brett had agreed to the sleepover, brightly promising to call from Ithaca.

Leafing through the newspaper as she drank her coffee, Brett noticed the date. She'd officially begin her new life in Ithaca on Independence Day. Images flashed through her mind. Sailing on the ferry with Jackie. Making the guest room into her own. Stumbling upon the Ithaca job posting. She'd felt giddy, almost intoxicated with freedom. She tried to dredge up a remnant of those feelings, but when it was permanent and final, independence was a lot scarier.

Carrying her coffee cup to the sink, she looked out the window to the bird feeder, hanging empty and still in the thick summer air. The moving truck was due in fifteen minutes. She had only one task left, and then she'd be ready.

When Amanda came home, she found a gift bag on her bed. Inside was a cell phone and an envelope. Her mother's neat handwriting filled the lined paper inside.

Dear Amanda, she read. *I know you're unhappy with me, and scared, and angry. If I could make this easier for you I would, but that would mean more lies.*

I'm going to miss you terribly, and I'm worried about you. I'm going to call you often. I got you this cell phone so we could talk privately. You might not want to talk to me, at least for a while, but when you do, you'll have it.

In the meantime, I'm leaving you something else that helped me all these years, when I was feeling unhappy and scared and angry. You got me the bird feeder for Christmas when you were about four. I'm sure your dad helped you pick it out, but I'll never forget your face—so excited—when I opened it on Christmas morning.

Filling that feeder all these years, I've learned that when someone else depends on you, you take care of yourself. That's how I coped. I knew you were counting on me to be there.

You'll always be my daughter. But you don't need me like that anymore. It's my chance to spread my wings. I hope someday you can understand why I have to do this now.

Please feed the birds for me, Amanda. I'll know you're OK if you're feeding the birds. I love you.

Mom

Tucked inside the envelope was a twenty-dollar bill with a Post-it note stuck to it, also in her mother's handwriting. *Wilson's gets bulk feed in end of September.* And a second Post-it, with two phone numbers. *Mine. Yours.*

Clutching the letter in one hand, Amanda dropped onto her bed, her sobs echoing in the empty house.

～

"Good afternoon, Deborah DeWitt-Goldman."

Christopher exhaled with relief. After what seemed like half a dozen rounds of phone tag, he was finally speaking to her.

"It's Christopher."

"Christopher. Can I call you back? I'm right in the middle of something."

Her urgency sounded manufactured. *It's not too late*, Arthur Felk had told him. But it was only getting later.

"No, you can't call me back. We've been talking to voice mail for two weeks now."

"I've been busy. I've kind of got a lot going on now, in case you hadn't noticed." Deborah was not normally sarcastic. Neither was he, but he couldn't squelch it now.

"I had noticed. You showed me a picture, in fact."

"Oh, so you looked at it, then?"

Only about a hundred times since, he thought but did not say.

"Of course. And I wanted to talk to you about it. But you dropped that picture in front of me and then just left."

"Kind of like you did, back in February."

Touché. And ouch. He didn't know what to say. A pause stretched between them. Deborah spoke again, sounding apologetic.

"This is silly. We sound like children ourselves."

"I guess so," Christopher conceded.

"I'm sorry about all the messages. I really have been busy, and I guess I just don't know what to say anymore."

Christopher didn't know either, so he steered the conversation away from themselves. "Dr. Felk wants to meet with you."

"He already came to see me."

"He did?"

"Right after your hike."

"Such as it was." Christopher thought back to the abbreviated trek. "Did you set up the endowment for him?"

"I'm helping him get started. A joint endowment is complicated. Then after I'm gone, the medical school development staff will take over."

"After you're gone?" Christopher sat up.

"On my maternity leave." He caught a prickly note in her voice again, as if he'd forgotten the main subject.

"But that's not till November, right?"

"Actually, I'm starting at the end of September. I've got vacation and sick time I need to use before the end of the year, so I'm going to take it easy for a bit before she's born."

Before she's born. There it was again, that feminine pronoun that made everything feel so much more real. And September was next month already. "Phillip's OK with that?"

"I don't need him to be OK with it, Christopher. I'm entitled to the leave. It's policy."

"And it's three months?"

"Four. And I'll be entitled to more vacation at the start of the new year that I'll tack on. So I expect I'll be off until at least the first of April."

"You've made a lot of plans, haven't you?"

Deborah laughed, but there was no humor in it. "Someone has to, Christopher."

"How's Helen?" He allowed a note of accusation in his voice. He wanted to remind her. She was as responsible as he for their split, for bearing the burden of planning the future.

He reached for his wallet and found the picture. The black-and-white print had faded to a purplish-brown, like a bruise. The date stamp was three months ago. How much would she have changed by now, his daughter? As much as her mother? As much as him? Less than three months to go now. Was it enough time for him to get over Deborah's deceit? Could he ever, if she continued to refuse to accept any responsibility for their circumstances?

"She's doing fairly well, all things considered. I'm going out to see her in October, after my leave starts." The manufactured urgency returned to her voice. "Really, Christopher, I've got to get to a meeting now."

"You're flying to Seattle? That late in the pregnancy? Is that safe?"

"The doctor assured me it'll be fine."

"OK. Well, I . . ." He paused. He'd what? See her later? Talk to her later? Call her later? Soon? Nothing sounded quite right, yet he wanted something that implied future contact.

"I miss you," he said suddenly.

The words surprised him. There was a long pause. He heard what sounded like a choked-off sniff. Then, "Good-bye, Christopher."

On her end, Deborah leaned back, one hand still holding the phone, the other splayed over her belly. Her brain and heart reeled in opposite directions. *Leave the door open*, Dr. Felk had implored. Though she had agreed, she honestly hadn't expected Christopher to knock.

A real rap sounded on her door. Angela peeked in. "Phillip's waiting for you."

"Tell him I'll be five more minutes." She needed to pull herself together.

"OK." The secretary nodded, concern in her eyes.

"I'll be fine, Angela. I just need a couple minutes." Deborah forced a smile. "Close the door, OK?"

After a soft click assured her of privacy, Deborah laid her head on her desk and felt the tears pool. Lots of plans, Christopher had said. She put up a good front. Even Julia didn't see the whole truth: That she had no plan for handling the moments of terror, the moments when doubt stained her certainty that protection of the embryos rightly superseded honesty with Christopher, the moments when the quicksand of her culpability in her daughter's future started to pull her under. No plan for after March, except that she would not be returning to her office here in Myron Taylor Hall. No plan for how she would cope if she lost both Christopher and Helen, who was really not doing well at all.

And worst of all, no plan for her daughter if fate decided that she, Deborah, should have the Huntington's gene, too.

～

Peeling off her garden gloves, Linda saw Robby's phone on the kitchen counter, vibrating with the alert of a new text. "Robby, you've got a message," she hollered.

Robby pounded down the hall from his room, just in time to pick up the phone as it actually rang. "Hello? Yeah, hi, it's me."

Linda tried to remember when she last heard Robby talk on the phone. He almost always texted, a giant leap forward for people on the spectrum, removing the mystifying facial cues, vocal tones, and inflections that typically stymied communication. Yet here he was, practically chatting.

"Didn't get it. Didn't have my phone. Half an hour?" He looked at Linda. "Can you take me to the library?"

Linda looked at the clock. "I guess so. What's going on there?"

"OK." Robby spoke back into the phone. "I'll bring my laptop."

"What's going on?" Linda repeated her question to Robby's retreating back.

He re-emerged from his room with his laptop bag. "What's going on?" Linda asked again. For some reason, it felt like Robby was deliberately, consciously ignoring her, not just occupying his zone of isolation.

"Meeting Paula to work on Audubon stuff." He pulled his Lions sweatshirt over his head and draped his headphones around his neck.

"Paula?" Linda said anxiously. "What do you two have to work on together?"

"We're running for offices."

Linda blinked. "You mean for the club?"

Robby nodded.

"What are you running for?"

"Vice president."

"And Paula?"

"President. We're meeting to build a website for our campaign."

"You need a website for that?" Linda recalled a hazy flashback of a high school student council campaign, a speech in the auditorium, hand-lettered posters.

"The club's site is ten years old and runs on Dreamweaver." Robby snorted. "No member database, no blogs, hardly any pictures. Building a new one is our top priority. Paula says a campaign site will show people we can do what we promise. Come on, let's go!"

"Um, sure. Let me grab my keys," *Robby was running for a club office?* Linda felt like she did when awakened by a phone call, grogginess clouding comprehension.

"What, um, made you decide to run for office?" she asked casually, in the car.

"I need leadership skills," Robby said, cryptically.

"Who says you do?"

"Cornell."

"Cornell? You mean for the camp?" After returning from Lansing, Robby moped for a while about being too young to go that summer. But after their trip to see the piping plovers, Sam explained how he could use that experience and this whole school year to improve his chances of acceptance. He had Skyped weekly with the park ranger, Ruth, until they released the captive chicks. They e-mailed that professor, Goldman, who had promised to send a current application as soon as it was available. Meanwhile, Robby had scoured the old one, which he'd found on the Cornell website.

"Leadership potential comprises twenty percent of the applicant's total score," Robby now recited. "Vice presidents are leaders, right?"

"Um, yeah." Not really, Linda thought. "You didn't want to be president?"

Robby shrugged. "Paula wanted that. That old guy, Ed, he's the vice president now. She didn't want to work with him. So she asked me."

"So everything's fine now with you and Paula?" Linda asked cautiously, pulling into the library parking lot.

"Uh-huh," Robby said, opening his door. "She said she'd drop me off later."

Automatically, Linda started to object, then cut herself off. She could complete her garden work if she didn't have to return for Robby. Maybe she'd call Sam and see if he wanted to pick up Chinese for dinner, too. Or even go out to the restaurant together. A real date.

"OK," she agreed, marveling at how light her heart felt. As if it had suddenly sprouted wings.

Robby tripped up the library steps, feeling happy. Paula's beat-up Toyota wasn't in the parking lot, so he must be there first. Everything was better than fine with Paula. She'd asked him to run for office with her, after all. So she did like him. And now he would get to sit next to her in the library. One of his favorite places.

He walked through those tall plastic things that beeped if you took a book without checking it out first. He had done it once, when he was in third grade. The shrill sound was awful. He had dropped his books and just stood there, covering his ears. He wouldn't do that now, though.

They were supposed to meet upstairs, in the reference section. He remembered standing next to her in the hotel lobby in Lansing, thinking he wanted to kiss her. What would it feel like? He ran his tongue over his lips. In movies people closed their eyes. How could they do that and be sure they kissed? What if one person's mouth wound up on the other's nose? And Paula was taller than him. What if her mouth landed on his hair?

He walked past the spinning globe at the top of the stairs. Wait, there she was already, at a table by the window. Then where was her car? And someone was sitting next to her already. A guy wearing a Michigan T-shirt. His chair was pulled up close to hers. Really close. His arm was stretched across the back of her chair. Her brown hair brushed his hand. Robby halted, tugging on his sweatshirt strings as he stared.

Paula looked up. "Hi, Robby! Come and meet my boyfriend, Alex."

TWENTY-SEVEN

The plane glided smoothly onto the runway at Sea-Tac International. Deborah relaxed her grip on the seat arms and exhaled a breath she hadn't realized she'd been holding. Safe on the ground, dry, upright. Life jacket untouched. The other passengers were already standing, opening the overhead bins, impatient to move on to the next leg of their journey, oblivious to the miracle within the mundane landing. Would she ever be the blithe flyer she had been before the crash? Probably not. Not much was left of her pre-crash self, in fact. A husband but no marriage. A career she no longer cared about. Imminently, a baby, but perhaps no future as a mother.

Matt met her at baggage claim. Even though he'd told her Helen wouldn't be up to the trip to the airport, Deborah was still disappointed not to see her sister, smiling and waving next to the stainless steel baggage carousel.

"She can't wait to see you," Matt reassured her on the way home. "But I've got to warn you, she looks a lot different."

"Different how?"

"She's lost weight. And muscle tone. She's pale, because she's hardly ever outside. She can still get around on her own, but she moves much more slowly. You have to be careful when you hug her or touch her, because she's very sensitive to pressure."

Deborah nodded. It didn't sound that bad. Not the feeding tubes and wheelchairs that Christopher had prophesied.

But Helen looked that bad. The healthy, vibrant woman Deborah had last seen a year ago was transformed into one faded and worn-out. In Helen and Matt's foyer, she pulled her sister into a hug, trying, over Helen's bony shoulder, to erase the shock from her face. Just as Matt had said, Helen flinched.

It was better when they talked. Sitting on the family room couch, wrapped in a red afghan, Helen fired questions at Deborah about her pregnancy. The afghan gave her body more mass and reflected color onto her face. When Hannah and Mariah came home from school, the mood lightened further, and the five of them laughed through dinner.

Afterward, Deborah sat with Helen and Matt while her nieces went out with friends. She was about to excuse herself for bed, pleading jet lag and pregnancy fatigue, when Helen cleared her throat.

"So tell us your plans for after the baby."

"I wish I knew." She sighed and placed her hands on her belly.

"Are you going back to work?"

"I have to. But not in the law advancement office. Not with Phillip and a capital campaign. Too much pressure. Maybe not even at Cornell."

"So you're going to look for a new job? With a newborn around?" Helen looked skeptical.

"I guess so." It all seemed so far away. "I haven't thought much past November ninth. I've got some money saved. Christopher said he'd put her on his health insurance. So I don't have to worry about that, anyway."

"What else is Christopher doing?" Matt spoke up.

Deborah tried to smile. "Same as always. Teaching. Research."

"I see." Matt pressed his lips together and looked away.

"Deborah, Matt and I want to propose an idea." Helen sat up, her breathing growing more rapid. "It might sound crazy at first, but if you think about it, you'll see there's a lot of potential advantages." She paused. "We'd like you to think about moving to Seattle."

Deborah's jaw went slack. Nonplussed, she looked from her sister to her brother-in-law, then back at Helen, who sat rigidly upright, gauging her reaction. Deborah opened her mouth, then closed it, too flummoxed to speak. Helen nudged Matt.

"It makes sense for you to be close to family now, Deborah. You're already thinking of leaving your job. You could find another out here. We've got a lot of connections at the University of Washington now. Hannah and Mariah would be able to help with babysitting, especially in the summer. And we could use your support, too." Matt put his arm around Helen.

She nodded. "You could even live with us for a while, until you're ready to find your own place. We've got plenty of room. It would be nice to have a baby around again. Something to remind me of the future."

Deborah found her voice. "But Seattle—across the country? I don't know. Christopher and I are still so unsettled." And there was her house, and the job she still did have, after all. And Julia. And— Matt was talking again.

"It seems like Christopher's settled himself into that apartment," Matt said, disdain in his voice.

"Yes, Deborah. It's been almost six months now, right?" Helen said. "Is he even going to be at the birth?"

"I don't know," Deborah said softly.

"How long will you let him try to figure things out?"

Deborah thought of Dr. Felk again. *Leave the door open.* Christopher would step up when the baby was born, he'd told her. She looked down at her belly. What if Dr. Felk was wrong? *I miss you,* Christopher had said. But she needed more than talk. Helen and Matt's idea was appealing. The door couldn't stay open forever. She looked up.

"All right. I'll think about it."

～

"Amanda! Amanda!"

Mrs. Hamilton was coming at her, waving a red sheet of paper and smiling broadly as Amanda stood at her locker.

"Good. You're still here. I've been trying to catch you all week, but I've kept missing you."

Amanda shrugged. "Got stuff to do." Stuff was usually hanging out at Abby's or Kelsey's, or the library if her friends were busy. She spent as little time as possible at home, in the too-quiet house that was starting to smell musty.

That morning, though, her dad said she had to come straight home. He wouldn't say why, just "it's a surprise." Guessing that his idea of a surprise—a good one, anyway—wouldn't match her own, she was dawdling at her locker.

"Oh." Mrs. Hamilton looked like she expected more explanation. "Busy semester?"

Amanda shrugged. "Just being a senior and all. College applications. You know."

"Right." Mrs. Hamilton nodded as Amanda slammed her locker. "Speaking of college. I think you need to do this." She handed Amanda the red paper.

"Scranton Cultural Center presents Irving Berlin's holiday classic *White Christmas*," Amanda read. "Open auditions October tenth, eleventh, and twelfth." She looked up into Mrs. Hamilton's beaming face. "You want me to audition?"

Mrs. Hamilton nodded. "You need more experience to get into a college drama program. You were fantastic as Rizzo last year. But our production this year won't be a musical. And it's not until the spring. It's the perfect time for you to get another show under your belt."

"But the Cultural Center? Isn't that almost professional? And October tenth is next week!"

"This is a community production. There'll be some talented folks, but no professionals. I know the director. He graduated from here ten years ago, actually. I've already told him about you."

"You did?"

"He couldn't promise anything, of course, except for a fair audition. But it's a fun show, and I think you've got a great shot. So what do you say? I've got a copy of the script with your name on it if you want it." Mrs. Hamilton held up a folder.

Inside, Amanda felt excitement percolating for the first time since *Grease* closed. Her dad would be unenthusiastic. Her mom would think it was great. Well, she guessed that's what her mom would think. Amanda hadn't returned her last call, so they hadn't talked in almost two weeks. She could feel Mrs. Hamilton watching her.

"Amanda? Is everything all right?"

"Sure." Amanda cleared her throat. At least Mrs. Hamilton expected something from her. "I'll take it."

It was after four when she got home, the script buried in her backpack.

"Amanda. There you are." Her dad was jingling his keys in the kitchen. "Didn't I tell you to come straight home? Come on, we don't want to be late."

"Can't I put my stuff in my room? What's the hurry? Where are we going, anyway?"

"You'll see." Her dad was in the best mood he'd been in for months, almost cheerful.

She tried again as they backed out of the garage. "Why can't you tell me?"

They were headed downtown. She tried to guess, but her dad refused to answer. After fifteen minutes he turned on the blinker for the next exit.

"Lackawanna College, Next Right." Amanda read on a road sign. Trepidation lurched inside her. Scranton's community college.

"Dad, are you taking me to Lackawanna?"

He didn't answer for a moment, staring out at the traffic. The light turned green.

"Dad, are we going to Lackawanna?" Her voice rose.

"Amanda, please. There's no need to yell."

"Are we?"

He looked over at her, his mood somber again. He nodded. "The business division is hosting an open house for prospective students tonight."

"A business open house? What, accounting or something? Dad, that's not what I want to do!"

"You don't even know. You haven't tried it yet."

"I don't want to try it. I know what I want to do, and it's not at Lackawanna."

"Think of your future. A business degree means security, Amanda. If you want to, you can always do drama as a hobby."

"A hobby? Dad, are you serious? Have you, like, paid any attention to my life lately?"

He bristled. "At least I'm here, you know."

"You mean Mom isn't."

"That about sums it up, doesn't it? I'm here. Doing the best I can. She's off a hundred miles away, doing God knows what with God knows who."

"What do you mean, doing God knows what? She got a new job at a food pantry."

"I sent her divorce papers, Amanda. I told her it was her last chance." He steered the car up the exit ramp. "She could rip them up, burn them, destroy them any way she wanted, and I would forgive her if she came home. But if she signed them and abandoned her vows forever, then I couldn't forgive her. Ever."

He glanced at her, his face melancholy. "She signed them. I got them back two days later. She didn't even consider coming back to us. For all we know, she's having another affair with some other sinful soul up there."

Amanda felt sick in the front seat. Was that why her mother hadn't called lately? The car turned into the Lackawanna campus. No. No way. Her dad was just an unfair, imperious jerk.

"So now that you couldn't make Mom do what you wanted, you're going to try to make me?" She crossed her arms. "This was a waste of a trip." She rummaged in her backpack for the script. "Mrs. Hamilton wants me to audition for a new musical. If you want to go in the open house, fine. But I've got lines to learn."

TWENTY-EIGHT

"Pickup for Goldman," Christopher told the kid behind the counter at Campus Cantonese. Rifling through the row of brown paper bags, he yelled back to the kitchen. The Chinese reply obviously displeased him.

"Big order. Ten more minute. Sorry." He disappeared into the kitchen, yelling in Chinese.

Christopher sighed and dropped onto the bench next to the cash register. He flipped through one of Ithaca's weekly freebie rags restlessly, then stood again. Two of his grad students had volunteered to pick up the food. He wished he'd let them. Campus Cantonese was one of his and Deborah's regular haunts. *Had been one of their regular haunts.* They always sat in the middle booth along the back wall. *Had sat.*

Out of habit, his eyes drifted there. He blinked once, then twice. There was Deborah, in her usual spot, opposite another woman who looked vaguely familiar. They leaned toward each other, deep in conversation. But it was what was between them that pinned his gaze.

A baby's car seat.

He was across the restaurant in half a dozen strides, moving on pure adrenaline, pure instinct. "Deborah."

Both women turned toward him, startled. "Christopher!" Deborah gasped.

He looked from her to the car seat. "Is this—did you—"

A strange look crossed Deborah's face, and she leaned back against the booth, revealing her swollen belly almost touching the table's edge. A cocktail of emotions swirled. One part disappointment, one part relief, one part foolishness. "Oh."

"Christopher, this is Julia Adams. I think you met her at the dean's picnic last summer." Actually it was two summers ago now. "You know her husband Michael from bio, too, of course." Deborah paused, then deliberately nodded at the car seat. "And their son, Nate."

"Nice to see you again," Julia said.

"You, too," he managed, before he was saved by the kid from the counter.

"Goldman? Your order's ready."

"Thanks. I've got to go," he said to Deborah, almost stepping on the kid's heels in his haste to follow. Drumming his fingers, waiting for the credit card to go through, he heard her voice.

"I wouldn't have the baby and not tell you, Christopher."

The cocktail swirled again. Was it two parts relief this time? He looked at her. "OK."

"OK?"

"I mean, good. I'd want to know."

"You could have fooled me," Deborah said.

"Actually, you did fool me." The words were out of his mouth before he knew it. Deborah drew back as if he'd struck her.

"Sign here," said the kid. "Sorry for the wait."

"It's all right." He felt Deborah watching him as he scribbled his name. The kid punctured it on one of those pointy spears. He turned, bracing for Deborah's retort.

But none came. They stood looking at each other for a long minute until Christopher spoke.

"I've gotta get back. I'm taking this to campus for a student group meeting tonight."

Deborah looked surprised. "I didn't know you advised any groups."

"It's my first meeting. For students who want to be instructors and advisers in the summer ornithology camp."

"Bird camp? For middle school kids?"

"Thirteen to sixteen, actually."

"Really?" Deborah blinked. He read the puzzlement on her face. Was there a hint of pleased surprise, too? But what good would his practice attempt at parenthood do now anyway, with the real thing so obviously imminent, and so many months wasted?

"Yeah. So I've got to get back."

"OK. Well, good night, then," Deborah said. He felt her eyes continue to follow him, out into the cold night.

In the car he tried to settle his nerves. He was finally comfortable in the fellow's apartment. He turned toward it when he left his office, rather than toward Cayuga Heights. He remembered to buy coffee before he wanted to make a cup. He caught almost all his waking second guesses before they could slip out, like "I miss you" that day on the phone. They only caught him at night, when he woke up alone and had to recall that it was now normal.

Yet this one encounter had easily seeped through the mental sandbags he'd so carefully placed around the events of the spring. He tried to identify what remained of that emotional cocktail. Relief he hadn't missed the birth? Fear she wouldn't want him at the birth? Did he even want to be at the birth? What *did* he want?

His car had arrived back at the Lab. Trudging upstairs with the food, he wanted to be back at the apartment, wrapped in the trappings of his solitude again, repairing his sandbag bunker. Maybe they could handle the meeting without him.

But no, Peter was already there. He couldn't leave now. The best he could manage was a few moments in his office to regroup.

In the sanctuary he automatically checked his e-mail. Four new items, which all looked like they should have been caught in Cornell's spam filter. He paused over one, then clicked. It was another message from Robby Palmer. Like the others, he skipped a salutation and plunged right into what was on his mind.

"I've been elected vice president of my Audubon club," it read. "Do you think that's enough leadership for the camp. Please let me know." It was signed Robby Palmer, with a link to what looked like the club's website.

Christopher clicked on it automatically, then minimized the window just as quickly. Camp was competitive, and admissions policy called for all applicants to be reviewed blindly, as he'd reminded Dr. Felk repeatedly. Technically, even Robby's e-mail broke the rules. In fact, that night's meeting was to review the rules for the applications expected to start arriving immediately after the New Year. Christopher had been struggling with how to disclose the matter of the thumb drive, which he had kept locked in a drawer since that day in April.

But as he massaged his temples, Christopher recalled the story Arthur Felk told in the hotel bar, about his brother. *The story has a happy ending. Robby needs somebody younger.* He remembered Deborah, in the taxi after the crash. *Is work really more important than family?* Dropping the photo on the table at the restaurant. *Not just a girl. Your daughter.*

He hit "Reply" and began typing. "That's great, Robby. It'll really help your application. Keep track of everything you accomplish as an officer. We'll start taking applications after Jan. 1."

Hitting "Send," Christopher went to claim his lo mein.

Deborah put her leftovers in the refrigerator and went to the baby's room. It drew her every evening now. She sat in the glider rocker, leaning her head against the green gingham cushion, her arms cradling her belly. She was adamant that the nursery not become a pink straitjacket, even though Julia told her it was hopeless. "Every single outfit Nate got—I mean every single one—had either a vehicle or a ball on it," she'd told Deborah at dinner. "And eighty percent of them are blue."

How odd that babies were immediately divided into their separate camps, yin and yang, black and white, when the world they would inhabit was filled with shades of gray. Her baby's more than most. That was what Christopher couldn't appreciate, either. To him, it was right or wrong to have a baby. It couldn't be both. Helen and Matt's perspective was just as stark. They couldn't understand why she didn't cut ties. Move on. Why live in limbo?

She sighed heavily, shifting in the chair. There, that was more comfortable. She still cared for Christopher, that was why. She couldn't let go of the dream she'd envisioned for them, that they were so close to living. Tonight, though, it was again clear that Christopher didn't understand that she was compelled to do what she did in February: protect the embryos at all cost. That was what mothers did. Especially when they knew the fathers cherished hopes as fragile as Christopher's.

She shifted her hips again, wincing. Heartburn? She deliberately ordered *moo goo gai pan* because it wasn't spicy. Did she have any Tums in the house?

Then there was the practical reality of their situation. If she did have Huntington's, the baby would need someone. Would need her father.

The pain flared again, longer this time, then ebbed just as the baby kicked. The jolt reverberated up, up to her brain, which suddenly lit with comprehension. A contraction. Not heartburn, but a contraction. Labor. Happening now. She had to call Dr. Dunn. She had to call Christopher. She had to—but as she stood, the pain of the next contraction pushed her back into the chair.

Immobilized, Deborah held her belly again and stared at the green glowing numbers on the digital clock. Timing. She was supposed to time the contractions. Or was it how long in between? Or both? She had to ask Dr. Dunn.

"Both. And when they're a minute or longer and five minutes in between, come on in. Or if your water breaks. OK?"

"How long will that be?" said Deborah.

"First baby, hard to tell. Could be a while."

"Oh," said Deborah, feeling forlorn.

"Your friend Julia's bringing you in, right?"

"Right."

"All right. You can do this, Deborah. I'll see you soon."

After the doctor hung up, Deborah didn't hesitate. She dialed Christopher.

TWENTY-NINE

Thanksgiving morning, Brett woke to the first dusting of snow. One more thing to do on the Alliance's busiest day of the year: shovel the walk.

Since no one expected her to fill a pew, she watched the Macy's parade on TV for the first time in twenty years. Midmorning, as she made a Western omelette, the pangs of loneliness hit. Dropping the knife next to the piles of diced ham, green peppers, onions, and cheese, she dialed.

Amanda *would* be expected to fill a pew, she realized, as the voice mail greeting began. "Hi, Amanda. It's Mom. I just wanted to wish you a happy Thanksgiving," she said to the silence. "It snowed here today. I heard it might there this weekend. I hope you're feeding the birds, sweetie. I'm so thankful you're my daughter. I know it's been a hard year, and I hope that you can still count me as a blessing, too," she finished hastily, before hanging up to wipe away her tears.

She missed Amanda terribly. They had talked a few times, when Amanda chose to answer the phone Brett had given her. Many other messages were not returned. Brett went back to Scranton twice: in August, before school started, and again in October, for school conferences. Both times Amanda kept herself busy almost the entire visit. Brett accepted the passive-aggressive punishment resolutely, vowing to give Amanda the time and space she needed. In lieu of a real relationship, she found herself monitoring the weather, imagining Amanda trading shorts and tanks for jeans and sweaters and now, her winter coat.

Otherwise, she felt exactly as Elizabeth said she must. Committed. Fulfilled. Energized. And free. Richard had sent her divorce papers, which she had signed and sent back in the next day's mail, officially casting off the pastor's wife yoke. But after almost five months of Amanda's aloofness, she was starting to wonder if she had miscalculated the trade-off.

Thanksgiving dinner service began at four. She left the apartment at noon and walked to Immaculate Conception, where the posse of cooks was just putting the turkeys in the oven. As excited as another mother for a bat mitzvah or a sweet sixteen, Brett circled the dining room, fluttering here to straighten a tablecloth, there to make room for another serving dish, back to the kitchen to make sure the salad was tossed with the right dressing.

A line snaked around the building when the doors opened. Brett and the greeter and server volunteers played the role of host to the hilt: taking coats, writing nametags, ushering guests to the buffet lines, and helping find available seats at the crowded tables. Turkey was carved. Potatoes scooped. Pumpkin pie sliced. Coffee flowed. The afternoon flew. The last guests were soon gathering their coats and saying their own thanks.

"Good job, Brett," said Pastor Sue as she collected her coat.

Brett's exuberance exited with the crowds. She sent the volunteers home and washed the last dishes herself, stewing that Amanda had not called back. *You're the mother. You have to keep the door open*, she reminded herself, dialing again.

"Hello?"

"Amanda." Hearing her daughter's voice for the first time in weeks made Brett's voice crack. "Happy Thanksgiving."

"Mom? Is that you?"

"It's me. I wanted to wish you a happy Thanksgiving," Brett said, clutching the phone, wishing for the words that would allow this one phone call to fill the void of the lost months.

"Oh. Well, um, thanks." Her voice was flat again.

Brett pushed on. "Did you get the message I left earlier?"

"Earlier today?"

"Yes. I called about ten."

"We were at church."

She wasn't answering the question, Brett thought. "Well, it doesn't matter now," she said aloud. "How have you been, sweetheart?"

"Fine. I'm fine." Amanda sounded automatic. "Busy."

"Busy with what?"

"I've got rehearsals all weekend."

"Rehearsals? During the holiday weekend?"

"Not for a school play. It's a Scranton Cultural Center production."

"You're kidding. You're cast in an SCC play?"

"Yeah." Amanda sounded like she was smiling now. "*White Christmas*. Mrs. Hamilton talked them into letting me audition. I'm in the chorus, and I've got a few lines."

Brett was more delighted that their conversation was still going than at the news. "That is just wonderful, Amanda."

"Dad doesn't think so."

Brett frowned into the phone. "What do you mean?"

"He keeps preaching Lackawanna College."

"He does?" Anxiety surged through Brett.

"'Business is security, Amanda,'" she intoned, imitating Richard. "'You don't have to give up theater, but you have to be realistic, too.'" She sighed.

Silently, Brett cursed Richard. "Amanda. Listen to me. This is important. You have to listen to yourself first. Your father can have an opinion. I can have an opinion. But you make the decision about your future.

"After the experience of the musical last spring, after everything Mrs. Hamilton told you about your talent, and now being cast in this community production, can you imagine going to Lackawanna? Entering a business program now?" Brett waited.

"No. No way," Amanda finally said.

"I understand. I get that. I sat in the audience and watched you. You can't deny what your soul wants." Brett paused. "Well, I guess you can. But it's not worth it. Believe me, sweetie. It is just not worth it."

There was a long pause.

"Amanda? Are you still there?"

"The show opens December fifth," Amanda said. "If I got you a ticket, could you come?"

≈

Robby hunched his shoulders inside his sweatshirt as he sat in the chilly backyard, parked in the one lounge chair he'd insisted stay outside for winter, aiming the Sears binoculars at the sky. His yard list was on his lap. He was at ninety-six now. He wanted to get over one hundred by the end of the year. Not impossible, but unlikely. At the Audubon meeting last week, everyone compared their December totals. Most people got two or three. Paula had the most of anyone, with six.

Paula. His stomach felt funny when he thought about her. They had won the election and were officially officers. But every time she was around now, Robby couldn't think about blog posts and a member database and all the stuff they'd promised. He just thought about her boyfriend sitting next to her in the library, his arm wrapped around her. And then the funny feeling in his stomach started.

"Hey, Robby." It was his dad's voice, next to him all of a sudden. "Finding any to add?"

Robby shook his head, keeping his eyes on the sky. A single dark shape arced across his field of vision.

"There, what about that one?" his dad asked.

Robby shook his head. "Just another sparrow."

"Hmmm." His dad dropped something onto his lap. "Maybe it's time to take a break."

Robby lowered the binoculars. The paper in his lap was an ad, its red and green capital letters screaming at him: *SALE SALE SALE! Hurry in for holiday savings! Best deals of the year!*

Grunting, he handed it back to his dad. "Hate shopping."

"Turn it over," his dad said.

Rolling his eyes, Robby turned the paper over. *Cameras, binoculars, accessories! Bushnell, Nikon, Canon, Olympus! Best brand selection, best prices!*

"Binoculars?" Robby looked up at his dad.

"I think you're ready for an upgrade," his dad said. "It'll be an early Christmas present."

"Really?" Robby fingered the pebbled surface of the Sears binoculars. Up north, he'd tried Ruth's. On hikes at Kensington Metropark and the Nichols Arboretum in the fall, he'd borrowed some from other club members. Theirs were all so much lighter and sharper.

"Really." His dad nodded. "Come on."

The mall parking lot was packed. So were the hallways inside, echoing with recorded Christmas carols. Robby pulled his hood up, yanked his sweatshirt strings, and kept his eyes pinned on his dad's green quilted coat.

The binocular store, which looked mostly like a camera store, was much quieter. "Help you?" asked a man wearing a denim shirt.

"We're interested in binoculars," his dad said.

"Over here." The man led them to a case in a back corner. "They're not my specialty, though. I'll get someone who can help you. Alex?" He drifted toward an open doorway.

Robby leaned his elbows on the case. Inside, binoculars were displayed on two shelves, arranged left to right in order of size. They all looked better than the Sears pair at home. He grinned, feeling happy. This would be a great present. And he'd have them for the club's annual Christmas bird count, coming up in a few weeks.

"Looking for binoculars today?" Another man's voice spoke above his head. It sounded familiar. Robby looked up. He wore the same denim shirt as the first man, but unbuttoned. Underneath was a Michigan T-shirt. His eyebrows furrowed as he gazed at Robby. Then the lines straightened.

"Robby, right? From the Audubon Club. I'm Alex. Alex Daugherty. We met at the library that one time."

Robby nodded. *Alex.* Paula's boyfriend. He looked down at the case again, but this time he could only see his face reflected back. It didn't look happy anymore.

His dad was talking. "I'm Sam Palmer, Robby's dad. Are you in the club, Alex?"

Alex shook his head. "Not officially. But my girlfriend is. Paula. Paula Lynch."

"Paula. Right." Robby felt his dad put a hand on his shoulder.

"She just got elected president. And you're the new vice president, right, Robby? Congratulations."

Robby could feel both Alex and his dad looking at him. Waiting for him to say something. His dad squeezed his shoulder and cleared his throat, filling in the void. "Well. You're right, Alex. We're looking for some new binoculars."

"Great. We've got a good sale going this weekend. Are you looking for pocket-sized? Full-size? Image stabilizer? Do you have a budget in mind?" Alex took a key from his pocket and unlocked the case.

"Anything here would be an upgrade from what we've got," his dad said. "I was thinking between two hundred and three hundred dollars. I'll leave the features up to Robby."

"Do you go to Michigan?" Robby heard himself ask suddenly.

Alex glanced down at his T-shirt. "Yeah. Dearborn. That's where I met Paula. In biology class."

"Do you know Josh?"

"Josh?" Alex looked confused. "Josh who?"

"Yes, Josh who?" his dad echoed.

"Josh—" Robby paused. He never got his last name. He just remembered that the plover chicks went to the U of M biological research station. He looked at his dad.

"Josh from Skype. The one who took care of the plover chicks."

"Oh." His dad nodded, vaguely. "He went to Michigan?"

Robby shrugged. "It was a Michigan research station. He was a biologist."

"The research station up in Pellston?" Alex asked. His voice had changed a little. There was a note of admiration. "He was probably a grad student. Not many undergrads go up there."

Robby nodded, feeling slightly better. He had met Josh and talked to him, and he wasn't even a college student. "Yeah. He was a grad student."

"And you saw plovers? Piping plovers? That's really cool. They're endangered, right?"

Robby nodded again, feeling pride swell inside.

"All right. So it sounds like you're doing a lot of hiking. You probably want pocket-sized. And waterproof. I'd recommend one of these here." Alex reached into the case and set two pairs on top. "Both fall in your budget."

Robby lifted the first pair carefully. It weighed less than half of the binoculars at home. He turned the focus dial, aiming it out the store entrance, into the mall. He could see the line of little kids waiting for Santa in the mall courtyard.

"What do you think, Robby?" his dad asked.

"Nice." Robby put them down and picked up the second pair.

"These have a slightly larger lens diameter. Twenty-five millimeters instead of twenty," Alex said.

Robby could tell. This time he could see Santa and the elf hovering at his shoulder. He sharpened the focus. A little girl was crying on Santa's lap. He felt sorry for her. Even being here in the store with Paula's boyfriend was better than that.

"These are better," he said.

"They come with a storage case, too," Alex said.

"Looks like you've got a sale," his dad said.

Alex swiped his dad's credit card and handed Robby the bag. "Thanks. And good to see you again, Robby."

Robby looked at his shoes.

"Paula's talked me into doing the Christmas bird count thing. So I'll probably see you there in a few weeks."

"Oh." Robby's voice cracked. "OK."

"Thanks for your help, Alex," said his dad.

And then his dad's hand was on his shoulder again, piloting him out of the store, through the hot, noisy crowd in the mall, into the brisk air outside, and finally the refuge of the car.

His dad sat silently behind the wheel for a moment. "Phew," he said, exhaling the word. "You OK?"

Robby thought. Alex and Paula went to U of M–Dearborn. So they were old. Older than he thought. Almost as old as some of his teachers, probably.

"Robby?" His dad was looking at him.

Robby sighed. He shifted in his seat. The plastic bag on his lap rustled. He reached in and unzipped the binocular case, fingering the sleek, dark gray shell. He looked out the window. It was a perfect day for birding, sunny and clear, the trees free of obscuring leaves. And it was still early afternoon. Lots of time left to look for four more birds in the backyard.

He looked at his dad. "Let's go home."

THIRTY

The White Christmas performance was the best show Brett had ever seen. Amanda's part was minor, only a few lines. But for three hours, Brett could watch her. Afterward, backstage—where Richard was nowhere to be seen—they hugged for the first time in five months. As they rocked cheek to cheek, tears filled the brown eyes they both shared.

"I miss you at home. Dad's never around," Amanda said, stepping back and sniffling.

"I miss you, too." Brett took a deep breath. "I want you to spend your Christmas break with me."

"Really?" Amanda hesitated. "I wouldn't . . . be in the way?"

"Of course not." Brett was puzzled. "How could you think that?"

"You're not . . . um . . . seeing . . . dating . . . anyone?"

"Oh." Brett's forehead cleared. "No, I'm not. Not now. I didn't leave to be with anyone, Amanda. I left to be me. And being your mother is a huge part of me." She squeezed Amanda's hand. "Anyone I might be interested in—in the future—would have to understand and accept that. OK?"

Amanda gave a tiny smile and squeezed back. "OK."

"I haven't had time to meet anyone, anyway. I've been kind of a workaholic. In fact, we're planning to start a new project over the holidays, and I could use extra help."

To her surprise, Pastor Sue had suggested they launch Project Stork during the holidays. So many other Ithaca charities offered holiday programs that the Alliance's regular clientele dropped, she explained.

And so, two weeks later, she and Amanda were loading the Alliance minivan for Project Stork's inaugural run. Just a half dozen deliveries were scheduled, most to mothers Julia Adams knew.

The first five went fine. The families thanked them profusely. Brett and Amanda smiled at the babies, all of whom were quiet and angelic. *All is calm, all is bright,* Brett thought as they headed to the last house. It wasn't how she remembered her first months of motherhood.

The sixth delivery was to a home in Cayuga Heights. "Deborah and Grace DeWitt," Amanda read aloud from the delivery list.

"A lot of Cornell faculty live in this neighborhood," Brett said as she scanned the addresses, pulling up next to a neat bungalow. Snow blanketed the eaves. A Christmas tree glowed inside the leaded glass windows.

"It seems weird to be making meal deliveries to a house like this," Amanda said.

"That's the whole point of the project. To expand the Alliance's reach," Brett said. "But you never know. Appearances can be pretty deceiving."

Through the windows, the lights cast a weak glow on the unshoveled walk and steps. The porch light was dark.

"Is this the right place?" Amanda asked doubtfully.

"The address is right. Let's just ring the bell and see."

They could hear the baby crying before they even reached the snowy porch steps. Brett pressed the bell. The crying climbed a notch.

"Wow, that's loud. Think they can hear us?" Amanda asked.

Brett pressed the bell again. Again, the baby's wail crescendoed. Her intuition tingled. This was the house they were meant to visit tonight. Someone here did need help. Another long minute passed until the porch light came on. The door was flung open by a woman about her age, holding a baby who shrieked again, and then suddenly went quiet.

"Hi, I'm Brett Stevens from Project Stork. This is my daughter, Amanda." Brett looked into the woman's face. Pure exhaustion, no sign of recognition. "We're with the Ithaca Interfaith Alliance?"

"Oh! Julia's group. I forgot you were coming tonight. Come in." The woman stepped back, closing the door behind them. The baby resumed her screaming.

"Oh, no, Gracie, please, don't start again." she begged in a raw voice. The baby took no pity.

"One of those days?" Brett asked the woman, evidently Deborah.

She nodded. "She's been at it for the last hour and a half, until I opened the door."

"Sounds like colic. This one had it, too." Brett nodded at Amanda. "Opening the door might have helped, actually. Going outside always soothed her."

"Not really practical this time of year," Deborah said tartly.

"May I hold her?" Brett asked, ignoring the tone. "My jacket's cool, anyway."

Deborah handed the baby over. As Brett rocked the little body against the cool, quilted material, Gracie's cries again quieted. She blinked and opened her wet eyes, blue like her mother's.

"Oh, thank God," Deborah said, her shoulders relaxing visibly. "I don't think I could've taken much more."

"Well, you don't have to take it alone for the next couple hours, anyway," Brett said briskly. "You're the last delivery of the night, and you're going to get the deluxe Project Stork treatment."

She held Gracie while Amanda unloaded the food and Deborah ate. While Deborah nursed the baby and put her to bed, Amanda shoveled the porch and the walk. Brett cleaned up the kitchen, filling the dishwasher with stacks from the sink and doing the rest by hand. She folded the laundry in the dryer. Amanda finished shoveling and was stamping the snow off her boots when Deborah re-entered, alone.

"She's asleep. Thank God." She had changed her clothes and brushed her hair, Brett noticed, and looked transformed from the woman who had opened the door. She seemed familiar, too, though Brett was sure she'd never seen Deborah around Ithaca.

"Hallelujah." Brett agreed. "Well, thanks for having us stop by. We'll see you tomorrow night, same time."

"You're thanking *me*?" Deborah's eyebrows rose as she looked around the spotless kitchen. "You called yourselves Project Stork. Tonight you were more like Project Sanity. Even after I was rude."

Brett laughed. "Everybody needs a hand once in a while. Glad we could help."

"I'm serious." Deborah shifted in the doorway. "I've never felt so incompetent before. I'm used to being good at what I do."

"Amanda, would you go out and start the car?" Brett waited until the door closed behind her own daughter. "Gracie doesn't know what's good or bad. Right now, all that really matters is that you're here. Feeding her. Keeping her warm. Safe."

"Really?" Deborah stared out the window, at Amanda's back.

"Really. I know it's hard. I'm a single mom, too." Brett held her breath, then relaxed as Deborah's nod confirmed her hunch. "But it's going to be the most worthwhile thing you've ever done."

Fleetingly, a hopeful smile crossed Deborah's face. "I hope you're right."

"Just take it a day at a time." Brett opened the door. "Now promise me you'll go to bed yourself."

"Promise." Deborah held up her hand. Her smile stayed a second longer. "See you tomorrow."

In the car, Amanda held her red fingers in front of the heating vents. Some vacation for her, Brett thought. Running around a strange town delivering food, shoveling a stranger's porch.

"You must be freezing, sweetie. Thanks for being such a good sport tonight. I'll make hot chocolate at home, OK?"

"OK." Amanda seemed preoccupied.

"Wishing you stayed in Scranton?" Brett asked, carefully not looking at her.

Amanda shook her head. "I was just thinking how cool that was. When we showed up, that lady was a wreck. The baby, too."

"Being a new parent's tough with two adults. I can't imagine doing it alone."

"Then, after dinner and a couple hours, they're both, like, acting human again."

"This kind of work is called human services for a reason," Brett said, mildly.

"I guess." Amanda looked at her. "I can see why you like it. It feels pretty good."

"It does, doesn't it?" Brett felt like singing again. "Joy to the World," this time.

Together they made the Project Stork rounds for the ten days of Amanda's visit, saving Deborah and Gracie for the last stop each night. Though Deborah was never as distraught as the first night, she was tired and worn out and always as grateful for their visit as for the food. On Christmas night she handed Brett a check.

"Julia told me you're just getting this thing going. I've worked in fundraising, and I know it's hard to start new projects when the other ones don't stop."

"You've worked in fundraising?"

"A bit," Deborah said briefly. Upstairs, Gracie started to cry. Brett filed away the information for another time.

Amanda left for Scranton the morning of New Year's Eve. Brett ached thinking of her return to Richard's cold home, even though she seemed excited about a party at Abby's. But it would only be for five more months, since they had decided that Amanda would spend her summer in Ithaca. Still, the clock dragged until it was time to do the Project Stork deliveries. She saved Deborah and Gracie's for last, as usual.

Deborah answered the door, her eyes red, clutching a tissue. Seeing Brett she smiled but then broke down, backing into the house, huddling into a lump on the couch. The TV was on.

"Deborah, my God, what's happened? Are you sick? Is Gracie?"

She wept louder, shaking her head.

"She's not sick. Not yet. But she could be. I'm such a bad mother, I've been so selfish."

"What are you talking about? You're anything but selfish."

"No, I am, I am. You don't know, you don't understand . . ."

"Deborah, you're not making sense. What do you mean, Gracie could get sick? Can I turn this thing off?" Brett searched for the remote. Deborah cried harder.

"That's what did it. That stupid TV. I turned it on after Gracie went down. They had a show on, the top news stories of the year, you know, the kind they always do this time of year." She took a deep breath and blew her nose. "Just give me a minute. I can stop. I'll get hold of myself."

"Take your time." Brett brought a glass of water while Deborah found the remote, muted the TV, and exhaled deeply.

"OK. By any chance, do you remember that plane crash last January? The plane that landed on the Hudson River?"

It was Brett's turn to struggle for words. "Um, yes. I remember it

289

very well. Was that"—she stammered—"was that one of the year's top news stories?"

Deborah nodded. "And I was on that plane. With my husband. Gracie's father. Christopher." Tears started flowing again, and she brushed them away fiercely. "You must think I've gone crazy."

"Deborah, no. Definitely no." Brett couldn't believe the coincidence. The foggy familiarity she felt the first delivery day cleared. "I was in New York that day, too. In fact, I was on a ferry in the river. We were—I was—going on a sightseeing cruise around Manhattan. Our ferry got pulled into the passenger rescue."

"You're kidding." Deborah stared at her. "We were picked up by a ferry."

"I'm not kidding." Brett stared at her friend, remembering, too.

In the silence, the clock chimed. Six more hours left in 2009. Deborah was probably as eager as she to put the year behind her.

"This is incredible," Brett said. "But you see, I do understand. That was an awful day. Seeing that show, and now having Gracie, it must have brought up all kinds of scary, terrible memories. And what-ifs."

"Yes. Both," Deborah said. "But the crash isn't the worst memory. It's everything that started that day. What I refused to admit. Because I was selfish. I just wanted to have a baby. It's all I could think about. But I didn't think enough about being a mother. A good mother would never endanger her child. And I've put Gracie at risk."

"You're not making sense again. You would never do anything to harm Gracie. What started that day?"

As the tears slid down her cheeks, Deborah confided everything. Her sister Helen's panicked call on the wings. Her husband wanting to stop IVF. Persuading him to try once more. Learning of Helen's Huntington's diagnosis and withholding it from Christopher. The pregnancy. Christopher moving out. Gracie's birth and the hell of these first two months. And now, just as things finally started improving, the future. A new year staring her in the face, taunting her with the uncertainty of how many more she could share with Gracie.

Brett listened in mutual, mute sympathy. When Deborah stopped talking, Brett said, "My turn."

She told Deborah how her life swerved off course that same day on the Hudson. Told her about the guilt and fear of losing Amanda. Told her about the five months of limbo, and how that risk only now appeared over.

"Amanda's a wonderful young woman, Brett. You've been the best mother you could possibly be, sacrificing your own happiness for the sake of the family you thought was best for her," Deborah said. "But Gracie will probably hate me. What mother brings a child into the world with fifty-fifty odds she'll become an orphan?"

"The odds aren't your fault. Stop punishing yourself for something you can't control," Brett said, empathy infusing each word. "And she wouldn't be an orphan. She has a father. A father who needs to step up to the job, even though you didn't ask me."

"You think I should try to get back together with Christopher?"

She sounds hopeful, Brett thought. *Like she wants me to talk her into it.*

"That's not my decision. Do you want to get back together?"

"I'm not sure. Helen thinks I'm crazy to even consider it. She wants me to move to Seattle. And I was angry at him when I was pregnant. Furious. But then when I went into labor, I just called him automatically."

"So he was there? At the birth?"

"Not the birth. I couldn't reach him. By the time he got the message, it was over. He came to the hospital the next day."

"That didn't make you angry all over?" Brett said.

"At first it did. I told myself it was his fault I was so exhausted and miserable. But then, just getting through the day drained every

291

bit of energy I had. He did call a few times, asking what I wanted him to do. But she was always crying, or needing her diaper changed, or needing to be fed. I didn't have enough energy to call him back, let alone be angry."

"And what about now?"

"It's all just gone. It sounds so corny, but all I feel inside is love for Gracie."

"So is there any love for Christopher?"

Deborah bit her lip.

"You don't owe me an answer. But love or not, he has a responsibility to Gracie. Your beautiful, *healthy* baby Gracie, safe upstairs right now. The child you're sacrificing yourself for, trying to be two parents. Asking what you want him to do, that's a cop-out. He has to figure out what he needs to do. He's Gracie's father, not you."

"I want to believe you." Deborah wiped her eyes again. "But that still leaves Gracie at risk."

"Then get tested," Brett said, without hesitation.

THIRTY-ONE

Christopher squinted at the Ivory Tower's menu, one of those blackboards scrawled over with colored chalk and hung so high it was almost illegible from the floor. He gave up. He wasn't really hungry, anyway.

"Just coffee," he told the girl with the nose ring behind the cash register. He sat at the counter in the window, watching for Deborah. Ten o'clock passed. 10:05. 10:10. 10:15. He was about to call her when she breezed in.

"Happy New Year." She hung her coat on the chair next to him and sat down, so quickly he didn't have a chance to stand and hug her. "Sorry I'm late. It's a little harder getting out the door on time these days."

"It's fine. Still Christmas break." He tried to ignore the wish that he would have been able to hug her. She looked pretty much like she used to on weekends, her hair in a ponytail with workout clothes and a Cornell sweatshirt on top.

"Right. Just coffee for you?"

He nodded.

"Well, I'm starving. I'm going to order." She pulled a wallet out of a giant pink polka-dot bag he'd never seen before and went to the counter, not even looking up at the blackboard.

"Morning," the nose ring girl greeted her. "The usual?"

"Yes, thanks, Molly."

"Large dark roast, black, and a breakfast egg sandwich with cheese on an everything bagel. Coming up. How's that little angel?"

"Angelic. Most of the time, anyway." Deborah answered. Christopher couldn't see her, but he could tell she was smiling.

"Sounds like you're a regular here," he said when she sat down.

"I guess so. I started coming with Julia after prenatal yoga classes. I like it. It's cozy, friendly."

"And you've brought the baby, too, sounds like."

"Yes."

"Where is she now?"

"Grace, Christopher. Her name is Grace. I call her Gracie. At Julia's."

"Grace. Right. You said. That's pretty." It was, though the nickname surprised him. Deborah and he had always shared a distaste for nicknames, politely but firmly correcting colleagues who inevitably shortened theirs to the expected Debbie or Chris.

Nor could he really believe they were sitting there, talking about their daughter, whom he hadn't even seen awake yet. She was born by the time he got Deborah's message the night she went into labor, sleeping when he visited the next day and every other time since. They had talked a few times, but conversations were always curtailed by Deborah needing to change a diaper or feed her or tend to some other need. Sitting there now, Deborah no longer pregnant, it was all starting to seem like a crazy dream.

"I have some news," she told him, sipping her coffee.

"News?" His internal guard went up.

"I'm not going to get Huntington's."

Huntington's. Emotions galloped through his head. Blissful confusion for a moment more. Fleetingly, happiness. Then the dawn of comprehension, of memory, of polarized positions. Of the mocking magpie ringing in his office last winter. He had to unclench his jaw to speak.

"You had the test."

She nodded.

"And you don't have the gene."

"No."

"So Gracie's not at risk, either?" He was back in the kitchen the day when Matt called with the name of the Columbia doctor. Valentine's Day, it was. He had discovered his wife had undermined their marriage on Valentine's Day.

She shook her head. "Huntington's doesn't skip generations. She's safe."

Faintly, Christopher registered relief. But her deception felt as raw as it did almost a year ago. He knew she was trying to meet his eyes, but gazing out of the shop window, he saw only their unresolved past reflected back. And Deborah, sitting there, unapologetic.

"Christopher? This is good news. Right?"

Christopher unclenched his teeth and closed his eyes. "Why should your news mean anything to me now, Deborah?"

She pushed her plate away and laid her hand on his arm. "You told me you miss me."

"I said that." It seemed like a lifetime ago. It was a lifetime ago. "I missed us. But we don't exist anymore, do we?"

She didn't reply. But her eyes were crestfallen. *Unbelievable.*

"You thought this was going to change things. You luck out and don't have Huntington's. I'll come home, we'll be a family and live happily ever after."

Slowly, Deborah nodded.

"Damn it, Deborah. The end doesn't justify the means. It doesn't change that you lied. Or that you put the baby at risk, too."

"No, it doesn't. But that's done. Over with. We have a daughter now." Deborah spoke angrily now, too. "I'm sorry I disappointed you. But *you* were the one who decided it ruined our entire relationship. You were the one who decided to move out."

Christopher opened his mouth. Deborah held up her hand, cutting him off.

"I can't keep rehashing the last year. I called you about the future. If you don't want to be a husband anymore, well, I can handle that. But you said yourself she deserves two parents. So give her that much. Give her a father. Not a drop-in, once-in-a-while father, either, but a dependable one."

They sat silently, both staring into their coffee.

"I don't know what to say," he said finally.

"How about, 'I'd like to meet my daughter. When's a good time?'"

Christopher stared out the window again. The sun had broken through the clouds, and he could see past his own backlit reflection now, out into the street. With the students gone for break, it was quiet at this time of day. He had said all throughout her pregnancy that he'd fulfill his role as father to the child. To Grace. Unbidden, Dr. Felk's face rose in his mind. *Don't let it get too late.*

He turned to Deborah. "All right, then. When's a good time?"

Robby stepped down from the school bus, his boot sinking into four inches of fresh snow. Maybe a snow day tomorrow. He hoped Paula wouldn't want to cancel tonight's Audubon meeting. They had a lot of work to do, planning the Big Day.

The diesel engine's roar faded as he plowed to the front door and opened the mailbox, flipping through the envelopes. Nothing from Cornell. March 1, when they had said accepted applicants would be notified, was still more a month away. Still, he couldn't help looking.

Inside, he dropped the mail on the kitchen counter. His parents were still at work. The house was quiet, just the way he liked it.

He laid his headphones next to the mail. The bus ride home hadn't been too bad. After his mom found out about his walks home last year, she insisted that the school escort him to the bus. That made him mad. He had refused to get on a few times, delaying the whole line of buses until she came to pick him up, her face tired, her voice strained.

This year's route was more tolerable, though. It was shorter, and the kids were less rowdy. No one tried to steal his preferred seat—driver's side, six rows back—where he'd settle down with his headphones and one of his field guides. On days like today, the bus was a lot better than a wet, cold walk. Robby poured a glass of chocolate milk and went to his room.

The new snow formed a soft peak on the bird feeder outside his window, as yet undisturbed by feathered foragers since he'd filled it that morning.

His phone vibrated with a text. Paula.

"Should we cancel?"

Robby typed back. "No. Gotta talk about the Big Day."

The website and the Big Day were what they promised the club. The website had been easy. But the Big Day, a twenty-four-hour race where members competed to see and record the most bird species, was a lot more complicated, even with Alex helping. He had officially joined the club and was planning to turn the Big Day into an extra credit project for his advanced biology class.

"I know . . . OK. C u at 7."

After dinner, his dad drove him to the Central United Christian Church. The headlights cut a swath through the dirty white fishbowl of the evening.

"You and Mom are both driving on the Big Day, right?"

"Right. We'll take turns. Six-hour shifts, probably."

"And we'll take the SUV." This car didn't have a GPS.

"Right."

"You'll make sure the gas tank's full before we start."

"Right."

"And we've got the Michigan atlas, and the county maps for Wayne, Macomb, and Oakland."

"Right."

"And backup maps. In case something happens. One gets wet. Or ripped. Or something."

"Right."

"OK." Robby put his hand on the door handle as his dad pulled into the church parking lot. "See you later."

Sam watched him disappear inside. They had been through the check-list already, and would countless more times until the Big Day on May 1. But Sam knew he would answer Robby's repetitious questions without complaint. With each one, the memory of the silent, sullen son who had become so obsessed with geese a year ago grew fainter.

It wasn't that birds cured Robby. He was wired differently than the neurotypical majority, and that would never change. Like the piping plover was a rare bird, Robby was a rare boy. But he was a boy, not a diagnosis. And birds were proving to be the bridge he and Linda had hoped for, a perch from which their boy could safely venture beyond the bunker of his brain to form real-world relation-ships. Dr. Felk. The ranger up north. Paula. Eventually, maybe, Alex. Maybe this professor at Cornell.

Maybe even his own father.

THIRTY-TWO

"All right, everyone. Let's try to keep on schedule, shall we?" Lab director Peter Hawkins brought to order the meeting of the Cornell Bird Camp Oversight Committee.

"We'll start with the good news. You'll remember we talked about the upcoming feature in *Audubon* magazine."

How could we forget, thought Christopher. Peter had mentioned it at every meeting since October. *Audubon* had pushed it back from the November issue to January to March. Each delay had amplified his dramatics about the future of camp. Now, he brandished a copy of the glossy cover above his head.

"The piece is in the current issue, which hit newsstands last week. Already, our camp website hits and inquiries are up by double digits," the director recited the numbers with relish. "We can expect to see the same spike in applications, especially after subscribers begin receiving it this week.

"I'd like to personally thank Christopher Goldman," he continued. "As the article's primary source, he's done us all proud. Christopher, thank you." To Christopher's chagrin, Peter began applauding.

Blah, blah, blah, thought Christopher. *Get on with the meeting, already.* He thought of Robby, and hoped his application would measure up in this stiffer competition. Since Robby's November e-mail, he'd monitored the applications. Robby's had arrived January 4, post-marked January 2, the first date applications were accepted. Acceptance letters would go out March 1, now less than three weeks away.

"As you know, we hoped that this piece would appear earlier in order to benefit our recruiting," Peter continued. "Given the circumstances, I'm proposing that we extend our application deadline through March fifteenth."

A stir reverberated through the room. Christopher caught the eye of Michael Adams. He was moonlighting on the bird camp faculty, too. Michael shook his head slightly, then nodded at him. Christopher glanced at Foster, who repeated the gesture.

Christopher understood. As the one singled out with thanks, he stood the best chance of successfully protesting this unfair change in the rules. He sighed, wishing he were out in the field, away from academic office politics, then raised his hand.

"Excuse me, Peter, but changing the application deadline at this point? That's unfair to the applicants who abided by the rules."

The director's eyebrows shot up. "Unfair? How about canceling bird camp at the last minute? Does that sound fair?"

"But that's not going to happen. That's not a real risk."

"Absolutely it's a risk," Peter retorted. "Over the last five years, five to ten percent of camp spots have gone unfilled. That's our profit margin, right there. We need to fill every single one of those spots." His gaze swept across the faces. "Eventually, we have to make it competitive enough that we can raise tuition."

Another murmur went around the room. Anger surged in Christopher's gut. Michael Adams spoke up. "Can't you change the deadline next year? We're all aware the bottom line is important, but—"

"Are you?" Peter Hawkins almost seemed amused. He looked around the room. "Do you know how much it would have cost to buy this kind of space in *Audubon*?" His words barreled out. "Over one hundred thousand dollars. That frees up money that we can now spend half a dozen ways. Hire a couple graduate assistants. Upgrade the software for the acoustic library." He looked pointedly at Christopher. "Provide housing for visiting professors, gratis.

"You did your job. You did it well. My job is to maximize the opportunity. We'll be taking applications through March fifteenth."

Dismissed and disheartened, Christopher slipped out the door.

Michael Adams followed. Pale sunlight streamed through the corridor windows that overlooked Sapsucker Woods.

"Man. What a prick. Glad I don't have to work for that guy year-round."

That about covered it. Christopher exhaled, rubbing his temples.

"I'm not even sure this bird camp gig's worth it, but with a new baby, I could use the extra cash, you know?"

"Mmm-hmm," Christopher replied.

"Yeah, diapers, doctor's visits, they all add up, and Julia's still not working. But she loves being at home with the baby. She's got a whole schedule worked out—play groups three days a week, library story time, all that. I thought all the kids in Ithaca were in college. Never knew there were so many little ones." He laughed. "Deborah's been over a lot. Gracie's a real cutie."

Christopher froze as Michael spoke their names. He and Deborah were old news on the Cornell grapevine. It couldn't have escaped Michael Adams. Did he just assume Christopher was like other part-time dads, picking up the kid on weekends? Since the coffee shop meeting, he had spent six mornings with Gracie, but she slept through three of them. The most interaction he'd had was giving her a few bottles. Still, it took his breath away to hold her and realize she was part of him and Deborah. One time she'd fallen back asleep while drinking from the bottle. He'd sat there until Deborah returned, marveled at how beautifully everything worked, from her quick, shallow breaths to her steady heartbeat to the grasp of her tiny fingers clenched around one of his.

"She is, isn't she," he said cautiously.

"Yeah." Michael chuckled. "Tiny little thing. Quiet, too. The rest of the kids will all be crying, howling. Gracie, she'll just sit with Deborah, nice and quiet, content as can be. I think she was born a couple months after my guy, right?"

"November tenth." Christopher repeated Michael's words to himself. *Tiny. Quiet.* Like him, perhaps? Would she prefer the solitude of libraries and labs, or take after Deborah and be able to chat up a lamppost?

"But Nate's a little quarterback already. Nineteen pounds, I think Julia told me. Gracie looks so delicate next to him. An owl and a hummingbird, that's what they remind me of."

"Owl and a hummingbird. That's good." Christopher smiled, recording the detail.

"But then, she's got tons of hair, and Nate's still practically bald. Who knows how it's all going to work out. Girls are supposed to grow up faster. Maybe Gracie will be pushing him around on the playground in a couple years. Or—"

Michael's phone interrupted him. "Speaking of," he said, glancing at the screen. "I'll see you around. Hi, honey," he spoke into the receiver, loping down the hall, unaware his proud father small talk had shaken terra firma beneath Christopher Goldman.

Christopher stared out the corridor window. Freshly fallen snow reflected the weak winter sunlight filtering through the barren branches of Sapsucker Woods. It was a view he loved, but faces filled his mind instead. Deborah's. Gracie's. Down the hall, voices intruded on Christopher's thoughts. The bird camp meeting was adjourned. One more face floated into his mind: Robby Palmer's.

Imagining the *Audubon* magazines landing in mailboxes nationwide, Christopher felt a rush of urgency. Deborah and Gracie would take more time. This he could do now. He reached for his own phone.

Skimming to his contacts list, Christopher punched up Arthur Felk's number. He got voice mail. "Dr. Felk, Robby needs something to put his application over the top. Can you write a letter of recommendation for him? I'll see it's added to the application package."

"By the way, don't plan on us next week. I'm taking Gracie out to Seattle, to meet your aunt Helen," Deborah said as she snapped the baby into her snowsuit a few weeks later.

Deborah's new habit of speaking, where she would start a sentence addressing him, then finish it talking to Grace, was the oddest thing. Did all mothers do that? Christopher wondered idly.

"That's a long trip with a baby." He remembered ending more than one West Coast flight ready to mutiny against a squalling child and its parents.

"I know. But at least I got a direct flight out of New York. And I don't have much choice. Helen can't come out here."

"She's not doing well?"

"It's hard to tell over the phone, but the conversations are getting shorter. Neither she nor Matt say much. That's another reason I want to go out myself. And I'm hoping Gracie cheers her up. You will, won't you, sweetie pie?"

There it was again, another split-sentence pivot from him to the baby. And it always was from him to the baby, not the other way around.

Deborah lifted Grace, who looked as ready for dogsledding as she did for the twenty-yard trip from front door to car door, and kissed her before settling her into the car seat. "So we'll see you the first week of March, then."

"OK." Would it really be March? It sounded far away. "Give me a call when you get out there. I'll miss you both." The words came out unbidden, as they had on the phone last year.

303

Startled, they both stared at each other. Deborah seemed ready to say something when Grace yanked on a toy hanging from her car seat handle, triggering "Twinkle, Twinkle, Little Star." Distracted, Deborah simply nodded and tucked the blanket more firmly around the baby. Then they were gone.

Deborah texted him from Seattle, fulfilling the letter, but not the spirit, of his request. It was now Wednesday morning, his usual time with Gracie. With a free morning, Christopher had planned to sleep in and then relax and read before his afternoon classes. Online newspapers, ornithology journals, the latest draft of his own paper he was preparing to submit.

But instead of savoring the unscheduled quiet, he couldn't concentrate, reading the same article three times before giving up. All right, then, breakfast. He scraped the last of the coffee from the can. Opening the fridge, he pushed aside containers from Campus Cantonese, ketchup, and mustard in search of eggs. Spotting the carton in the back, he reached for the last small, odd-sized jar in front of it.

Holding it up, he recognized Deborah's small, precise printing on the label. "GDG—Jan. 31" The white liquid inside frothed when he shook it. Leftover milk, he realized. Deborah stocked him with bottles of her pumped breast milk to feed Gracie, who usually sucked down everything provided. This one had been forgotten, evidently.

January 31. A month ago. Could it keep that long?

Her phone rang through to voice mail. Disappointed, he left a short message. It was barely six a.m. in Seattle, but weren't all babies early risers? He put the milk back in the fridge and started scrambling his eggs.

Deborah didn't answer when he called again an hour later or an hour after that. His free morning was being chewed up worrying about his family in absentia. He took a shower, keeping the phone on the sink.

It was almost time for him to leave for his afternoon classes when she called at last. "Christopher, what's going on? You've called three times."

"I found a bottle of Gracie's milk in the fridge. Dated January thirty-first. I wanted to know what to do with it."

"January thirty-first? Dump it." Deborah sounded surprised, but not annoyed. "Is that all?"

"Yeah. Well, no. Not really. You hadn't called, and I wanted to talk to you." He paused. "How's it going out there? How's Helen?"

"She's OK. She's got a couple good hours a day. She stays home, mostly. But we did get out to the girls' school concert the other night. That was big for her."

"And how's Gracie? How did she do on the flight?"

"Better on the flight than I thought. The time change has been awful, though. Her naps are all off. I—"

"Deborah! Are you ready? We're supposed to be there at nine thirty." Christopher heard Matt's voice calling in the background.

"Going along on a doctor's appointment today?" he asked.

Deborah shouted back to Matt. "Be right there!"

"I've got to go," she said into his ear again.

"Headed to the doctor?" Christopher repeated, not wanting to end the most civil, unloaded conversation they'd had in months.

"Deborah, the Realtor's here." Matt's voice was louder now. "We've got these showings stacked pretty tight. We need to get going."

"OK. I'll be right there." Deborah spoke away from the phone again.

"Realtor? Showings? As in, real estate showings?" Could Helen already need alternative housing accommodations? Why else would they move at a time like this?

"Christopher, I'll explain when we get home." Deborah's voice was clipped, abrupt.

305

"Explain? What is there to explain?" Suddenly, a horrifying thought grasped him. The hair on his arms rose.

"Deborah, is that Realtor there for you?"

Her silence said everything.

"You're moving to Seattle?"

"I'm not moving yet. I'm considering it. I need support, Christopher."

"I'm supporting you!"

"Because I practically drafted you. And I need more than babysitting. I need emotional support, too." Deborah spoke tightly. "And so do Helen and Matt. And the girls. We're in a position to help each other. That's what family does, you know."

Christopher felt sucker punched. He sat down heavily, sinking into the sofa with its worn-out cushions, and swallowed hard. He could barely breathe.

"You're taking Gracie across the country."

"It's not a final decision." Deborah's voice softened. "Matt suggested it couldn't hurt to look at houses while I'm out here. See what's available. I'm sorry you heard about it like this. We're leaving day after tomorrow. I'll call you when we're back in Ithaca."

"What time does the flight get in? I'll come pick you up."

"I've already made arrangements. I'll call you, I promise. Yes, Matt, I'm coming now. Good-bye, Christopher."

Sitting concave on the sofa, his knees halfway to his chin, he remained immobile until habit sent him to the kitchen to replace the phone on its charger. The refrigerator reminded him of Gracie's bottle. He unscrewed the yellow cap and poured the milk out in the sink. Watching it drain away released an inner valve, the one he had screwed over his soul a year ago. He loved them. Both his wife and daughter. He couldn't nurse his pain and injustice anymore. Their future was at stake, and he needed to be part of that future. He couldn't let any more time drain away, either.

For the first time in his life, Christopher Goldman missed a scheduled class, as he drove to Ithaca-Tompkins, without luggage, and bought seat 14B on the 1:05 p.m. flight to Philadelphia, with continuing service to Seattle.

As Christopher flew west, his cell phone and other electronic devices dutifully turned off, his voice mail recorded an unnamed caller.

"Dr. Goldman, this is Dr. Felk's assistant at the museum, returning your call from a few days ago. I'm sorry to tell you Dr. Felk isn't able to write the letter you requested. He fell last week and broke his hip. I relayed your message, and he asked that you call him at New York-Presbyterian.

"I'm sorry to leave bad news in a voice mail, but I don't want to risk waiting to reach you directly. Please call him as soon as you can."

THIRTY-THREE

Ladies and gentlemen, this is the captain speaking. On behalf of the crew, I'd like to be the first to welcome you to Seattle, where the local time is 3:40 p.m." Christopher reset his watch as they taxied down the runway.

"Portable electronic devices may now be turned on. We know you have a choice in air travel, and we thank you for choosing United. Flight attendants, cross-check for arrival."

His phone showed one new message, but it wasn't from Deborah's number, and she was the only person he wanted to talk to now. He'd listen later. Now he needed to find a taxi.

Matt and Helen's garage was closed, and the entire street looked deserted. Most of the neighbors were probably still at work. Compared to Ithaca, the weather felt balmy, and he shrugged off his winter jacket.

The doorbell echoed inside. No answer. Matt had said the showings were stacked tightly. Could they still be out looking? He rang again. Would they have taken Gracie with them on the house-hunting expedition?

He cupped his hands around his eyes, trying to see into the sidelights surrounding the front door. A baby's bouncy seat sat on the dark wood floor, next to the staircase. His stomach tightened, and he reached for the doorbell again. A moving shadow caught his eye. Christopher looked up. The door opened. There stood his sister-in-law, shock on her face.

"Christopher."

"Hello, Helen." His hand was still on the doorbell.

"Don't. She's sleeping."

"OK." His hand fell to his side. Helen looked shrunken compared to the last time he'd seen her. Despite the warm day, she was shrouded in a turtleneck and a University of Washington sweatshirt, a red afghan pulled over her shoulders.

"Can I come in?"

She hesitated only a fraction of a second. "Of course." She backed away from the door, allowing him to step through.

In the silence of the house, they faced each other, mutually wary, then spoke simultaneously.

"What are you doing here, Christopher?"

"Deborah's still out looking at houses?"

"Looking at houses?" Helen looked cautious.

"We spoke this morning, Helen. She told me."

"Told you what?"

"That she was going to look at houses. That it was Matt's idea. That it 'couldn't hurt.'" His stomach clenched again. "It does, Helen. It hurts."

"Good. It's past your turn to know what that feels like." She crossed her arms.

"What are you talking about?"

"For the last year you've made your ideals more important than Deborah. Than your family. 'She tricked you, she deceived you.' She had to ask you to meet your own daughter, for God's sake. Do you know how much that hurt her?"

"My marriage is none of your business, Helen." But he was taken aback at how much she knew.

"'My' marriage. Still thinking singular." She snorted, which triggered a coughing fit. She sat on the staircase. "If there's any marriage left, Christopher, it's in shreds. Deborah had a job interview here, did you know that?"

Her words were blows. "An interview?"

"At the University of Washington. For their annual fund. She's eminently qualified. They'd be crazy not to make her an offer. And she'd be crazy not to take it, if you ask me."

Silence fell in the hall again, until a cry broke it. Gracie, upstairs.

"She's up from her nap," Helen said, standing again.

He dodged in front of her easily. "I'll get her."

"Deborah left me to babysit."

"I'm her father, Helen." He was halfway up the staircase. "I'll take care of her." At the top he looked back, raining the words down on her, forcing her to believe him. Swearing it to himself. "I'll take care of her."

Still in the upstairs bedroom a half-hour later, Christopher heard the front door close, and then voices. Helen's excited one. Matt's deeper one. Last, Deborah's. Gracie looked drowsy again. He laid her gently in the crib—another piece of the baby kit Helen had all ready and waiting—and then stepped out, quietly closing the door.

From the top of the stairs he faced down the trio, Matt with his arm around Helen, who gripped Deborah's arm. She turned to her sister and with one hand, gently freed herself. "Christopher and I need to talk, Helen. May we use the kitchen, please?"

Helen started to answer, but tears began to fall. Matt nodded at Deborah. "We'll be upstairs, then." He led Helen up the stairs, steering her past Christopher silently.

When their door closed, he descended, each footfall taking him through the past year, rewinding it before Grace's birth, before the hike and warning from Dr. Felk, before his move, before Deborah's pregnancy test, to the crash. The "Miracle on the Hudson," the media had called it. If the pilot could salvage that situation, convert disaster to miracle, there must be hope for them, too. He stood next to Deborah.

"She's asleep. I gave her a bottle when she woke up, and she's just drifted off again."

Deborah nodded. "Let's get something to eat. I'm hungry."

She led the way to the kitchen and removed leftover Chinese containers in the refrigerator.

"Mariah's the lo mein lover here. There's plenty left."

Christopher looked into the white box. He hadn't eaten since his eggs at home in Ithaca, but he wasn't hungry. He folded the cardboard flaps again and pushed it away.

"Helen said you had an interview out here."

She met his eyes as she chewed, then nodded.

"Why didn't you tell me?"

She answered with another question. "Why should I have thought you'd want to know?"

He grimaced as his words at the Ivory Tower echoed.

"Well?"

"I was wrong." The words tumbled out. He saw Deborah's lips quiver. He groped for more words, better words, words that would unravel the cocoon Helen was spinning here, with the bouncy seat and the crib and who knew what other baby trappings. "I was too angry to say so. Too proud. Scared. Dumb. I'm sorry. Don't take a job here. Please. Please say it's not too late for us." He spoke Dr. Felk's words from the woods with anguish.

Her lips quivered once more, and she asked again. "Why should I?"

"Because I still love you. And Gracie. This morning, when you didn't bring her, I realized how much." He fumbled for his wallet, pulling out the faded ultrasound photo. "I've kept this here since the day you gave it to me."

"But you were right. I could have passed on the Huntington's gene." Deborah's voice trembled. "I risked her life. If she got like Helen it—it would have been my fault."

She still felt guilty, too. He shook his head fiercely. "No. It wouldn't be your fault. It would be life."

"It would. I got lucky, but I was selfish. I can't stand that I was." She gripped her elbows and shivered.

"You were brave, too. Going through the pregnancy alone." Christopher stepped close to her and rubbed her arms, understanding that the cold she felt was emanating from within.

"And there's something else." Momentarily, she looked down and then straight into his eyes. "I did something else unforgivable. I risked denying her a father by deceiving you." She was crying. "I'm sorry, Christopher."

Waves of relief, cleansing, baptismal waves, swelled from his gut as he held her against him. They were both crying now.

"It's not unforgivable. You're not unforgivable. I have. It's done. It's over. And we're going to take care of her. No matter what happens. She's our daughter. Even if she had Huntington's. Or gets—I don't know—food allergies. Or she's nearsighted." He tapped his glasses. "Or has autism. Who knows. Whatever. We'll handle it together. Two parents. One family. Right?"

He stepped back, looking into her teary eyes, waiting for her concurrence.

"One family," Deborah repeated, and they kissed in the strange kitchen, awed at the abundant beauty of second chances.

THIRTY-FOUR

July 2010

Through the car window, Robby watched the hive of activity on the sidewalk as his dad pulled up to the curb in front of Mews Hall. Parents and kids shouted to each other as they unloaded cars. Sweaty people in red Cornell shirts threaded their way through the throngs of kids there to move in for bird camp. Robby recognized one.

"Hey! There's Professor Goldman!" In an instant, Robby was out of his seat and out the door, sprinting toward a sandy-haired man wearing glasses and one of the red shirts. "Professor Goldman!"

Christopher turned.

"Robby! You made it. Welcome to bird camp." He put out his hand.

Robby grasped back, reminding himself to look at the man's face.

"I barely recognize you. You've gotten a lot taller."

"He's grown four inches this year," said his mom, walking up behind him with his dad.

Robby shrugged. "When do we see the birds?"

"Not till tomorrow. Let's see if we can find you one of these luggage carts," Christopher said, casting about for one unclaimed. He explained, "The Ornithology Lab's actually separate from main campus, about a ten-minute drive. Starting tomorrow, there'll be shuttles going over every day."

Robby's face drooped. "I wanted to go today."

"You'll have plenty of time with birds, Robby. I promise. Today we just want to get you settled, meet your roommate."

Trepidation rushed through Robby. His heart beat faster. "Is he here?" He knew his roommate's name was James, thirteen years old, too, from Pittsburgh. That was all.

"We'll find out upstairs."

The elevator was too small for the cart and the four of them. "Why don't you and Robby take the cart and go first. We'll get the next one," Linda said to Sam.

"Thank you for contacting us about Dr. Felk," Linda said after the stainless steel doors closed.

"Of course. How did Robby take it?" Dr. Felk had never left the hospital after the February fall that broke his hip. Pneumonia followed, potentially a flare-up of a low-grade respiratory infection that had abided for some time, Christopher was told.

"He didn't say much. Of course, he never says much, especially about feelings. But I have to imagine he felt a loss. Dr. Felk was the first adult who accepted him just for who he is."

Christopher nodded, wondering if Robby's parents knew about Benjamin Felk.

"Dr. Felk requested a memorial service here on campus. At Sapsucker Woods, the sanctuary around the Lab of Ornithology. We've scheduled it for the end of next week." Christopher paused. "I think he would have liked Robby to be there, if that's OK with you. I was able to tell him about Robby's camp acceptance before he died in March, and he was so pleased."

Linda hesitated only a moment. "You'd be there, too?"

"Yes. And my wife, Deborah. She helped execute the terms of Dr. Felk's will. He's endowed a chair here." The endowment had been one of Deborah's last projects before she took a job at the Ithaca Interfaith Alliance. She could work from home and be with Gracie, or from Seattle and be with Helen. Brett's daughter Amanda helped with babysitting. It had been a good change for all of them.

"All right, then," Linda said, pressing the button for the elevator. "I think Robby should be there."

Upstairs, Robby opened the door to room 224. A fan whirred loudly. A skinny boy wearing a baseball cap was sitting at a laptop at the desk in front of the window. He turned.

"Hi."

"Hi," Robby managed back.

"You're Robby, right?"

Robby nodded.

"I'm James."

Robby nodded again. His dad reached over the luggage cart to shake James's hand. "I'm Robby's dad."

"Nice to meet you," James said.

On the desk next to his laptop, Robby saw a pair of earbuds, like all the other kids at school wore. He looked at the floor.

Professor Goldman and his mom walked in. James helped them unload his stuff, and his parents took the cart to bring up another load. Robby opened his laptop bag, placing his computer, brown notebook, and Sibley's guide on the other desk.

"Oh. That reminds me." Professor Goldman said. Reaching into his pocket, he drew out Robby's thumb drive, the one he'd given him at the Lansing conference so long ago. "I think this belongs to you."

Robby accepted it silently, his head down.

"I've made some notes in some of the files," Professor Goldman continued. Robby's head flew up.

"I think you're on to some interesting ideas. That database you set up comparing the bird strike crashes over the last ten years was especially intriguing."

Robby smiled.

"Bird strike plane crashes?" James asked.

Robby nodded.

"Cool."

Robby felt his smile grow wider.

"The file organization is sloppy, though. I renamed the files I worked with, adding my initials and the dates. That's standard scientific file naming protocol," Professor Goldman said. "Got it?"

"Got it." Robby nodded.

"I've got to get back downstairs. I'll see you guys later, OK?"

"OK," James said. Robby nodded, turning the thumb drive over and over. He could feel James looking at him.

"Can I see the database?" James asked. "My laptop's all ready to go."

"Sure," Robby said, sitting down in James's chair, smiling so hard his cheeks hurt.

Robby shifted in the folding chair, the last in the front row set up on the observation deck. Professor Goldman's jacket was on the next one. A pink polka-dot baby bag staked a claim to the next chair, and a purse on the one next to that. Since the deck was crowded with people in black and the day was too hot for his new, hooded Cornell sweatshirt, Robby felt grateful for the three-chair buffer.

He gazed at the pond and the sanctuary before him. He tried not to look at the table covered with the plain white cloth and the urn precisely centered on it. At least there wasn't a coffin, like at his great-grandfather's, the only other funeral he'd attended in his life. As he bounced his knees up and down, he spotted a reedy strand of grass growing between the planks of the deck. As he twirled it first clockwise, then counterclockwise, clockwise then counterclockwise, his knees steadied.

"How's it going, Robby?" Professor Goldman slid along the empty seats to the one beside his. "We'll start in a few minutes."

Robby nodded.

"You're sure about doing your part?"

Robby nodded again, vigorously.

"OK, then. I'll introduce you like we practiced."

"Dada!" Even at a memorial service, Gracie's nine-month-old voice drew smiles. Behind the chairs, she squirmed in the arms of Professor Goldman's wife.

"Dada!"

Professor Goldman waved at his daughter.

"Dada!"

Robby looked back. Gracie's voice was getting louder, her squirms more insistent.

"I'd better go see to her." He squeezed Robby's shoulder. "This would have meant a lot to Dr. Felk, Robby."

Robby looked at the urn again. It was hard to imagine a body fitting inside. What was being dead like, anyway? People said heaven was in the sky. So Dr. Felk was closer to the birds. That meant it had to be good. Still. He twirled the weed, wishing he could talk to him again.

Professor Goldman was standing back at the podium positioned next to the white-covered table. "If you'll all take your seats, please, we'll begin."

Robby listened to speaker after speaker. A Cornell chaplain. Fellow alumni, former students, colleagues. The chaplain again. An old woman who said she was his sister and cried as she talked about some new chair that she said Dr. Felk was endowing. Robby didn't understand why a new chair would make her cry. He felt Professor Goldman stand up next to him and return to the podium.

"We've heard a lot today about Dr. Felk's lifelong vocation as a teacher and mentor. I experienced that more than twenty years ago. I'd like to introduce you now to the young man who had the privilege of being his final pupil. Robby Palmer. Robby?"

Robby slid off his chair and walked to the podium. He twirled the grass between his fingers until he could force himself to look out over the crowd. He saw James, sitting in the back. Next to him was Sophie, that red-haired girl from Ohio who always wore owl T-shirts. Today she had on a dress, though. She looked nice.

Besides James and Sophie, everyone else there was an adult. Robby didn't see any of them. He saw Dr. Felk. He saw the man he remembered from the museum's basement, the man who shared his books and birds. The man who believed him at the Lansing conference. He lifted his audio recorder from the podium shelf and poised his finger over "Play."

"Canada goose. *Branta Canadensis.*" His voice enunciated each syllable of the bird's common and Latin names. Then came the recording, a flock of noisy, reverberating honks that Robby imagined were heard over Manhattan eighteen months earlier.

"Trumpeter swan. *Cygnus buccinator.*" Like the geese, another member of the Anserinae family that Dr. Felk had quizzed him on in the museum archives. More honking.

"Swamp sparrow. *Melospiza Georgiana.*" The familiar high-pitched trill of one of the Sapsucker Woods locals.

On it went, Robby's narration alternating with the birdcalls. The waterfowl that had first engaged him. The birds of New England, the territory of Dr. Felk's life's work. The birds of the Great Lakes that Robby was just beginning to explore.

In the midday heat, the resident population of Sapsucker Woods remained mute throughout Robby's tribute. Later, the chaplain would tell Robby it felt more sacred than any prayer she could recall.

"Piping plover. *Charadrius melodus.*" The sequence of clear, paired peeps, unheard in the wild to everyone there but Robby.

"Bicknell's thrush. *Catharus bicknelli.*" The short, low notes followed by the longer, higher song of Dr. Felk's favorite.

The mourners remained reverently silent as the last echo of the Bicknell's thrush faded into the pond and the woods and the thick, humid air. Above their bowed heads, a silent, streaking jet painted a gauzy white stripe across an almost perfect, blue summer sky.

ACKNOWLEDGMENTS

Sincere thanks to Chris Baty, founder of NaNoWriMo, which led to the first draft in November 2010. Also, author Audrey Niffenegger, whose answer to my question at the National Writers Series allowed me to develop Robby, my protagonist, in a new way.

My very first readers: Sonja Somerville—who went on to read multiple drafts—Mary Pollock, Kimberli Bindschatel, and Carolyn Lewis. More beta readers: Lois Orth, John Pahl, Christine Noga, Joyce Duell, Meg Young, Marsha Buhr, Nancy Gray, Anna Bachman, Maureen Botteron, and Amy Hartzog.

Carrie Bebris, Christine DeSmet, Jennifer Rice Epstein, and Arielle Eckstut.

My book club: Linda Butka, Diane Lundin, Janet Wolf, Flora Biancalana, Misty Sheehan, and Lynn McAndrews, whose comments led to one of the biggest, best changes in the plot.

My writing group members: Mardi Link, Anne-Marie Oomen, Teresa Scollon, and Heather Shumaker, who put up with reading bits and pieces out of sequence.

The birders: Daniel Kerby and Bill, the Grand Traverse Audubon Club, which hosted me at meetings and outings; and Alice Van Zoeren, piping plover expert at the Sleeping Bear Dunes National Lakeshore.

The Ithacans: Jocelyn Bowie, Lynette Hatch, David Stewart.

Anie Knipping, for sharing her talent on my original cover. And David Drummond, for this newly created one.

Editors Tiffany Yates Martin, Zane Schwaiger, and Heather Shaw for their keen attention to detail. Of course, Danielle Marshall and the Lake Union team.

To my family—my son, for serving as my inspiration. John Irving's taken the title "A Prayer for Owen . . ." but that doesn't make this any less of one. My mom for providing the extra childcare that allowed me to push through the key first draft. My daughter for providing respite. And my husband who hung in there with me on the roller coaster ride it's been from page one through draft nine to self-publication and now re-release with a fantastic publisher. I'd have gone off the rails without you.

BOOK CLUB QUESTIONS

WARNING—SPOILERS!

- Do you agree with Deborah's decision not to have genetic testing before getting pregnant? Why or why not?

- Do you think Christopher's reaction is justified? Why or why not?

- What do you think about the portrayal of the female characters vs. the male characters? Does one gender seem more sympathetic than the other?

- Despite significant strains, both of the heterosexual relationships in Sparrow Migrations are resolved, while the lesbian relationship is not. Why do you think that is the case? What do you think about that as a reader? Is it fair?

- Did the novel change any perceptions you held about autism? How so? Why do you think Robby is an only child?

- Does the likelihood/risk of special needs factor into whether you would have children, as it does for Christopher?

- What do you think about the depiction of Christianity in the novel? Which character better upheld Christian ideals, Richard or Brett? Why?

- What meaning do you derive from the title?

ABOUT THE AUTHOR

Award-winning author Cari Noga has been a professional journalist for twenty years. She is the author of *Road Biking Michigan*, a nonfiction book, as well as essays in *Chicken Soup for the Wine Lover's Soul*. *Sparrow Migrations*—a semifinalist in the 2011 Amazon Breakthrough Novel Award contest—is her first full-length work of fiction. She is also the author of "Plover Pilgrimage," a short story that serves as a companion to *Sparrow Migrations*. The mother of a child with autism, she lives in northern Michigan with her family.